In April of 1155 B.C. the Egyptian Pharaoh Ramses III — historically considered the Last Great Pharaoh — died. As death eventually finds each of us, a cloud of mystery has always surrounded this particular demise.

While the mummified body of Ramses III was discovered in 1881, it was not until 1937 when Egyptian text was translated from the ancient *Judicial Papyrus of Turin* did the world know of the Pharaoh's deliberate murder. The assassination plot involved several of his wives, dozens of his palace staff, and respected citizens outside the great walls of the Royal Palace. Historians have dubbed it "The Harem Conspiracy".

Within the writings of the papyrus are four carefully detailed trial transcripts of the accused and their motive. Two other papyri detail the black magic used against the Pharaoh and subsequent punishments of those found guilty. Since the *Judicial Papyrus* also recorded the Great Pharaoh's death ten days into the trials, it was widely believed a slow acting poison was used to murder Ramses III. Not until 2012 did modern technology finally reveal the definitive cause of his death. Yet no amount of expertise or unearthing of ancient scriptures has answered the key question: who actually killed Ramses III? As an author, I find this an exciting opportunity to devise a fictionalized — albeit plausible — perpetrator to this ancient murder.

Although a dead language for centuries, our best documentation of their ancient writing is classical Egyptian from the Middle Kingdom era. Translations of religious and medical texts, remarkable poetry, and hieratic writings from this time were quite formal in style. While the exact phonetics of this lost language is unknown, I have attempted to convey the flavor of the period by incorporating this flowery and elaborate speech into the dialogue and narration of this novel.

Some redundant historical individuals have been compiled into a single character for the sake of brevity. Others are completely fictionalized to act as a transition between events and key historical characters. All in all, however, names of the recorded accused are used and the facts are presented accurately in one of history's oldest unsolved murder mysteries.

I hope readers enjoy this 3000-year-old "Whodunit".

# Cast of Characters

Pronunciations are approximate since vowels only existed in the spoken ancient Egyptian language and not in the written. We can only approximate each vowel and where it would have been placed in their words.

## Historical Figures

Ramses III (RAM-zeez) —The Pharaoh to all Egypt, reigning from 1186 BC to 1155 BC. He was the second Pharaoh of the Twentieth Dynasty in Ancient Egypt's New Kingdom era

Iset Ta-Hemdjert (EYE-set Ta-HEM-jert) — First Royal Wife and Queen to Ramses III. She is simply called Iset within this novel for the ease of the reader

Amonhirkhopshef (AH-mon-hirk–hop-shef) — Nicknamed Amonhirk within this novel, he was the son of Iset and Ramses III and named as successor to the throne.

Tiye (TEE-yuh) — Second Wife and Queen to Ramses III, she was fixated upon her son inheriting the throne

Pentawer (Pen-tah-wer) — Son of Tiye and Ramses III and second in line to the throne

Pebekkamen (Peb-e-kah-men) The Chief of the Chamber to Ramses III, he controlled the messages to and from the Harem and became an ally of the conspiracy

Perneb (Per-neb) Royal High Priest who joined the conspiracy, bribed by decidedly un-holy actions from Queen Tiye

## Fictional Figures

Ari (AR-ee) — A childhood friend of Queen Tiye's

Akar (ah-CAR) — As the Keeper of the Royal Guards, he used brutality in his official role

Pentu (pen-too) — He served as the Foreman of the Left Side for the construction of all Royal Tombs

Asim (ah-SEEM) — A trained handmaiden to Queen Tiye

Joba (HO-ba) — A Royal Palace Audience Chamber Guard and a loyal friend to Asim and Pentu

Tamin (tah-MEEN) – A Harem wife who comes to Asim's aid

# HAREM CONSPIRACY

## Prologue

### Museum of Egyptian Antiquities, Cairo
### 2012

For decades, the mummified remains of Pharaoh Ramses III rested in an antechamber commonly termed the Mummy Room of the Cairo Egyptian Museum. He was remarkably well preserved having never been subjected to grave robbers or the environment during his entombment. He remained in slumber for over three thousand years until his discovery in 1881. The old boy was trotted out occasionally to wealthy benefactors willing to open their fat wallets for the grotesque thrill of viewing The Last Great Pharaoh of ancient Egypt. A celebrity in his own right, the mummy of Ramses III was the basis for Hollywood's tales-of-tomb-curses. His mummy was considered so ugly, it provided the perfect inspiration to Hollywood for Boris Karloff's character in his mummy-risen-from-the-dead horror movies.

Since 1985, the most desiccated ancient kings and queens were placed in clear hermitically controlled cases within the museum proper for all to see. Tourists and students alike marveled at what their remains revealed. This day, even though confined within the museum for decades, Ramses III would have much to say.

Today esteemed professors, Egyptologists, and members of the Egyptian Ministry of Culture were gathered here hoping to find a definitive clue to one of the oldest recorded mysteries — the murder of Ramses III. The fragile *Judicial Papyrus of Turin* scrolls of 1155 BC concisely related the conspiracy surrounding his murder. While revealing the guilty parties and detailing the trial, Egyptologists could only surmise the cause of the king's death. Irritatingly, the most burning question was never addressed in the scrolls — who actually killed the Great Pharaoh? Was it a member of his harem or someone else entirely?

An elder and esteemed Egyptologist was walking at a quick pace to the conference room. Today was the day, he thought. Perhaps all our questions will be answered on this day.

He picked up his pace when he recognized the know-it-all intern with a nearby group of tourists. The younger man had apparently barged into the group, taking it over from the poor tour guide who stood off to one side looking annoyed. The bespectacled intern was not so much informing as he was holding court, thought the tall stooped man. He hoped this particular intern would not see him. Perhaps while he was talking, thought the elder, I can slip quietly past. The intern was indeed busy with a rather lengthy explanation of an Egyptian mummy in the display case. The man stooped a bit lower and kept going.

". . . and their belief in an Afterlife, that which we call Heaven, is the earliest historically recorded religion promoting a life after death." Warming to his topic, the young man continued, pushing his glasses against the bridge of his nose. "This belief was so all-consuming in their lives, as was the importance of having one's body properly preserved by mummification, that most Egyptians refused to travel far from their home country in case they died. They feared if they were away from the priests and embalmers they would not be properly embalmed, ergo, never have everlasting life. This was the same reason why military campaigns were not fought far from Egypt.

"Even the poor, if they could afford it, were embalmed based upon what they could pay. You see, there were essentially three embalming services with three varying prices. The wealthy — and of course royalty — always received the most expensive treatment. It took 70 days to fully mummify a corpse if one chose the top process. All care was taken with expensive ingredients and wrappings. Special masks would be worn while the holy spells and prayers were said over the body. Of course, the extremely poor folk would be buried without any embalming process whatsoever. Probably buried in the desert but the dry sands would still cause a mummification of sorts.

"In fact . . ." It was then the intern spied the elder man as he walked quickly away. "Actually, your tour guide will finish explaining it to you. I have another appointment," and he made a mad dash to follow the official to the museum conference room.

The squatty young intern was struggling to keep up with the longer strides of the taller man. "Sir," said the younger man, "Sir, I must again protest to any further testing of Ramses and the other mummy. You know, the mummy we call 'Unknown Man E' found with the king. I am truly concerned about the effect the computed tomography scan —the CT scan — and other invasions that technology could have upon the remains." Rather than feeling any true historical concern, the intern voiced his objection hoping to enhance his position within the museum. Should anything actually go awry with this decision, he was on record with an "I told you so." Everyone in the museum was aware of this intern's self-serving attitude. He was not particularly liked because of it.

"I know what a CT scan is, young man," said the Egyptologist caustically. "I assure you, all care was taken," replied the older man with a surprisingly spy gait. "Special containment clothing was worn and a forensic radiologist was on hand. Even for Unknown Man E." The man hoped this would be the end of his conversation. He was deep in thought over what implications today could bring.

He had always been keenly interested in the 'Unknown Man E' mummy, as he was officially christened. Why was he buried with the king? He was covered in goatskin, not linen wrappings, and not expertly mummified. His jaw sagged open lending to his descriptive nickname of 'The Screaming Mummy'. Death by poison might have caused that agonizing expression yet that was only conjecture. He might have died from suffocation or strangulation. Still, considering this lack of attention, why was he placed next to the king? Why bury him in a place of honor? I hope the DNA test performed on him will answer some of these questions, the older man thought with anticipation.

The younger man was about to continue his argument yet the Egyptologist squelched that quickly. "And Ramses III. We will finally know, young man, how he died. Even if he suffered a coronary, the scans and other testing will tell us. Of course, we may never know the 'Who' in this murder. Who actually assassinated Ramses III? But this should be a most enlightening bit of information. I believe. Most enlightening."

"But," said the intern taking a double step to catch up, "I thought the scientific community was fairly certain he had been given a slow acting poison. Ricin, perhaps. Otherwise how did he live through the trials? We know he did according to the translated documents from their court transcripts."

"Death by poison was only an assumption, young man," said

the elder, truly miffed that he must keep up this conversation with the intern. On the other hand, he thought graciously, perhaps the boy will learn something providing he had the patience to teach it. "We could merely fill in historical gaps from what we know of the times, you see. Poison was often used to eradicate enemies and we've assumed it was so in the king's case especially since we believe he didn't die until the tenth day of the perpetrators' trials. And the extra layer of linen about his neck and feet — well we'll see about that too." They approached a large gathering hall and the Egyptologist opened the door allowing it to close upon the tag-along intern. This egotistical young man was becoming tiresome.

"Those extra bundles could mean nothing, yet samples of the material was taken for further testing. It was far too dangerous to continue our invasion upon the mummy here without the proper technology. It's a moot point, really. Specialists in London performed the DNA tests on both bodies and they've returned unharmed from their examinations. England had the best equipment for handling him, you see. I hope we get the answers we seek. If not, we're at a standstill until further technology is invented."

As the younger man was about to speak again the elder said, "My comment was merely rhetorical. It's no good to protest now, my boy. The director of the Supreme Council of Antiquities authorized the tests and the mummies are home. We are about to find out the results from the Great King's examination."

As murmurs and greetings subsided, attention was given to the dais and the Minister of State for Antiquities Affairs who stood before them. His ever-present battered hat sat upon his head as if he had just come in from a dig. He had a thick large packet in his hand and the room went still as he gently opened the flap with a smile. It was reminiscent of the Academy Awards, thought the tall Egyptologist humorously.

Reading the contents silently to himself, he met the eyes of his audience and said in astonishment, "This," said the Minister succinctly, "changes everything."

# BOOK ONE

## Egypt
## 1151 BC

### Chapter One

The People-From-The-Sea were foolish enough to rely upon old familiar battle tactics and today it would be their ultimate undoing. Numerous cities had been laid to waste by these ferocious intruders as they swarmed territories like locusts upon crops. Egypt could not fall to these marauders in this confrontation.

These would-be conquerors had been beaten back before in hand-to-hand combat — Egyptian troops were never undermined upon the land. Yet the Sea People did justice to their name. They were excellent sailors in open water with large fighting ships, much more advanced than any Egypt had to offer. Yet this was Egypt's own Nile River, the lifeblood to the land of the Pharaohs. The Egyptians knew her well and built ships to maneuver her passages. Slim and swift, they were powered by both sails and oars and were additionally manned this day with the skilled bowmen of professional soldiers.

He felt his chariot lurch as his steed pawed at the ground and snorted. He felt the muscles of the powerful haunches ripple with excitement. "Ah, you are as anxious as I to see battle, are you not?" said the Pharaoh to his horse. "Calm yourself, old friend. We shall soon see the result of my plan."

Instead of engaging these enemies on open waters, the preparations by Pharaoh Ramses III for this encounter had been cunning. The People-From-The-Sea had been allowed to sail unchecked into the Nile Delta. Egyptian bowmen knelt at the edge of the shore. Chariots were positioned on either side of the river, equipped with soldiers who could both draw their bow and ride over the roughest terrain. Their horses were carefully trained for such maneuvers, communicating silently with their driver as if blessed by the gods themselves.

He watched from his vantage point at the front of the chariot division, waiting just a few more moments until the bulky battle ships were in range. Even now, his cruising vessels were preparing to attack from the intruders' flank. Thousands of Egyptian soldiers prepared to defend their land were here at his command.

He watched as the first ship eased around the nearest bend. Then another and another, each nearly scraping against the shallow sands with their bloated wooden bellies. Closer, closer, thought the Great King. Just a bit more . . . now! He prayed yet again to the falcon-god of war, Montu, for a glorious victory as he signaled for the horns to blare and the battle to commence.

The bowmen shot first, lighting their arrows with oil and setting them aflame. Sunlight was nearly obliterated with the onslaught of the smoking shafts soaring towards the ships of their enemies. They found their marks and Ramses saw flames rise from the wooden crafts as if from the Nile itself.

When the ships began sinking, great grappling hooks were projected onto each by a separate division of Egyptian military, dragging the charred ships to shore. Now the land combat would begin.

As he rode through the sands towards the foray, he saw nearby steeds lower their heads, their muscles stretching and flexing as they turned towards the shore. The smell of smoke and burning flesh assailed his nose as he rode faster towards those who were now fighting on the sands. Ramses raised his heavily forged sword as an enemy troop approached him. With a cry of battle, Ramses tensed his muscular arm, and lowered the heavy sword to find its mark upon the man's head. Blood erupted from his skull and stained the sand as Ramses turned his attention to the second doomed interloper approaching from his left.

Slowly these visions faded into the past and Ramses III — Ruler of all Egyptian territories, Pharaoh of Upper and Lower Egypt, political and religious leader of his land, the keeper of all he surveyed, the second ruler in the 20th dynasty of Egypt, and a living god to his people — woke from his slumber.

In this mood of half-sleep, he could yet hear the zing of his archers' arrows as they rained a great volley of shots upon his enemies, and feel the sand pelting his skin from the horse's hoofs. Like many dreams, the colorful escapades had seemed so genuine he had trouble differentiating them as slumber imaginings or conscious reminiscences.

The gods had seen fit to bestow upon him pleasant memories while he slept. The visions that tumbled in his thoughts had been those of himself as a younger man, riding proudly and fiercely into confrontation, saving his country from ruin. He preferred the dreams and the glory days to those of today which were fraught with political decisions, drought, and financial shortcomings.

When sleep was fully spent and not to be regained, he opened his eyes to the early dawn of the morning. He saw the gossamer fabrics of his bed and draperies at his terrace window stir in the warm morning breeze. He inhaled deeply the smells of Thebes, Egypt's capital city. While the most sweltering season was several months hence, today was destined to be a wonderfully hot day in his Kingdom. He thrived upon his country's heat and bright sunlight from above. It gave him vitality and strength, personal blessings from the sun god, Ra. After all, the name Ramses meant "Ra has fashioned him" and he welcomed the connection to this great divine being. His official title also connected him to Amun, the god designated as the creator of all things and was announced loudly at the most formal of events — "Powerful in the Justice of Ra, beloved of Amun".

It was a recognized fact that from the god Horus, the protector of Egyptian Royalty, sprung the first Pharaoh. Consequently, Ramses III and all Pharaohs who came before or after could claim a direct bloodline from Horus. Thus Ramses III was a living god and as such was worshiped as an earth-bound deity.

He reached down and scratched his protruding stomach. He was now in his 31st year as Pharaoh. He had lived 67 years on this earth and was admittedly not in the same enviable shape of his dreams. Thankfully, Egyptian artisans of frescoes and statues always depicted gods and Kings as thirty-year olds. An odd tradition yet one he was thankful for as he aged. He would be remembered throughout history as the virile, muscular figure of his youth.

Although, he thought with a slight smile, he was surely not *that* aged. Why, only last year, upon his 30th year of rein, he ran a great race on the feast day honoring him. While he may not have been the first to cross the finish, he was certainly not the last. In fact, he performed quite well, he assured himself.

Last evening's sexually rhythmic activities gave no indication of his age either. Time spent with his secondary wife, Queen Tiye, had been satisfying for them both. Admittedly, she took the reins when his libido failed to stir (too much drink, he reasoned) yet in the end, he triumphed amid much vocal enthusiasm from the woman beneath him. With so many wives clamoring for his attention in the bedchamber he still satisfied them all, he thought with the enormous ego only a King could possess.

The evening had been so enjoyable perhaps he should repeat the occasion tonight. There was no denying Tiye was accomplished in the bedchamber. Perhaps he would allow her to conduct the festivities once again. He felt his loins swell at the thought.

The King walked through the fluttering fabric framing his short terrace and welcomed this glorious day. From his vantage point he saw the sun rise above the intricately carved obelisk at the edge of Thebes. This giant marble needle had been erected 300 years ago and the ancient towering structure still confirmed the power and strength that was Egypt.

Ramses watched as the shadow from the obelisk slowly reached out to envelop his city, end to end, like a gentle hand cradling a child's face. It was a good omen, thought the King; one he interpreted as continued protection and prominence of Egypt.

Adjacent to his own viewing terrace were two windows belonging to his primary Queens. Their quarters were sumptuous in their own right with magnificent paintings and reliefs filling the walls and ceilings. This area of the Royal Palace contained these combined Royal Bedchambers, wet rooms, dressing areas, parlors, and private audience rooms of Ramses and his two highest-ranking Queens.

His Mortuary Temple and combined Royal Palace here in Medinet Habu was a short distance from the heart of Thebes. He had commissioned the temple to honor the god Amun in his 12th year of reign and was well pleased with the attention to detail by the craftsmen. His temple alone had required over 3000 stonecutters with a finished expanse of over 70,000 square feet. He convinced himself the enormous size was out of necessity, not vanity.

This Palace was more municipality than single building. Not only did the complex contain his Temple constructed in the center of the long complex and the private residences of the Royal Queens, it also held administrative chambers, buildings for the production of rare and intrinsic goods, storehouses, kitchens, servant quarters, stables, and the Harem suites for his other wives and offspring. The education of Royal Children and favored non-royal children were conducted in adjacent school buildings. The sons and daughters of distinguished aristocrats were often raised together with the Pharaoh's own, creating a close personal bond between the future ruling class and the successor to the throne.

Natives of other countries thought residing within one's mortuary temple morbid. Foreigners considered facing one's own mortality in such close proximity to living quarters a depressing idiosyncrasy of the Egyptians. "Yet we Egyptians are not like other people," said Ramses to himself.

While the rest of the world considered the Egyptians obsessed with death, his countrymen knew the truth. They were not fixated upon dying; tombs were constructed in a life-affirming belief in immortality where the deceased enjoyed an eternity of peace and contentment. The term 'ceasing to live' better described the Egyptian's viewpoint of dying. Indeed, the Egyptian language did not contain the word 'death'. They believed existence did not end here on this world; time on earth was merely a transition from one life to another. It mattered little to the Pharaoh how others viewed the Egyptian beliefs. A new consideration or method was often met with initial scorn — until those who once ridiculed it came to favor the idea. For centuries, Egypt had been the most powerful and sophisticated civilization in the entire world. Other Kingdoms bowed to him and overlooked any oddities to have Ramses' protection and trade.

The opulence and grandeur of Thebes shone in the unfolding sunlight. Gold and azure blue reflected off the rooftops of nearby temples. The markets were humming with early merchants preparing to hawk their wares and penitents were making their way to the Temple of Karnak for worship. Early day activities of this nature remained unvarying for generations. It would surely be thus for generations of Kings to follow. By then Ramses III would be reborn in the Afterlife, watching these worldly proceedings with the other gods.

He shook himself free of these disturbing thoughts. He was not old, he convinced himself. Occasionally tired yet he had many concerns and duties. He still had enough energy to continue his rule of this great and noble country. His Royal Physicians constant medical care and the Royal Magician's spells of protection that encompassed him ensured his longevity and health. No, this was not the time to dwell on bleak and nonexistent worries. Not on this splendid day presented to him.

In the distance, he could see rows of traveling camels — those sturdy ships of the sands — and their undulating riders. Tied in bundles on the rump and sides of the animals were rolls of tightly wrapped goods, ready to bargain with at the marketplace or trade with the boatmen along a Nile estuary. The day was beginning as it should and he prayed it would remain as calm and languid as those dependable camels.

He turned from his terraces as his manservant entered his chambers and accompanied the man to the ornate Robing and Wet Room. Here he was met by a second servant with the lofty title of 'The Chief of Secrets of the House of the Morning'. This senior aide insured all rituals of he King's morning cleansings were completed according to stringent rules and customs. The man's eye missed nothing as he observed other servants called 'Chiefs of the Scented Oils and Pastes for Rubbing His Majesty's Body' as they conducted the complex grooming and hair removal.

Every morning, this large antechamber was abuzz with Royal staff attending the King. Handlers of Royal linen, crowns, jewelry, and the 'Director of Royal Loincloths' would crowd the area. Each man was well trained, silently and efficiently manipulating the Royal tools of their craft. The process was long and tedious necessitating the King's awakening to begin at dawn each morning. Even so, this allowed him time to clear his thoughts and prepare for the day ahead. Additionally, the flowing water upon his body was refreshing and he had never been one to complain of too much pampering.

While standing with limbs akimbo upon his tiled floor, water mixed with scented powders were poured over his head, burbling into the drain below him. Servants known as The Cleansers gently ran soft linen cloths across his skin as fresh rinsing water fell upon him. Fragrant and rare oils were likewise applied to his body keeping his skin soft, supple, and sunburn free in the arid climate.

Shaving implements, depilatory creams, and an occasional scraping with pumice stones were carefully used to render the Pharaoh's head completely bald. Every three days his entire body would be removed of hair. It was a monotonous process however Egyptians believed cleanliness was above seemliness.

Finally came the carefully applied dark kohl makeup under his eyes to hinder the glare from the sun. A heavier layer would be applied today since the great sun god Ra saw fit to shine more brightly above the kingdom.

When his gold-overlaid sandals were finally slipped upon his feet, he would be as comfortable as any King could in a sweltering day under the Egyptian sun.

While the life of the Pharaoh was seen as one marked by pampering, prestige, procreation, and immense power, in truth his time was not his own. Laws and rituals structured every aspect of his life. Ramses' official duties, his domestic life, and his daily schedules were rules of conduct and traditions followed by Pharaohs throughout the ages. Even his strolls on the Palace grounds and marital cohabitation with a wife had their subscribed hour. This particular Pharaoh often changed the schedule of the latter if he felt the need, which had been often in his younger days.

The King was never completely alone. During the day, bodyguards were always near his side. High Priests, the Vizier, courtiers, servants, and a variety of government officials surrounded him during the day while family and favored officials dined with him in the evening. Butlers known as the Pure of Hands managed his meals and acted as his food tasters, sampling everything before the Pharaoh consumed it. His safety and good health surpassed all other duties in the routine of the Palace. Even his private chambers were adorned with the images of protective gods guarding him from otherworldly danger while he slept.

A plethora of specialists guarded his health. The Chief Royal Oculist routinely examined his eyes and the Palace dentist his teeth. Another physician cared solely for the King's belly and digestive concerns with herbs and tonics. The Chief Royal Magician cast protective spells over his whole being on an annual basis. These shielded him from earthy elements that even he, in this mortal form, would be susceptible to.

It was no surprise that Egyptian doctors were sought out in the rest of the world. While most did not receive such extensive care as the King, Pharaohs willingly sent medical specialists to treat royal households in surrounding kingdoms. Doing so not only promoted good will between trade countries, it also created an obligation from the foreign king towards Egypt.

While staff completed their tedious routine upon his body this early morn, he thought again of his second wife, Queen Tiye. It would be a simple task to carve out some time after breakfast and before his scheduled audiences to pay her a visit. He knew she arose late from slumber so the timing would be perfect. Yes, he thought, that is an excellent idea. His initial daily duty was prayer in a temple, yet today he would first pay a visit to his Queen and ensure her lack of official obligations tonight. If she had other commitments — well, he had dozens of other wives from which to choose; servants as well if he so desired.

He instructed the Royal Overseeing Chief to hurry this morning's process along. No reason was given; none was needed. He was the Pharaoh, after all, and his demands were always met.

## Chapter Two

Queen Tiye languished in her bed longer than usual this morning. She curtly shooed away her handmaiden opting for further slumber rather than greet the day. She eventually rose when the sun was fully in the sky, a fact that assuredly had the Palace staff's tongues wagging by now. It mattered naught; even a Queen second in precedence was entitled to her desires and extended sleep was one of hers.

It was to be another suffocating day in Egypt. Naturally, thought Tiye. When was it not in this nearly rainless country? She hated the heat — had done so all her life — which might be construed as odd considering Egypt was her birthplace. Being of noble birth she had options when the heat was overpowering; servants to fan her, bathe her in cool water, or apply cool cloths to her head. And yet, the heat still affected her.

As a child, she would sneak out of her home where the walls only confined the heat even further. She and her friends would climb upon the roof in the twilight to stay cool and catch the occasional breeze. Of course her mother chided her, comparing her to the commoners, and not a lady of noble blood. Only the common masses, said her mother, built their homes with flat wooded roofs for the purpose of storage and slumber during the warmer nights. Many such homes also canopied this space as an area for entertainment and cooking when the heat became unbearable within the brick walls made of mud and straw, the formation for all Egyptian buildings.

With the heat, came the flies, those constant, buzzing and biting nuisances. Every abode, rich and poor alike, had at least one flyswatter to rid the home of the horrid insects. The various rooms of her Royal Bedchamber contained three of the useful items and she had no qualms in summoning a servant to swat at the pests whenever they bothered her. And this particular Queen was frequently bothered.

Her meal consumed and enjoyed, she was now ushered to her own prescribed morning cleansing and hair removal ablutions. Some citizens subjected themselves to this as many as five times a day since Egyptians placed the purification of one's body to the highest degree. To some of their allied countries, the Egyptians' penchant for complete lack of body hair indicated a type of deformity and a fanatical behavior. To the Egyptians, body hair was believed to be shameful and unclean. They reasoned that wild animals and barbarians had body hair, not sophisticated and advanced societies. Still, the Egyptian so-called proclivities did nothing to deter the amount of trade conducted between countries, no matter their opinions of each other.

With this climate came a predicament, especially for the women of wealth— how to stay comfortable yet stylish with a full head of hair in the blistering heat and sun of their country? One could not. Yet baldness was out of the question: it was not fashionable or practical with the sun's rays. The women needed a temporary head of hair that didn't trap heat and could be shaped into fashionably acceptable styles. The answer was an airy, hand-woven wig, many of which were in this Queen's cabinet.

The lack of hair helped somewhat in the continuous insufferable heat. The other less refined motive for the hair removal was not often discussed yet it remained true nevertheless — lice. Apparently, several outbreaks of body lice occurred throughout the decades, both on the head and body causing not only great annoyance but also constant itching. The learned medical practitioners believed hair and sweat might cause the contagion of these bloodsuckers, hence the nearly addictive behavior for hair removal.

Whatever the original reason for hair removal, less hair led to less sweating and body odor, something reviled by the Egyptians. When evening banquets and close proximity with guests was imminent, citizens placed perfumed cones atop their bewigged heads to emit fragrant scents throughout the night.

Local artisans took great liberties with the size of these cones when painting frescoes and carving inlays upon stone. Artisans often took liberties with a great many renderings, considered the Queen. In truth, the cones were no more than little blobs of shea or beeswax butter mixed with flower petals and oils. The waxy butter would soften in the perpetual heat, releasing pleasant aromas as they melted.

Tiye had little faith in any of this morning torture and the waxy head cones. As a child, she seemed to constantly sweat. Not a mild perspiration as a proper lady might; the moisture emanating from her was as a peasant boy running in the desert. Her mother had been critical, clicking her tongue when she came home drenched in sweat. Even her brothers, her mother constantly informed her, never produced such an inordinate amount of moisture from their bodies.

She was taken to physicians and magicians to aid in this unbecoming defect. She was given a mixture of incense, lettuce, fruit, and myrrh to be rubbed under her arms for four days, morning and afternoon. The concoction only made her underarms sticky. Nothing particularly helped, actually becoming worse as she entered the age of her monthly bleeds. She would, her mother often admonished her in disgust, find the necessity to be cleansed several time a day to remain attractive to her pre-ordained future husband. Thankfully, the pouring sweat finally subsided as she matured yet the heat still affected her more than others.

Tiye was positioned in the wet room above the drain for bathing, the first of several ministrations in the daily ritual. Egyptian soap was made from a mineral salt called natron mixed with a paste containing clay or ash and worked into a lather for cleansing. Various scents were added to the mixture for the wealthier buyer. Suffering through these cleansing purifications twice daily was sufficient for Tiye. It was not only dreary but she was reluctant to stand nude before a roomful of servants feeling keenly vulnerable to do so. Therefore, she allowed only two women to attend her — the overseeing Palace Woman and a trusted young novice-in-training, Asim. The two women in attendance to her were dressed in loose fitting thin linen shifts that would dry quickly. They were often drenched as much as the Queen while working in such close proximity to splashing water.

Her novice was one of many spoils of war. Defeated indigenous people would be taken as booty to victorious Egypt to live. All captives became a Royal resource and as such the Pharaoh had authority over their distribution. Many were conscripted into the army, others given to temples for service, relocated to colonies of waged labor, or presented as a reward to deserving citizens. Asim was given to the Queen by her husband to train in whatever task Tiye deemed appropriate.

Yet, these people were not considered slaves. Indeed, there was no Egyptian concept for such a term. While some worked without a monthly stipend other than room and board, they yet had rights under Egyptian law and many eventually became citizens. In households of nobility and wealthy citizens, they were often trained in household duties and business positions. They were given room and board, and could own property of their own. If their masters abused them, it was well within their rights to file a complaint in court to be removed from that household or to seek punishment towards the owner. The courts usually sided with the worker and as such, most were treated fairly and unharmed to avoid courtroom drama. Oddly enough, it was not unheard of for an Egyptian born citizen, deep in debt, to sell himself as chattel until his arrears were settled.

These details were beyond Tiye's interest; in fact, she showed little notice in the workings of her country. Her only concern towards Asim was training her in the tasks at hand.

The scraping and rubbing completed, the worst task lie ahead: it was hair removal day. She insisted upon keeping her head of hair to a manageable style. Her thick hair must be cut to no less than the length of her little finger.

Tiye remembered the first time her mother had shorn her head. She had been very proud of her luxuriant hair as a child. Her thick and lustrous waves were the envy of all. She openly cried as she watched the locks fall about her feet while her mother reproached her for such vanity. According to her mother, this was one of several undesirable traits held by Tiye. She would never be first in her husband's heart, her mother often warned, if she did not learn to curb her many offenses to the gods. While the wigs she now wore were woven into the most intricate hairstyles (each woman tried to outdo the other in extreme designs and ornamentation) she still missed her own hair.

Yet, here she was — Queen to the Great Pharaoh Ramses III. Her mouth lifted in a slight smile. She once informed her mother that her talents were favored in the bedchamber over those of the First Queen, Iset. (Of course, Tiye's mother knew not how she acquired such talents.) Naturally, her mother's response was to point out she could not be _that_ skilled — she was still Second Queen. Tiye frequently bit her tongue to stop herself from lashing out at the woman. She wanted to remind her that the arrangement of seniority was based upon the order of marriage, nothing else.

"Queen Iset, is called The Kings' Great Royal Wife and Lady of The Two Lands," her mother would pronounce with a sniff. "And you? Are you aware the people refer to you as The Lesser Queen?" Yes, this term was familiar to Tiye. The Pharaoh told her it was not said in a disparaging way, as her mother intimated, yet as a means to simply identify her as the second ranking Queen behind Iset.

Lesser indeed, she thought. She hated that moniker. As a strong-willed and headstrong woman — two more faults with which Tiye's mother applied to her — she was intent upon securing what she desired. She could wheedle anything from the grasp of the King— jewels, gowns, and the finest quality of everything that caught her eye. She may be called 'The Lesser Queen' yet she was still a Queen. As such, her power was immense within the court and her every order was met unhesitatingly by any servant with whom she came in contact.

She and her Sister Queen, Iset, had more in common than merely marriage to the Pharaoh — they were both members of the Pharaoh's immediate bloodline. It was important the succession of rulers be uncontaminated, never tainting the lineage with simpler minds and inherited illnesses from foreigners or merely highborn Egyptians. Some Kings had married their own sister, niece, or even their eldest daughter to ensure the purity of the line.

As she stood ramrod straight with eyes closed while the two women continued her morning purifications, she allowed her mind to drift to more pleasant thoughts. She recalled the vision of her husband riding across the dessert into battles during the early years of their marriage, his great horse leaving a scattering of sand in the wind, the Pharaoh's body glistening in the bright sun. Ramses had been a great warrior in his youth and images of this virile man amid his victorious battles were on display throughout the land. He had been a remarkable sight, often causing her to gasp at such earthly beauty.

This was the man she had been joined to in marriage and this was the courageous individual she strove to keep in her memory. It was always a shock to see him in his current human state. His golden glow had long been snuffed. His vitality had waned as well. For one who had shown great passion for his people and the world surrounding him, he now often strode lackluster and uninterested through daily events. It was embarrassing to the Pharaoh's name and that of Egypt to see a growing disrespect from the rest of the world.

Their prior evening's sexual exercise in her bedchamber had been a perfect example of his lack of involvement. Of late, with his aging and extra weight, she was less confident of her sexual performance in bringing pleasure to her husband. Prior to a scheduled appointment from him, she pled for the gods' assistance. Thus far, her prayers had been answered — Ramses always left her bedchamber satisfied.

Last night, however, he had surprised her by bursting into her room wearing that familiar lewd smile, his signal of a need for sexual gratification. She was certain the panic in her eyes would be seen if the room had not been in evening's gloom. He would not have been pleased had he witnessed that emotion cross her countenance. She quickly said prayers to the goddess Qetesh, the deity of sacred ecstasy and sexual pleasure. For additional protection, she also prayed to Isis in her role as goddess to marriage. With such short notice from her husband, it was the only measure she could take for her well-being. She had little faith in these entreaties yet she hoped they would ensure pleasure to her husband. Even with those godly appeals, it had taken sweet talk and cajoling on her part to see the act reach fruition. Towards the struggling climax, she finally resorted to fantasies upon sexual escapades of her youth. Those thoughts eventually brought about the desired finish.

Egyptians had very little taboo in anything sexual and premarital sex between single people was not considered shameful in any way and even socially acceptable. This openness towards sex was likely the explanation for the lack of prostitution in Egypt. Marriage, however, changed that attitude dramatically as monogamy after marriage was expected. Most marriages were formed from love and women were respected as partners in life rather than as subordinates, yet adultery was not tolerated. The stigma was far more serious and dangerous for a woman than for a man as the bloodline was passed through the woman. If the woman was faithful, the man was assured of passing his property to his blood heirs.

Tiye was constantly fearful, even with her talents in the bedchamber, she would fail someday. Even a Lesser Queen could find peril at the whim of a ruler. Her safety was the main reason she had never strayed from the marital bed, although she had been tempted to do so over the years. The reasoning for self-restraint was simple: she wished to keep her head.

Even as her thoughts raced, the object of her consternation entered her chamber. Her first instinct was to quickly cover her breasts and near hairless genitalia as her husband crossed the threshold of her private chamber. She caught the scowl forming upon his brow at her actions. Slowly and, she hoped, seductively she removed her arms from around her voluptuous body, saying, "My apologies, My Husband. You startled me." Her skin glistened with the water upon her body and she saw the frown slowly disappear.

Ordering her women servants from the room, she caught the admiring eye of the Pharaoh directed at her young maidservant, Asim. Her wet garment was clinging to her body, putting her nakedness underneath on display to him. He had an eye for the young ones, mused Tiye, and Asim was rather pretty. Still, she would not tolerate his attention to yet another woman and vowed to keep any familiarity between those two in check. She could do nothing about conjugal visits between Ramses and his twenty other wives yet she would not loose another novice due to her husband's sexual appetite. She was brought back to reality by her husband's voice. He was expressing his desire to visit her again this evening. Not asking, of course; merely informing her.

Coming to her senses, she replied, "Of course, My Husband. I shall be delighted to have your company. We do, however, have a dinner arranged with your newly appointed minister and his wife. I believe several of the Royal Prefects and the High Minister of Finance shall also attend. I fear it could be a lengthy affair. Perhaps the morrow might be better suited for us. I do not wish to embarrass My Pharaoh in front of his guests by departing early from the meal." Again the scowl darkened his face. "However, if you do not mind leaving the others to entertain themselves, then neither shall I," she smiled as she reached out to caress his arm.

The familiar glint appeared in his eye, telling her she had corrected her misstep. "It is settled then," was his only reply. She would wait for his move to leave the dinner party and then — what? A repeat performance — or lack thereof — as the previous night?

Participation on his part would be insignificant at best following an abundance of drink and food. She inwardly shuddered.

"Wonderful. I shall plan something special for you," she said, hoping the gods or her imagination would strike her with a pleasurable idea before the night fell. She had labored far too long last evening and rejected another exercise in exhaustion for tonight.

He left with a look of happiness and anticipation upon his face and she began steeling herself for tonight. It was not that she found the sexual act unpleasing. In the early years of her marriage — indeed, even prior to that union — all things sexual had been uppermost in her thoughts. Even now, she could occasionally find pleasure with her husband yet not when she worried of his displeasure and her safety. The entire event was becoming simply too much work on her part. Sighing, she recalled her servants to finish their ministrations to her person. After drying her skin in the softest linen, she prepared for the last task of this routine — application of fenugreek oil.

The seeds of this remarkable common plant were the basis for many uses. It transcended magic, medicine, and cosmetics with almost god-like powers. One of the oldest foliages to be used for medicinal purposes, the seeds had been utilized for over 2000 years. Physicians applied poultices of the seeds mixed with clay to treat cuts, wounds, skin irritations, and swollen glands. Mixed in a tonic, it provided relief for bronchial infections and tuberculosis. Fenugreek tea was a principal remedy to increase mother's milk and some thought the tea also acted as an aphrodisiac.

In the cosmetic venue, fenugreek oil aided in keeping skin smooth and supple, chasing away those dreaded wrinkles that came with older age and dry climate. The process of creating this expensive unguent was intensive while strictly adhering to an ancient recipe. It required two full sacks of the plant and several days' effort to produce a minimal amount of the precious substance.

Those who could afford this luxury used it judicially, normally reserving a few drops for a facial treatment. Tiye, however, preferred to have the oil applied to her entire body after bathing. It was time consuming yet she believed it was well worth her effort to stand with limbs extended while her two women gently massaged it into her skin. Her body looked as youthful as it did twenty years ago.

Wrapped in a linen sheet, she sat before her gilded table in an ornately carved chair with a leather sling forming the seat. Her morning chair was not only one of comfortable structure, it was a piece of beauty. The back of the chair was made of cedar from Lebanon with inlaid pieces of ivory in the shape of a large lotus blossom. The legs of the chair ended with the paws of a lion carved from Nubian Blackwood. The sides were open with intricately fashioned twists of wood sheathed with thin sheets of gold binding the frame together.

The next step in the morning routine was far from favored: the cleaning of her teeth. While it was usually painless, she was not fond of anyone poking about in her mouth or moving her lips aside for a better reach within. Her servant skilled in the care of her mouth and teeth began by spreading paste made of ground rock salt, mint, and dried iris blossoms upon a toothbrush. Her servant gently and carefully rubbed this mixture across Tiye's teeth until they gleamed. The woman was well trained in this task and took care not to inflict the Queen with pain.

This was not a task reserved only for the noble. On the whole, Egyptians' cleansing routines involved their entire body. Most citizens of Egypt used a simple twig with worn ends for their morning teeth cleaning ritual yet as Royalty, her brush was a carefully designed length of wood with bits of frayed twigs wound tightly upon each other.

While the teeth of nobility and wealthy citizens were in decent condition, the common man did not fair so well. The reason was simple enough. Grain in all its forms was the main staple of food in the country. The stone wheels that worked the seeds into flour could only grind them to a certain degree of refinement. The resulting grain was in a usable texture, yet sand attached to the plants and even tiny stones were often incorporated into the sacks of flour and then into the food. Chipping one's tooth was not uncommon for the simpler folk.

On the other hand, the Palace had granaries on site that ground and reground the grain until they became a finely sifted powder. The wealthy, too, often paid for further grinding of the grain. It was a more lengthy and costly process yet those who had wealth often had vanity as well. Retaining one's teeth spoke to this conceit.

Having completed this oral cleansing routine her attendant trained in cosmetics, commonly called the 'Royal Face Painter', retrieved her portable case of scents, creams, and various colors of facial cosmetics. The ivory and gold leaf cosmetic chest was opened and ministrations upon her face began.

Upon her table stood a bronze statue of a scarab beetle, positioned upright upon a stand with outstretched wings. The statue was covered in precious gems and an exquisite silver mirror was positioned between its open wings. She watched her reflection in the polished surface as her face came alive with color and shadings. Another servant brought fresh fruit for her to nibble upon in between application strokes.

An easy breeze caught the hem of her covering and she extended a delicate and pampered foot towards it. Considering Egypt's behavior towards women, she was better off as an Egyptian than a woman of the Hittite or Athenian Empires. In Egypt, women were allowed the freedom to own businesses, enter into legal contracts, buy property, serve on juries, and were generally considered equal to men. Other parts of the world treated women like chattel; property to be owned and constrained by men. To be controlled in such a manner would be difficult for a strong-willed woman such as Tiye.

Moving a few brightly colored bottles aside, the Queen searched for the fragrance she wished to wear this day. Egyptians were fortunate to have an abundance of plant life with which to compose aromatic scents. The roots, blossoms, or leaves of such plants as cinnamon, iris, lilies, and roses were soaked or cooked then mixed with rare oils to produce perfume. Many perfumes had more than a dozen ingredients. She chose the lily infused perfume oil and applied it liberally to her throat, temples, and wrists.

Her nails were attended to with a red henna dye. Occasionally she had this same red henna applied to the curled wigs she wore in the evening. She watched as her skilled face-painter applied coloring to her eyebrows and darkened her lashes with kohl powder. The dark kohl makeup was carefully painted under her eyes and extended from the corner of each in delicate angled patterns. All Egyptians, high or low ranking, wore the carefully applied black mixture under their eyes. With the sunlight glaring off the white sands, it was a maneuver with which the citizens protected their vision.

Tiye pointed to the alabaster pot filled with bright blue pigment. It was known as Egyptian Blue and had been first concocted in the 4th Dynasty, over 2000 years before Ramses III sat upon the throne. The color was not available in nature — it was the first man made pigment in the world and considerable talent and skill went into its development. The Egyptian technicians had safeguarded the secret of its creation for generations. It was a magnificent concoction and one that spoke to the skill and ingenuity of the Egyptians.

The Queen cared little of the cost or the many man-hours involved in developing this perfect blue. She cared only for the way it enhanced her eyes.

Now she was considering her *kalasiris*, the gown she would wear for the morning appointments. "Bring me the white gown with the golden threads today," she ordered one of her attendants. "No, not that. The one with the gold braided belt and ties at only my left shoulder. Yes, that is the one." The gowns of late were extremely form fitting and either tied at both shoulders or upon only one as the dress she now chose. Egyptians were very fond of curves and the gowns accentuated the womanliness of those wearing them. Occasionally, gossamer fabrics would be fastened at the shoulders to flow behind the wearer. At evening celebrations, a sheer gown would be worn under a glittering cape providing both cooler attire and some displayed nudity.

"Tonight I wish to wear the blue gown with the many pleats," she instructed. As pleats were a current trend, Tiye was not to be outdone by another woman at tonight's evening meal. This particular gown of which she spoke had three different pleating styles. From the waist down, tight pleats only a few centimeters apart were formed. Crisscrossing over this first set were more pleats that were less narrow in width while the bodice of the gown was set in chevron-patterned pleats. The gown was a miracle of handwork and extremely labor intensive yet she only appreciated the way it draped around her voluptuous body. "Ensure it has been cleansed," she continued, "and the gold buttons polished." Buttons served no purpose on any gown other than adornment, another current whim in clothing design.

Linen had been the fabric of choice of Egyptian garments for thousands of years. Living in such hot climate, this inherently cool light fabric was the perfect choice. It could also be woven into many different degrees of thinness. Of course, those of more meager means wore coarser woven linen dresses with a cut not as close to their bodies. For those willing to pay, it could be woven so thin it became transparent if they so wished. When the weather grew cooler, a linen shawl could be effortlessly tossed about the shoulders for warmth. It was the easiest of fabrics to wash and dry, an important factor to the cleanliness-obsessed Egyptians.

In the hot Egyptian summers, people often wore as little as possible. Partial nudity was never thought indecent and breasts were often exposed in styles past. For some, especially servants and women dancers, it was the norm to wear only short breeches with necklaces. Field men wore loin clothes while those working in the waters were usually nude. Children, in the hottest of months, usually went about naked until their twelfth birthday. Throughout the existence of the Egyptian empire, artists had been painting frescoes of nudes: simple people in their daily routine. It was not meant to be obscene or even titillating. It simply depicted the way of life in Egypt.

Tiye, however, was never one to dress scantily. Many decades ago, the women's *kalasiris* were held upon the body by two straps between the breasts and tied at the neck. The breasts were left uncovered. Following that design, the trend was the use of a single strap over a shoulder attached to the back of the gown leaving one breast exposed. Today, most women of means wore gowns that covered both breasts. This, too, was Tiye's choice. While offering her more modesty, it also presented her the opportunity for further embellishments upon the bodice of the gown. While she did not mind nudity in more intimate moments, she preferred to not feel as though she stood on display, believing in public modesty always. Well, perhaps not always, she smiled. She remembered a time when others who reveled in her nudity pleased her immensely, even provided her a feeling of power. Memories best left for another time, she sighed.

She finally realized her 'Royal Handler of the Queen's Jewelry' stood by patiently, holding one of several jewel boxes waiting for the Queen to make her choices for today. Not only was her jewelry the finest in Egypt, so were the decorated and inlayed boxes in which they were placed. They were cleverly constructed with sliding lids and drawers. Some divides were hidden so well within the boxes, only the owner knew of the secret compartment.

Men and women of all classes wore jewelry. It was much more than a matter of ornamentation. The choice of one's jewelry and the more one wore made a statement as to one's wealth, social status, or favored gods. The wealthy were often laden with anklets, armbands, wrist bracelets, necklaces, pendants, and earrings. Naturally, the jewelry boxes of Royalty contained only the finest pieces of gold and precious gems.

"The ivory and gold bracelets. Also the brooch in pink quartz and the matching earrings." Large brooches were often worn at the center of the shoulder ties with additional jewelry around the neck. Tiye was never above flaunting her station in this life and engaged the most talented artisans for her jewels.

Pointing to another piece she told her handler, "And that lapis lazuli necklace. Yes, that is perfect for this evening." The opaque deep blue of the lapis stone and its gold pyrite flecks held a special attraction for all Egyptians. They equated the blue with the color of the night skies and the gold reminded them of the stars. It was not a native stone to the land of the Pharaohs but imported from Badakhshan, a great distance from Egypt yet manageable through the waterways of the Nile. Exorbitant quantities were brought into Egypt and used in every aspect of their lives — from jewelry and artwork to cosmetics and healing. It became almost of godly importance to them and iconically Egypt. It happened to be Queen Tiye's favorite stone and she owned many lapis lazuli pieces of jewelry. The particular necklace to which she indicated had been a gift from someone extremely dear to her. It was her most treasured piece of jewelry.

Leaning towards her intricately designed table filled with cosmetics, she plucked a freshly picked fig from a bowl. "My knife," she commanded to any servant nearby.

Tiny fruit knives were common in all Egyptian homes. Women of wealth often owned such a favored implement with hilts of gold and gems. Using these sharpened blades to slice open fresh fruit ensured the often-juicy fruits could be eaten in a refined manner. Queen Tiye was no exception to this display of good breeding. She was extremely proud of her little knife designed for her by her husband, The Pharaoh, for smaller fruits.

Taking a sip of orange juice from a cup, she watched her Royal Face Painter. Yes, she thought as she observed the application of pink pigment to her cheeks, it was not difficult to be treated like the Queen she was. Choosing a large date, she began to slice it into dainty pieces with a pleased smile upon her face.

## Chapter Three

The Pharaoh completed a most fulfilling breakfast carefully planned around his health and well-being. He was in an excellent mood, anticipating this evening's private entertainment with his Queen. Now he strode through the marble halls with his entourage close behind to begin the long and occasionally boring task of receiving visitors clamoring for his attention. He passed the myriad of exquisite carvings outside the grand dinning area and a lapping fountain placed within an interior garden.

While public structures were decorated in reliefs boasting of Ramses' many military conquests, the interior design of the Palace differed greatly with calming nature scenes. Carvings of animals and flora covered the walls and ceilings painted in bright reds, blue, and greens. Support beams of date palm or acacia wood were also covered in similar images. Gold leaf was applied to tops of columns and borders of the walls. Several gods — always depicted in gold leaf — were in relief offering blessings to the Pharaoh and Egypt.

The Royal Audience Chamber where Ramses held court after early prayers was enormous. The raised dais centered at the far end of the room was carved from the finest alabaster, each of the six steps adorned with bits of carefully inlaid gold. Nestled atop this platform was the throne, carved from cedar with ebony and ivory inlay. The armrests ended in the head of a lion and the feet of the chair legs were carved claws. A small footrest was situated directly in front of the chair, equally carved and richly inlayed. Under the careful scrutiny of Palace magicians, artisans had painstakingly carved hieroglyphic spells of protection on the back of the throne and upon massive pillars and arches surrounding the grand seat.

The overall size of this dais encompassed the entire end of the grand hall. This imposing edifice lent import to all official proceedings and reasserted the powerful reign of the Pharaoh. Royal Marble Craftsmen toiled nearly a year to complete this room of power. Each morning the marble floor was polished until it gleamed by those trained in such details. Costly incense of frankincense, myrrh, and shaved fragrant woods from the Land of Punt were lit within their specially crafted pots in the corners of the room.

The down-filled pillow seat had been carefully fluffed and dusted before most men rose in the morning. Upon this chair more than a dozen Pharaohs had ruled, each handing out justice to those poor unfortunates gazing up at him. This morning Ramses III would do the same.

His Majesty was announced to the court by several Royal titles. Today, the Pharaoh had been dressed in the finery officially and generationally dictated to him. He also wore his most impressive adornment this morn; a wide collar necklace. It stretched across his chest to over each collarbone. He owned several styles, each golden piece inlaid with precious jewels in intricate patterns. In the past, these heavy pieces slipped and moved irritatingly about when worn. The solution was to create another smaller amulet-like piece tied to the rear of the collar to serve as a counterweight, keeping it in place and the Pharaoh happy.

Men's clothing consisted primarily of a linen tunic/loincloth called a *shendyt*. It was fashioned from a specific cut of white linen fabric, wrapped around the waist, drawn up between the legs, and tucked or fastened in the front. Yet the Pharaoh had a standard of dress that was his alone. While Ramses' garments were essentially white to deflect the beating sunlight, they were fashioned with different weaves, large patterns, threads of gold, and carefully dyed colors woven within. Each cost more than the common workingman would see in a lifetime. The Royal Tunic was also longer than standard length and entailed a fully pleated panel in the front with beading and precious threads woven in. While he often wore the tail of a lion around his waist as a belt and the skin of a leopard about his shoulders, today he was unencumbered by such articles. It was much too hot this day for such a display.

With his crown designated for this day's hearings, he also wore a long rectangular fake beard attached to his chin with straps around the back of his head. He completed the Royal attire with the gold and blue striped Royal Crook and Flail held crossed against his chest. These two additional symbols indicated his role as shepherd to his people and herdsman of humanity.

Surrounding councilmen were also officially adorned for today's session. The scribes sat in the Pharaoh's peripheral vision near well-placed oil lamps. They had already begun scratching upon their papyrus rolls with sharpened reeds from the Nile dipped in black ink. These men spent years in the practice of their craft beginning with cheap materials to inscribe upon as pieces of wood or pottery. Papyrus paper was expensive and could not be wasted. Only when a scribe had mastered his craft could he write upon the precious paper. These Palace scribes had been writing for the Royal Court for many years, each one extremely talented. They would record every utterance and small gesture that took place with efficiency and speed whenever court was held.

The use of hieroglyphs was extremely time consuming and a very artistic form of writing. These exceptionally detailed drawings were reserved for religious texts and the adornment of Egypt's buildings and monuments. The scribes used another faster method of writing transcripts: hieratic script. Even with this method of cursive writing they could yet fall behind in their transcript and often they would compare notes to ensure accuracy.

Seating himself with a flourish upon his throne, the Great Ramses III signaled to his Vizier: he was prepared to hear entireties from those on the official docket.

On any given day, scheduled individuals would be permitted into this intimidating chamber according to rank. First to come forward were representatives from other countries who either wished to introduce themselves as their country's official, or those who wanted something from Egypt — a trade treaty, a boundary dispute, or a volume of other requests. Each brought gifts, hoping to outdo one another with the most interesting, lavish, or sometimes outrageous offerings. It was monotonous at best. Over the years he had lost interest in this bowing and scraping of dignitaries. He was, in a word, bored. The only interesting break in this task was the gift each official brought.

The Royal Department of Ministers would then be granted access to the Pharaoh, some needing approval of current construction projects, others offering reports on the financial and employment status of the city. Every branch of his ruling departments had at onetime or another come before him with concerns, plans, maps, and charts. It was never a meeting of equals at a table or in a council room. Here, the Pharaoh was the only one seated; all others came to him at his pleasure. He was, after all, the only deity in the room.

After the ministers, his trusted generals would enter in their imposing military garb to provide updates on conflicts, borders, and troop rations.

Following his generals came the common man, looking for justice and the occasional vengeance for a wrong perceived against them. Usually his Vizier — the second most powerful man in the Kingdom — would oversee such proceedings. Today, Ramses waved away the man's move to replace his King as judge. It had been some time since Ramses had the chance to connect with the common man and he was feeling altruistic this morning. His sworn oath was to judge fairly and impartially, while valuing reason above emotion. How could he be effective to his people if he never sat in judgment over them, he reasoned convincingly to himself. Besides, occasionally it was expected of him.

First on the docket was a local baker. "My King," began the man after prostrating himself upon the floor, "this man," the baker turned and pointed to the accused in the case, "set a deliberate fire to my business. My wife was nearly burned."

Obviously there was more to this man's story. The Pharaoh looked at his Royal Chief Counsel to begin the questioning before he passed punishment.

"And what reason would this citizen have to commit such an act?" asked the official of the baker.

The complainant merely shook his head in response. The official tried again by asking the accused a question. "Is this accusation a fact?"

The second man replied in the affirmative explaining further. "Some months ago I built and installed a small grinder for this baker. He had no complaints and indicated he was saving a great deal of time and expense by preparing his own grain rather than purchase it from the local miller. He has since refused what is owed in payment. I have respectfully requested payment in the amount we set upon yet I have not seen a deben-worth of goods. We agreed upon twenty deben as my pay. He has made false statements regarding payment of the debt, assuring me he would eventually do so. Yet, I say again, he has not."

Since the beginning of the Egyptian empire, the country had been a cashless society relying upon the barter of goods to consummate payment. A deben is a three ounce measurement of weight. Values of items are based upon a number of debens. Bread was baked in roughly the same sized loaves throughout the country, each one equaling the price of one deben making it a uniform price through the realm. If, for example, a pair of sandals sold for twenty deben, those same sandals could be traded for any other item also worth twenty deben.

The barter system had made Egypt a wildly prosperous country and the practice was thought to be scrupulously honest. As it was for the most part. Depending, however, upon various circumstances — trading illegal or perhaps stolen goods, an overwhelming product need in a community, or the social status of each trader — it could be unjustly profitable. Often, it was entirely a subjective matter, usually based on a strong desire to own an object and another's greed for gain in return.

The same practice was used throughout Egypt's trading associates. Egypt's natural resources like gold, papyrus, linen, and grain allowed for the trade of olive oil from Crete and Greece, cedar wood from Lebanon, and ebony and ivory from Africa. The Egyptian metallurgy experts were so adept at compounding metals, they created bronze with tin and copper traded with Anatolia. From the Iberian Peninsula they acquired silver, a scarce and expensive commodity, to combine with the alloy electrum to produce a metal with beautiful gold and silver properties. Trading between countries for such items was most equitable to each side.

In this particular case set before the Pharaoh, the builder of the mechanism was to be paid six deben of fabric, a straw mattress worth five deben, ground wheat flour worth seven deben, and two deben of bread. "Again I respectfully say to your majesty, I have not received these agreed upon goods."

The official now addressed the baker. "Think carefully upon these questions, Baker, before you issue your answer. Did you notify this builder of complaints concerning the efficiency of the machine he constructed? And since having this mechanism at your disposal, have you seen the need for visits to the local miller to barter for his services?"

The baker could only answer in the negative to both questions. At this, the room looked upon the Pharaoh for his decision.

"Enough," said the Pharaoh in displeasure. "This grows tiresome. Baker, you shall provide fifteen deben-worth of payment to this builder.

"And Builder, you shall put the remaining five deben worth of your time and materials to repair this bakery. This is your Pharaoh's decision on this case today." The King leaned forward and looked at each man squarely. "Yet listen well to what I say. Baker, you made an arrangement with this man for services and payment. You did not uphold your end of the contract. Indeed, you offered false statements and promises to him.

"As an Egyptian, you know your word is a sacred trust involving all aspects of your life. Honesty is how a man's worth is measured.

"As punishment for this, Baker, I could render great physical and financial penalties to you today. Yet your position in our society is one of great import. It is also a fact that you require your hands to continue making this nutrient for our people. You do not, however, require your tongue to do so. If ever another falsehood of yours be presented before me, I assure you that part of your body shall be severed from the whole."

The great King now turned his scowl upon the builder. "As for your actions, Builder, this solution was not yours to make. The violence you have shown indicates a man who yields to his temper rather than guidance from the gods or an inquiry of your Pharaoh to settle such discourse. Lesser offences have resulted in severe sentences.

"You, too, are an integral part to our country's prosperity and as such, I am unwilling to eliminate you from this task. And while you require your hands for your livelihood, I believe the loss of a finger or two shall not present an undo hindrance to that endeavor. Even now my scribes are writing of my condemnation of any such further actions by you, and my promise of this future maiming should you not heed my words."

Having lost interest in any other disputes brought to court this day, the Pharaoh stood, signaled that the Vizier should carry on, and made a grand exit through massive doors to the rear of the dais. As the great King left he heard a court attendant verbally close the Baker/Builder case and call the next.

## Chapter Four

Fittingly adorned to begin her first assigned task of the day, Tiye finally emerged from her bedchamber. Once each day, she traveled to a temple for prayer and meditation. Today, she mused, she would travel to the Temple of Karnak. It was the largest religious complex in the world: more a small city of temples than one single building. She was fortunate the place of worship was so near to this Palace. The Pharaoh had several Royal Palaces throughout the country, places to maintain his regal lifestyle while traveling up and down the Nile. This Palace, however, was Tiye's favorite and she seldom left it.

Ramses insisted upon an unusual overall entrance for this Royal compound based upon citadels he saw during his military campaigns in the Mesopotamian region. His builders constructed a magnificent tower in the form a fortified gatehouse as the main entrance to the site. The entire city-sized Royal Palace/Temple was enclosed within a double mud-brick wall 35 feet thick and 60 feet high, having the look and fortification of an impenetrable fortress.

The possibilities of war had been a threat for many years past. Indeed, thought Tiye, even in these enlightened times there was always such a threat; hence the walls. Open apertures allowed archers easy aim at intruders from high above. The walls were thick enough for soldiers to stand upon and pour oil upon any interlopers while archers would shoot flaming arrows at the gooey mixture.

Images of Ramses defeating the People-of-the-Sea and other marauders were etched upon the entire perimeter of the enclosure and rose high upon the tall gatehouse. The reliefs were viciously detailed, alerting all would-be raiders the horrors in store for them. As such, this establishment provided great security for the Pharaoh and Royal Family. No earthly harm could possibly befall this building or those within. The edifice had a slightly prison-like exterior, yet the inside offered all manner of modern conveniences and luxuries to those in residence.

Before beginning her forced time of prayer, she would allow herself the pleasure of visiting her son, Pentawer. His favorite place in the Palace was an open atrium garden encircled by splashing waters and exotic foliage brought from far away lands as gifts to the

Pharaoh. The breezes that traveled through the semi-enclosed area were scented with fragrant flowers. Here she would begin her search for her beloved son.

As highly sensual people, it was no surprise that the major themes in Egyptian religion were fertility and procreation. The family was the core of Egyptian society and there was tremendous pride in one's family. In fact, a child's lineage was traced through both parent's ancestry, not merely the father's as in other countries. Egyptians adored children, considering them great blessings to the family and the country.

Women who failed to conceive often sought help from the goddess of fertility, Isis. Several years following the birth of Pentawer, this had been Tiye's course of action as well to conceive another child. Alas, no amount of prayers or sacrifices softened the heart of the goddess and, while she rejoiced in Pentawer's life, he was destined to be her only child.

Seeing him at the far end of the room brought a smile to her face. A long ago memory suddenly walked through her thoughts; that of her young son sitting upon the lap of his father, entranced by Ramses' stories of ancestral Kings and their heroism in colorful remote lands. They would spend hours thusly, father and son, placing the country's needs second to their own enjoyment

Pentawer adored his father and their bond only strengthened over the years. She had observed the two deep in conversations regarding matters of state one minute and in loud raucous laughter the next. Pentawer had a magnificent grasp of mathematics and Egyptian laws and Ramses would often seek him out to confirm suggestions from the Royal Financiers or Lawmakers.

Tiye looked warmly at her brilliant, compassionate, and loving son — the son who would never be Pharaoh.

Pentawer's birth placed him sixth in line for the throne. One by one, the elder four bothers had succumbed to death; maladies, battlefield injuries, and accidents had taken them to the Afterlife. The remaining two candidates were Iset's son, Amonhirkhopshef, and Tiye's own beloved son. Pentawer was only slightly younger than his brother and because of the obvious preference Ramses had shown towards her son, Tiye had thought Pentawer would be named Crown Prince.

Yet plead, cry, cajole, and bribe as she might, the son of Iset was named successor by Ramses in his 25$^{th}$ year of reign. Her beloved Pentawer was positioned second in line to the eldest son, Amonhirkhopshef.

Tiye frowned as the name of her son's competitor came to mind. It was a pompous, pretentious name for a miserable excuse of a man who was more intellectually dense than a stone in the great pyramid, more useless than a barren woman. Most Palace residents referred to him as simply Amonhirk. On official events, he would be announced by his full name, syllable by syllable with much emphasis on each, together with his full title as successor to the throne. Bile rose in Tiye's stomach whenever she heard this.

And yet, when they were boys, the brothers were tutored by the same teachers and played together for hours. They had been very close until Ramses announced his heir. Once the formal decision was announced, Amonhirk became intolerable. The climate changed very quickly between the brothers at that time.

One day after their class discussion of Egypt's affiliation with neighboring countries, Tiye found her son here, upon the same bench as he was now seated. When the Queen approached her son that day, the look of pain and disbelief was evident upon his face.

"Mother," he began on that long ago day, "today we studied Egypt's relationships with other countries like Nubia and the Hittites." He took a deep breath and continued. "We barely began the class. I had just answered my tutor's question correctly when Amonhirk said something spiteful. He said he would talk to Father regarding my need to continue with these studies. He said since I would never be Pharaoh, I should be banned from this subject, as only he needed such knowledge. He told me I would be better off in the soldier's training schools. Mother, is this true? Am I no more useful than any other warrior?"

Tiye thought she would cry for her son's pain. He had always been quiet to his brother's boisterousness and studious to his brother's athletic abilities. While her son preferred to spend time in her animal zoo with her, Amonhirk enjoyed sports of all types. Pentawer had always been such a gentle boy with feelings easily wounded. The brothers were as different as night and day: Pentawer solemn and lanky, Amonhirk sturdy and agile. Yet for all his strength, Amonhirk seemed to suffer a constant runny nose or some slight malady. Her son was seldom ill and in Tiye's opinion meant he would lead a long life as the Pharaoh.

She swallowed her pain and attempted to reassure him of his other talents. "My son," said the Queen on that day, "that is not so. You are intelligent and talented, loved by everyone in the Palace. Please, speak to your father. He shall reassure you of your place in his reign. He loves you dearly — you must know that. Amonhirk has always been a most headstrong boy." She chose a gracious portrayal of him, as Tiye could never state her true feelings of the Prince: she believed Amonhirk was consumed by jealously towards her son.

"Did you not say he only spoke thusly after you correctly answered a question? As you always do?" Pentawer nodded. "So you see. Even he is aware how quick-witted and talented you are. He is embarrassed when he does not know the answer and takes his anger out upon you." He is spiteful, that one, thought Tiye; spiteful even as a small child.

"Hear me, my son. Amonhirk is greatly mistaken. Your father surrounds himself with those schooled in many subjects. He requires their knowledge for him to rule successfully. He is a great Pharaoh and cannot be wrong in this. He is often in discussion with his learned advisors, guiding him upon the best path for Egypt. It has always been thus and always shall be. I know he shall teach you all you need know if you only ask him. You are invaluable as advisor to the Pharaoh." She stroked the frowns from his forehead. "Do not brood so, my son. I trust your father shall set all to rights."

Pentawer simply nodded and rose from the bench. "I thought my brother loved me," he said. As he walked away, Tiye heard him say, "That was my favorite subject."

Tiye teemed with hatred towards Amonhirk from that moment on. To this day, she found it painful to speak to the man yet forced herself to treat the heir with the respect his position deserved. She did not behave in this civilized manner for Amonhirk's sake yet rather for her son's and Ramses'. She was ever hopeful of changing the Pharaoh's appointment and to look favorably upon Pentawer as the chosen son to become Ramses IV.

Of course, Tiye's own mother had much to say on the subject. At every opportunity, the women let Tiye know the situation was most likely her fault. "My grandson should be King," she whined constantly. If only she had given birth a few months earlier, her mother complained, he would have been the first-born. And how, Tiye would question of her mother, could that have happened? Babies are born when they wish to be.

"If you had visited the witch, we would not be in this untenable situation," her mother often pronounced.

She was referring to women who practiced questionable magic and resided in most areas of Egypt. While not formally educated magicians, for the right price they would cast any spell, one of which could result in an early delivery.

"She would have performed the necessary magic to induce your son to be born before Amonhirk. This is all your doing," finished her mother.

Naturally it was Tiye's fault. According to her mother's bleating, most of the unfortunate things in the woman's life resulted from Tiye's blunder. Tiye could indeed have made the trip to the local witch yet at what cost? An early birth could also mean death.

One in ten women died in childbirth in Egypt and 30% of newborns never saw their first birthday. Seeking unnatural inducements could increase those chances. Tiye could never have subjected herself or her unborn babe to those odds.

She now looked at her grown son seated upon the favored bench and was thankful she had never succumbed to the demand of her mother's. Sliding a smile upon her face, she walked towards him in greeting. He was her motivation for all things in this life. She would do anything for him. Anything.

## Chapter Five

The town was two days' journey on foot from Thebes and within two miles distance of the building site, a large deep valley. The town was created for one purpose — to house those talented citizens to construct and decorate a necropolis for the deceased Pharaohs and their families. Those who lived here called it simply The Village yet in official correspondence it was referred to by its formal name of Set-Maat. The town was named for a deep-seated principle in the lives of Egyptians. The desired qualities in an Egyptian's life were truth, justice, harmony, and balance. This was a concept known as ma'at, hence Set-Maat was also known as The Place of Truth. It was so named for the honorable and truthful works of art designed here by generations of artisans. The residents held great pride to be known as the Servants in the Place of Truth as they built the tombs of the Pharaohs.

Currently, sixty-eight houses were spread over three miles in a completely walled-in uphill establishment. Many generations of craftsmen had lived and worked here as paid citizens. Due to the importance of their work, they were paid up to three times that of a field hand and their homes were assigned to them as part of their wage agreement. Unmarried workers and whole families were assigned house here as part of their stipend. If a workman died, the wife no longer had the use of the house and she was forced to leave the town. Since Set-Maat was rather cut off from other communities and women were scarce, finding a wife could prove difficult for a single man.

The positions and skills of the men were inherited, taught by father to son. The construction of the tombs had been honed and improved upon over time yet the designs still followed a basic plan of elaborate twisting tunnels leading down to the final burial chamber of the Royals. They were built on specific mathematical principals and with absolute precision. After all, this was the Pharaoh's final resting place as he fought his way to the Afterlife. As such, they were built to last for eternity.

It took the hands of many men to build the tombs and those from Set-Maat were quite specialized and diverse. The architects supervised the operation, the artisans, and the unskilled men. These usually numbered 30 to 60 to a crew, one crew assigned to each side of the tomb. Occasionally this number could increase to twice as many depending upon the size of the tomb being constructed.

The progression of each tomb was efficiently planned for left and right side crews working simultaneously. The quarry gangs would begin first, digging the tomb side by side into the mountain. Using only a wooden shovels and bronze chisels, they managed to dig into this limestone hundreds of feet down to the burial chamber of Ramses III, their current build. Citizens had great respect for these human moles dedicated to their craft.

As the tunnel widened, wooden scaffolding was erected for other crews to reach highpoints when their turn upon the tomb began. The first to use these structures were the plasterers who would smooth out the walls using a mixture made from clay, quartz, and crushed straw. Once this coat dried, the next specialized gang would carefully smooth thin layers of clay and limestone whitened with diluted gypsum over the walls and ceilings.

Following this group, the draftsmen would outline the designs agreed upon by the priests and the Pharaoh. They used red ochre to divide the walls and ceilings into squares for accurate placement of the decorations and text then create a rough outline of the designs within the squares. A chief draftsman made any corrections and added detail to these designs using black charcoal. Finally, the sculptors and masonry men would start carving the bas-relief figures around the black drawings, etching the cuts deeply into the walls. The completed reliefs looked as if they were about to leap from the walls, so dimensionally real did they appear. Finally, each design would be painted in six basic colors in accordance to the holy law, each one detailed and breathtaking. Gold leaf was reserved for accentuating the many images of the gods.

As these trained artists worked, other men assigned to more menial tasks were constantly in and out of the tunnels. Some waited with large baskets in and around the scaffold to bring out excess stone and debris. Others acted as laborers assisting the craftsmen. Many would be distributing water along the line of men and some would keep the torch lamps burning. Eliminating the excess smoke from the tomb had been an ingenious discovery when the pyramids were first constructed. Baked clay containers were filled with either sesame oil or animal fat and then adding salt. The salt limited the amount of smoke from the oil-induced flame, ensuring the paintings remained bright and clean. Additionally, it had the added benefit of easier breathing for the workers.

Generations ago, some clever man discovered that by cutting lamp wicks into specific lengths, they could judge the passing of time. When the first wick of the day gave out, the men knew it was time for the mid-day meal. When the second wick was lit and died, it was time to end the day's work.

Scribes detailed everything from the amount of supplies used or needed to the names of those present for the day's shift. They detailed the amount of work completed, any unexpected problems with the tomb, and each man's workday hours. Bits of discarded limestone flakes could be found littering the tunnels depicting charcoaled reminders to a change in direction of the dig, architectural ideas, or sketches of the painted designs. Some even found the time to draw comically lewd images upon chips to share with fellow workers.

With this work progression along the line of men, it was possible for the entrance of the tomb to be completed even as digging was beginning at the deepest point of the tomb. This seemingly simple method of so many men working on one tomb in complete synchronization was a marvel of cooperation, knowledge, and habit. It was reminiscent of an anthill, each tiny insect going about his business with a full understanding of the finished result.

Since one tomb could take decades to complete — and Royalty continued to die — the town's longevity was assured. One of the first tasks of a new Pharaoh was to commission his tomb. The building of this structure took precedence over any other, even that of his royal residence. Life in an earthly Palace was fleeting — life after death was everlasting. Years were spent upon the construction of these completely man-made underworlds, staggeringly complex to build and beautiful to behold. The trick facing the construction project for the Pharaoh was two-fold — living long enough to see the tomb's completion and having it properly funded before he died. Upon the Pharaoh's demise, workers had an additional 70 days during the embalming period to complete the tomb. Some sites could be rushed into completion during this timeframe, although the original grandeur or size might suffer.

The town of Set-Maat was fully self-contained to eliminate lengthy travels and maintain full concentration upon the task at hand. In years past, water was delivered daily from the cisterns around Thebes, a difficult task for the government-paid water carriers. Now a deeply dug well in the middle of the town provided a constant source of fresh water. The townspeople had their own bakers and brewers, specialized medical men and magicians, dozens of chapels dedicated to the gods, and even a scorpion charmer who specialized in only one malady — providing magical cures for scorpion bites.

The members of the community could come and go as they wished yet only those with certain work related business could enter. The reasoning was simple — plans and renderings of Pharaoh's tombs were kept in strictest confidence and security. No one must know of the many bends and turns to the burial chamber within the tombs. Ensuring the safety of the Pharaoh and his belongings was of the utmost importance.

In decades past, Kings and their families — even favorite pets that had been mummified and saved for this purpose — had been buried deep within the walls and tunnels of pyramids. A small village had been established near these massive buildings for the sole purpose of housing the paid workers of these massive monuments. Year after year, decade after decade, these men used their talents to create the tombs with great precision and adherence to specialized methods. Constructed on a square base with four corners, the alignment of each pyramid is near perfection. Great care was taken in the designs on several to ensure each corner faces a cardinal position: North, South, East, and West.

These great four-sided structures would increase in size with each new Pharaoh, each one demanding a grander resting place than those of their predecessors. Over 1400 years before Ramses III reigned, the largest such edifice in Giza had required over two million stones to satisfy the giant ego of Pharaoh Khufu. The pyramids were immense structures befitting living gods, telling the world of the inhabitant's great power and importance. The easily seen formations also alerted others who were not so law abiding or pious — tomb robbers.

These monuments were, unfortunately, the most pretentious advertisements to the wealth hidden within. For all their detailed design and twisting tunnels, these holy structures had been forced open and robbed by thieves unafraid of the gods' retribution for their act of sacrilege. Even Pharaohs' remains were occasionally stolen, the most heinous of crimes.

It was no secret that as burial processions became more elaborate, the value of the items interred grew exponentially. Most of the looting occurred directly following the burial when priests and family had traveled home. Mandated sentries were placed onsite to protect the tomb. Unfortunately, since greed is a strong human vice, these guards were easily bribed for a cut of the bounty.

Egyptian courts dealt with such criminals almost on a daily basis yet they would never discover all the perpetrators. Torture was often employed, convincing the accused to confess and inform upon their cohorts. Punishments ran from floggings or the amputation of a hand or nose to those who were privy to the information or received the stolen goods. The sentence of an agonizing death was the norm to those who either orchestrated or entered the tomb. Still, few were deterred from this monetary windfall. More went unscathed than were apprehended.

In fact, looting of these burial sites became so severe, then-Pharaoh Amenhotep had been forced to take immediate measurers to halt this despicable crime. The original settlement housing workers for the pyramids was abandoned and this desolate specialized town was constructed over 300 years ago. Because of its lack of accessibility, Set-Maat was to be the key to this problem of tomb robbing.

A second solution was also brought into play — stop the construction of the pyramids and begin underground tombs. This limestone-rich valley was the chosen site, hence the Valley of the Gates of the Kings near Set-Maat. Of course, the looting was not altogether halted and possible reasoning lay behind this. Who knew the layout of any tomb better than the tomb builders themselves? It was a reasonable assumption to believe many valuables had found their way into the hands of such employees yet it was never proven.

The artisans and their families lived as they worked — personnel assigned to the left side of the tomb walls lived on the left side of Set-Maat. Reversely, the right-sided staff lived on the right side of the town. There were two different foremen for each project, one for the left and one for the right, who lived among his assigned staff. It seemed to make traveling to the site easier and communications locally situated. Whatever the original reasoning behind this divide, it had been thus since the city's inception.

Pentu was the Foreman of the Left Side Gang for each tomb. Since the work period was a ten-day cycle with two days off, many men stayed in a tented encampment during their time-on period rather than travel back and forth from the town. The women managed the family and household affairs until their men returned home for their free period.

As Pentu passed one side of the walled-in town he came across script etched into the stone He looked closer and saw it was a love poem. Poetry was one of the best-unknown treasures in Egypt. The people had poems and verses for everything. Poems were traditionally said or sung as a funerary verse to protect the Pharaoh after death. Some were written as a cry for justice, commemorating the death of a loved one, or in honor of the gods. Yet the subject matter most often written of was love. That emotion brought forth great writings of love found, love lost, and everlasting love. Pentu read this poem aloud:

*To hear your voice is pomegranate wine to me*
*I draw life from hearing it*
*Could I see you with every glance,*
*It would be better for me*
*Than to eat or to drink* [1]

It was beautifully poignant and to Pentu spoke of something he fervently desired: a love to call his own. His daily prayer to the gods was a plea to find a wife and have children to love. He was yet searching. Most of the women in the town were married and he did not reciprocate the attention from the single women who found interest in him. I have been blessed with health and stability, he thought. Perhaps that is all any man should expect from life. Yet he hoped for more. Some day, I wish to shower a woman with love. I shall know her at first sight.

---

[1] Excerpt from the poem *The Flower Song* discovered in the town of Set-Maat. First written during Egypt's New Kingdom (1539-1075 BC) but likely composed much earlier.

For now, he must be about his business. Today he was making the two-mile walk to the tombs from the town and past the impromptu tents. Pentu preferred his own bed at night and enjoyed the quit of his solitary abode to that of a camp full of men. Additionally, he could not hear the constant complaints from the workers when he was within his own walls. To avoid such grumblings for as long as possible, he walked a bit slower today. The men were becoming tiresome yet there was naught he could do other than commiserate with them.

Circling around the tented encampment, he strode down the hill to the valley below. In the middle of the site was a large clearing, a center point of sorts. Branching from this spot into the cliffs and hills surrounding him were the tombs built by generations of his family.

Nodding to some of the workers, he made his way to the tomb currently under final construction, that of Ramses III. The underground tunnels and chambers were located down a narrow path from the center point.

He stood looking at the squared-off opening surrounded by blocks of stone held together with mud and acacia beams as support. Walking inside the cool entrance, he rubbed his hand upon one of the eight stone pillars leading down to secret chambers. The columns were smooth and cool to the touch. The stonemasons had done an excellent job, thought Pentu.

He took his time to marvel at the artistry along the route to the burial chamber. The colorful renderings of the Pharaoh's triumphs and tales of his bravery began upon the base of the pillars and walls, finally stretching above his head to the curved limestone ceiling. Magnificent, thought Pentu. The colors were vibrant and detailed. Messages to the gods, passages from holy books, and magical spells had been inscribed throughout the tomb. When the gods viewed these, they would know the righteous character of the Pharaoh. This was as it must be for Egypt's own living god.

As he walked, he picked up a few tools someone had mislaid. One was a bundle of rope with one side frayed, creating a brush that was now crusted with dried material. It had been used to add thin layers of plaster to the tomb. The other item he found was a wooden plumb bob used for alignment. It was a large wooden framed triangle with a cross piece of wood just under one peak. Hanging from this was a carved, pointed clay bob tied to the apex with a string. Simple, yet quite accurate.

He made an abrupt turn in one of the annexed corridors, a turn not originally planned upon. This tomb had once been under construction for the Pharaoh Setnakht, father to Ramses III. When digging broke through to a tomb of another deceased King, the hole was repaired, and Setnakht's tomb was abandoned to dig elsewhere. Unwilling to waste the work that had been accomplished so far, Ramses III claimed it, removed traces and images of Setnakht, and replaced them with his own. Using their shovels and chisels, the crews simply dug around the old tomb and this sharp offset corridor was the result.

Limestone is a strong material, one that could withstand the exposure to the Egyptian sun and temperatures, yet could be unpredictable and stubborn to their plans. The formation of many natural tunnels and chambers occasionally occurred and the men used these rather than dig out others. For all the copious notes and plans of the engineers, they were always at the mercy of the limestone.

As he ventured through these long sloping corridors down to the burial hall, Pentu heard the sounds of tapping and voices. Only a few men would be working on the tomb now. It was almost complete yet there were always finishing touches or another painted scene Ramses had commissioned. The longer he lived, the more embellishments they added. It mattered naught: this tomb was large enough to accommodate any changes the Pharaoh would have.

He passed through an arched opening and into the actual burial chamber. He had walked over 400 feet from the entrance to this point, the end of the tomb. Here were more detailed reliefs of His King in vibrant colors. He was pictured in glorious battle, his bow raised, his enemies scattering before his golden chariot. In the corners were life-sized statues of the gods carved from obsidian with gold accents.

The statue of Anubis, god of the dead, overshadowed the others in size. It would be this god's task to guide the King into his eternal life. The god's large jackal-head was also of obsidian while his garments and headdress were inlaid with precious gems like lapis lazuli, obsidian, garnet, and red carnelian.

In the center of the room stood three caskets, carved from wood and gilded with gold. They were nestled inside one another according to size, the final lid leaning against one wall. The innermost one would hold the mummified remains of the King. Before the Pharaoh died, Priests would carve magical spells within the largest casket to guarantee a quick journey to time without end. These multiple coffins would ensure the safety of the great ruler.

The focal point in the room was the rose granite sarcophagus. The top of this long stone box stood at shoulder height to Pentu and was longer than he was tall. The sides were completely covered in religious texts, images of Ramses vanquishing his enemies by decapitating them, journeying on his barge to the Afterlife, and massive carvings of the goddesses Nephthys and Isis, the protectors of mummies. The full sized relief of the King dressed in Royal finery was centered upon the top flanked by two additional carvings of the goddesses. The lid alone weighed over 1300 pounds. Several men and a pulley system would likely be utilized to place the granite lid upon the entire collection of nestled wooden coffins.

The adjacent chamber would hold the Kings personal items, one of which would be the very chariot pictured in the wall reliefs. Other smaller statues representing the King's servants were already placed in abundance. This staff would be needed to serve him throughout time when the gods raised his body. There was once a period in Egypt's history when members of the Pharaoh's staff were killed and buried with him for their servitude in eternity. Over time, that was considered barbaric and reproductions representing servants were utilized instead.

A multitude of treasures would fill this room since whatever a person had enjoyed or needed in life he would also require in the Afterlife. Taught by the holy priests, one's inner being, called his *ka,* would join the Pharaoh's body after death and it would rise again to enjoy the familiar surroundings of home and deceased loved ones in the Afterlife. This King had reigned for 67 years and would surely have an abundance of required possessions for his eternity.

Pentu could only imagine such glorious items resting here with him. Then he shook his head — no, he thought, I could not. My imagination is not that great. Try as he might he could never imagine such splendor since he had never witnessed it. His father told him of jeweled beds, golden chairs, mummified pets, and food to ease hunger placed for Kings past. He knew the Book of the Dead would be in position near the King's resting place although he had only heard of such a text.

Looking to the right he saw the large alabaster chest that would hold the Royal canopic jars. He knew an internal organ from the mummification process of the King would be placed in each ornate container. Each piece of flesh would be waiting to be rejoined with the King. Only the priests would cross this threshold and view the room at it's fullest, issue the final prayers, and recite the last spell. He longed for such sights and although he had an asset in building the tomb, he was merely a simple foreman — and only a foreman on the left side at that.

Since Ramses had ruled throughout Pentu's life, he had never seen a Royal Funeral Procession. His uncle, who along with his father had been stone masons from the village, told of furniture dripping with gold, dazzling jewelry, enormous alabaster bottles filled with rare ointments and oils, golden battle armaments, hammered gold thrones, even a full-scale barge. His father described golden sandals with hammered gold finger-and-toe covers. Ornate garments would be placed in the antechamber so the deceased would be properly dressed when he met the gods.

While pondering all this, he heard voices grow louder as some of his team approached the treasure room. He had specifically tried to avoid them since he could well guess their topic of conversation.

"Here," shouted one man. "He is here. I was sure he walked this direction. Pentu, our wages are another day late," said the artisan without preamble. "No supplies for a week now. We are rationing as well as any other family yet the supplies grow scarce. I have four children. We need our deserved pay."

The other men nodded in agreement. Pentu knew of this oversight of the Vizier's yet tried to reassure the men.

"I am sure it is merely a delay. Perhaps the Vizier has not been able to collect fresh goods. Have we not always received caravans each month? He shall arrive, I assure you," he said without conviction. He too was beginning to wonder of the delay.

By now several men had gathered including the scribes, men from the camp, and the second foreman.

"And how is it you know of this?" asked one man belligerently while thrusting forward his prominent chin. "Have you received a message to notify you of a delay?"

Someone must go to Thebes and complain to the Vizier," said another man.

"No. The Pharaoh must know of this directly. I do not trust the Vizier," said another.

Pentu tried to restore peace, wondering why he was suddenly assigned to bring level thinking to this crowd. "The Vizier seems like a good man. *Is* a good man," he corrected himself with more conviction. "Remember, he is at the behest of our King in both Upper and Lower Egypt. Perhaps he is simply overwhelmed this month or is traveling and did not leave proper instructions." In times past, one Vizier was assigned to Lower Egypt (which oddly enough was to the north) while another to the Upper Kingdom (located in the southern portion) of the country.

Several years ago, the Lower Vizier was removed and punished for corruption. The Upper Vizier, Hewernef, was suddenly in charge of maintaining the wishes of his King throughout the entire country. His duties were vast — financial matters as well as judicial, military, and architectural were only a few. He took up residency in Thebes to be closer to the King yet he was seldom in his own home. Pentu often wondered how one man could manage such a feat. Indeed, the last time he saw the Vizier the man was looking quite drawn and wan.

The men were beginning to quiet down and listen to him. "Perhaps," said Pentu, "one of our scribes should journey into Thebes if payment does not arrive soon. That is one of their duties, you remember, to settle differences between us. I believe this should be in their prevue as well. I think two more days' wait might be in order." With that, he began to walk away, feeling he had done all he could and more than he was obliged. Remembering the pitfalls taken by the residents of Set-Maat in the past, he really wanted no part of this discussion.

Two years prior, the problem of past due wages had become critical when the town's supplies were two months late. Pleading had led to naught but silence from the Pharaoh so the men gathered as one to commit a most unheard of act. The workers had refused to continue construction upon any commissioned tomb or structure.

For the first time in recorded history, common craftsmen brought the government of Egypt to its knees, a most dangerous act to workers and families alike. If that bold endeavor would not yield the outcome they desired, replacements for their jobs could be found or, worse yet, they could be arrested for committing a crime against the King.

By the power of the gods, the King had seen fit to acquiesce to their risky maneuver. The Vizier personally brought a wagon laden with past due food and supplies. The look in his man's eyes, however, told Pentu that such a risky move should never be taken again.

"I think you should travel to Thebes and speak with the Vizier," said a hulk of a man in the back of the chamber. "You are a man who thinks calmly."

"Yes," chimed in another. "Pentu is the man for the task. You have always been fair to us, even sharing your portion of goods with others."

"I think he should go directly to the Pharaoh."

"Yes, Yes! The Pharaoh. He is the only one who can provide us relief."

"The Pharaoh will fill this burial chamber with all manner of riches and yet we have no food or blankets. Surely he can trade some of his gold for supplies."

The men were becoming loud and angry. It would be easy for a riot to break out if this continued. While both scribes faired well with problems among this settlement, they often made rulings based upon emotion rather than evaluating the problem. Pentu had not always agreed with the decisions rendered, especially when it concerned his own crew.

"Yes, I shall go," he said loudly over their raised voices. The men looked expectantly at him. "I shall go," he said again. "Yet you must agree to a two day wait. If the Vizier arrives before that time, I shall speak to him here. If not, I promise to travel to Thebes. If you do not agree, you can find someone else to do your negotiating." There was some grumbling yet in the end, there was accord all around. They would wait for two days.

## Chapter Six

This morning, Queen Tiye opted for her covered caravan along with her personal guards to transport her to the temple. It was not a lengthy journey since her destination was the compound of Karnak, just at the end of Thebes' city square. As often as she journeyed this short distance to the temple, the sight of it always caught at her breath.

Pharaohs began commissioning the building of Karnak several hundred years ago to honor the great god Amun, the creator of all things. Since the initial dedication, each subsequent ruler added to it, proclaiming his own show of power. Its size and magnificent artwork stated quite plainly the devotion and prominence religion held to the people of Egypt. This massive temple establishment was easily seen from the Royal Palace. Like the Palace, the temple facility was comprised of a series of Pylons, monumental gateways that tapered into carved horizontal moldings called cornices. Each of these entries led into courtyards, halls, and temples. One pylon led into the great Hypostyle Hall, containing sandstone support columns 75 feet tall. Designs of limestone-carved clusters of reeds such as papyrus, lotus and palm leaves flared out at the top of each colorful column and onto the ceiling. Or so she had been told. Only the Pharaoh and selected priests were allowed at the religious rituals held deep inside this particular hall. Her husband told her of its glorious details. The hall itself, he said, was over 50,000 square feet with 134 of those tall majestic columns lending their support to the carved and painted ceiling.

As Queen, she found no reasoning why she should not be a participant in these rituals. She had tried cajoling her husband into — at the very least — providing her a peek inside this wondrous hall. She was uniformly refused. The priests, he said, would not allow it. The priests, she often thought, overstepped their bounds with their increasing power and wealth. She had yet to meet one that did not repulse her. She considered them all patronizing vermin.

There was no separation of religious beliefs from the daily life of an Egyptian. From morning prayers to evening devotions and each task throughout their day, religion did not simply surround the Egyptians; their lives were consumed by it. They believed all events were the actions, or the non-actions of the gods. Water fell from the sky, fishing was plentiful, and children were born healthy because the gods rewarded the proper conduct of the people. Conversely, punishment was issued for earthly wrongs to another person or slights to the gods. A farmer might pray for a healthy crop, yet it would not be forthcoming if the man had cheated his neighbor. The gods could be cruel and many prayers were never answered. Or, thought Tiye, perhaps the prayers <u>were</u> answered only not in the manner the penitent had hoped.

This designated time in a temple was a daily duty of hers and she performed it half-heartedly. She tried to believe in the gods and their power over mankind — had wanted to all her life. If one did not believe and act righteously in this life, one could never experience the joy of the Afterlife. And all Egyptian beliefs began with the expectations of the Afterlife.

While she firmly believed in an eternity, she was dubious of the gods. "Yet how can I reconcile one without the other?" she thought, befuddled by the contradiction within her. Of course she would never mention such doubts. Risk being called a blasphemer or disloyal to the Pharaoh? Never. She was Queen and as such was held to a higher standard than others. Part of that lofty pedestal she stood upon was loyalty to her Pharaoh, the gods, and their priests. Silence was the only option. Still, the turmoil often churned within her.

For the most part, Tiye agreed with the teachings towards tranquility among Egypt's people. She found it difficult, however, to pray and adore a god with a body of a human and the head of a bird or a jackal. Some gods were a combination of two or even three animal parts. While she loved animals, she found such a creature questionable and was unable to form affection for such a god. She prayed to them anyway hoping her doubts proved false. She believed in taking no chances.

Most Egyptians did not live past their early thirties so they took great comfort in knowing life continued after one's physical death. Observations of surrounding occurrences gave truth to this belief: the sun died in the west each night and lived again on the morn in the east. So too did the order of their world: it was eternal and constant. The gods controlled the sun as they did the ebb and flow of the Nile river and every living creature. The world functioned with predictability and regularity, as should their everyday life.

For that reason, Egyptians were concerned with interactions with their gods and the ethics of dealing with each other. Mankind must subdue their baser desires for the good of all to live in a society that would not only benefit them on earth yet be rewarded after death. It was a widely held tenant of Egyptian morality: purity was rewarded by a joyful paradise and wrongdoing was punished.

And yet, thought Tiye, what of the greedy, the lustful, and the dishonest people? Were they prepared to gamble away their chance at salvation through misdeeds? Tiye knew firsthand of those who went about their daily lives with disdain for all others. They prayed in the morning then cheated a neighbor before the noon meal in the most nefarious of business dealings.

She knew of priests — allegedly above all worldly faults — who were the most offensive. Greed seemed to be infecting that group of men in an incredible rate. How, wondered the Queen, could they ever hope to sit with their families and the gods after their death? Perhaps they were even more skeptical of a godly existence than she. If one did not believe, she reasoned, they would have no fear of death as long as their earthly body was properly prepared for burial.

Disembarking her coach, she instructed one of the sentries to shield her with protection against the sun. He shot her a sarcastic grin in response and assisted her from the pallet, brushing his fingers against her ample bosom as he did so. She disliked this caretaker and had mentioned as much to her husband only to be told of the man's abilities to protect her. This man had been in her small division of guards sporadically for over one year. Whenever he stood at her side in protection, he had regarded her with insolence and lewdness. His eyes often held another emotion she read as cruelty and dislike which had shocked her. She regarded him with indifference as she did any other servant so his decidedly negative reaction towards her remained a mystery.

Also, while his touching of her body — sliding his hand against her full buttocks or across her waist — could be misconstrued as accidental mishaps while in her proximity, she did not believe that was the case.

No, she thought, she was sure these actions were deliberate. Rather than dismiss him from her entourage, she merely smiled. Familiarity had become a habit with this man; an unacceptable habit she planned to use against him when she needed. As a child, she had developed an excellent memory of other's slights towards her; a talent she had honed through the years.

Coming from a family of great wealth and blood ties to the Royal Family, she had never been denied the comforts life could offer. However, she was not raised by nannies, unlike other children in families of stature. She often wished she had the attention of a nanny. Her mother had rules for every facet of her life, from morning until night. If she ever disobeyed, her mother effected punishment as only she could. Beatings had been the least of them, she reflected.

Tiye knew from a very young age she was destined and contracted for marriage to the Crown Prince of Egypt and would one day become Queen. Once, after her mother had slapped her face for a less than respectful tone to her childish voice, she had made the mistake to disagree with the treatment. When I am Queen, she told her mother insolently, I should see you beheaded if you treat me in such a shameful manner. The look upon her mother's face informed her she had made more than a slight error. For her words, Tiye had been locked in a small storage cabinet for two days, sans food or water. It was a lesson well learned by the young Tiye and she had never spoken of the mortification to another. She had curbed her tongue from that point on towards her mother.

*Her Mother*, she thought with distaste. How those two words stuck in her throat. The woman had the appeal of a scorpion. She had never been much of a mother to Tiye, preferring instead her two brothers.

And yet, her two enlightened siblings had taken their wives and children out of the woman's grasping claws to be employed elsewhere in one of her father's many business interests. Even her father had left, choosing another residence in Lower Egypt pursuing a more enjoyable retreat. Tiye was the lone survivor, the only family member remaining to endure the serpent's tongue. She missed her father dearly: and resented him for leaving her alone.

In spite of her harsh upbringing — or perhaps because of it — she discovered a method to gain her own power in life. She considered herself a collector, yet not of trinkets. She was a hoarder of other's misdeeds. Holding these snippets of information, either real or construed, had given her control over another. When the time was right she would request payment or favors from victims in return for her silence.

In her youth, she occasionally threatened a child in her social circle of friends with their misdeed and a promise to tattle. Tiye was an accomplished liar and her natural look of innocence only added to her believability. Parents always accepted her tale hence her victims always yielded. Only once did anyone refuse. One unfortunate playmate had found herself severely punished when her transgression came to light. The girl never rejected another request from Tiye again.

Perhaps, thought Tiye, it is in my bloodline. When she was a small girl, she overheard her mother conduct this very same technique with another woman of means. From what she remembered, the conversation concerned a necklace her mother coveted. The words were not easily distinguished from between the thick walls of the home. She only remembered the malicious tone her mother used and the other woman's swift exit from the abode. That night at the evening meal, her mother was wearing the woman's necklace. Yes, thought the Queen, it must be in my lineage.

She would savor the actions of this soldier; perhaps encourage them as well. A most important favor would be collected from him for holding her tongue. After all, she did have the ear of the Pharaoh and he naturally believed whatever she chose to whisper in that ear. "Yes," she murmured under her breath, "this man could be very useful." She smiled to herself again as she walked the steps to the temple. Hoarding her secret close was almost as fun as presenting it to the unwitting victim. She would allow his contrivances to continue, committing them to memory in great detail.

Rousing herself from these pleasurable thoughts, she faced the task at hand. She must pray for guidance and use her ingenuity to develop a pleasurable evening for her husband. May the gods — or good fortune — help her if she did not.

## Chapter Seven

His given name meant 'killer' and 'victorious'— two graphic adjectives that coincidentally described his character. He was proud of the moniker and his life exemplified his name. While he professed himself to be an honorable man, those around him knew the truth: his cruelty knew no bounds.

Akar began his service to the King acting as a Royal Tax Collector. In a barter society, taxes were exacted by seizing a portion of the crops grown, merchandise made, or even a piece of one's property. A usual amount for taxes was 10% of the total. Innovations and growth could not occur without a steady source of income to finance Egypt's great achievements; hence the high taxation rate in Egypt.

The agriculture sector was the easiest from which to estimate taxes. The field was measured belonging to the landowner and the yield of crops assessed. Additionally, bulky crops were not hidden particularly well, even those harvested and bound for market. If the owner disavowed ownership to a portion of land to avoid taxes upon it, the land was seized for the Throne.

Whatever Egypt lacked in resources it could easily gain through the trade of grain, the most profitable commodity in the country. When a farmer had a surplus of grain, it was stored in community granaries. However, each time the farmer made a withdrawal of his portion, he was charged a fee dependent upon the quantity. This fee was divided between a cost to feed the needy, payment to those who maintained the granary, and the balance deposited into the Treasury of Egypt. Residents of the rich Nile farmlands also provided crops to the Pharaoh who then redistributed the product to each class of people based on rank and status. Essentially, the rich became more so.

While most Egyptians paid their taxes without dispute, some were not so amenable. Granted it could be difficult for a farmer to pay promptly what was owed in times of drought. The most elaborate of excuses, however, came from statesmen and wealthy mayors who, Akar believed, had more than enough in their reserve. This was the element of his position he enjoyed most. It was perfectly legal for him as Master Tax Collector to induce the cheater to pay by whatever means necessary. Breaking arms was a favorite tactic of his. Another method of persuasion was to issue several lashes to one's back. Once, when a city official was adamantly refusing to pay, he beat the man to death. It was all in a day's work for Akar.

To be a tax collector was to have the most hated job in the country. Most men in this profession lived in isolation, fear, and exclusion from society. Usually, the Master Official took an assistant to each home for support. Not so with Akar. Large and burly, he never feared for his well-being. Indeed, he often flaunted himself in public, daring anyone to offend or threaten him. He pushed through life taking what he wanted from each position and then moved on to another as any other natural predator.

He shifted from tax collecting to the prison system. Proving an aptitude in the control of prisoners, he was quickly promoted to Chief Punisher of Criminals within the country's police force. To Akar it not only meant higher wages, it meant prestige as well. He was now permitted to bring his own particular form of justice and punishment to those imprisoned unfortunates.

Occasionally, citizens were incarcerated until a debt could be repaid yet usually minimal offenses were resolved in the courts with fines assessed. Those convicted of theft or a more offensive crime usually faced the Vizier himself in court. Occasionally their physical punishment was dispensed in a public display as an example. All in all, Egypt did not have a substantial group in a prison at any one time. The exception was the hardened criminals — murderers and deserters for example — who were held until their day of reckoning arrived.

If prisoners were not to be the subjects of a public exhibit, the Vizier passed the criminals with their assigned sentences to Akar. He in turn would assign his underlings to mete out the minor punishment. Some payment was due in flesh and his subordinates easily handled simple tasks as flogging or issuing the usual punishment of five bleeding cuts upon the person's back. The more involved and pain inducing penalties he performed himself, often improvising in these bloody tasks. Akar believed all prisoners needed punishing, yet there was a more sinister reason for his personal touch: he enjoyed it.

He was particularly pleased when a sentencing involved disfigurement or mutilation and he took great care with his knives, ensuring the victim did not soon forget the lesson taught. Slicing off an ear or a piece of a nose was an art to Akar. The screams and pleas of the unfortunate who found himself at the hands of his artistry often brought him to physical arousal.

Then there were the women. He was not often lucky enough to have females in his care as very few were ever sentenced to the prison system. When they did, he found time to give them special attention. Occasionally, if time permitted, the attention lasted several days. Even if their time together was brief, he always allotted a moment to take a special keepsake from each one. The handcrafted box hidden within the walls of his domain held many such tokens. Often running his fingers through his collection or adding a fresh memento to the box, he was continually amazed at how nipples could differ from woman to woman. Even the tiny bits from his first subjects, now long shriveled and dried, still showed variety.

When women prisoners were not available, he took to one of the few established brothels in the country. He had a reputation to uphold, after all. His pleasures in the bedchamber involved depravity and pain, usually ending with a beating upon the woman. The extra payment he tossed at them always ensured their silence. If that did not hold their tongues, they knew he had other methods with which to do so.

When he was an adolescent, perhaps twelve years of age, his father declared himself through with the boy, calling Akar a degenerate, emotionally deficient, and a failure as a son. He was banished from his childhood home to live with a distant relation on his mother's side. After one year, when he was caught branding his small cousin, they too washed their hands of him.

Perhaps, he thought, I *am* emotionally deficient. He should have been grateful to his relative for merely casting him out. The man could have informed the authorities and had Akar arrested yet he cared naught what his family thought of him. Throughout his life he knew he was capable of reaching great heights.

On his own, he began meagerly enough as an apprentice to a sword maker. He was especially interested in the variety of blades and their purpose. This one could slice off an ear with ease, that one would slide through a man's body like porridge. It would be a study for his future triumphs, he felt. Such knowledge would be useful throughout his life.

He had succeeded in becoming a great warrior for the sake of his country and His Pharaoh, battling his way through the enemy and leaving destruction and blood in his wake. Glorious days!

Having proved himself on the battlefield, he had become a member of the bodyguard corps. Now he was a captain and the Keeper of the Royal Guards, the man overseeing an entire company.

Because of his position he was entitled to special benefits. He resided in a sumptuous suite of his own within the compound of the troops. The Pharaoh was fond of Akar's humor and often invited him to partake of evening food and drink, much to Queen Tiye's displeasure. He presented a lascivious grin at the thought of Tiye. She was not a beauty yet attractive enough, with a large bosom and hips to match. A body he could truly devote many exceptional nights to.

And today, he said to himself, I am assigned to that Royal Pompous Bitch. She seldom traveled outside the confines of the Palace and when she did, it was never exciting or dangerous. Still, he had asked for this — literally. Royal Guards were often rotated and if a space needed filling for a time, he sought out this post. It pleased him to silently torment her with his casual contact. So far, she had never chastised him for his random touch. Perhaps she did not care. Or perhaps she enjoyed it. Either way, his taunting would continue until he was directed otherwise.

## Chapter Eight

For the King, evenings at the Palace were often enjoyable, filled with exotic food, scintillating conversation, drink, and musical entertainment. Sometimes the true pleasure came privately after the evening meal. Following his visit to her cleansing room two days past, the King had been especially pleased that same evening in the bedchamber of his wife, Tiye. Her imagination was seldom boring yet remembering what she had accomplished that evening with feathers and fine linen bands brought a smile to his face.

Daytime duties, however, had become complete drudgery to Ramses these many years. His advisors continued to present him with unpleasant and occasionally dire news. Today the Pharaoh was not in an intolerable mood anticipating more of the same. He became even more foul tempered after hearing from his Vizier.

His Royal Council Ministers were gathered in the Audience Room, each wearing their amulets, armbands of gold, earrings, and massive rings. Some of these pieces were for adornment or vanity. Others proved more useful to their position.

Rings were not only fashionable but served a more practical purpose for those in ranking government positions. Originally, each official had a short stubby piece of metal with his own particular crest crafted onto a flat end. These left a distinctive mark of one's position on a tiny blob of wax or dipped into black ink to seal official messages. These sealing sticks were often misplaced, lost, or stolen. Someone eventually had an idea to incorporate these crests upon the top of finger rings. Always worn, members of the Pharaoh's council and his officials throughout the country never feared of loosing their assigned seal again. As expected, other fingers were adorned with more valuable rings to complete the look of said official.

Today, some of those rings were twisting in anxiety, fearing the current disposition of the Royal Pharaoh

"Am I to understand this employee of my tomb has the audacity to threaten me, His Pharaoh and Ruler of all Egypt?" he said menacingly.

"Sire, he has been sent as an envoy by the entire community of Set-Maat," said his Vizier carefully. "I assure you, he is not behaving in a threatening manner. When we spoke yesterday he expresses great adoration for you. They have not ceased construction, My King, only suggesting to do so if payment should not be made.' This was, of course, an over exaggeration on the part of the Vizier to protect his own skin.

The King pounded both arms of his chair and half rose from it. "Threat or suggestion, I will not have this. Not again," he yelled.

He well remembered the previous occurrence when the work upon his tomb and that of others had screeched to a halt. Only when carts laden with goods had arrived at the settlement did operations begin again. The people of Set-Maat had succeeded to strike against the throne in an unthinkable act of treason and humiliation towards the King. It had been the first such recorded act against any world ruler. He would not suffer so again.

"And what say you, my Master of Finance? How stands the treasury and the solvency of my land?" said the King sarcastically. The man addressed disliked delivering bad news to his King yet he would be forced to do so now. Clearing his throat he said, "My King, as you know during your reign we have been involved in several battles and all-out wars. While your guidance and the blessings of the gods have seen triumph on each occasion, war has it consequences no matter the victor. Conflicts are a most expensive business." For hundreds of years Egypt had enjoyed a singular prestige throughout the world. They were second to none in their pre-eminence. Yet this prominent position came with a price. Military clashes were expensive and the treasury was draining at an alarming rate. Financial stability was a continual concern to his advisors. Yet how to put this inoffensively to the King was the question facing the Minister. "Provisions for war — food, clothing, weapons for our soldiers, temporary tenting facilities, among so many others — are quite costly. Add to that the loss of many good men on the battlefield and you can understand the drain on the treasury. Of course a soldier's additional pay for each enemy killed is of a further cost."

The Minister was referring to the method of counting the number of enemy lives taken while on the battlefield. As proof of their killings, each soldier brought back the severed hands of the defeated troops. For each kill, they were rewarded additional sums. Off the record, the Egyptian soldiers often severed another enemy body part as a personal trophy — the uncircumcised penis of their dead victim. This was more of a novelty, an oddity for others to behold since most Egyptian males went under the blade as an adolescent for the sake of cleanliness.

"And yet," declared the Pharaoh, "our many wins have produced much wealth to the treasury and should have been more than adequate to pay for further conflicts. All symbols of wealth and power were collected from our defeated enemies and transferred to the Royal Treasury. Since I know this to be so, I fail to understand why we do not have an abundance in our reserves.

"Then too, it was on my command the copper mines of Canaan and Sinai be quarried for the glory of this mighty country thereby providing further resources. It was through my negotiations an organized trade route was developed with the Land of Punt. These accomplishments brought in goods and riches never before seen in Egypt. Why have these funds been consumed?"

"Unfortunately the decrease in collected taxes has not added to our reserves. Perhaps," the man suggested at the Kings scowl, "we can offset these losses by an increase in taxation. That would depend, I believe, upon our production of crops."

"So now we arrive at you, my Royal Minister of Taxes and Levy." The Mighty Pharaoh Ramses looked directly at the minister, waiting for a clear response.

"My Royal Majesty, the drought we have suffered these several years has not been profitable for crops or consequently the taxes collected upon them. As you are aware, crop production composes the greatest work force in the country and the most profitable to Egypt in trade. Since our crops have not been as plentiful of late, trade and production in all areas have steadily decreased. Your citizen's income has lessoned as a result. It is impossible to collect on income not earned or held. It would lead to a complete break in the lives of your people."

"You have attempted to pass blame from one council to another," said the King in anger. "Very well. Let me hear from the Readers of the Waters. Perhaps they will have news to brighten this outlook of doom you present me."

So important was the Nile to his country, Egypt developed a yearly calendar based upon the three cycles of the river. Each time frame consisted of four months with 30 days in each. The first season was the flooding period, when the river overflowed onto the lands leaving behind layers of fertile silt. The second was the planting season and the last the harvest period.

When his land was blessed with the yearly great flooding period, the rich earth produced such crops as flax, figs, melons, pomegranates, barley, and numerous varieties of vegetables. The herbs produced were used in cooking, medicine, cosmetics, and embalming the dead. Papyrus was the most versatile of crops, which not only grew wild but was also cultivated. It had been harvested in Egypt for thousands of years. The root of the plant was edible while the stem was used to craft parts of boats, mats, and paper.

From wheat and other grains, the Egyptians made porridge and bread. A low alcoholic beer made from barley was thick, nourishing, and sweet. It was part of every Egyptian's central diet. Without the Nile overflowing her banks, all expectations of earnings would be crushed.

Throughout the history of Egypt, a group of Priests and Magicians were tasked with the duty of reading the level of the Nile River to determine the rise and fall of its flooding periods utilizing their god-given talents and the use of ancient Nilometers. The country maintained three basic types of Nilometers. One was a vertical column build into the sides of the river bank, the second was a magnificent stone carved structure with a corridor stairway of steps leading down to the Nile, and the last was a deep well with a culvert. By reading the specifically notched measurements in the stone, this group of trained men could successfully determined the extent to which the river would overflow and feed the soil with nutrients. If the water level was low, famine could ensue. If the level was too high, the flooding could be destructive. The men, by whatever means used, were never mistaken in forecasting the rise to come.

In this land of sand and heat, water also meant power. The control of this precious resource was the heart of Egypt's political system and their strength among other countries. Egypt's complicated and inventive irrigation system had maintained that strength for thousands of years. Canals, basins, dams, and reservoirs provided irrigation from the Nile River to crops for trade and to cisterns holding fresh filtered water for his people. It also provided water to private gardens, fruit and vegetable groves, and elegant ponds and fountains to those of wealth. Water was also used in trade with other countries, some who had seen worse devastation than Egypt from the drought. The Pharaoh and all of Egypt needed these upcoming floods.

One Official Reader was brave enough to answer. "Most Revered Ruler of all Egypt," he began, "once again, the amount of melting snowfall from the mountains has not been adequate enough to bring the Nile to its much-needed levels. Based upon our readings, the flooding season will not extend over our banks to an extensive land mass." The King's scowl deepened and the man continued hurriedly, "Crops generated will be barely adequate to feed our people and many farmers are planting further inland with crops needing less water. They are often hand delivering the water from the river, as our irrigation system does not reach this newly planted area. Naturally we cannot invest in the needed canals without the necessary funds. We pray, however, their ingenuity and hard work will aid us in our harvesting bounty. Of course, trade crops to our neighbors will be lessened and rather limited. The taxes collected on profits from trade will remain much the same as last year; low. For whatever reason, the gods do not see fit to release us — and, I might add, neighboring countries as well — from the continual drought."

"Unacceptable!" roared the King. "You have misread the Nilometers. They are ancient and in need of repair. I have seen the crumbling stone with my own eyes."

"While my King is correct as to the age of some Nilometers, we have constructed new level readers in other locations and repaired several of the old. We have relied upon the newer marks and architecturally sound levelers. I assure you, with much respect, that we have traveled the length of our river and recalculated our findings. We are not mistaken."

"And yet," stated the Pharaoh with annoyance, "my earlier question remains unanswered. What has happened to our spoils of war? I wish to know the accounting of those funds."

One man began speaking with much trepidation. What he was about to say would surely be misconstrued as criticism yet it must be voiced. "My Pharaoh, with the collected spoils from our victories, the country began an enormous amount of building projects, a most generous undertaking by you, Great One. Much has been spent on your construction projects, including enlarging Temples extending over the most fertile of soil. Perhaps, My Great King, if some of this temple land was reestablished to produce more crops, we may yet see a healthy harvest."

Another Minister spoke up, believing he had latched onto a wonderful solution. "My Pharaoh, regarding the Priests of Amun and their temples, there is more we should discuss. Many of these temples now sit upon these fertile lands. A generation ago they were declared non-taxable. Field hands work portions of this land for the good of the people, yet they are forced to relinquish a share of their crops or other deben-worth of goods to these priests. If they do not pay these fees, they will loose permission to grow crops. These fees to the priests do not profit your Throne as they too have been contracted as non-taxable. Adjusting the ownership of this land is a viable solution to many financial difficulties we now face. However, the Priests of Amun have become extremely wealthy and wield considerable power from these agreements. Any decisions in this matter should be handled cautiously as they shall not welcome our interference."

Egypt and all its glory belonged solely to the Pharaoh. Only he could portion off land or allocate it for the betterment of his people. This minister hoped these lands could be re-designated by His Pharaoh.

The Pharaoh's face darkened and his eyes narrowed. "Are you not aware," the Great Man began, "of my Royal Responsibilities to my people and to our gods? I am to give land to temples for expansion. This I have done. I donated vast amounts of land and gold for new Temples constructed in the cities of Thebes, Memphis, and Heliopolis, again as my duty entailed. I enacted a tree planting enterprise throughout the country to provide needed shade for my people and beautify the temples. Rescinding any of this would be an insult to the gods and the people

"When the gift of these many plots was initially arranged, did you voice concern? Was I informed of the valuable crop resource of this land? The answer is no. Now you dare voice your disapproval and analysis. It is an impossibility.

"I too am disgusted with the financial gain of these priests due to the long ago signed and sealed contract. They are becoming too powerful and wealthy. In their minds, they are almost as powerful as their Pharaoh yet I alone control this world. I am the only living god of Egypt. Sickened as I feel towards the priests, I cannot repeal a gift to the gods. And I will not chance eternal damnation for doing so."

That was indeed the truth, reflected the Royal Reader. The Pharaoh would be forced to answer for such an act. So too would the country. Curses would be meted out to the good people and the land. Currently the situation of the country was somewhat grim yet if temple grants were removed from the gods' glory the outcome would be dire. The gods took great displeasure in being cheated.

"Perhaps with nationwide prayer we will be granted a abundance of snowfall in the mountains next season. As for this harvest . . ." The minister simply raised his arms in vagueness.

The King spoke as if to children, deliberately and slowly yet with an undertone of anger in every word. "Yes, you should continue to do so. Pray for the snow and floods that do not appear. Yet even a deluge of water will not ease my foremost concern, the initial topic of this conversation — my tomb

"Without a tomb built by the people of Set-Maat in which to receive my worldly body I will not join my fellow gods. I am to make the needs of my people known to the gods once I have reached my paradise. It is my final responsibility to Egypt. How am I to speak to the gods if I am not among them? I have been a noble ruler yet my Afterlife is threatened in spite of that. This is unacceptable to the point of obscenity." The Pharaoh's size seemed to increase as a puff adder swells with air when ready to strike. It was an alarming sight.

"I shall have my Royal Magicians place a curse upon your heads if this is not resolved. If I am doomed to wander the earth after death, I shall haunt you until the end of time itself. I say to you here and now, those wages shall be found and my tomb completed.

"And yet, while you agree the wages must be paid, you cannot enlighten me as to the source from which we will glean this payment. From the Treasury? Apparently not. From taxes? No to that as well. What then? Do you expect me to pull debens-worth from my ass?

"Each of you casts culpability upon the other. For all your wagging tongues, we have come full circle with no solution." Ramses turned to his Vizier. "You say this representative came to the Palace. Is he still within these walls?"

"Yes, My Great One. He waits for a reply in the antechamber to this very room."

"I would speak with him. Now."

The Vizier signaled to a sentry who excited and quickly reentered with the man in tow.

"Your name," commanded the King.

"I am Pentu," he said with a low bow.

"You are the messenger from Set-Maat? You threaten my everlasting life by ceasing work upon my tomb? How dare you strike against me in this manner! Do not think I will succumb to your demands a second time." Pentu remained silent. "Loosen your tongue, man. If you have no need of it, you will find it separated from your mouth."

With another bow, Pentu said, "My great and noble King I swear by the gods I — that is the people of Set-Maat — wish you no ill will and do not threaten you. I am here as their voice, to inform you of the need to our families. We are your loyal subjects and do not dishonor you. It is with great sadness, however, I must tell you of mothers putting their children to bed with the sounds of hunger in their bellies and cries upon their lips.

"Parents are foregoing food so their children may have a meal. The men have difficulty continuing their daily tasks when they are weakened from lack of nutrition. Our medical men have a shortage of herbs and potions for the sick. We have little oil for lamps within homes and the tombs. Our tools are in need of repair. We humbly request only what we've earned, nothing more.

"We are very proud of the workmanship passed from father to son. We are anxious to return to our glorious task in your honor. It is difficult to do so when we are hungry and filled with worry for our families."

The King sat silent for a moment. "Perhaps the lesser men should find themselves expelled from the town and their position. Then the resources could be found to pay the remainder."

"We pray the gods will allow you to find a way in bestowing upon us all our just due. However if eliminating jobs is your decision, I believe you care too much for your people to not provide those families their past due wages."

"Waged positions are difficult to find to even those with talents. Our drought has wrought difficulties to rich and poor alike.

My Royal Council has just advised me of the need for prudence in Egypt's expenses."

"Alas, my great King," said Pentu, "I am not acquainted with financial issues on such a grand scale. I can only assure you the people of Set-Maat have been rationing until there are no provisions with which to ration."

Ramses III sat back in his ornate chair. "Tell me of yourself and family."

"I have not much of an interesting tale to tell, My King. As my father and his father before him, I trained in the art of design, specifically that of statues and relief carvings. By the blessings of the gods, I have made my way through the ranks of tradesmen and have risen to the Foreman for the Left Side of Tomb Building. At this point in my life I am unmarried and without children."

Ramses pounced upon this bit of information. "So," he said, "you live a solitary life yet receive payment befitting your position in authority. Almost twice that of the average stone mason. Yet you have the temerity to demand more from me."

"My King, since I have no extraneous obligations or familial ties, I have been distributing my additional goods to families in need.

"I swear to you on my honor as a loyal subject and an honest Egyptian, I make no demands. I am not here to threaten your good health in this life or the next. I only seek that which is past due to the citizens of Set-Maat, to those families who create the most magnificent tombs and chambers for the glory of the Pharaohs."

"I believe you to be an honest man, Pentu, and you seek such remittance for others," said the Pharaoh more calmly. "Yet I would ask for a proposal none of my Royal Council members have given me — where should we find these wages you request?"

Pentu surreptitiously glanced at the royal chair, coated with gold leaf and precious jewels and quickly averted his eyes. Certainly he could not suggest His Royal Majesty relinquish his own treasures for this cause. It would be his undoing if he proposed such a notion. Instead he said, "My King, again I apologize to you yet I am not educated in such complicated matters. I can only mention to you what the people of Set-Maat — indeed, of all lower ranking citizens as myself — do when faced with financial decisions. We refrain from purchasing that for which we do not have the fair trade value of in hand. Additionally, if service or goods are poorly received, we do not favor that person with further business. Your citizens of Set-Maat provide excellent craftsmanship for you yet we must survive to continue to do so." He was prepared for the wrath of the King upon his head now. To think he, simple man that he was, would say such a thing to the King. It was madness.

The Pharaoh sat back in his glorious chair staring at the man beneath him. "You have made a clear case to me, Pentu, and it is not without merit. You seem to be as well equipped in diplomacy and negotiating as any of these men gathered with me today."

Leaning forward the Pharaoh declared, "I have made my decision. My Vizier shall meet with you before midday tomorrow with full payment. In the meantime, you will be given accommodations in my Royal Palace. Now leave me. We have much to discuss as to the source of the funds needed."

With that Pentu was miraculously dismissed with his head intact. Bowing and backing from the room, he hurriedly made his exit to contemplate his reprieve.

When the King was once again with the Royal Council, he spoke primarily to the Vizier yet his words were meant for all. "As your Pharaoh it is solely my responsibility to delegate responsibility. As well as blame," he said pointedly. "Here is my decree. Vizier, tomorrow you will procure the entire lot of back stipend for these people. Gather food, medicine, clothing — any and everything you should have brought to them weeks ago.

"As for the rest of you, I am disgusted with the guilt you so easily impart upon the other's head. This simple man, Pentu, answered my every question forthright and without fear. Your mewling and crawling accomplishes nothing. You tie the hands of progress and find no solutions when difficulties arise. My people and the country's well-being depend on our decisions in this chamber and yet I am surrounded by a chorus of fools. I expect honest answers from each and every one of you from this point forward.

"It is apparent to me that you are overpaid in your positions as Ministers to my council. You grow rich and fat while my Eternal Life is threatened." None of the Ministers dared stare at the Pharaoh's own protruding stomach. One man had the good sense to cover the many valuable rings upon his fingers within the folds of his garment. "Therefore, as to the expenses needed for this back payment, each and every one of you present here today will forsake ten days worth of wages to be placed into a special allotment for the town of Set-Maat. I expect to collect that amount from you before the evening meal tonight. This amount is hereafter forfeited from your pay each month to deposit into this cache. I shall personally review the sums offered. Pray they are not short.

"The Vizier will use your contribution today for current requirements. The remainder will stay intact for future payments to that community. Minister of Finance, you shall select three of your best clerks to oversee this fund. I shall have the final word as to their qualifications and appointment. They shall serve as check and balance. Nothing shall be withdrawn from the allotment without the tacit approval of the three. You shall present me with their names on the morrow after awakening.

"My Vizier shall have a cart readied with supplies at the Palace gates on the morrow. He will journey to Set-Maat with Pentu to make distribution and a tally of the paid wages.

"Payment shall never be past due to those men again. If so, you shall forfeit more than ten day's wages. It is done." To his scribe who had been quietly recording today's every word he ordered, "It is now written as Royal Decree."

## Chapter Nine

As Pentu left the Royal chamber he released a long sigh of relief and strove to keep his hands from shaking. I am intact, he thought; I spoke out treasonously to the Pharaoh and I am unscathed. Not only intact yet I accomplished the task set upon me. My town shall have the goods they need and deserve.

"I have never heard any commoner speak to Our Pharaoh in such a manner," expressed the man escorting him to a chamber for the night. "I considered it foolhardy until the King released you without harm. Not even a warning was issued. You left his presence gaining his admiration, I believe, yet a word of caution— I do not believe you can escape unharmed a second time from a similar speech."

"I shall never know what evil force possessed me," said Pentu, now beginning to sweat, "however, I agree with you fully. A god was assuredly providing entertainment at my expense. I am only thankful another greater god took pity upon me and stepped in."

"Most certainly. I have never seen the Pharaoh's foul mood change to one of agreement so quickly. You must be blessed with luck.

"Indecently, my name is Joba. I am one of the Royal Audience Chamber Guards."

"I am grateful for your acquaintance," said Pentu with courtesy. "I am also thankful for your advice and kindness. I must tell you, I am quite ill at ease within these walls. Never could I have imagined such splendor in the Royal Palace. It is so overwhelming. This must be a wondrous place to work."

His guide nodded. "It is indeed. The household staff is quite friendly as well. Most of His Majesty's Harem wives are cordial and quite lovely. Of course, surreptitious glances are best. Pharaoh Ramses is very protective of his family."

"I have heard Queen Iset is quite beautiful. Have you even seen her? It that true?"

"Words cannot describe the loveliness of the First Queen. You have seen artistic renderings of her?" Pentu nodded. "Believe me when I say those are only half truths. Additionally, she is most kind and gracious to us all. You will never see one such as she."

At that moment, Tiye's handmaiden, Asim, walked down the corridor. She smiled slightly and greeted Joba as she passed the two men. Pentu turned his head to watch her walk away. Never before had he seen such loveliness. The First Queen could surely not compare to this creature of the gods. Something struck Pentu deep within his core and he knew he must see her again.

"Who is she?" he asked Joba.

"Ah, you have just seen one reason why views within the Palace are so pleasant. Her name is Asim and a good friend. Yet I warn you; she is the personal servant to Queen Tiye who closely protects her innocence. She is being saved for one of noble stature. There is no hope for you with her, I assure you; no one crosses that Queen."

As they continued along their path, Pentu was silent as he listened to his newfound friend point out several architectural elements and various Royal chambers. Hope or not, he only knew that he must make the beautiful Asim's acquaintance no matter the cost.

## Chapter Ten

Asim continued along the ornate corridor to her mistress, Queen Tiye. Today's task — bringing her mistress a basket of fresh fruits to nibble upon — was an unusual duty for her. It was, in fact, well beneath her station and she had departed her Queen's chamber in a mood of some pique.

Now however, she realized the gods had seen fit to send her on this errand. How else could she explain the chance meeting between herself and the handsome stranger walking with Joba? She could not; therefore it must have been destined by the gods.

She wondered who he was and why he was in the Palace. His clothing was well worn and his face browned from the sun yet there was kindness and humor in those eyes. He looked out of place within these walls yet he comported himself well. In that brief moment she had noticed everything about the man and liked what she saw. It was also quite apparent he had an interest in her as well. She hoped they would meet again and have time for conversation. She did not believe the gods would ordain this meeting only to tease their emotions. Perhaps she should aid the gods with the path they had set her upon. What harm could come of it? She would merely make inquiries about him. Joba was a dear Palace friend. She would begin with him.

Deep in thought, she rounded the gilt edge of a column and ran headlong into Akar. Grabbing her by the shoulders before she fell he said, "My dear Asim. Are you taking flight from someone or — dare I hope — fleeing to me? If it is the latter, I assure you it could have been accomplished in a more subtle manner."

Asim stood with Akar's hands tightly grasping her shoulders thinking how much she abhorred this man. Occasionally acting as Queen Tiye's personal bodyguard, she had seen him within the Palace walls. This frequency, however, did nothing to allay her aversion towards him.

"I assure you that I am quite able to stand of my own accord, Akar. I am perfectly fine. There is no longer need of your support, although I am grateful to you for doing so."

He made no move to release her. In fact, his grip tightened as he brought her closer to him. She could feel his hot skin through their thin garments and was repelled.

"Indeed, I see you are quite perfect, Asim."

"Let me loose, Akar. I beseech you. I wish to avoid untrue gossip." She was trying to be cordial to him. He was a very strong and powerful man, outweighing her by almost thrice. She did not know what he would do if provoked.

"Sweet Asim, do you not see how comfortably we fit together? I find this quite enjoyable. Please tell me you do not find it objectionable." He increased his hold upon her with his arms around her back. "Think of the loving relationship we could have with each other."

The look in his eyes was anything yet loving. The glint was more than lust alone — she had seen desire in other men's eyes before. No, there was something else behind those brown orbs, a sense of danger from which to run. She was suddenly frightened and panicky, feeling the tightness of his arms about her.

"By the gods, Akar, if you do not unhand me I shall kick, scratch, and scream. Guards in each of these corridors shall come running." Cordiality was gone. She was truly fearful now.

He attempted a laugh yet she knew he was irate. "Apologies, *my lady*," he said sarcastically. "I shall allow you to be about your errand." Looking down at her basket, he asked, "For the Queen? Well, we do not wish hunger upon her." Before she could object he grabbed her hand and placed a kiss upon the inside of her sensitive wrist. "Although she will not miss one from your basket." He took a ripe fig from the top of the pile and bit into it with gusto, the juice dribbling from the corner of his mouth. With great deliberation, he slowly wiped his mouth with the back of his hand while baring perfect white teeth, never removing his look upon her. "Perhaps on another occasion I shall sample all your wares."

She took that to be a threat. Taking her hand back with a jerk she merely wished him good day and hurriedly went on her way. Her hands were shaking and she held tightly to the basket handle.

I should speak to the Queen of his advances, she thought. Perhaps she could thwart his attentions. Perhaps she could even dismiss him from her staff. No, that would not do. The Pharaoh assigned Akar to this position of authority and only the Pharaoh could dismiss the man. Ramses held Akar in high esteem, although Asim could find no reasoning to this. What if I went to the Pharaoh directly? The niggling voice within her answered that suggestion with derision. Hah, it said to her, Ramses III should believe a servant girl over a great warrior? Never! And if she caused his dismissal, what then? She was sure angering a man like Akar entailed consequences. And she had the impression he would enjoy meting out those consequences. She shivered as she remembered those tremendous hands encircling her. She would never know the end to his attention. She must continue to rebuff him as safely as possible.

Asim tried to reconnect with the memory of the other man, the one with the kind smile walking with Joba. His attentions would be most welcome, she thought. I pray I am able to locate him.

## Chapter Eleven

Shortly after Asim extricated herself from the arms of Akar, the second Royal Palace collision of the day was transpiring. It occurred where the long hall met the edge of the official dinning room directly across from elegant gardens. With so many maidservants in attendance, one might have expected a word of warning. None was forthcoming and the two Queens both turning the same corner at opposite sides slammed into each. At least they each found steadying hands to prevent the indignity of landing on their backsides.

While composing themselves amid many apologies, Tiye had the opportunity to regard her rival, the First Queen Iset. This Queen never seemed flustered, mussed, or hot. Indeed, Iset seemed to favor the blistering heat as a lizard did upon a rock, although her skin was of the pale tan much favored by the Royals and the rich. To have darkened skin signified one who worked the hot fields and a member of the peasantry so those of stature stayed out of the sun as much as possible. If one were to acquire wealth, one wanted it known by whatever means possible, even lighter skin tone.

As far as beauty among wives of Pharaohs, The Great Royal Wife Nefertiti had reigned more than a century ago and to this day she was still regarded as the most stunning Queen who ever lived. The many reliefs and statues of her throughout the country bore this fact out. Yet if Nefertiti were historically the most beautiful, Iset would place a very close second.

Statuesque and slender with large dark eyes and youthful skin, she captured appreciative glances wherever she went. She made the simple act of walking appear as a graceful dance. As if beauty was not gift enough from the gods, she was as lovely inside as out. She genuinely cared for the people around her, often sacrificing hours tending to the needy within and without the Palace. Over the years, her soft temperament was often called upon to halt silly clashes between the Royal Children. On special occasions, she presented her handmaidens with gifts, treating them as friends rather than servants. Everyone loved and respected the Great Royal Wife Iset.

Everyone expect Tiye. Tiye loathed the woman.

Were it not for her and her wretched son, Tiye and Pentawer would be sitting at Ramses' side at official and social gatherings rather than a step lower as their position in life dictated. Without the woman, Amonhirk would never have been born and Tiye's son would inherit the power of the throne. And yet, other than the woman simply *existing*, Tiye could find no personal fault with her.

And then Queen Iset smiled and revulsion shimmied down Tiye's spine.

It was her teeth, those overlarge pieces of polished alabaster flashing in her mouth. Tiye often witnessed those considerable teeth ripping and tearing at chunks of meat at banquets and had always found them menacing. The eating habits of crocodiles in the nearby Nile came to thought.

Even now, while her Sister-Queen spoke, Tiye could not look away from those large white cubes. "My Sister," said Iset, "I am making a journey to the house of a handmaiden. Her son is quite feverish and I am bringing a junior physician knowledgeable in such illnesses to aid in his recovery."

If a person became ill, there was no better country in which to recover than Egypt. The medical practices were second to none with a specialized physician treating each illness or disease. For over 3000 years, from the recorded 1st Dynasty of Egyptian Pharaohs, the medical practices had changed little and were yet highly advanced. Their approach was examination, diagnosis, treatment, and prognosis. Remedies were closely related to magic and religion since the causes of illness were the work of the gods. Herbs were given for pain and symptoms, while the final cure was administered through the aid of magic spells and prayers. Coriander had digestive qualities while cumin was a stimulant and used to eliminate flatulence. Castor oil and dates aided as laxatives and patients with tapeworms were fed an infusion of pomegranate root. Garlic and onions aided endurance and the Egyptians consumed them in great quantities. Raw garlic was especially helpful to asthmatics and those with other bronchial complaints. Honey and animal dung were applied to wounds to prevent infection. The application of raw meat was effective to stop bleeding and sutures were used to close wounds. Mint was used to terminate vomiting, mustard seeds to induce it.

These scientific approaches were taught to healers in tutorial establishments called The House of Life. In this centuries-old educational facility, men studied ancient medical papyri. The texts outlined cases of illnesses and injuries to the head, neck, arms, and torso while instructing the various treatments used for maladies such as intestinal disease, parasites, dentistry, skin, eye problems, and broken bones. Over 700 magical spells and medicinal remedies are noted in the teaching texts. Additionally, 35 sections deal specifically with gynecological problems and procedures including the diagnoses of pregnancy and labor contractions during birth. Other areas laid forth mental disorders including dementia and depression. Those suffering from epilepsy were given camphor

The Egyptian healers had great knowledge of human anatomy and while surgery was not often practiced, many qualified surgeons did so when there was no alternative. Their tools of the trade included saws, forceps, scales, shears, hooks, spoons, drills, and flint or obsidian edged knives.

Injuries were separated into three different categories: treatable injuries were handled immediately, contestable injuries not considered to be life threatening were merely observed for further development, and the final category was untreatable predicaments. In this instance, doctors did not intervene other than tempering the pain while keeping the patient comfortable until the end.

So advanced was the Egyptian's understanding of the human body, they realized the pulse's connection to the beating of the heart and that bronchial tubes worked in relationship to the lungs. They understood the correlation of some diseases between ill livestock and humans. Even notions of the nervous systems originated with Egyptian teachings. Still, with all their knowledge, some illnesses like malaria and lockjaw knew no cure. Hence the very secure occupation of the embalmers.

During Ramses III era, the word 'brain' was used for the first time in any written language. Specialized Physicians understood that injuries to this organ within the skull could be life threatening or cause unique symptoms to the rest of the body. Cases in the text centering on the brain describe head injuries that affected a person's ability to speak, to walk, and how well the person could track objects with their eyes. With conservative treatment, doctors could treat injuries to the brain without killing the patient.

While brain injuries could cause death or disruption to a person's actions, on the whole it was deemed rather worthless. Indeed, when one was mummified, the embalmers would remove the brain with a hook or a rod inserted through the nose. The bits of gray matter were promptly discarded while the essential heart was left intact within the body for one's life to continue in eternal paradise. In the opinions of specialists, the heart was the source of human wisdom, emotions, memory, thoughts, one's personality, and a person's very soul.

Diet was well known to play a large part in preventative health. The richly irrigated soil resulted in a diet that was more balanced than that of other countries. Vitamins from fruits and vegetables, proteins from fish and game, oil from linseed plants, as well as carbohydrates from cereals and grains, all aided in maintaining a healthy body.

Many Egyptians had a garden of their own with a small selection of fruits and vegetables. A more varied selection of these could be found in town markets throughout the country. Additionally, fish was caught from the Nile, and were often preserved with salt, roasted, or boiled. Wild game such as deer, antelope, ibex, and gazelles were also hunted for family food. From domesticated animals, milk was acquired as well as the production of curd, whey, and cream.

Every home served bread. Flour was mixed with yeast, salt, spices, milk, and occasionally butter and eggs. Some of the thicker loves would be hollowed out and filled with beans or vegetables. Flat breads were often made with raised edges to hold eggs or other fillings. These could be carried with ease in daily travel.

Aside from bread and porridges, the Egyptians enjoyed beans, chickpeas, lentils, green peas, Egyptian lettuce, and leeks among other vegetables. Dates were the most common fruit and were used in a variety of ways to sweeten bread or food. While spices were usually expensive, even the common man could enjoy some of the more wild growing herbs.

Of course, those in a position to afford it had the best combination of food. Various meats were easily accessible to the wealthy along with exotic fruits and expensive spices. Seeds from the fenugreek plant went beyond the use as a cooking herb and skin conditioner. They were also utilized in some of the oldest medicinal remedies known.

Physicians were acutely aware of the nutritional benefits of proper foods and often used such fundamentals in their treatment of illnesses. From the blessings of the gods and the gift of the Nile River, the Egyptians were regarded as the healthiest people in the world.

While the common man did not often see doctors for their health, medical care was not completely out of their reach when illness occurred. Such was the case today with the Queen offering the assistance of a Palace Doctor to a citizen. 'Junior' though he was, the medical services he offered would be better than no aid whatsoever.

"Would you care to join me in prayer with the family or assist the physician?" asked Iset to her sister Queen.

Tiye shook her head, lowering it as not to show her horror at the suggestion she travel to a home where someone was ill. She could not fathom putting herself in such harm's way. Those who came in contact with maladies or diseases often became ill themselves. She would only nurture her son back to health. Or her pets.

That last thought brought about a legitimate excuse to voice. "Apologies, my Sister, yet as you know the life of my beloved Minx has ended and I wish to pay my final respects to her while she is preserved."

Her Sister Queen showed surprise and said, "Oh, I had forgotten. My sincere apologies. I remember how you loved that cat. You do have more though, correct? You should not dwell upon the dead when you have others to love."

A flash of anger passed through Tiye yet she hid the emotion and nodded. Would Iset feel such coldness if her precious Amonhirk died? After all, she was blessed with other children. She bit her tongue from voicing her thought.

Few people understood the love Tiye had for her pets. Egyptians as a whole loved animals, especially dogs and cats, and they mourned deeply when a pet passed from this life. Dogs, especially greyhounds and Pharaoh hounds, were highly valued in this life and the next. They were used to herd cattle, aid in guarding, police enforcement, military actions, and most often as household pets.  Most collars and leashes were fashioned from leather or papyrus rope.  Over time they evolved into works of art with wealthy owners creating gold or silver collars, gems and ornate bows for fastening with the dog's name inscribed upon it.  They were embalmed with great care so they could once again romp with their masters in the Afterlife.   Killing a dog carried with it severe penalties.  If the dog was collared, and therefore assumed owned by another, the pet's murder was a capital crime.

Ramses III preferred dogs to other household pets and many roamed throughout the Royal Palace and its grounds.  Tiye preferred cats.  Household cats were prized not only for their companionship yet also for their usefulness in ridding the home of unwanted vermin.  Additionally, the goddess Baset had the body of a human woman and the face of a cat.  A protector of many virtues and ideals, she was also a goddess of pregnancy and childbirth, possibly due to the high fertility of felines.

Cats were so loved and cherished that the crime for killing a cat, even by accident, was death to the perpetrator, a fact that Tiye thought fitting.  Additionally, it was against Egyptian law to export cats to other countries.  A special branch of the government sought out and recovered any illegally exported cats.

When a beloved pet died in Egypt, family members shaved their eyebrows to denote mourning.  Since the shaving of ones body was common in the country, the lack of eyebrows was the most recognizable outward sign of grief.  The period of mourning was considered past when the eyebrows grew in.

Most did not feel an animal's companionship as strongly as Tiye, who loved animals over most people. Actually, over *all* people except her son. She felt their loss more deeply than others; a deficit in her character perhaps, yet she was not about to show this flaw to Iset.  The pain she felt was hers alone and she would never exhibit this weakness to another person, particularly to Iset.

"My gratitude for your understanding," said Tiye.   "Please inform the family I shall recite a special prayer for the boy." The conversation over, each wished the other a fine day under the gods' protection, and continued to their respective assignment.

Tiye made her way to the high priest conducting the mummification of her precious cat. She had witnessed preservations of her pets in the past yet it was never easy for her.  Each one was a part of her and she mourned them profoundly. She tried to take solace knowing she would hear her gentle purrs and stroke her soft fur once again in the Afterlife yet for now, the ache was devastating. She would cry for Minx in private.

Perhaps, she thought, a visit with the Harem might lift my mood. As Second Queen, they accorded her the respect and awe she deserved and Tiye never tired of such displays. Since her private chambers were located in the Palace proper, a walk along extensive hallways was required to the Harem quarters. Here resided twenty of Ramses' wives, their children, servants, wet nurses, and surrounding guards.

A Pharaoh's marriage was either seen as a duty to carry on his lineage or for political reasons. Marriages uniting royal houses from different countries ensured vast trade agreements or changed enemies into allies. Women who entered the Harem from other royal families controlled considerable wealth in their own right and employed knowledgeable men to assist them in administering it. Many of the women in the Harem were less than a true wife yet more than a consort. Even with such a complicated status in the House of the Pharaoh, they all bore his legitimate children.

In some respects, it was a normal household with children running about and anxious mothers or nannies in pursuit. The building was an exceptionally large portion of the overall Palace compound. The size was also the most efficient method in coping with the number of women who were in some way a part of the Royal Household. The Harem was a self-contained institution in its own right. It had its own economic assets, income generating activities, and administrative officers who handled their funds.

A handful of these secondary wives were born in other countries. They were usually a member of a royal family, a family of great position and wealth, or related to someone in a powerful governmental assignment. All the women of Ramses' Harem were of breeding and well educated. Their quarters were carefully protected and sequestered yet adult males of the Royal Family were permitted to enter these quarters. Non-relations were completely barred. The Chief of the Chamber to Ramses III, a man named Pebekkamen, remained within the antechamber to the official entrance. The needs of the many wives were voiced through him although strict regulations existed as to what those needs might be.

According to the law, messages were carefully scrutinized before their release from the Harem. Governmental conversations, sensitive information, or details regarding Ramses III, his staff and family must never be released to the outside world. If Pebekkaman deemed the communications appropriate based upon the criteria he was given, he would hand them to one of the exterior guardians. They in turn would summon a courier to deliver the message. To send a simple greeting to family members outside of the Royal Palace was a lengthy and intrusive process.

While these quarters were set apart from the main Palace, the unit was within the same thick protective walls. An ornately carved bridge over a large pond linked the Harem to the main Palace. The entrance opened into a lush garden filled with fruit trees, flowering plants, ponds and palms. This was a favored meeting place for the women to gather and chat about children or gossip about the Palace goings-on. Branching off from portions of the gardens were comfortable living spaces for each woman, the sizes of each designated by their order of marriage to the Pharaoh.

While Tiye occasionally visited the gardens within the center of the women quarters, she had not taken time to do so lately. She had been remiss in this and she reproached herself for the neglect. It was not through any great sense of love that she assigned herself these social calls; she wished to be seen as their benefactor. It was of great import to maintain good will with the Harem women. To be seen as an advocate and friend to these women — she choose not to consider them Sisters — she hoped to be privy to their misgivings and complaints. To court their concerns might provide a path to seek a favor if she required one.

As she entered, it was obvious the languid atmosphere usually present in this area had disappeared. There was great excitement among the women, each speaking in astonishment and surprise. Taking one of the wives aside, Tiye inquired as to what had ensued to cause such activity.

"Oh, My Queen Tiye," said the junior wife, "it is most unusual. Our husband and Pharaoh of all the land has divined to pay special tribute to his son, Amonhirk. We wonder what it means. Will Amonhirk take the throne from Ramses while he yet lives? Do you have any explanation for this, My Queen?"

Tiye was without knowledge of any such tribute yet it would not do to let this lesser wife know of her ignorance in the matter. She was Second Queen and should be privy to any news regarding the throne.

"I cannot imagine Ramses relinquishing his rule in any manner. What reasoning do you have for such a notion?" said Tiye

Another junior wife approached and said, "Our Pharaoh has given orders to the Royal High Priest for an additional aura of magic spells to be incanted over Amonhirk. They are to be the same superior protections the Pharaoh himself receives every year. What can it mean?"

While Tiye was seething inside, outwardly she remained calm and reassuring. "Oh, that. Yes, it is to be. Amonhirk has been appointed as the chosen successor. We all are aware of that; it was decided several years past. The Pharaoh simply chooses caution."

"Why should he do so with only Amonhirk?" asked another wife. "If something should happen to the Crown Prince, would not the Pharaoh simply choose the next son for successor?"

"Is that not correct?" said one of the newest wives. "Would not Pentawer be King?"

"Does this mean he has no faith in Pentawer if something should happen to Amonhirk?"

"I always believed Pentawer was his favorite. He has always been such a joy. Is this not a slight to your son?"

"What does that mean to our country if Ramses is afraid of another walking in Amonhirk's sandals?" The comments were being thrown at Tiye from all the women now.

"Yes, what has Pentawer done to render him untrustworthy? He seems to be a good man in every respect. I had hoped he would sit on the throne instead of Amonhirk"

Tiye tried to contain the situation and said more loudly than needed. "Sisters, I am sure there is more to this bit of gossip — and this is simply gossip in which you are engaging — than you know. I assume my son will be included in this added protection.

"Now, let us go about our business. Ramses dislikes such household tales spread about his Royal Palace. Speaking as you do is bound to cause trouble. You must lower your voices if you discuss this." She saw a hint of fear reach some of their eyes and many nodded in agreement with her.

"Yes, My Queen," said the youngest wife. "My abject apologies. We obviously only received a partial truth. The Pharaoh would never forget Pentawer in such a manner."

Many voiced their agreement with this statement and Tiye smiled at their realization of this fact. Bidding them a day blessed by the gods, she continued on her way as though nothing worrying had occurred. "Composure," she whispered to herself as she strode through the corridors of the Palace. "Above all, maintain your composure."

She felt the hot tears of anger burn against her eyes. Her fury was palpable for she knew the tale of the Harem wives' as truth. "Why," she said aloud, "why would Ramses plan such an act against our son?" She clenched her hands at her side as she walked with purpose to her husband's location. After the mid-day meal, he usually took a brief respite in his chambers before other duties and evening festivities. She would have this out with him. She would have to be circumspect with the conversation, however, while not informing him of the source of her information. She would not bring the wrath of Ramses down upon the Harem for divulging this to her. Yet it was imperative she know his reasoning. Had he completely washed his hands of Pentawer ever gaining the Throne? Or could she yet entice him to make a favorable decision for their son?

Taking a deep breath and slowing her pace, she approached the door to his chambers. Seeing her arrival, the sentry at the end of the long hallway walked to the entry door and announced her. She strode in regally with a smile on her face that did not reach her eyes.

Bowing to Ramses she said, "My Husband. Would you have a moment to spare me? I would have a brief conversation with you if you permit."

The Pharaoh was still wearing his morning attire and the fabric headdress patterned in gold. Even the false beard was yet attached to his chin. He was seated upon his favorite chair and gazing at his land. When he turned to her, she could see the younger more virile man he had been. She said as much to him hoping to ease her way into the conversation.

"My Pharaoh, you have taken the breath from me. Seated as you are, I see my young King ascending the throne for the first time. You are truly full of glory," she said.

Her comment had hit the mark, judging by the smile spreading across his face. Rising and kissing her cheek, he said, "Ah, my sweet wife. I am very pleased to hear you still regard me as such."

She began by informing him of the evening's guests for the supper hour and asked his approval of the menu choices. She had selected his favorites — steamed fish fresh from the river, roasted fowl caught by his personal hunters, lentils, and seasoned green vegetables. From the Palace orchard she had selected fresh figs soaked with honey, and warm baked breads sweetened with dates. His only addition was cheese and butter for the breads, and an abundance of roasted garlic mixed with onions for his health.

Finally arriving at her true reason for this visit, she began by saying "My Husband, the time for special blessings and magical protection spells is soon upon us. Would you have any special directions to the Magicians and Priests this year? Any special preparations the family should undertake?"

The Pharaoh raised his hand to a nearby servant, and the man poured Ramses a cup of beer from a side table and brought it to his King. "The family shall gather as usual for the combined ceremonies. As before, the Priests shall lay their blessings upon my family and the magicians will then proceed with their own magical babble. After the family leaves the room, Amonhirk and I will remain for further ceremony."

"I see," said Tiye. "Will these be the usual protective spells or of a more specific nature?"

"Are you questioning me, Wife?"

"Of course not, my King. I am simply wondering if I should order a second room for your private ceremonies."

"This year, Amonhirk and I will receive the additional blessings and spells. I would see my successor protected against harm. No further preparations need be made." He had already lost interest in the conversation and had returned to his seat, gazing out at his realm.

"My King, should not Pentawer also receive the protections of the Pharaohs? If Amonhirk should fall, Pentawer would succeed, would he not?"

Now he turned to her with flashing eyes. "With the added protection, Amonhirk shall in no way fall. Pentawer will not succeed me. This fact you have been told."

Placing her hand upon his shoulder, she pushed recklessly ahead. "My Great and Noble King, I know that you and Pentawer have always had a special connection and that you value his judgment. I would respectfully request you further consider him as your successor. He is a good man, caring and intelligent. You and I both know he would make an excellent ruler of this magnificent country. I beg of you, My Husband, as his father, do not eliminate him from this decision."

"So. That is your reasoning for this intrusion?" With a deep sigh Ramses III continued. "Yes, I do have a most special relationship with our son. He has always had my interests in heart with any and all problems. However, is this what Pentawer chooses or is it your voice alone I hear? If he feels so keenly about ruling, why is he not pleading his case?" He raised his hand to forestall her interjection.

"I shall tell you why. While he has always been brilliant, he is sensitive to the point of weakness. A Pharaoh must be strong in body and spirit, to make difficult decisions that might bring about the pain of others, limit a person's freedoms, or mete out harsh punishments.

"Pentawer does not have that ferociousness in him. He is barely able to squash a bug.

"Amonhirk can not only be ferocious but cunning and brutal in his pronouncements when required. That is necessary to be a ruler in my country — indeed, in any country. It is essential a King can bring those qualities tempered with fairness to his rule. Additionally, it is our tradition and law the eldest son inherits the throne."

Seeing the pain and sadness upon his wife's face, his own softened as did his tone. "My dear Wife, do not look so forlorn. Our son is a good and kind man. Those are wonderful traits. Amonhirk has been made aware that Pentawer shall always offer just and intelligent options to the Throne, as he has always done with me. While he is not to sit upon the Throne, his place is secured in the new reign as Amonhirk sees fit. I shall attend to it."

Tiye smiled at her husband yet the turmoil inside her did not waver. As Amonhirk sees fit? The Crown Prince shall not see fit to consult her son, she was sure of it. And how shall Ramses 'attend to it' when he is a mummified corpse deep within his tomb?

Still, she made her request for forgiveness while wrapping her arms around his neck and giving him a gentle kiss. "My sincere apologies, My Husband. Thank you for making considerations for him while you remain in this life and I pray you protect him in your next.

"I beg you forget my impertinence. Let us instead look forward to the wonderful entertainment and meal I have planned for us." Planting another kiss upon his neck, she left him to his interval of peace.

She was shaking with anger and frustration as she left the Pharaoh. She decided to walk to the only area in the Palace that brought her serenity — her zoo.

It began with a gift from the Pharaoh. As so often happened, a visiting dignitary presented the Great Ramses with a gift. This particular offering was a small tame monkey. Ramses promptly gave the sweet creature to Queen Tiye, well aware of her captivation for animals. So began her zoo

Over the years, she housed baboons, falcons, various fish, hippopotamus, gazelles, mongoose, and lions in a special enclosure outside of the Harem quarters. Palace residents were allowed unlimited access to enjoy her collection, entering it through elegant gardens. Once a year, Tiye opened the zoo to the citizens of Egypt who entered at the front of the structure through tall gates detailed with wooden sculptures of animals. It had become a much-anticipated event, which pleased the Queen immensely — she never overlooked the opportunity to ingratiate herself to the commoners. It was a sign of wealth to maintain a grouping of various animals at one's home and the Royal Zoo was the largest collection of local and exotic animals in the country.

As she walked among her many pets, offering fresh vegetables and frequent scratching to their heads, she was contemplating her next move. For a move must be made — one final shove to see her son upon the throne.

Ramses had delivered his final word on the matter and she would be more than foolish to return to such a conversation. "Yet I must do something," thought the Queen aloud. Ramses believed his final decision stood yet she would not retreat. Anything is possible with the correct motivation to the best people. It was only a question of finding them.

## Chapter Twelve

It was late evening before Asim had the opportunity to seek out Joba. She was wearing one of her favorite gowns; form fitting as the current style dictated, with pleating below the knees and blue threading throughout. Servants of the Royal Palace must be dressed as their station deserved, and she was, after all, a handmaiden to the Queen.

She cinched in her narrow waist even further with a hand tooled gold belt. She knew how lucky she was and thanked the gods daily for her good fortune. Had she stayed in her own country she could never have dressed so finely nor lived in a Palace. Some mornings she felt the need to pinch herself, to wake up from this comfortable dream. She was a novice to the Queen of Egypt. The gods were surely happy with her devotion to have bestowed such a destiny upon her.

And yet she was of an age where she looked at children with envy and couples with longing. She wanted a family of her own yet that notion relied upon the whim of the Queen. Queen Tiye was waiting for just the right man for her, Asim was told; the type of man from a noble family with riches in his own right. Many had made an overture to the Queen for Asim to live by their side. They had been men of note yet none satisfied the Queen. Asim wondered why. What was the Queen waiting for?

She knew it was unkind and evil of her to wonder at the reasoning behind the Queen's motive. Could it be, thought Asim, the Queen would receive compensation in return for relinquishing her? If so, it must be a monumental exchange she seeks. She was the Queen of Egypt — what could she possible want?

Knowing she was courting the Queen's wrath would not keep Asim from seeking out the man who had stolen her heart with one glance. She recognized that thought as truth and knew the gods had sent him to her.

And so she sought Joba, the only one who might provide her with the information she desired. She looked in the staff dining area realizing it was time for his evening meal. Those present had no knowledge of Joba's whereabouts. Perhaps he was retrieving liquid refreshment from the massive wine collection below ground. Alas, the servants sorting the wines were no more informed as to Joba's location than she.

Finally, she traveled to his post located outside of the Audience Room and Judicial Chambers. Ah, there he is, though the weary Asim, simply early to his position. So relieved was she to find him, she grabbed eagerly for his arm.

"Asim," he said softly. "What brings you to this area?"

"Oh, Joba," she said, "I have been searching for you throughout the Palace for hours."

When he looked stupefied as to any reason behind her hunt, she clarified her action by asking of the man she had seen him with.

"Ah, I believe you are referring to Pentu. The man wearing work clothing, yes?" She nodded. "He is from the community of Set-Maat. He completed a most amazing action earlier today. He came here to ask our King for past due payment to his people. They have not been paid for some time. Pharaoh Ramses actually agreed. He leaves tomorrow at dawn with the Vizier and a wagonload of necessities."

He lowered his voice even further to keep his conversation from being overheard in the Royal Audience Chamber. "Our Pharaoh's mood had been most foul this morning. I believed the man would suffer for broaching the King in such a manner. Yet the gods were with him, it seems.

"I pray the gods continue to surround him as he is with the Pharaoh in the Chamber as we speak." He tilted his head to the door of the Audience room. "I wish him luck. I have not known Our Pharaoh to request an audience with anyone so late in the day."

So, thought Asim, this attraction has been for naught. He is set to leave on the morrow. The gods had not been in play with their brief meeting. On the contrary, they had been toying with her.

Seeing her fallen expression, Joba said, "Ah, so *that* is the direction you follow. My apologies, Asim. Unless plans differ in there," he pointed to the great room, "he leaves for his home on the morrow."

He cocked his head and looked at her sternly. "Need I remind you of Queen Tiye and her desire for you to become a lady of society? Perhaps this is the best solution to your hunt. It would not be prudent for any covert actions in this respect. The Queen shall know and not forgive."

Asim was about to protest, voicing her earlier misgivings regarding Queen Tiye when Interior Guards of the Great Room opened the doors. Through the massive wooden doors strode the object of their conversation: Pentu.

They looked at each other in astonishment and began speaking in unison, each of them overlapping the other's words until Asim laughed and looked to Joba for the proper introductions. With some reluctance, he did so.

When Asim was properly introduced as servant to the Queen, he bowed to her with respect, unfamiliar with the proper greeting to someone of such importance.

Inane comments from the nervous pair were sure to follow, thought Joba. Asim began speaking first. "Joba has informed me that you were in the Great Audience Room."

"Oh, yes I was," said Pentu.

Asim's turn again. "And you were with the Pharaoh."

"Indeed. It was a great surprise."

They stood staring at each other for a moment when Joba rolled his eyes and said with annoyance and sarcasm, "We do not have the entire evening to stand here listening to such scintillating exchanges. Pentu, tell us what transpired with Our King."

He gave a bashful smile and said, "When I was called from my room to see him, I knew I would surely receive the punishment I avoided earlier today. And yet I did not. The gods are still with me. Instead, I have been offered a position — or perhaps ordered to take a position, I am not entirely sure which …"

"Get on with it, my friend," said Joba.

"Ah, my sincere apologies. At any rate, I am to be one of the consultants to the Royal Ministers. The Pharaoh said he appreciated my voice of reason and lending a straight tongue to my words. He informed me his Ministers did not often speak thusly. He said he would expect me to always speak truly to him. I was told to swear by the gods to do so."

"And you accepted the rank?" asked Asim while thinking, Of course he did. Who would not?

"I most certainly did. I am to receive quarters here in the Palace," Pentu said with glee and wonderment.

"And what of your trip to Set-Maat tomorrow, to your people with their back payment?" said Joba. He could see where this situation was going and did not approve. Asim was a good friend and he would despair if she received punishment from the Queen. Perhaps Pentu would miss his home and he would return from whence he came leaving Asim to her own destiny.

"I said I would trust the Vizier to make payment in Set-Maat. I would forgo the journey if I could include within my duties the monitoring of the workers wages and see to the regular distribution."

Joba looked shocked. "By the gods, you did not speak so to the Pharaoh! And you yet stand? With a new post? My friend, the gods surely sprinkled you with good fortune the day you were born."

After more congratulatory comments, Pentu asked if Asim would permit him to speak to her. Privately.

"Of course," she said. She attempted to sound indifferent to his request yet she was giddy inside. She saw Joba shake his head with a warning frown. Asim knew she should take heed yet, after all, this was the gods' design, not her own. She merely tilted her head at her friend and shrugged her shoulders in reply.

"Have you seen the temple courtyard yet? It is most beautiful at night," she asked of Pentu as the two of them left Joba's company. She was glad when he replied he had not. "In fact," he replied, "I have seen naught but hallways and the Audience Room." She smiled at him in delight. This would be something special they could share.

Once there, she led him to the most remote part of the area, deep within the foliage and pillars of the second temple courtyard. The clay braziers were alight aside the great statues, lending a gentle glow to the scene. Pentu was astonished at the beauty and said as much.

"The Royal Gardens are equally as splendid." Said Asim. "I can assure you, gardens of the Royal Palace put all others to shame. I should be very pleased to show it to you. It is filled with exotic plants and trees brought back from foreign travel by The Pharaoh. Cabbage roses and lotus blossoms are in abundance within the ponds and their scent fills the enclosure. Delicious and succulent fruit from other countries climb the walls along with native figs, dates, melons, and pomegranates. Now that you are a member of the Royal Ministers, you may partake of these rare delectables whenever you wish."

"I can hardly absorb all that I see today and I cannot believe my good fortune. I prayed to the gods that I would see you again and here you are. And now I sit with you in this most magnificent courtyard."

Asim smiled. "Yes," she said, "here I am."

"Before I was called to see the Great Pharaoh, I was determined to ask Joba to find you tonight," said Pentu. "Please say this is not a dream for if so, I wish to never awaken."

Asim reached for his hand and held tightly to it. "Do you not feel this? The warmth of my hand in yours, my thigh touching yours? I assure you, this is not a dream yet the direction the gods have led us."

"Perhaps this is too forward," Asim continued, "my utmost apologies if it is, yet when I first saw you today, I knew we were destined for each other."

Pentu agreed, tightening his hold upon her hand. "I have never been struck so soundly by Hathor. The goddess of love has truly blessed us this day.

"Yet I am concerned, my lady, of your position to the Queen. I am unaccustomed to such beauty and behavior. I have been working on the Royal Tombs all my life in some capacity. So it was with my father and his father before him.

"There was no other course of action for our family, you see. We were allowed to move up within the ranks, as did I to a foreman, yet it would always involve the work of Royal structures. One might say we went from womb to tomb in our own world of craftsmanship." He smiled at his silly joke. "As such, my knowledge of social niceties is sadly lacking. And you are a lady of the Palace. I feel I shall embarrass you."

Touching his face Asim reassured him. "As of today, you are no longer a builder or foreman. You have been given a position of great import. You are a member of the most revered council in all of Egypt. I am most fortunate to be sitting by your side. No one, not even the Queen, could object to you."

"And yet. . ." He looked at his palms. "My hands are as course as I."

She took his hand in hers again and said, "From your life's tale, I believe you to be a kind and intelligent man, qualities I have long searched for. You say your hands are rough yet I would wager your lips are soft."

With that, he could no longer resist her and the two enjoyed each other's company until dawn broke through the night sky.

## Chapter Thirteen

Tiye and her group of tag-along servants and guards left early the following morning to travel the Nile to her birthplace. Today she would utilize one of her smaller barges, currently waiting at the private Royal Harbor for her. She was thankful the Pharaoh had the remarkable notion to commission this dock and pier situated at the rear of the Palace compound. Hundreds of men had dug this very wide canal, climbing up and down various lengths of wooden ladders to reach deep into the sands, before anchoring the docks firmly into the ground. There had been a great celebration when men finally broke through the remaining ground at the banks of the Nile connecting the waterway to the mighty river. Citizens and Royalty gathered to watch as the final dig through the narrow piece of land was made to release the rushing waters. Amid loud cheers from the people, the water gushed through the sand, swirling and tumbling into the new channel. The largest of the barges gently bobbed and rocked as the water settled about it.

Tiye appreciated the convenience of boarding her ship in such a private area, requiring only a few steps from the Palace proper. She had several barges in her private fleet, all neatly docked alongside many others belonging to the Pharaoh and visiting dignitaries. The use of each ship depended upon the distance traveled. While small, today's particular conveyance was built for speed yet the opulence appointed to it was not lacking due to its size. The finest elements of gold leaf and statues adorned the ship. Her private chamber on the top deck consisted of golden columns strung with drapery to hide her from common sailors. The food and drink were plentiful and rare, served upon gilded platters and within silver cups. The Queen disliked travel yet if she must, she did so in comfort and luxury.

She thought of her mother's request for this voyage. The message from her had been unusually demanding. Her mother had made the pronouncement that a late afternoon gathering of old friends was planned. Tiye, the note stated, was expected to attend. This, unfortunately, involved the Queen to stay overnight in her childhood home under the same roof as her mother.

It was a comfortably smooth journey on her well-crafted ship. She enjoyed hearing the water splashing against the wooden ship and the sound of wild water birds calling to each other. Perhaps, the Queen thought, I might leave when the festivities had concluded. "A most unlikely idea," mumbled Tiye. Her mother would insist on an overnight stay.

Tiye knew the event was not altruism on the part of her mother. It was the woman's opportunity to flaunt the Queen of Egypt/Her Daughter to others, even if Tiye was only 'Number Two'. Assuredly tonight was to be one of those occasions when her mother clamored for attention.

While the Queen would never admit it to her mother, she had a perverse enjoyment to these affairs as her mother honored her with respect even if the groveling was merely an empty display to guests. The gatherings of her mother were very lavish and truthfully Tiye enjoyed the attention and the sight of childhood faces. The best of food, drink, conversation, and entertainment was her mother's standard which acquaintances often attempted to outdo, much to the delight of her mother. The Queen would just make the best of the situation and leave on the morrow, she vowed to herself.

Tiye ordered the curtains be lifted from her chamber atop the barge so she could view her childhood home upon approach. It had always been a most beautiful home. And why should it not be so? Her family was extremely wealthy and her mother had always demanded the best of everything.

She sighed when the first glint of the grand building amid a grove of palms came into sight. Her father had commissioned every detail of this house during construction and Tiye always loved it because of that. She also found herself looking forward to seeing the multitude of servants. They had genuinely loved Tiye, even if her mother had not.

Tiye's nearly forgotten memories were emerging within herself. Rather than tamp them down as she often did, this time she gave rise to them. Most of her favorite memories came from time spent swimming in the nearby cove. She could almost see it to the west just past the crooked palm. She and her friends spent full days there, alternating turns to watch for crocodiles while the others swam. Their swimming spot was an unlikely space for those monsters to sun as the small sandy beach was surrounded heavily with rushes and bushes. Whatever the reason, crocodiles were not particularly fond of this secret swim locale. Still, it was much better to be safe. Those giant reptiles were known to rip off a man's arm with one chomp.

Those rushes had served another purpose for the younger Tiye; they hid the more grown-up games that occurred behind them.

Old stirrings were awakening within Tiye as she remembered those games. What began as "If you show me yours then I shall show you mine" developed into much more intimate activities. She had learned the art of what pleasures a man and used this newfound expertise willingly and often.

What fun those days had been. She had a variety of boys upon which to practice and soon found them willing to do her bidding for a taste of her later in the secluded rushes. She had used her sexual prowess as a weapon to wield whenever she so desired; withholding from one and giving to another as the mood struck.

One young man in particular, Ari, had been her most ardent admirer and the two of them enjoyed each other's bodies for several years. Indeed, they delighted in such activities prior to her journey to the Royal Palace in preparation of her marriage to Ramses.

On that final cool evening, they lay among the damp rushes, listening to the water lapping on the short sandy shore. Ari was gently drawing a length of fresh wild grass against her naked thigh. She was gazing at the stars, lying upon her back with one arm crooked behind her head.

"Ari, do you think the gods live among those twinkling stars?"

"Possibly," he said as he tickled her stomach with the grass. "Not upon all of them, of course. Even we do not have enough Egyptian gods to fill all the lights in the sky."

"Then of what use are the rest if not homes for the gods?" Tiye asked.

"That is simple," he said as he bent his head to kiss her neck. "They provide a wonderful glow in which to reflect upon your naked form. You appear most radiant tonight and I rejoice in your perfection." His lips traveled to her full bosom then he looked into her eyes and smiled. Turning on his back alongside Tiye, he too, gazed at the evening sky. The damp grasses were cooling to his back. Even with sunset, nights in Egypt remained exceedingly warm. "It is truly a night created by the gods."

"I wish this night would never cease, Ari; that you and I could stay here within our small oasis, gazing at the sky, feeling each other's warmth. Then travel to the stars for all eternity. I very much like that notion."

"Alas, my sweet lotus blossom, that is not to be. You shall be my Queen, the Queen of all Egypt," he said with a lopsided grin. "We have different paths to follow in this life, my pet. I only ask that you not require me to bow exceedingly low when next we meet."

Tiye giggled and looked at his face, glowing in this evening's light. "Ah, yet you must bow lower than the rest, my love. If you do not I shall surely see your silly sweet grin and then burst into laughter. Not proper deportment for a Queen I am sure." Ari grinned at her jest.

"It seems such an untruth, a fabricated story to tell young children," she exclaimed in disbelief. "Me, the Queen of Egypt, the wife of the future Pharaoh. Oh, I know it has been arranged since I was born, yet now . . . after all these years . . ." Tiye sighed deeply. It would be an enormous adjustment for her. There would be no more evenings like this one; no longer could she swim in the Nile whenever she choose; no longer run and play all day. What would her future hold, she wondered with some trepidation. She sighed again. "I shall miss you, Ari, my love." She stroked his face, hoping to forever secure his visage within her memories. She had learned the art of pleasing a man from him — from others as well, if truth were known— and she hoped it would serve her well with her new husband. Yet she cared deeply for Ari and would indeed miss him.

He took her hand in his and kissed her wrist. "And I you," he said. She was a bit stung by his nonchalant attitude but then their relationship was never meant to be serious.

Attempting to lighten the atmosphere, she reached between his legs and said, "And I shall unquestionably miss this." She felt him come to life under her touch.

With a lewd smile, he took her in his arms to enjoy her one last time.

Before they left the tall rushes that night, he presented her with a small leather pouch. Something to always remember him, he said. Inside was a beautiful lapis lazuli necklace, the one she yet kept in the now-battered bag within her jewelry case; the possession that spoke to her above all other pieces.

He had been her first love and that term conjured up youthful desires as only memories of a first love can. She recalled the rush of excitement when she would see him, and the desperate longing when they were apart. It was an aching and exhilarating experience in one and she knew no two lovers could ever felt thusly. Yet, instead of a union with one love, her marriage had consisted of arrangements, contracts, and dozens of other women with whom she must share her husband.

"Ah, dear Ari," Tiye sighed as she forced herself to the present. He had been the most handsome and wealthiest young man in the area. She shuddered as she remembered his muscles rippling as they engaged in their physical pleasures. He had been several years older than she and she wondered if, over these past years, he had become as soft and flaccid as her husband.

Putting aside such thoughts, she climbed into her magnificent carrying chair. She was held aloft by four servants to cover the short distance of land to her home. She was arriving in the highest style to the door of her mother, hoping to display her prominence and power.

She agreed to attend this party not only for the chance to greet old friends but also for a purpose of her own. She planned to discuss the Pharaoh's words regarding the Throne and their son with her mother. She was dreading the conversation yet it must be broached. *Something* must be done and her mother had the most cunning and ruthless mind of anyone she knew. Certainly not a compliment to the woman yet in this instance it was a fortunate flaw.

The house was a flurry of activity and she heard her mother issuing demands. Servants were dashing about with bowls of flowers, great platters of roasted foods, hunks of cheeses, fresh bread, jugs of beverages, and the freshest of fruits. She received bows and smiles from the servants as she passed, searching out her mother.

"At long last," her mother greeted her. Tiye was actually early yet refrained from saying so.

"Hello Mother," said the Queen. A kiss or hug did not pass between them and Tiye made no attempt to initiate one. She knew how her mother disliked displays of affection. She often wondered how the woman had conceived three children.

"The house smells delicious."

"Yes, it does," agreed her mother. "The flowers are from the garden as is the fresh fruit. The new trees have born the most delicious figs and citruses. I've been working very hard for days preparing all this for our guests." The Queen almost laughed aloud. She had never seen her mother so much as cook an egg or arrange a single fragrant bloom.

"Whom shall I see tonight? The regulars?"

"Some," answered her mother coyly. "With a few surprises." Tiye inwardly cringed. Mother loved her surprises. Occasionally they led to an unfortunate blunder that would bite her in her plump ass. Tiye recalled the time she invited the mistress of not one man but two. Both men were in attendance at the gathering with their wives. It became quite a debacle with harsh words and even food flung about.

Her mother insisted the overlapping invitations were an error yet she was never included in either of the couples' social gatherings after that incident. Even though Mother lamented about her ostracism, Tiye had a suspicion the invitations had been issued with clear thought; her mother enjoyed seeing the embarrassment of her social rivals. What she had not considered was her position as a pariah afterwards. Tiye always thought the punishment to her mother was befitting the mortification suffered by two esteemed families. Her mother pleaded for aid from Tiye yet she uncharacteristically refused to step in as Queen to set order to her mother's societal woes. Her mother had been peeved with her daughter for some time, which meant Tiye happily disbanded these obligatory visits for two months.

After she was prepared in a glittering bejeweled gown and a wig dripping with strands of gold chain, Tiye entered the public salon area of the home in time to have the first set of guests pay her homage. While many who gathered here this evening were old and loyal friends, she was their Queen and as such it was written she be accorded the respect her position warranted. As Queen, it was she who must take the initial step to transition a stuffy situation to one of casual friendliness. Today, she strove hard to lend that atmosphere to the gathering. She might need such loyalty if she hoped to accomplish recognition for her son.

She was in the midst of greetings when she heard giggling from her mother. She knew that laugh. It was meant to be coy and flirtatious. Her mother was apparently making overtures towards a man. Hopefully, he is not another married man, thought Tiye.

When she looked up to see her mother's prey, Ari stood by her side in the doorway of the great salon. The sight of him almost made her swoon. He was easily recognizable, still strong and handsome as ever. The gods had undeniably blessed him.

Her mother had her arm in the crook of his, fluttering her eyes at him and keeping up a constant stream of useless chatter as she led Ari to her daughter. When he approached, he did so with the familiar lustful look in his eyes. She nearly buckled at the knees.

"My dear Ari," she said, "this is indeed a very great surprise; one I am pleased my mother arranged."

He bowed extremely low to her and presented his lopsided smile, reminding her of their long ago private joke. She chuckled discreetly at his antics and realized it had been some time since she had laughed. Seeing her old love was indeed a cause for joy.

She offered her hand with an indication that he should arise. Ari kissed her wrist and said, "I am glad you approve of the invitation extended by your mother. I am confident this surprise shall not leave her ostracized from local society."

She smiled wider. "Ah, you remember that fiasco."

"Certainly. I also know the outcome of that evening. One husband left his wife for the popular mistress. They moved to Lower Egypt within a fortnight after your mother's party."

"By that time I had left this house for Thebes yet I often wondered if the families had reconciled. Obviously my mother's surprises have not always been as pleasant as tonight's."

With the addition of Ari, the evening became even more enjoyable for the Queen. Once the greetings were made to other guests and her mother insisted upon introducing her to new acquaintances, she managed to escape with Ari to the rear gardens. Her watchful guards followed at a discreet distance.

The night had grown cooler and they walked slowly among the arbors and trees. Tiye inhaled deeply; fragrances were abundant from the blooming plants and hanging fruits.

"It has been some time since I wandered in the garden," said the Queen. They found their way to the center of the garden and seated themselves upon a marble bench in front of a fountain. "I cannot imagine the dwelling of the gods having a more heady scent."

"We played here as children, remember? Your mother was constantly cautioning us not to damage the flowers yet we skipped across the plantings when she was not looking. We played Senet here as well if memory serves me," said Ari. Senet was a very old board game loved by all walks and ages of Egyptian people.

The board was actually a box with 30 spaces carved into the top, three rows of ten spaces each. One side of the box contained a small drawer in which the gaming pieces were kept. While there were no particularly set rules, most games were played much the same as it had been for hundreds of years. Adults often played this as a game of chance.

Gambling had been a pastime for Egyptians from the dawn of time. Some individuals were so overtaken with the madness they placed bets upon anything; from the date rain would fall, to the gender of their unborn child.

Naturally, there existed a god dedicated to the gamblers fate, although how or who created him was a mystery to Tiye. Thoth is credited as the author of science, religion, mathematics, writing, magic, and philosophy. According to his story, he is also credited with adding five more days to the old yearly calendar. He did so by gambling with the moon to win a small portion of its light so the sky goddess could deliver her child. During these five days, the sky goddess gave birth to four more gods.

Now how, wondered Tiye with surprise, did I ever remember that teaching from childhood? As little as she believed — birthing four babies in five days is complete nonsense — she could still recite their tales, ridiculous as they were. It was no wonder she had little faith in deities.

At any rate, it was this winning bet of Thoth's that further denoted him the god of gamblers. Pleas and promises to him did not often see a gambler's prayers met — many a good man had lost entire estates and fortunes with their addiction.

Loosing, however, never seemed a deterrent to the inveterate gambler. The sport became such a problem that laws were enacted aimed at controlling the spread of this vice. Tiye was doubtful it curbed the problem. She often witnessed Royal military men tossing colorful cubes against Palace walls in wager.

Yet to the children in Tiye's circle of friends, the game of Senet had merely been an innocent way to spend a hot afternoon within cool surroundings. Bets placed were never monetary: only silly dares given to the looser. Once she was made to walk around the edge of her fountain on tip toes while the others laughed and cheered her on. Ari was continually challenged to physical activities should he loose. It seemed he was always climbing some structure or tree as his losses outweighed his wins. Yet it was all in harmless fun.

Leaning back, the Queen ran her hand across the cool water in the base of the fountain. "Life was so very simple then, was it not? Occasionally I wish to relive those days." She was thinking specifically of the times spent in the rushes yet would never say as much to her companion. Those memories were best set aside for the most part, only to be brought out when she was completely alone.

Ari nodded at her statement yet changed the topic. "I have often wished to pay attendance to you on your visits here. Alas, you never seemed to stay but a day with your mother."

Tiye frowned. "Would you wish to lengthen your stay if she was your mother?" she said. He shook his head with a mock look of horror upon his face. She could not help yet laugh.

"Which brings to mind your family, Ari. I was very sorry to hear of your parents passing. I pray they are watching you from the Afterlife." She took his hand and remarked, "You wear your fathers ring, I see."

"It is my way of remembering him." Then he laughed and said, "It is much too tight for me and I could not remove it even if I wished. Unless my finger is removed from my hand, I believe I shall take it to my tomb." He made an effort to wiggle it upon his finger to prove his statement to her.

Proper conduct dictated she should ask after a possible wife and children, yet she was reluctant to do so. She did not wish to know of another woman who shared his bed. Somehow, knowing he had taken a wife would lesson the intensity of their young love affair. Besides, she thought wryly, her mother would surely inform her later. Instead she said, "I know your father is very pleased in the honor you bestow to him. They were very good people. I am sure they quickly passed the necessary tests by the gods to enter their eternal life."

"My gratitude for your sympathies. My sisters have moved with their families to an estate west of Thebes. I am the only one carrying on the family traditions in this area."

Those traditions, Tiye knew, involved many successful business and concerns including granaries, farms for livestock breeding, ships, and trade throughout neighboring countries. Ari would now control it all.

"Your mother informed me that it is your intent to stay for several days this time. Is that so?" Tiye had never considered this thought but now she nodded, suddenly deciding this idea had merit. "That is most welcome news. Perhaps I could interest you in dining at my home on the morrow. Either the mid-day or the evening meal. I am sure a Queen's busy schedule precludes mine, your humble admirer," he said with a grin.

They settled upon the following afternoon. With a kiss on her wrist, he begged departure from her. There were many duties needing his attention. "Additionally, I have been monopolizing much of your time. I am sure the other guests wish to garner attention from you. I shall, however, anticipate our time together on the new day."

He was correct, of course. She must not devote undue attention to one guest, no matter the length of their friendship. Idle gossip would not do. Straightening her shoulders and placing a smile upon her face, she and her guards re-entered the salon to conduct pleasant conversation with others.

## Chapter Fourteen

Tiye rose from her slumber remarkably early by her standards. She was anxious to speak to her mother of Pentawer. "Oh please," she prayed to the many gods she doubted, "please let us arrive at a solution to my husband's oversight."

Her mother was rendered nearly apoplectic with anger when Tiye voiced the decision of Ramses.

"My grandson shall not be King?' she shrieked. "That is the information you would inflict upon me? That pompous, selfish, arrogant . . . *nek tchew a-a*." She spat out the words as though they were bitter herbs. Tiye had never heard her mother speak in such a manner. Essentially, in polite terms, she had just wished for a donkey to copulate with the Pharaoh.

Tiye sighed. Many years ago, her prearranged marriage to Ramses had been a delicious opportunity for her mother to boast of her daughter's importance. It was a match blessed by the gods, she would claim. Today she slings insults in her King's direction, Tiye thought. "Yes, Mother, he is all that. He is also the Pharaoh of Egypt and as such, he can be whatever he chooses."

"Something must be done. Do you hear me, daughter. *Something must be done.*"

"Indeed, Mother. That is exactly why I have broached this subject with you. I am in full agreement, yet what do you suggest I do? I have begged, enticed, and appealed to his reasoning to no avail. He refuses further discussion. Even if he should become dim witted with age and was ousted from the Throne — hardly plausible yet a mere hope of mine — Amonhirk would yet inherit. I have lost many nights' sleep attempting to form a solution of sorts. I was hoping you might do so where I have not. You have friends in high social standing. Perhaps you could entertain their assistance. I am spent with emotion and have no notion short of murder . . ." Her thought trailed off. Mother and daughter stared at each other. "No, Mother. I misspoke. Cleave it from your thoughts immediately. It is a most treacherous and dangerous suggestion to follow. Moreover, the King is never alone. It would be extremely difficult," she said rather unconvincingly.

"Yet not impossible, correct?"

Tiye stared into the dark conniving eyes of her mother. She had hoped for a solution, but murder? Kill the Pharaoh of all Egypt? She laughed aloud.

"You are more perverse than I imagined, Mother. Have you any notion of the horrible punishment we should receive if we attempted such a thing? We are merely two women, not an army for that is what we require to kill Ramses.

She rose from her seat and strode about the room. "And if the King died, what then? Amonhirk still inherits the throne."

Her mother replied quietly. "Not if they both died. Timing would be all-important, though. Timing and opportunity."

Tiye turned and stared in horror at her mother. "Have you not been listening to my words? The King is never left to his own devices. Never. You have become quite demented."

"So be it, Daughter. Yet tell me — what course of action do you suggest? For you are correct in your assessment: both King and successor must be removed in some manner. Concurrently, I would reason. Or perhaps not. If Amonhirk should die after the King, would not Amonhirk's eldest son inherit? If that is true, the Prince must pass first. His mother, Queen Iset, might need elimination as well. She would be trouble, I am certain of it."

Tiye was frightened now. "Mother, you must curb your tongue. The servants are near. We are not alone in this house. It is treason to discuss such ideas and now you have dispassionately added another to your mad scheme. Why not simply remove the entire court and begin anew?"

"Servants," she sniffed with a dismissive wave of her hand. "They are in the far wing of the home. Besides, they would support such a move. They are completely loyal to me. To you as well, Daughter. They have always loved you for some reason."

Tiye winced. The woman could never resist a slight hurled in her direction. With a sigh, she replied, "So now we have accumulated servants as well as we two. What a formidable lot we shall be.

"Tell me this, Mother. If Amonhirk were eliminated, why would we do so with the King? He would surely appoint Pentawer to the throne with Amonhirk dead."

"You are as shortsighted as ever. Even as a child, you demanded instant satisfaction with no caution to a subsequent problem.

"Imagine, *Daughter Dear*," she said sarcastically, "what Ramses would do if his heir to the Throne died suddenly. Is not Amonhirk in perfect health? Also protected with enchantments? Do you not think his death would be considered extraordinary? The first individual suspected would be your son. Should he remain ignorant of our scheme, he would still be the cause and hence be blamed. Either way he would be asked to name the conspirators. And Pentawer is weak of character."

She raised her hand to stem the protest Tiye was ready to give. "Do not misjudge me, Daughter. I love my grandson dearly yet he would incriminate us both. Oh, yes: he would talk. Imagine the scandal — the mother and grandmother of the Prince of Egypt murdering the named heir to the Throne. Pentawer would appear a pathetic man. Allowing women to perform such an act for his benefit would not sit well with the people. He would never be named Ramses IV under any circumstances.

"Do you not see the advantage of cultivating doubt and insecurity towards Amonhirk? He must be believed incompetent or self-serving. Faith in him must be tainted in some way. My servants in this house are acquainted with others in several wealthy homes. They have their own way of communicating news and gossip. Our plan would catch hold when the rumor mill begins. Any appalling tale of the heir apparent would spread throughout the city.

"And my hold on society is not without bonus. Once the servants begin talking within their dwellings, their proprietors should begin questioning the Prince's capabilities as well. Naturally, as mother of the Queen I shall be sought for corroboration. It shall be only too easy providing details to my friends — friends who travel for business and holidays to Thebes and Memphis along the Nile. Stopping, you see, for conversation and supplies. The stories shall spread.

"Others could be enticed to join our cause given the right motivation. Ari comes to my thoughts, as well as the Amundi and Puniri family. Both extremely wealthy families and connected to powerful people.

"You must spread rumors of Amonhirk among the Palace staff, naturally, for we must create suspicion of him in Thebes as well. Perhaps Thebes particularly as it is the country's capital and seat of the most powerful citizens. Luckily, I yet have many connections there.

"Conversations must be done quietly and covertly, of course. There must be no indication of your lips telling the tale."

Tiye thought of the worry she witnessed in the Harem. They, too, did not appreciate Ramses' show of favoritism to Amonhirk over her own beloved son. Perhaps she could acquire some assistance in that area. Several of the women had connections with their homelands. Perhaps a spark could be brought to flame in other countries.

Tiye was slowly warming to the idea but voiced some trepidation. "Ramses is protected by magic and doctors who care for him always. The Royal Priests pray for his good health and longevity and also conduct sacrifices on his behalf. The magician's spells must be removed for him to become defenseless. The mighty Pharaoh must be replaced by an old mortal man. Only then shall he be susceptible to death. I do not see how this can be accomplished, Mother, without our necks caught under the executioner's blade."

"Poison," said her mother decidedly. "Ricin or a combination of ground poppy seeds and portions of the hemlock plant. Apricot kernels can be ground into a most effective poison. I believe the seeds from the fruit of a Persea tree could do the deed although we would require a multitude of them to be effective."

"You amaze me, Mother. You have quite an arsenal of dangerous knowledge at your fingertips." Tiye wondered idly if her mother had ever put these potions to use. At least her father yet lived. "That idea is not a viable one. His food is tasted at every meal," said the Queen.

Her mother waved Tiye's reasoning aside as she would an irritating gnat. "And what of your time alone with him? Surely you partake of wine in those moments. Delicacies too, I should think. Are those sipped and tasted beforehand as well?"

"The food would have been tasted. Indeed, every morsel to pass his lips is tasted beforehand. A cup of wine from the bottle would also be sipped. Adding poison to the food could be messy and noticed. Yet the wine . . . perhaps if I slipped it into the cup, not the bottle. That would be somewhat simpler as I usually serve the beverage. I would only require a small vial hidden upon my person or somewhere nearby."

"And the doors. Are they not locked for privacy?"

"Naturally, Mother. Good solid wooden structures with enormous locks. Complete privacy unless a guard or servant is called."

The extent of wood grown in Egypt consisted of acacia, sycamore, fig, palm, and other small trees. These species were too knotty and fragile to build anything of strength and were used for items such as furniture, statues, ship masts, and sarcophagi. Timber of cedar, ebony, and fir were imported for larger items like ships, rafters, and doors. Yet wood was costly — costly to others yet not for the wealthy and certainly not to the Royal Palace. The Pharaoh favored thick and artistically carved doors throughout the Palace. The locks attached to these sturdy impenetrable doors were of a simple pin-tumbler design invented nearly 2000 years earlier. The only drawbacks were their size — nearly two feet in length — and the equally bulky key.

Coming to her senses, Tiye said, "Yet this is madness. We are considering murder. I was seeking a solution or an assurance from you yet never had I thought you might suggest such a course of action."

"I see," her mother said coldly. "Ultimately this is your decision. Perhaps you should consider more discussions with Ramses, hmm? I could assist in the discussions. Why, I must send a messenger at this moment to schedule a time in the Pharaoh's routine. Should I request four days hence? Is that acceptable with your duties, Daughter?

"Ah, another thought. Your father should be contacted as well. He is not without power in Egypt. Naturally, I shall make inquiry as to his timetable. Alas, I do not know what date he has available without consulting the man yet I am sure he would accommodate us. He is, after all, related to the Pharaoh. It would become a pleasant family affair. Yes, your father should be immediately contacted.

"Naturally, if our conversation does not show Ramses the truth in our request, perhaps we could schedule a second and then a third meeting. Surely, continued discussions must change Ramses' decision. What say you, Daughter? Shall that ease your emotional sensibilities to our initial plan? If not . . . well, I am at a loss. What suggestion would you make?"

Her mother was employing her tactic of drama and sarcasm, a method proven to be very satisfactory to her over the years. Tiye found it tiresome and extremely irritating yet not without merit. Try as she might she had no other thoughts on the matter. She could not voice this subject matter again to Ramses unless she had little concern for her own well-being. She was not anxious to incur his wrath further.

"I believe we should continue these thoughts at a later time, Mother. Tonight, perhaps. Meanwhile, I have an afternoon meal with Ari. I vow to give this further thought." Her mother looked sideways at her with skepticism.

"Truly, Mother, I do. And you should pray for alternative methods while I am absent. A <u>safe</u> alternative to our desire end."

"And you, Daughter Dear," replied her mother, "should test the waters with Ari. He might be extremely motivated to do your bidding."

With a spiteful look at her mother, she left the walls of the cool morning room to prepare for her meal with Ari.

## Chapter Fifteen

The domicile of Ari was within walking distance and Tiye choose this method of travel rather than her riding chair. Only one bodyguard accompanied her and she planned on posting him at Ari's door upon arrival. She now used this brief walk to digest the outrageous idea of her mother. It would require a great deal of thought.

Ari had always been the dearest of friends. She would speak to him of her mother's idea. Cautiously, of course, and in broad strokes. She must not divulge the actual plan her mother presented; only view his opinion of Amonhirk as would-be Pharaoh. Individual political opinions were surely held yet seldom discussed between people, even among friends. Ramses III was Pharaoh and as such had complete dominion over his subjects. Long standing laws determined the successor to his throne, not the people. It was a simple fact and had been so for thousands of years. Tiye could not recall a documented revolt against any Pharaoh. And yet, she was thinking of embarking upon such a course.

Arriving at the magnificent home of Ari brought back many feelings of happier times, times when poison and murder were unspoken. Ari was there at his door to greet her and it brought a smile to her face. How very sweet of him, she thought, to greet me personally rather than assign a servant. Yet he was always very attentive to his guests.

He greeted her with the requisite bowing from his waist and a grin. Tiye protested this formality to him.

"Never let it be said that I do not pay honor to My Queen," he replied.

As she crossed his threshold, she was pleased to see Mery, Ari's longtime attendant. The servant began her occupancy within the home as Ari's nanny and was now Keeper of the Home with authority over all other servants. Intermittently bowing and curtsying, she was quite aflutter and tongue-tied. Tiye quickly put her at ease while Ari laughed heartily. "You do seem to have an overwhelming effect on people," he said.

Tiye was so pleased to be around her youthful surroundings, she did not immediately notice the lack of seating and tables about the room.

"Ari," Tiye eventually asked, "what became of your massive seating arrangement under the ceiling canopy? Oh, and the ornamental chest your mother so loved? In fact, I remember this room was overcrowded with family artifacts and furniture."

"Some pieces have been placed in my siblings' homes. Others were pieces I was never fond of. Mother loved to collect furniture and I prefer a sleeker, uncluttered way of life."

"I should very much like to greet some of your other servants." She named a few of her favored women.

"Alas, they too have seen a transfer to my sisters' services. They each have several children and much more care is needed in their abodes. As I am unencumbered in that area, Mery is all I require. Come let us enjoy our meal." So, thought Tiye with some satisfaction, he is without a wife.

They sat and were served by Mery who, Tiye was told, also prepared the food. The meal was simple with fresh fish and fruits and a very flavorful sweet wine upon which to sip. After the completion of the meal, Tiye expressed a desire to explore the grounds of his estate. His land had a flourishing garden and crops of trees that she and her friends often climbed — without her mother's knowledge, of course. Even now she could still imagine the berating from her mother. Always behaving more as a peasant than of nobility, she would have said.

The main garden area seemed to be rather ill kept yet the orchard trees were flourishing. As they continued their walk, the Queen strove to avoid stepping and crushing much of the fruit upon the ground. "It would seem you have missed the best of the harvest, Ari. The fallen pieces are now food for wildlife rather than the market."

"I had a most abundant crop this season. This is actually the second growth. You are correct, however, I must gather the pickers directly. Too much fruit is wasting away and a tidy sum could yet be had for the remainder.

"I confess I rely upon others to notice the gathering seasons. My time is devoted to other concerns." Reentering the cooler, tree covered portion, the couple sat upon a very old marble bench located near a quite empty and crumbling fountain. As much as she adored and trusted Ari, she felt something was amiss in his home. As one of the wealthiest men in this region, she doubted the veracity of his many excuses. For the present, she put those thoughts aside and opted to take her mother's suggestion and speak of her son. She had the perfect opportunity to do so when he asked about the details of her life in the Palace.

After a few amusing anecdotes of the residents, she began her task. "Pentawer has grown into a fine, brilliant man. It saddens me that our country can not know the success Egypt could have under his rule."

"He is second in succession to the Throne, is he not?"

"He is. He is also the most beloved of Ramses' sons. The years have only brought them closer, with our King often seeking out Penatwer's unique advice. It is a great shame that Amonhirk must rule. He is a spiteful, lazy man, more interested in hunting and fornicating than the status of our country." She was forced to voice a plausible reason why she disliked the Prince so intensely rather than merely due to his right of succession.

Ari was not as attentive to Tiye's conversation as she would have liked. "I suppose line of inheritance to the Throne is a directive for a reason. The lineage of the Pharaoh has always been for the best, I believe. Although, it would be pleasant to admit I am on close terms with the Mother of the Pharaoh. Considering how close we really were." The familiar lewd look on his face brought chills to her.

Curse him, thought the Queen. He has always had this effect upon me. My emotions are not my own when he is near. She hoped this effect he had upon her would have dissipated by now yet it was not so. Idly, she wondered if she should allow her body's reaction to be put to practice. It had been a decidedly long span of time since she had enjoyed sexual contact. With Ramses it was always a chore. An exhausting chore. Wasn't she allowed a brief interlude of pleasure as well?

Ari leaned in to the Queen. "My sincere apologies. I have not been as conscientious to your conversation as I should. I have a pressing reason, however." He reached out to hold her hand gently. "Shall I tell you?" Tiye nodded, wondering what he was about to divulge. "It is your presence, my lotus blossom. Since your mother's evening affair I cannot vanquish your memory." He ran his fingers up her bare arm and across the bodice edging of her gown, ever so lightly touching the crest of her bosom. "I am flooded with images of our times together near the river."

"Ari, lest you forget, Mery is in your home. She could overhear us. I would not want to see you victimized for speaking such lovely sentiments. Besides, we were only children."

"I must tell you, I cared for you deeply, more than you can imagine. And I was fully aware of your affection for me. Alas, I could never reveal my feelings — you were destined to be Queen. I could not possibly compete. Instead I lost you to the people of Egypt."

"Ari, why did you not show me a sign of this?" she said with anguish. "You might have told me on our final day together. Perhaps the promise my father made might have been broken. Or, we might have left Egypt for a life together." And I, thought the Queen, would not be in this present quandary contemplating murder.

"Ah, my sweet. I have been to Thebes and have seen your face rendered on the many buildings. The artists must love you dearly to create such pieces of beauty. How could I have robbed you of the nation's love? No, my dear one, you were placed here to be honored by all men, not myself alone, and to one day sit at the side of the gods."

His fingers began tracing their way up her neck. He knew of her sensitivity to this area and she cursed him again. She felt a bead of sweat trickle down between her breasts and experienced a shortness of breath as his lips assumed the movement of his fingers.

"We cannot," said Tiye breathlessly. "Mery . . . she shall hear."

"Impossible," said Ari as he began nibbling upon her ear. "She has left on an errand." With that, he loosened the tie and brooch upon her gown, revealing her full bosom. "How convenient our garments are constructed. Do you think clothiers had these moments in mind when they designed them?" She giggled yet silently agreed with his reasoning. She slid her hand to the top of his tunic, unfastening the piece as a whole. Completely naked he carried her to a small patch of soft grass. I must not continue with this folly, she inwardly warned, yet who would know?

They remembered each other's bodies as a priest remembers his prayers, touching areas of naked flesh that brought delight and desire. She fully surrendered herself to him as in days of old upon the sweet turf.

## Chapter Sixteen

Having fallen into slumber, Tiye and Ari did not awaken until the sun had fully set. When Ari suggested she linger for the evening meal, she accepted. More time spent with him would be wonderful.

She arrived home quite late, saying a quick prayer of thanks to the gods — real or imagined — that her mother was not in the front parlor waiting to confront her for news. Their conversation must wait until morning, thought the Queen. I have much to sort out tonight.

She lingered the following morning in her comfortable bed. She waited until her mother increased the noise level of whatever task she was attending to in another room. It had always been her way — much to the family's annoyance — to create as much noise as possible, making it louder, if necessary, to awaken the household. If she was an early riser she saw no reason why all others should not be as well. One would think she could have more courtesy when Royalty was in the house, thought the Queen. By her estimation the cock had barely finished with his crowing.

Her maids prepared her as quickly as they could while the banging below grew louder. For someone who never took part in the household duties, her mother could sound extremely busy when it appealed to her.

Poking her head into the meal preparation room, Tiye made an announcement to the staff. "Cook, we shall have one guest at the morning meal today. Please have fresh eggs collected and prepare some of your wonderful sweets. I favor newly picked figs and berries upon the table as well."

Naturally, her mother was at her elbow when she turned, determined to hear every conversation. Tiye was startled nonetheless. "Mother, do not creep about the house in such a manner. It is quite unnerving."

Ignoring Tiye's irritation she plowed into the subject from the day prior. "Tell me, Daughter. What decision did you glean from Ari? Shall he support our cause?"

"It is too soon to tell. I have not yet fully broached our desires, only sought his opinion of my son. That is why I have invited him for our morning meal. I hoped we might have time to speak in the garden and further investigate his allegiance." Her mother was very enthusiastic over this development yet before she could interject her anticipated statement, Tiye continued. "And you, Mother, shall not interfere. In fact, I must to insist you find a reason to leave the house. Visit a friend or take Cook to market for fresh fowl. I fancy duck this evening meal." Her mother began to open her mouth yet Tiye continued, crushing what was surely to come. "No, Mother. Hear my words. You are not to be anywhere near this abode after we have consumed our meal. You do understand, do you not? Call this a Royal Request if you like yet you shall remove yourself."

Her mother scowled yet Tiye would not back away from this decision, no matter the chill running along her back. This defiance of hers shall surely call for her mother's retaliation, reasoned Tiye. However, the thought of such a delicate conversation held with someone as indelicate as her mother was non-negotiable. Her mother said. "When I return, you shall confide in me all that transpired." It was not a question but a demand, her way of regaining control. Tiye nodded in assent.

The meal was an inspired success. The three of them told old tales of friends and events, leaving each laughing with delight. Tiye had the presence of mind to thank and compliment Cook on her wonderful entrees and Ari took the old woman's hand and kissed the back of her hand. "The honeyed cakes were sublime," he said to her. The woman turned pink with joy.

Servants entered the room to clear the plates while her mother made a mumbled reason to leave the home. It was a rather odd exit for the woman but as least she was gone.

"Come," Tiye said to Ari. "Let us wander to the cool garden."

Once again they sat by the flowing fountain. Occasionally the water would splash upon their waists and Tiye leaned backwards to catch more of the cooling drops along her spine. The fountain was far removed from the front of the garden or the house yet unlike Ari's home, servants here were abundant. She must watch what she said or did.

"Yesterday was a most wonderful day for me Ari. I felt as though I had not a care or duty in the world except to enjoy myself."

Ari leaned in to whisper in her ear. "I too enjoyed our time together. You are an astonishing and desirable woman, Tiye. Yet I feel sorrow for you, my sweet, to not enjoy every day as we did. For one who is surely pampered in life, it surprises me to hear you speak so."

"Pampered, yes, yet never without responsibilities or watchful eyes upon me. I realize the guards are present for my protection yet they line the corridors and continually surround the family. I occasionally feel crowded and smothered."

"And the Pharaoh, your husband? Has he given you joy?"

Touching his cheek lightly, she replied, "Certainly not as you did last eve. Yet, for the most part I have been content with my life."

"What would he do," he said pensively, "if our recent activities ever came to light? For that matter, what of those in your youth? You were very accomplished for your age, pet. Does he never question you of your education in such subjects?"

Tiye snorted. "He is merely content with my gifts and has never been inquisitive. He might overlook my youthful indiscretions." Although, Tiye thought, the number of young men involved during my girlhood might be objectionable to him. She ran her hand under the splashing water of the fountain reflecting upon Ari's query.

While nothing was expressly written against a married woman engaging in extra-marital indulgences, privately the punishment could be divorce, beatings, and occasionally death. Court records confirm occasional involvement in such instances. In one such documented case, a woman accused of adultery was tied limbs akimbo, each to a stake in the ground. She was thusly restrained outside her home — the home she had sullied by her actions — and set aflame in front of her family, children, and neighbors. Such examples would surely deter others from offending the gods or promoting social turbulence.

Egyptians place great value on social harmony so it was understandable why special interest was given to stories that encouraged tranquility within the family. Egyptian literature often told of what lay ahead for the unfaithful wife. Monogamy was regularly stressed in stories of the gods as well; strong examples of truth and serenity within families.

All this ran through Tiye's thoughts as she searched for a succinct answer to Ari's complicated question. "Fidelity in a marriage is not to be toyed with, particularly in a Royal marriage.

Oh yes, I would come to great harm." She knew it was much safer to remain faithful to one's mate, especially when that mate was Pharaoh Ramses III.

Changing the subject matter Ari said, "I am so very glad you invited me to partake of the morning meal with you. I have something rather serious I wish to discuss with you." She looked at him quizzically.

"Various endeavourers of mine have seen trouble of late. You noticed my meager furnishings yesterday. I offer apologies yet the reason I presented to you was false. You see, I face financial ruin."

"Oh Ari, how? Your father surely left you in a most secure position financially, did he not?"

"So I believed. After his demise, creditors were upon my door like locusts, each one demanding payment for gambling losses incurred by my father. I think the anxiety over these debts drove my mother to her early death."

"Gambling? I had no idea your father was so inclined."

"Nor did I," he said sadly. "You witnessed yesterday just how much I have relinquished to my father's folly. I was much too mortified to admit my problem to you then. Now you see why the servants and the priceless pieces of family heirlooms are no longer present.

"I have been forced to sell several properties so I may at the very least keep my family home. I have postponed several creditors hoping to find something of more value to sell. Only my home and a vineyard in the north remain. Since the vineyard is yet lucrative, I have been able to ease those creditors with the profits from the wine. I have enough for the most meager of necessities and payment to Mery. I cannot turn her out. She has been with the family since my childhood. Where would she go at her age?" He shook his head in sorrow.

"Perhaps I can help you, Ari," said Tiye.

"I cannot ask that of you, my pet. To ask another's relief for such a family embarrassment is weak. And you, the Queen of my country, cannot be embroiled in this scandal."

Tiye thought for a moment. "No one need know of my aid, I swear. Next month upon my regular visit to my mother I could bring something of value for you. To provide you a small stake with which you may gain back what you have lost. Or rather what your father has lost for you."

Ari laughed derisively. "Are you prepared to skulk about, looting the Palace of golden artifacts to carry on your barge to me? That is unthinkable and puts you at such a risk I shall not hear of it. I merely wished you to know the truth rather than the falsehood I gave you. My guilt in lying to you was great. By the gods, I swear I have never lied to you in the past. "

"Ari, please listen." She grabbed his hand and said earnestly, "I have jewelry; many valuable pieces I no longer wear. They should fetch a considerable amount from those who know their value. They merely gather dust. No one shall miss them." Except perhaps her Guardian of Royal Jewelry to the Queen, she thought. No matter. She is the Queen and shall make a believable excuse.

Ari was practically in tears as he turner to her. "You would do that for me? You would take such a chance?"

She nodded happily. "Of course, Ari. You are my everlasting friend. And love." With that said, she began mentally deciding upon which pieces to bring to him. He would be out of reach tending to what little business remained, he told her, yet they promised to see each other the following month.

Shortly after Ari had left the home, her mother arrived, anxious for answers to her many questions. "So? What was the outcome of your conversation with Ari? Is he willing to lend assistance to our cause?"

She neglected to speak to him on that subject yet was not about to admit the blunder to her mother. She was also not about to reveal Ari's confidences to her. "Your mother always held such high esteem of my family, I would hate to disillusion her," explained Ari of his wish for secrecy. "It would be a sad occurrence to have her aware of my father's contemptuous behavior."

It was laughable to think she would divulge any secret to her mother. Everyone within the women's circle would know the tale before nightfall. To her mother she said, "I do not think he is quite prepared to do so, Mother." Seeing the look on the woman's face Tiye continued hurriedly, "At this time. He shall be gone until the following month. Perhaps I shall be better informed regarding our contacts and support by then."

Making plans for her return visit, Tiye and her various caretakers made their way to her barge for the journey to the Palace.

## Chapter Seventeen

Asim had her head upon Pentu's chest, listening to this rhythmic breathing and feeling his warmth under her. They had been meeting whenever possible in his newly allocated chambers within the Palace. When their time was limited they met in the gardens of the temple, their favored place. She was under many demands from the Queen and Pentu's new position to the Pharaoh took much of his time. They grabbed happiness together when they were able.

Pentu slowly opened his eyes and smiled at her. It was near dawn and she must leave his bed soon. "My love," she said, "the time draws near when I must depart."

He groaned and grabbed her around the waist while rolling her over and nuzzling at her neck. "I would have you stay with me forever in this bed."

She laughed at his playfulness. "Never to rise, never to eat or drink? However should we endure?"

"To feast upon your beauty would be food enough for even the gods," he said while selecting an area below her neck to place kisses.

"You are quite the poet."

"Ah, we are known to be a very poetic people, are we not?"

"Indeed. Yet I fear we have many other responsibilities demanding our attention. I cannot lie here and listen to your poetry, much as I would enjoy doing so."

"Ah, yes. The Pharaoh," he said with a wave of his hand and a chuckle. "He matters little. You are all I require on this earth."

She covered his mouth and said rather seriously, "Shhh, do not speak so. Someone might overhear and not realize your jest."

He smiled and stroked her face. "If we were in a home of our own we need not be concerned with passer-bys and those who poke into our lives. You would be free from chance encounters with that soldier, Akar. I would not have him maul you again," he finished with some annoyance.

A fortnight ago they met in the gardens for some time together. When he reached to hold her hand she had cried out in pain. After much cajoling, she finally told him how she came by the twisted wrist that pained her so.

Once again, Akar caught her in a corridor. He was adamant she should spend time with him while she was equally insistent she proceed on her way. A short struggle ensued with her wrist being wrung painfully in his clutch as she sought to flee. This version she told Pentu. What she did not divulge was the expression of excitement in Akar's eyes as he wrenched her small wrist.

"I should have reported the man when you first told me of his manhandling."

"No you must not. Word of us may find its way to the Queen's ear. If she were to learn of our dalliances, it could be the end of us both. I would not have your new position placed in jeopardy for such a trivial reason."

"I do not see a pained wrist inflicted upon you by Akar as trivial. I believe his attentions towards you shall only increase if he is not dealt with. And I see no reason why it matters to the Queen we have found love together. She should be more concerned if a Pharaoh's soldier was abusing her servant."

"You are very sweet to think so and under most circumstances that would be true. Yet situations are different here in the Royal Palace. Things are not always of one thought or reason. She has been grooming me for life as a lady since my arrival in the Palace. She is my mistress and my guardian."

"It is not so in my town. It is unheard of. People should have choices. Explain again why that dream of mine cannot see fruition. Why can we not be together? I should take you to Set-Maat. I have a home there, a position. We could have a life, just we two."

"We cannot flee from our pledges to the Royals. Such an action would not be appreciated and possibly considered treasonous. Until you have established yourself firmly in your position to the Pharaoh, we must have patience. Unfortunately I am closely controlled, as you know, and it is only by the gods blessings we have been able to meet unhindered. Indeed, she is also quite certain I maintain my virginity."

He looked at her lewdly. "I believe we have seen to that end quite satisfactorily, do you not agree?"

"Quite satisfactorily," she agreed grinning shamelessly at him. "And until we are able to escape this prison we have created for ourselves, she must never know."

"She cannot know by simply looking at you, my love. We are taking all necessary precautions to avoid pregnancy."

The understanding of contraceptives was included in Egypt's vast knowledge of medicine. The avoidance of pregnancy was considered a woman's responsibility and magicians or physicians offered many different formulas for sale. Some used balls of lint soaked in ground acacia leaves, or acacia fruit combined with honey. Others utilized a combination of honey, dates, and other substances mixed with crocodile dung. These blends were used by the female as a block and inserted vaginally to stop pregnancy.

Prophylactics were initially worn by Egyptians to prevent tropical disease before it was found to be somewhat helpful in controlling the size of a family. They were made of fine linen or sheep's intestines and held in place by ties at the man's back using cloth straps.

Egyptians were extremely fond of children and birth was considered a blessing even out of wedlock. They were all considered gifts from the gods and to be celebrated. In the situation facing Asim and Pentu, however, a pregnancy could mean great danger or even death at the hands of Queen Tiye. Asim was keenly aware of her mistress's wrath and power. The couple had no choice but to avoid a pregnancy.

Pentu had been quietly thinking while the two lie intertwined. "I wonder what she stands to gain with a courtship between you and a man of high social standing. What could anyone promise her that she does not possess or cannot own as the Queen of Egypt?"

"I have often thought the same. I cannot find meaning in such an idea yet I suspect the truth of it. I have never known her to be altruistic to anyone. She is always scheming for gain.

"As your own status with the Pharaoh grows she must consider you valuable enough for a husband. If you are one of high standing, she should allow you to take me as wife. It is my most fervent prayer to the gods."

"Then, as I begin another day knowing of your love for me, I shall pray for our cause as well."

## Chapter Eighteen

Tiye had her staff prepare her baskets and cases for the journey to her mother. However, she could not ask anyone to choose the jewelry she would bring to Ari; she must tend to that personally. Nothing too expensive yet valuable enough to assist him in his frightful circumstances. She chose a small necklace of lapis lazuli that was no longer considered fashionable, along with crystal and amethyst bracelets. She saw an old pair of carnelian earrings in a corner of one jewel case and decided upon those as well. Digging further, she also found a large necklace of garnet and turquoise and another rather dented brooch of rubies. The setting may be damaged yet separately the piece should fetch a hefty amount. He would be able barter these stones individually if he chose. Some were pieces owned prior to her becoming Queen; others were seldom worn and not particularly ostentatious. If the pieces were too grand, she reasoned, they might arouse suspicion when Ari bartered for their value. Reaching into a third case, she held the battered leather pouch from long ago. Pouring the piece into her hand she held it against her throat before replacing it in the worn leather. This piece she could never relinquish even if she returned it to Ari, the boy who had presented it to her in the rushes.

Packing the items for travel in her large case was problematic. She had more than one servant folding garments and tucking necessities within her baskets while others were rummaging about for the clothing she wished to include. She could never be seen undertaking such a menial task as packing when a servant would always do so. In the end, she placed them in a thick linen bag, drew the closure, and plopped it upon her dressing table.

As expected, her Royal Handler of the Queens Jewelry noticed pieces missing. The woman kept careful records of Her Majesty's jewelry; which piece the Queen preferred with a certain garment, which box each should be stored in, even the pieces she wore during the day and evening. The woman felt in doing so, she could never be blamed for any missing gems.

Bowing to her mistress, she said, "My Queen, I cannot locate a few of your jewelry pieces." She proceeded into a lengthy explanation of where they should be stored as well as when the Queen last wore each piece.

Before the conversation became too tiresome, the Queen pointed to the sack and said, "You will find those pieces in there. I have decided to purge a few of the older items and give them to my mother. You may make the necessary entries in your ledger to indicate my decision."

While only one in perhaps 100 people in Egypt were able to read, Tiye insisted her servants entrusted with greater responsibilities should be able to read and write. At least to the minimum needed for their particular duty. With this woman who cared for her valuable jewelry, Tiye had taught her to read to a satisfactory level and write, including numbers. It had been very good idea at the time yet now, with such meticulous records, she missed nothing out of place. Tiye felt as a thief of her own jewelry. Yet the girl accepted Tiye's tale, believing it to be of a daughter favoring her mother. The servant said as much to her Queen, praising Tiye for her most selfless act of kindness. If she only knew the truth, thought Tiye.

## Chapter Nineteen

"I believe these will trade for a goodly amount, Ari. It can be applied to the debt."

Once again Tiye and Ari were within his garden. They had just completed lovemaking and were both lying naked near his unused fountain.

She sat up and pulled her gown around her in a semblance of modesty. They were no longer intertwined and she felt suddenly exposed discussing the mundane topic of trade. He was holding a bracelet pulled from the sack of jewels she had presented him. Kissing intimately the tender inside of her wrist he said, "My dearest, I cannot thank you enough for this saving act. I shall know more of the value later today. Your mother has graciously invited me to your evening's meal. I shall be better informed at that time."

Putting the piece back into the bag, he gave her another kiss upon her palm saying, "For now, I must speak to my creditors and resolve this most worrying situation. Shall I see you home?"

With that they exited his home and made the brief walk to her mother's abode, her solitary guard walking a few paces behind his Queen. For some reason she felt rebuffed by him, as if she had participated briefly in a play and was quickly dismissed from the stage. And why, she speculated, did he display indifference towards the pieces she had offered him? Could he possibly be in so much debt that even a Queen's jewelry pouch could not extricate him?

She believed he would have be overjoyed to see her and marvel at the risky act she committed for his benefit. Neither had been the case. He must be more worried than I knew, she thought. She was unsure if she was disappointed, insulted, or angry. She decided upon all three. Perhaps the dinner hour will be more to my liking.

He bowed to her as she left his presence, keeping up pretenses of his great respect for his Queen in a most formal association. It was a cool farewell yet she attempted to understand his avoidance of gossip. With a sigh, she stiffened her back in preparation for her mother's company.

She barely stepped over the threshold when her mother accosted her in the entry, quite eager to speak to her alone. She would have to wait, thought Tiye. I shall not jump hoops for her. I am the Queen of Egypt and as such she shall comply with my whims.

She informed her mother of a need for rest prior to any conversation and made her way upstairs. Knowing the glare of disproval the woman aimed at her back, Tiye was unsettled when she entered her quarters.

After an hour had passed, Tiye felt refreshed and composed enough to engage with her mother. Naturally, the woman had turned the tables upon her daughter and could not be located. By the time she reappeared, Tiye had lost all composure while her mother was as cool and haughty as ever.

"Well, Daughter, to what do I owe such *honor*? Shall you now fit me into your busy schedule? Are you quite prepared to have a long overdue conversation with me?"

"Yes, Mother." A simple reply, yet one that would not set her mother's hostility on edge any further. One would think the woman was First Queen, thought Tiye.

They enlarged upon the plan previously discussed a month prior. Her mother had spoken to the servants who in turn had spoken to those of other powerful homes. Some had already made contact for clarification. "What tale did you spin of Amonhirk, Mother?" asked Tiye.

"A very believable one. Something to strike concern where they feel it most sorely — their wealth. I simply mentioned Amonhirk's plans to raise taxes. With the current instability of Egypt it was a plausible solution he might truly enact. I thought it quite clever."

Yes, thought Tiye. It was most plausible. She heard her husband broach that topic with her son.

"Of course, I was forced to invent that quickly since you did not provide me with other weaponry I might have utilized. At any rate, they not only believed it but were very put out by the possibility. The man with whom I spoke is extremely thrifty. Truly on the verge of tightfistedness. I have heard from his wife he considers taxation is beneficial only to the Pharaoh, his Cabinet, and the priests. He resents paying sums to someone else's coffers, even if he is the Ruler of Egypt."

"Are these his true words?"

"As I say, according to his wife. I did witness his anger when I mentioned such an increase. Trust me, my daughter. He would be pleased to see the death of Ramses and Amonhirk. There is not much this man would do to keep an extra deben to his name."

"I wish to ponder upon this further, Mother. Truthfully, I am frightened and cannot reason why you are not as well. This is murder we are discussing, and not simply the murder of some simpleton or criminal. This is the Great Ramses III, the Pharaoh god, the Enlightened One of Egypt. Do not these monikers chill you to the very bone? They do to mine." Her mother was about to speak. "Enough for now, Mother. My head aches and the hour grows late. Ari will soon arrive. Perhaps I will seek his counsel tonight."

The meal was enjoyable, as was any social gathering with Ari's sense of humor and wit on display. Afterwards, he and the Queen went walking in the family garden. Once again, her mother was under strict orders not to interfere or interrupt them. The woman sulked yet finally acquiesced.

"Ari, I have been so hoping my contribution helped your plight. Please tell me that is so."

Ari placed his fingertip upon her lips and walked deeper into the more solitary portion of the swaying palms. "The items were sorely appreciated, my little dove. My creditors were quite amazed I was able to procure such an amount."

"How did you explain the jewelry? Was there suspicion?"

"Ah, not at all," said Ari with a smile. "I simply told them they had belonged to my mother and I had not come upon them until recently. I said she occasionally hid items away in her dotage."

"Dotage? But Ari, she was not absent of sense. Your mother, when last I saw her, was still quite alert and quick witted. Unless she became so with time."

Ari laughed. "Of course she was not witless. However, I was forced to give them some excuse. They would have become ill tempered if they thought I had been holding back precious items. Do not look so horrified, my sweet. It was merely a ploy, a simple lie to protect our skin."

Tiye smiled back. Yes, she thought, only a small fib to protect us both. And who was she to condemn a lie, frowned upon by Egyptian teachings, when she was contemplating an act much more heinous.

"Alas," continued Ari, "I am yet lacking the total sum due. Indeed, I am short by a considerable amount." Seeing the questioning look upon his companion's face he said, "I am sorry, pet. Unbeknownst to me, interest has been accumulating on the original sum."

He let this sit with her for a moment, waiting for her to speak. Tiye's thoughts were racing. Did he expect me to give him more, she thought. The riches of the Palace were catalogued since they belonged to generations of Pharaohs, never just the one. How could she hope to bring any object out of the Palace for Ari? She would never ask her mother, did not even consider that an option. Perhaps a trusted servant might bring more jewelry to him. Was there a plausible reason for her to order such a journey from a gossiping servant? And what if the servant looked inside the parcel? It was not viable and she threw out that solution as quickly as a servant would remove a cricket from her bed.

"I do not know what more I can do, Ari. My move towards anything else would be questioned, placing us both in harm's way. Is there nothing you can find to ease this debt?"

"You were my last hope, my flower," said Ari sadly, "and I was deeply mortified to have asked you."

"Perhaps if I spoke to these collectors. They cannot hold you to another's debt even if he was your father. You did nothing to incur it and you should not be held responsible. Let me speak to them with you on the morrow. Together we can arrive at an agreement."

"No," he said hurriedly. She was taken aback at his definitive answer. Smiling he said more softly, "I do not want you to become so closely involved. Plus I would not have them know I sought relief from a woman, Queen though you are. In fact, that might be even worse for you. Think of the tale that might reach the Pharaoh."

"Then I shall come again to you with another parcel. I believe my agenda might allow for a subsequent visit in two weeks rather than waiting another month." She suddenly laughed. "How very silly of me. I am the Queen of Egypt. I shall travel this route if I deem it necessary. Would that time frame be agreeable to you?" Her words were rewarded with an enthusiastic kiss upon her full mouth by Ari, followed by his luscious lips traveling to the nape of the neck. It was quite some time before she reentered the parlor of her mother. She was not, after, accustomed to redressing without the use of servants.

## Chapter Twenty

Upon arrival at the Palace, Tiye was thrust into planning a most important event on the behest of the Pharaoh. It was a shared effort between the First and Second Queens for an elaborate banquet with officials from a trading country. It was being held on a holy feast day, in two days hence, and the foreign ambassadors had expressed a desire to attend the celebration. It mattered naught for whom the feast day honored since the dinner in the Palace was the main focus. The Pharaoh desired to continue the trade agreement with the other country so a memorable night of food and drink was demanded. Dancers, jugglers, acrobats, musicians, and singers were already scheduled for the evening's entertainment.

Working with her Sister Queen was not as difficult as she had feared. Queen Iset was most pleasant and acquiesced to every idea Tiye had to offer. Unfortunately Prince Amonhirk was also involved. His presence made Tiye gag with dislike and frustration yet she was polite as always.

"I hope you are agreeable to my son joining us. He will not aid in planning yet I thought it best for him to learn what preparations are needed for such an evening." Of course, thought Tiye with rancor, because your son will be Pharaoh and mine will not. "Perhaps as Pharaoh he will appreciate the Queen's endeavors to make such events function so flawlessly." At that she flashed those ominous teeth toward Tiye in what was meant to be a smile.

Tiye looked at Amonhirk, thinking how lucky he was not to have inherited those teeth of his mother's while gaining her elegant tall stature. He did, however, have a few unattractive features. His nose was wide and flat and his eyebrows were exceedingly bushy. He was known as a very pious man with complete devotion to the gods. Yet another item of discrepancy between us, thought Queen Tiye.

"I believe that is an admirable idea, My Sister," said Tiye although she firmly believed it was not. "I have often wished Ramses would attend such arrangements. Perhaps then he would not demand so much. At least he has not insisted the very moon descend from the sky."

Iset laughed at that, her teeth sparkling in her wide-open mouth. "Not too loudly, My Sister. If he should overhear, it shall surely be his next request."

Naturally the duties of each Queen did not extend to moving furniture or preparing any of the meals. Their involvement was devising a new menu or theme for each party and overseeing the servants.

Banquets were commonplace in Egypt as food and drink brought families and friends together. Lower ranking citizens often used glazed ceramic ware for plates and platters while the wealthier could afford table-ware of copper or silver. Using wooden dishware spoke of further status since only Royalty used the rare commodity in this fashion. The place settings of the Pharaoh out shone every other table in the country. The storage rooms held many different precious metals and marble carved into bowls, dishes, and cups.

It was from the valuable and varied dishware within the Palace that Queen Tiye hoped to find a solution for Air's financial difficulties. After all, she could not root about the Palace looking for items to nab. She had another idea that might succeed.

At this gathering, the Queens had decided to keep the colors light, using the alabaster dishware. Its translucency would look beautiful with firelight glowing in the room. "What say you, Sister — the large carved ebony or the smaller ivory goblets?" asked Tiye.

"The ivory would continue the pale color scheme. We can add color to the room with the wreaths of flowers on each table."

"Hmmm," said Tiye thoughtfully, "this plate is chipped. Do you see? We cannot use this with our esteemed guests." She wandered to another table and picked up a wooden serving bowl. "And this has a crack. It might be prudent if I inspected those we have in the storeroom and eliminate the worn pieces."

"If you have the time to do so, it is a wonderful offer and I thank you. You have a keen eye for quality. I trust your judgment."

"I shall make it a priority and do so after our time here." So, thought Tiye, that was simple.

"What shall you do with the broken pieces? I imagine they are yet of value."

Tiye feigned innocence and lack of thought. "I have a childhood friend who has fallen upon hard times since the mother and father passed from this life. Perhaps they shall be of use in the home." Iset simply nodded, commenting upon what a generous friend she was. Now she could take whatever chipped or cracked pieces she found and give them to Ari.

The two Queens were wandering within the largest of the banquet halls to view the seating arrangements. Low seats were customary at such banquets yet some preferred to sit directly upon floor pillows. Commonly used in all Egyptian households were folding stools; easy to use and store in even the smallest of homes. Such handy seats were originally fashioned after those at military encampments — practical wooden stands and simple leather slung seats. Those within the Royal Palace were also practical to fold and stash out of view yet hardly simple. Each leather sling was carefully hand tooled and painted. The wood they were wrapped around was imported with ivory inlay. Side tables would be scattered around the room with larger round tables positioned with studier chairs. Higher-ranking guests would be seated at slightly taller-backed chairs than the rest. The Pharaoh, his Queen, and Amonhirk would be seated at the tallest and most ornate chairs in the center of the room.

The aforementioned wreaths of flowers and small vials of perfume would also be added to each table. Also atop these, a covered bowl filled with water would be positioned for each guest to wash hands. Fingers could become sticky with greases and fruit juices, which were tasty when eaten yet unacceptable if clinging to one's hands. Indeed, every Palace bedchamber was brought a fresh bowl of water each morn for the purpose of maintaining cleanliness throughout the day.

"And the menu? Should we serve beef or opt for boar?" asked Tiye always deferring to Iset's choice. As if I cannot choose the complete menu alone, thought Tiye, as I have so often done.

"We have currently chosen goose, correct? Since goose is a fatty bird, perhaps boar would better suit the palate, as it is very lean."

"Nile catfish could be a welcome dish before the sweets are served. We have already ordered the figs as well as the grapes and dates. They shall be harvested on the morn. Do we have the watermelons? Yes? Excellent. Those will be sliced prior to the feast as well. Pots of honey for dipping, naturally, at every table.

"Fresh bread, of course, and many loaves will be baked that morning. Palm wine and mead as well as various beers. The less intoxicating beer shall be served first as well as citrus juice. I believe we have some of the Pharaoh's favorite wine in the underground cellar."

"Yes," agreed Tiye, "our Royal Wine Attendee has confirmed that. We have more than enough for this meal."

"Good. I have already instructed the cook to have whatever abundance of fresh vegetables the staff can acquire. I believe garlic, lentils, and turnips will be included in the order. Ramses is very fond of those." Herbs including aniseed, cinnamon, coriander, cumin, dill, fennel, marjoram, mustard, and thyme were often used in flavorful combinations within the Palace kitchens. The aromas emanating from there would be tantalizing and mouth watering.

"I have told the bakers to create their fabulous cakes with fruit and honey. Yeast cakes, naturally, baked light and puffy," added Tiye.

"Wonderful. Those will certainly provide conversation. They are unique to Egypt."

Egyptians were the first to recognize the value of adding yeast to breads and especially to a lovely confection called cakes. Baked on hot stones, the cakes did indeed rise as if by magic to double their original size. Other nations had not found this ingredient and Egyptians protected it greedily as their own. Combined with fruit and honey, the little cakes were served in times of celebrations and to impress others, often with festive decorations atop.

"I have organized the entertainment if you agree," Tiye informed her Sister Queen. "While the guests arrive and are awaiting the food, the jugglers and dancers will be performing. The acrobats next and while the meal commences, the boy with the lute shall play. Softly of course, so conversations may ensue. While the fruit is served, a singer with her harpist will perform. Then while remaining guests play board games the acrobats could return. They are quiet and would allow the players to concentrate on their respective games."

"Very commendable, Tiye. Some of the guests will, I am sure, take their games of chance most seriously. We do not want to interrupt those who wish to play. Separate tables away from the persistent revelers should be situated to that side of the room," she pointed to a far corner, "with additional food and drink. If one chooses to play a game, it does not mean one should sacrifice an appetite. However, how anyone shall fill one's stomach after this generous meal I cannot comprehend. At any rate, we shall have sufficient food for all."

Sufficient was quite an understatement, thought Tiye. The tabletops would scarcely be seen once the platters and bowls of roasted, grilled, baked, and fresh courses were brought in.

"My only concern," Tiye said, "is the betting by the players. It would not be prudent to have our honored officials leave with great sums lost. It has been known to happen, as you are aware. It may put the continued trade negotiations in jeopardy. I see no viable solution short of simply letting them win. However, the other Egyptian dignitaries might feel cheated. They would rightly feel so." She mentioned a few gentlemen guests who took gambling and games quite seriously. "These are important men in their own right, men who have befriended our Pharaoh. They would be insulted and irate."

"Hmm, you are quite correct in your assessment. One man you mentioned is on the verge of disaster. One large loss might tip him over. His ire would be very candid. I do not suppose we could have such activities absent gambling? No, I did not think as much.

"With our gambling laws in place, I think limited bets are required. We will simply defer to those laws and the desire of the Pharaoh if we hear of complaints. With a limit in place, we shall have neither large winners nor great losers. Everyone keeps their dignity and enjoys themselves." The crocodile teeth smiled at Tiye, who readily agreed. It was an agreeable answer to a possibly volatile problem.

"There is one more item I would request from you, My Sister." Tiye looked at Iset, expecting the worst. "At tomorrow's gathering I thought it fitting if you and Pentawer would sit with us at the Pharaoh's table in the tallest chairs. You are, after all, a high-ranking Queen and your son a chosen Prince. There is no need for you to be seated on shorter chairs. I hope that is agreeable with you."

"That is most agreeable. I offer you much gratitude for the offer."

Until this point in the day, Amonhirk had been wandering about the room and listening to the conversation between the two Queens. At this statement from his mother he turned to the women and scowled slightly. "I fear, however, Amonhirk does not think it suitable," finished Tiye noticing that scowl.

Iset turned to her son. "Is this fact, my son? Why is this suggestion met with disproval on your part? Tiye is your sister-mother and Pentawer your blood brother. They have every entitlement to sit as I decree. You would do well to seek this brother out for advice when you are Pharaoh as his knowledge is vast. You may cultivate his willingness to do so by this concession to such simple seating arrangements."

Amonhirk bowed to his mother. "You are quite correct, Mother. Pentawer is my brother and I love him as such. This outdated visual separation between us should be put to rest." He turned to Tiye and bowed to her as well. "Many apologies to you Queen Tiye. I was selfish to consider only myself and not of the future. You have my word upon the life of my father, I will forever take Pentawer in consideration in our country's future."

Tiye was astonished with this pronouncement from both of them. Never had she expected to hear such words. Then, as quickly as her joy appeared, so did suspicion. Might they have heard rumors of the impending assassination? Were they speaking with sweetened tongues to lower her defenses? She must consider these possibilities at another time. For now, she bowed to Amonhirk, expressing her gratitude and a vow that she and her son will do everything in their power to ensure his great reign.

She would also do well to inform her mother of this new situation. The visit to her home was two days hence and this information could alter their scheme drastically.

## Chapter Twenty-One

It seemed only a matter of days since she had made the trek to her mother's abode. The allotted two weeks had passed and today she traveled by barge once again. Never had she seen her mother twice in one month, she thought, and even her close servants were skeptical when they were informed of this visit. Tiye thought quickly and said the woman was slightly ill and needed attending. Telling this lie meant she must seize the first opportunity to warn her mother: the woman must act ill for the duration of Tiye's visit. Tiye knew her mother would not find it unappealing. Indeed, she would savor such attention.

Since Tiye offered her solution to dispense the broken dishware to those in need, she saw no reason to hide the items. She found many pieces that did not meet her standard for the Royal Palace festivities and had accumulated a considerable collection. Some were not damaged yet she pinched those as well. It was her word against servants, after all, and she would have these undamaged pieces for Ari. Wood plates, alabaster cups, even gold platters were making their way on board her barge within two large baskets.

At the last moment, she wrapped several amulets in pieces of linen and tossed them inside a case as well. Since they were for protection and religious reasons, they were not entered in any jewelry collection ledgers.

When her packing needs were met satisfactorily, she had time before embarkation. She decided upon a few moments with her animals.

"I will take a brief stroll in the gardens and around my zoo before we depart," she told her staff. "Finish packing while I am away."

It had been some time since she had personally seen to the care of her animals. She had chosen zookeepers who were like-minded in their love for animals and she knew they did an excellent job yet she enjoyed performing small tasks from time to time. Seeing the soft eyes of her many animals and their response to her touch was a calming moment for her. She would need to be calm, she thought, for these upcoming days. Her mother would always give her cause for discomfort yet this visit had more at stake. Presenting Ari with her second treasure trove and discussing the brewing conspiracy was already causing her insides to perform flips. Could it be the gods were punishing her for merely discussing such a scheme? No, thought Tiye, it was more likely caused by her morning repast. She would remember not to indulge in so much fresh fruit at such an early meal.

She was lost in thought while feeding one of her favorite goats. The doe had recently birthed a litter of five healthy kids. Tiye was wandering in their pen scratching each little one behind an ear, and receiving tiny bleats in appreciation, when she heard voices and footsteps in the attached garden. It sounded a bit like Queen Iset although she could not be sure. In a most undignified manner, she dashed behind the stable wall and crouched low.

Her guess had been correct as the voice of Iset could be heard coming closer to the zoo entrance. A second voice joined in with a tone of displeasure to it.

". . . why you insisted I present such a vow to her, Mother. I am the Crown Prince after all."

Ah, and that was the voice of Amonhirk. This could be enlightening, thought Tiye.

"True, my son. And I am the Queen. As such, while you are not yet the Pharaoh, you shall abide by my words. Amonhirk, can you not see this is a suggestion only for the benefit of your future and that of Egypt? No one man has knowledge of all things, even if that man is the Pharaoh. Your father surrounds himself with intelligent men to inform and advise in their particular area of expertise. Pentawer could be of great assistance in that respect."

There was a gapping silence before Amonhirk replied. "We were much more in accord when we were children. I do not wish his display of intelligence within my group of advisors. It would lend humiliation to my reign."

"Amonhirk," said Iset with a sad note to her voice, "you are jealous. Jealous of your blood brother who would only lend you aid. Jealously is a sin against the gods. If you allow it to eat away at your *ka*, there can be no Afterlife for you."

"I grow weary waiting for the crown. As does my wife. She yearns to be Queen as I do Pharaoh. I do not wish another to undermine me when I am crowned. However, I will strike a bargain with you, Mother," he said finally. "If you are yet upon this earth when I am Pharaoh, I will utilize Pentawer's advice for the glorification of my reign yet only at my discretion. That is the best concession I am willing to make."

"And should I be gone from these earthly sands? What then, my son?"

"Then he shall continue to live life within these walls as one with the Pharaoh's bloodline coursing through his body. He shall be Prince of Egypt yet he will not advise."

"I can see there is no changing you, my son. I am truly sorry for I believe you may not enjoy a seat next to mine in the Afterlife. I shall continue to pray for you."

With that they both walked out of the garden and Tiye emerged from hiding, her hem covered with hay. So, that is how it stands, she thought with anger. I should never have trusted his words, flowing like nectar from his mouth, trying to sway my judgment of him. He has not changed and has no intent to do so.

She had several ideas to offer her mother when they met. One thing they could both agree upon — Amonhirk must die.

# BOOK TWO
## Conspiracy

### Chapter One

"I fail to understand why you have not chosen to gain a commitment from Ari. He is not without power within social circles outside my own and our cause would do well to use that edge." Her mother began berating Tiye immediately upon entry to the home. She should have sealed his assurance two weeks ago. She should have names of other powerful citizens from him by now, complained her mother. And if this had not been done, why was she having such lengthy conversations with the man?

Taking a deep breath, Tiye grabbed her mother's elbow and drew her into an adjoining room. "Mother, that is the reason I have traveled here fully two weeks prior to my allotted time: to speak to him further. Oh and lest I forget, my reasoning to my servants for this unusual journey is due to your health. You are ill. Please act the part and take to your bed. I shall instruct Cook to bring your favorite honey and citrus drink."

So settled, Tiye pursued her purposes here; speak to Ari of her son as Pharaoh and offer him the goods she brought. Rather than carry the large baskets to his home, she sent a foot messenger to him indicating she would prefer to meet within her mother's house. She made herself comfortable in the morning room filled with the shade of palms in large clay pots. The sun rose on the other side of the house and this room stayed cool until midday.

She arranged the oversized baskets in the center of the room, almost as an offering of her love and support. Mother, naturally, asked many questions of the valuables, even attempting to commandeer several for her household. Tiye pointed out they were not in the pristine shape her guests were accustomed to. Indeed, these were broken, chipped, and bent; certainly not the quality her mother set out at societal parties. At the behest of the King, they shall be furnished to citizens who had fallen on sad times, Tiye explained. Since Ari's mother had been charitable to those in need, he would be the intermediately to this donation. It was a ludicrous and convoluted excuse yet she finally stopped her mother from asking too many questions or poking further in the basket. She was now exhausted from doing so. Mother sucks the life from me as soon as I enter this house, Tiye thought. The woman has a talent for such things.

It was at this point in her musings that Ari arrived "Ari, how nice to see you. Drinks have already been prepared for you as well as fresh bread and melons." She indicated the large platter on the center table, brimming with choice delights. "Also, a fresh catch of fish grilled with herbs and a sauce of spices. I remember how you enjoyed such fare. Come. Let us sit and converse."

Pointed to the baskets, she said to him "These baskets are for you." Softly she said, "My mother believes these are to be given to people of need. It was the only excuse I could dream of." She offered him a cup of wine and continued. "I do hope these will suffice. They have very little markings upon them and no indication of Palace ownership. There are, however, pieces of great value although some are ever so slightly damaged. Still, the wood plates should be of high interest to your lenders. I brought these as well." She handed him the amulets. "They are small yet well made of lapis and red jasper."

"Ah, my sweet dove. They look quite substantial." He moved closer to the basket and reached within to judge the craftsmanship of each. "The stones are of a singular beauty. However, I am not a particularly good evaluator of wood and alabaster. Perhaps you are?"

Tiye shook her head and said, "I am not. Yet I do know the value of one that was replaced, if that helps," and she mentioned a sum.

"That is a most satisfying evaluation. Hopefully others shall regard them so highly. There is the expected bargaining to be made, after all," he said while finishing a large piece of melon and then reaching for a slice of bread. "Alas, my sweet, when a final value has been offered by those stingy men, it will cover the amount due from merely one or two creditors. I am filled with remorse to say I shall need more from you."

Tiye winced at his tone, suddenly changing from one of affection to that of professional coolness. She could see no reasoning for the transformation.

She began removing her many pieces of jewelry — gold, ruby, garnet and carnelian — and handed them to him. "Here, Ari. Take these bracelets and rings. The necklace and earrings as well. These are surely worth more than the amulets. The Pharaoh commissioned them personally."

"My apologies, Ari, for I have nothing of my own to offer you. Anything, no matter the size, is accounted for. This was a difficult act," and she pointed to the bulging baskets, "and raised several eyebrows of staff. Other items would be missed. You could not imagine the effect a theft would bring upon the Palace. My offer to speak to each of your lenders is open to you. Please avail me of such assistance since that is the only option available."

"My answer was no to your offer when last we spoke. It is still no. My only resolve is to offer them items of great value."

Tiye sadly shook her head. "Of which these are — tremendous value, I assure you. Yet I can bring you nothing more, Ari."

He said nothing to her refusal, only frowned. "Oh Ari, please do not treat me so callously. I wish I could aid you further, truly I do." She reached out to softly touch his leg.

A cold gleam entered the eyes of the man she had called friend and lover for many years as he roughly shrugged away her hand. She was suddenly alarmed. "I am afraid, my pet, I must insist you find a way." He slowly ran his finger down her throat and into the crevice of her bosom. The manner in which he did so was not as enticing as it had been in their past. This movement was more calculating, as if he was declaring his ownership upon her rather than his love.

Attempting to reestablish control and hierarchy, she said, "You overstep, Ari. In words," she looked at his fingers and continued, "and in deeds."

He laughed and said, "You never objected to such deeds in the past."

"I object now and insist you stop. I am Queen, after all." There was a tremor in her voice and little confidence in her statement. She was extremely confused and could not reason his dispassionate tone or the complete turn of their conversation.

"Yes," he agreed with a sneer, "a Queen with much to loose. If you do not comply, I shall be forced to relate our, shall we say, recreational encounters to the Pharaoh. I do not think it impossible to be granted an audience with him. I yet have close friends who are able to arrange such a visit. Once the Pharaoh learns of my basis for such an appointment, I do not believe he will deny me the request." Reaching for another piece of fruit and his cup of wine, he asked sweetly, "Do you? You know him better than I. Would he refuse my request if, somehow, one or two details should reach his ear?"

This is not possible, thought the Queen. I cannot be hearing his words correctly. "You would threaten me?" she asked him. "Threaten me with our past friendship, our love? Ari, this is a most cruel joke to play upon me. How are you able to jest in this manner?"

"Ah, sweet blossom, I jest not. You are indeed a most desirable woman and our time spent together has been most enjoyable. Yet Love? My dear, I have never known of goods so used as yours. You were fortunate your husband did not realize this upon your marriage night. Perhaps he was too drunk to notice." She could do naught about the sudden blush rising in her cheeks. "Ah, I have found the mark. Excellent. That explains all.

"Now listen well to my words, pet. It does not matter how you accomplish this pilferage and I care little for your methods. What matters is my redemption. To that end I would see you in a fortnight with bounty of valuables, passing from your hands to mine."

"If you recite such a tale to the Pharaoh it will be yours alone," the Queen shot back. "My husband will believe mine as truth. We two are the only players in this game of yours, after all. And I am Queen."

"Do you think I would bring such a demand to you if there existed no proof? I lied that first day. Oh yes, truly I did. We were not alone. Mery was not only present in the home, but concealed so close all was overheard and seen. So you see, I do have proof. Oh, one more item to mention. I yet possess the brooch you wore that first day with the smallest bit of fabric yet attached. I must have torn your gown. My abject apologies," he said sarcastically. "Urgency was most important to us both that afternoon, if memory serves."

Thinking quickly, Tiye said, "My schedule precludes me from a visit so soon. Also, my mother travels to the Royal Palace next month and I have several functions thereafter. Therefore, my intended journey here will not occur. It must be three months hence. That is the only alternative to you. Suspicion will be aroused if my visits here become more frequent. And then what will you have in your hands if I am discovered? Naught. Those platters and my jewelry need suffice you for now. I suggest you barter wisely with them in the meantime."

Ari was obviously angry yet saw the truth of which she spoke. He must wait or chance having nothing. As he exited with basket in hand, he had the last word. "I shall admit to you, my sweet, you were a delicious distraction."

Tiye sat unmoving for some time with her hands shaking upon her lap. All these years, such a closely cherished and shielded memory she had held. And he had dashed it like fragile glass beads. Their recent encounters had been more than she could have dreamt. They meant nothing to him, while to her those moments had been the culmination of long overdue passion and tenderness. It had been the chance to relive the only moments of a love she freely gave and thoughts of what could have been. He knew her too well and had played upon those emotions of hers. The hot tears ran down her face and onto her throat, the same throat Ari had kissed so meaningfully. It pained her to realize this was merely a scheme to extort valuables, nothing more.

Anger finally reared its ugly head within her. He had called me 'used goods'. How dare he. *How dare he.* She beat her fists in fury upon the unsuspecting pillows at her side, nearly causing an explosion of goose feathers upon the room. He never showed qualms how often he had used her goods: nor others' as well, she recalled. I will not submit to his demands, she vowed. He believes he has close friends in power? He has no idea of <u>my</u> friends. He would soon find out, however. Indeed, that would be made quite clear to him.

Wiping the tears away and straightening her gown, she climbed the stairs to her mother's room. Opening the door, she saw her mother had given into playing the sad, ill patient and was obviously enjoying it. Well, thought Tiye, she shall not enjoy what I am about to impart.

"Mother, I am leaving directly for the Palace. You should be told this first: we cannot expect help from Air in our conspiracy.

Not ever. Additionally, I never want his name spoken again in this house." She began moving from the room when she turned towards her mother once more. "This I order, Mother, as your Queen. Suffer the consequences if you or the staff disobeys me. Oh, one more item of note. You will be traveling to *me* next month as you wish to see your grandson. Please remember that reason for your visit."

With that she was out the doorway, shouting for her servants to repack her trunks: she was leaving for her barge immediately. It was an exit worthy of a Queen.

## Chapter Two

Never had she been so relieved to return to the Royal Palace. The meeting with Ari had left her feeling violated and unclean. She was almost tempted to face the ordeal of a cleansing. Almost.

On the journey back on her barge, she spent her time alone in her bedchamber, ruminating over various vindictive measures she would take against her traitor, Ari. She reasoned her first course of action was to find the truth. She began to wonder if these debts actually existed. If so, did Ari's father truly plunge his family into such circumstances by gambling? Remembering the man's love for his family — something she once greatly admired — she thought not. Could it have been Ari who had mismanaged the family business and was ashamed to admit the fact? Or could it be something more sinister in nature? She must know the reasoning for his extortion.

Perhaps this was simply a mistake. Perhaps he was in danger physically and wished to keep her from the same. He said he had never lied to her. Was he lying to her now simply to keep her safe?

With a deep sigh she realized she was grasping at moonbeams. She recalled the calculated look in his eye. There had been no pity in that expression, nothing to indicate love or passion. He was quite intent upon the threats he offered. She would be forced to take action upon him, she realized, and it wounded her deeply. Grief descended upon her; grief for her foolish notions as a girl, for the loss of a believed love, and for the pain his memory would surely bring. She believed Ari had loved her as she had loved him, passionately and completely. Stupid child — how very wrong and idiotic she had been.

Her pain belonged in the past for now, she decided. Perhaps with time it would fade and memories would not stab at her heart. She must now protect her future. She would require further knowledge, she thought — knowledge of his daily routine, his friends, and even the temples he frequented. All this would be necessary before she could strike.

She would need someone whose eyes she could rely upon; to essentially spy upon Ari for several days until a pattern and the truth behind his financial struggles emerged. That would be her first task of the morning. Taking swift action in this regard would alleviate some of her current anger and pain. Only then could she set about her day with reasonable calm.

It was time to call upon the services of Akar.

## Chapter Three

A week later, she was seated across from the soldier in her private audience chamber adjacent to her own quarters. She and Iset were each allotted these private settings for interviews with citizens, meetings with staff, and daily discussions of schedules with their own Minister of Scheduling and Events to the Queen. Servants entered at the Queen's command through the connecting arches of her dressing room while her appointments attained entrance through a corridor door. With both doors locked, privacy was ensured for more confidential conversations. The dialogue she planned today demanded complete discretion.

"I have a special task for you, Akar," she began.

"Yes, My Queen. I am at your service," he said with a bow. She noticed his eyes did not leave her cleavage.

"Shall concern or suspicion be raised if you are absent from your duties and the Palace for several days?" she inquired. "Shall you be missed by anyone?"

"No, My Queen. Time away can be easily arranged. My schedule is my own, after all," he said, preening a bit.

"It will involve a short travel and your time involved could be more than one week. It all depends, you see, upon how much accurate information you discover and how quickly you discover it."

She named the town to which he would journey, failing to mention it was her place of birth. She also provided Ari's full name and the location of his home. "Something is awry with this man. I wish to know his financial circumstances and the why of them. If he is wealthy, I shall need to know his line of business, how he amasses his wealth. If he is in dire straights, I wish to know if he is in debt and the why of that as well. Discover to whom he is indebted, if indeed he is, and to what extent. Locate his friends and speak with them. Go into town and speak to the vendors of his purchases and payment habits. Investigate his pursuits of entertainment, where he spends his free time, and if he travels regularly for any reason. My name or your connection to the Royal Palace is not to be mentioned. You will wear commoner's clothing. Your attire must not have any Royal design or adornment upon it that may hint at your true position in this life. Have you any questions?"

Akar thought a moment before replying, "No, My Queen. You require any and all information I may acquire on this man. I may speak to anyone regarding his life providing I do not reveal my association to the Pharaoh, his Queen, or the Royal Palace. In short, a thorough investigation. If I may ask, what is the reasoning for this investigation?"

"You may ask —indeed, you have just done so — however it is of no concern to you. It is a Royal matter and as such no one is to know. Do you understand?"

The man nodded yet kept up the questioning. "Yes, My Queen. However, I am wondering what my compensation shall be for such a task. What shall you do for me if I accomplish this to your satisfaction."

The Queen turned an angry scowl in his direction yet the man did not flinch. "It is not a question of what I shall *do* for you, Akar, yet rather what I shall *not* do," she said with venom. "I shall *not* speak to the Pharaoh — my husband and your Supreme Ruler — of the liberties you so often take with me when you are assigned as my personal security. How you dishonor me with your leering glances and your personal touches that go far beyond your position of protection. I find these insulting and impertinent. I feel sure my husband will view them as I do; worthy of condemnation and termination."

She saw her statement had been met with some alarm, although not as much as she had hoped. "I see we understand each other," she continued. "I suggest you gather appropriate goods for travel and prepare your leave. Take nothing that leads to any speculation of your association here. Find some clothing of a more simple nature, yet establishes you as a man of substance. You will find areas adequate for tenting just outside the city proper. I believe the area has an inn and also taverns for food and drink. I have no notion as to their merit, however." As with most inns in the country, rooms were available to let for a night or more, yet privacy was not notable. Patrons usually slept in one room filled with beds. Occasionally, it was in the main room of the abode where others entered and left all hours of the day. Valuables were usually kept close to the guest for fear of theft.

She provided him with the date of his journey allowing him enough time to make arrangements for his absence. Tiye had decided upon the period when her mother would be visiting the Royal Palace. Should news of a man making inquiries of Ari reach her mother's ear, she might consider it her duty to alert him. Tiye would take no chances. She was pursuing risk enough by sending Akar without approval of the Pharaoh.

"You will portray yourself as a man traveling the area on business. Offer no specifics of your business, only vague innuendos. Specific details might require specific knowledge. You could easily be found out if you misstep with an inaccuracy."

She handed him an amount of small trinkets and amulets similar to those she had given Ari. "These are not overly valuable yet will allow you to purchase necessities. When you have information of value, return here and report to me. Now go."

As he bowed and turned to leave the room she called out to him. "Akar. No more than seven days. Do not disappoint me," the Queen instructed.

## Chapter Four

The morning sun glittered upon the solid headrest of the Queen. She was particularly proud of her headrest and reached past the abundance of pillows to slide her hand along the cool smooth stone. Originally designed to keep one's head off the ground and protect one's face against insects and vermin, these handy crescent-shaped headrests topped with pillows were used throughout Egypt. The Queen's, however, was one of marvel. The wooden framework was completely covered with inlaid squares of her favorite stone, the blue lapis lazuli. It was imperative the individual pieces of tightly positioned stones would not scratch the face of a Queen. Therefore, several talented artisans had repeatedly and carefully polished it to a smooth seam-free piece, resembling one massive blue stone as smooth as glass. Edging the cupped headrest was a symmetrical line of gold sheathing. Of all the hand-crafted pieces of furniture and statues in her chambers, this was by far her favored.

As if the headrest was not overindulgent enough, her bed was grander than even the Pharaoh's. The four-legged beds of the more affluent all utilized the same basic construction: slanted slightly from head to feet with a footboard to prevent sliding off. It had been originally designed to keep one's head off the ground while sleeping as protection from vermin and insects. Yet the Queen's bed was unique. The headboard had intricate wooden inlay called marquetry. Tiye's headboard comprised of finely sanded and hand glued pieces of rare and multicolored wood to create an image of gazelles and giraffes in elegant motion.

The footboard continued the animal theme with a large hand carved gazelle with elongated twisted horns for posts reaching several feet high. The golden seal of the Queen was positioned between the horns for strength. Leather straps were wrapped side to side on the frame and were topped with a linen mattress stuffed with goose down feathers. She once tried a mattress stuffed with leaves — the most commonly used stuffing in Egypt — yet the rustling of the leaves throughout the night prevented a sound sleep. It was discarded after one use.

Queen Tiye arose slowly and flirted with the notion to remain within her comfortable down bed when she heard a commotion in the halls. Tiye groaned in distress: she knew immediately who was causing such upheaval within the long, wide areas. It was none other than her mother although the question of 'why' could only be guessed upon. Peeking from behind the open door of her bedchamber, the Queen again groaned. Filling the anteroom to the Queen's suites with a surplus of servants and her enormous personality marched her mother. The woman was calling out in a strident voice for 'my daughter, the Queen', determined to deploy herself upon the very chambers belonging to Tiye.

Shaking her head and taking a deep sigh, Tiye opened the door wider and called out in return, "I am here, Mother. Why are you?"

"Ah, Daughter. You have not yet risen? I have traveled all morning to see you and you are yet abed?"

Ignoring this comment upon her supposed laziness the Queen replied, "Yes, Mother. I see you are here. I ask again — why? You are much earlier than expected."

Apparently, her mother was on a journey to visit her sister a few cities beyond Thebes and took the time from her precious schedule to visit her daughter. "I am sure you care naught that I have entered unannounced," stated her mother.

While Tiye did in fact mind, she neatly sidestepped this topic by asking, "Is my aunt aware of your impending visit?"

"She will not be concerned," answered her mother. Apparently her sweet and altruistic aunt was to have an unpleasant surprise, thought Tiye. The poor woman. She often wondered how two such divergent women could be sisters. "Unfortunately," continued her mother, "I shall only stay with you three nights." What a pity, thought the Queen sarcastically. "I feel it is time to visit my grandson. We have much to discuss with him."

Inviting her mother into her chambers, she was quickly dressed in the adjoining Royal Dressing Chamber while listening to her mother chatter aimlessly in the other room. As the last servant exited the room and allowed them privacy, the women turned the conversation to the death of the Pharaoh.

While Tiye and her mother had been manipulating fellow conspirators, they had not yet broached the subject to Pentawer. Today was the day to do so, her mother insisted, and the time was now. "Before he has begun another appointment. My grandson is surely up and about his duties early in the morn, is he not?" Tiye allowed this thorn to pass. Her cleansing ministrations must wait to do as her mother now insisted. She hated that particular routine anyway.

Tiye was more concerned of her son's reaction to this news they would impart to him. He was very fond of his father. Would he demand they cease such actions? Would he agree? Or, worse yet, was his love for his father so great that he would toss them to Ramses like so much rubbish? With amazement, Tiye found herself agreeing with her mother. Pentawer must know of their deeds and now was as convenient as any other time of the day.

"Oh," said Tiye's mother. "I spoke with Queen Iset as I came upon the long corridor. I found myself staring at those teeth. How do you cope with such a frightening visage? While she was most gracious, I thought she might bite me."

Tiye smiled slightly and said, "I find it best not to converse with her while in close proximity. A full step back is an adequate distance." Her mother snorted in reply, the woman's version of a laugh.

## Chapter Five

With her mother's prodding, the two women made haste to visit with Pentawer in his private chambers. The subject at hand was best approached behind closed doors.

"Grandmother, it is indeed a pleasure to see you once again. I did not expect you for many days."

"Yes," said Tiye, "neither did I. She shall return to us in a week or two. It is becoming quite the habit for her." Try as she might to remain civil, a touch of bitterness seeped into her tone. At her mother's raised eyebrow, Tiye plowed on to the subject at hand.

"My dear son. We have a most serious topic of which to speak. Many members of the Royal Palace are deeply concerned over the future rein of your brother, Amonhirk. I realize it may not occur for several more years, however . . ." She turned to her mother to voice their plot succinctly and convincingly.

By now, her mother had persuaded many of her societal friends to join their cause. While they would not actually storm the Royal Palace, they did bestow greats sums to be used as bribes to others. Tiye's mother set before Pentawer their primary goal — her grandson upon the Throne. She outlined the many families and officials of Thebes who supported the conspiracy. The individuals she identified surprised Tiye. Her mother had obviously spent inordinate time gathering like-minded followers.

Pentawer looked shocked as the full realization of their plan fell upon him. His eyes were wide and he often shook his head from side to side as his grandmother laid open their plan. When Tiye related the conversation she overheard in her zoo area, Pentawer's eyes narrowed and he became grim. "So," he said to the two women before him, "in spite of my father's order to the contrary, Amonhirk intends to remove me from all political dealings of my country." Tiye nodded her answer.

"You stand much to gain from our course of action yet Amonhirk must die as well." They explained the decision behind the death of both the Pharaoh and the chosen heir. "It is imperative Amonhirk's eldest son not be seated upon the Throne. Clearly, Amonhirk must die first to realize our intention."

Tiye was saddened for her son when he asked plaintively why his father must also die. "With Amonhirk dead surely he would appoint me his ascending prince."

Tiye remembered Ramses unyielding decision on that point. He would never name Pentawer as his successor. She chose not to injure her son further by relaying that conversation. "You love your father, I know," responded Tiye. "Yet we have looked at this from all sides. We cannot chance an investigation of Amonhirk's death and your father will surely do so. You know this to be true. You would never inherit having been involved in this most treasonous of acts." What was not said, yet understood, was the overwhelming fury of Pharaoh Ramses should he find the truth. Without question he would rain annihilation upon their heads.

Pentawer leaned back against the painted wall with his arms crossed. His mother knew of this pensive pose as he considered various decisions during his life. Tiye was surprised when her son suddenly leaned forward and spoke in an unusually fierce tone. "I am in accord with you. I have friends among the soldiers with whom I trained when Amonhirk considered me useless to the Throne. They will join me. There is much grumbling within that camp. Very few promotions have been awarded and certainly no rise in pay. Amonhirk will surely replace the council members with his own staff. Loss of position and wealth shall be quite motivating to those now seated. I shall speak to a council member or two as well. I am aware of irritation within their ranks.

"You say the Harem wives might be in agreement?"

"We believe several can be persuaded. There is considerable unrest in that corner. Those not born in Egypt could be concerned of their banishment if Amonhirk succeeds. With you in accord they should be in union with us. We plan to visit with them on the morrow."

"Excellent." said Pentawer. "They have always been kind to me. My schedule precludes such a visit however when next you meet with them, alert me and I shall attend with you. I do not wish to see them banished from the Royal Palace and shall say as much. Perhaps such a promise from my mouth would be the motivation they require.

"I must insist upon one path that differs from your own. I do not wish Amonhirk killed by another. I shall carry out his death."

He forestalled his mother when she would negate this. "No, Mother. It must be by my hand."

"So be it, my son."

They began in earnest to set the date and discuss the smallest of details. He proceeded to school the women in more governmental regulations and possible solutions for the poor financial situation in Egypt. This would allow them some facts to present to the Harem wives and anyone else who showed concern with Ramses' or future dealings with Amonhirk.

Pentawer mentioned the upcoming festival of Heb-Sed a few months' hence. It was held in celebration of the continued reign of the Great Pharaoh. Immense feasts and accolades were scheduled in Thebes and within this Royal Palace of Medinet Habu. With so many dignitaries and citizens in attendance, crowds and commotion would be more prevalent that day any other. How ironic, thought Tiye, the Great Man should meet the end of his reign on that night. They must not fail. To do so would mean their deaths.

## Chapter Six

The moon was aglow while small creatures were chirping and buzzing beneath Pentu's window. He and Asim were entwined upon his bed, speaking of their day and making promises as lovers often do.

"I find it difficult to sleep when you are absent from my bed," said Pentu.

Asim smiled up at him from the crook of his arm. "As do I my love. No pillow is as comfortable as the shoulder upon which I rest."

It had been a week since they found free time to share and this moment had been lusty and filled with longing "I do not wish to have our time together delayed for so long. I realize you have been consumed with the Queen and her mother yet I have missed you terribly."

Playfully, Asim nibbled at his chest. "I am only able to remain here for another hour or two. While the Queen has my accessibility most hours of the day and at night, her mother calls for my services even further. I am only with you now as they are feasting with the Pharaoh."

"I have not made the woman's acquaintance and I am not likely to," Pentu said in mock pomposity. "It is not in my job prevue, after all."

"Oh, hear the grand member of His Royal Advisors! Shall I bow to his words? How quickly you have adopted the language of the Palace," she teased him.

He smiled back. "I learn any lesson provided so I may make you mine. Everything I do is for you, Asim."

"As do I for you. Yet obeying the Queen and her mother is exhausting and I find the woman dreadful. It was a nasty surprise for the Queen to see her mother. She was not expected so early. Apparently, she leaves for a time and then returns to us. I shall never survive that woman.

"Her demands are quite outrageous, expecting more than her daughter. She is not the Queen of Egypt yet one would never know from her actions. 'Bring me fresh water, Asim. Bring me plumper fruit, Asim. This pillow is flat, Asim, bring me another.' I wish to scream yet I have held my tongue through it all. I do not wish the Queen to find fault with me. It is apparent the Queen holds no great love for her mother yet we are expected to jump when the woman snaps her fingers and show her great honor. I am always so incredibly tired. I cannot seem to sleep enough."

"Perhaps you are not eating well, my love."

"Food does not seem to appeal to me lately yet my weight loss is naught."

"Offering more of you for me to love," said Pentu nuzzling her neck.

Asim could not help yet laugh and push him away teasingly. "Pentu, I am serious. Perhaps it is the additional work of another demanding woman."

"Ah, well. She leaves soon, does she not?"

"Yes, thanks to the gods, yet it is not soon enough. The woman has already instructed me to have a morning meal brought to her when the cock crows and lay out her clothing for the morrow. She and the Queen are planning an early call to the wives of the Harem."

"Truly?" asked Pentu. "That is odd, is it not? If the woman is so self-absorbed, what does she care with the lesser wives? Her daughter is Second Queen."

"Yes, that is rather strange. Even Queen Tiye does not often rise so early and never to visit the Harem. The two of them have been in quiet and intense conversations as well; also unusual. I noticed them in her private Audience Chamber, behaving as children caught at a misdeed. When they saw me, the Queen was quite upset, instructing me to pay attention to my own tasks as she closed the door in my face. That was two days past and I am praying she does not take action against me."

"She would have done so by now, correct? Certainly the Queen would not wait a full two days to issue a reprimand."

"It is not the reprimand I fear, Pentu. If she so desires, she could transfer me to a lesser duty within the Palace, away from you. If I am assigned to the kitchens, for example, I could never find an excuse to be in this restricted portion of the Palace. I could not bear to be without you."

"Please, do not let it trouble you, my love. You have told me of her quick temper. One with such a temper would not wait two days."

"Furthermore, we have only another hour left together. I suggest we make the most of it." With that said, he reached for her, forgetting everything and everyone else in the Royal Palace.

## Chapter Seven

Mother and daughter arrived early to share the morn with the ladies and children of the Harem. Tiye's mother was perfection herself: complimenting the women's hair or gowns, patting small children on the head, even smiling at babes in swaddling. She never ceases to amaze, thought the Queen: so much artificial affection and concern when her heart is that of rough unhewn marble.

Her generous attentions served their purpose, however. The women voiced their greetings to the Queen's mother with smiles, commenting upon the length of time since they had the opportunity to enjoy her company. Tiye nearly choked at their misguided opinion of her mother.

After the children had been fed, a few the women gathered around the large pond and fountain centered among the palms, willow trees, and flowers. The pink, blue and white lotus blossoms were on full display, floating in the water. Many women sat on the edge of the water , drawing their hands back and forth in the cool water. The abundance of palms and flowing fountains kept this room cooler than most.

The Queen's mother cleared her throat; an indication to her daughter that her sociability had ended and serious matters would commence. Tiye was thankful she had always imitated approachability and friendliness with these members of the Royal Household. They should be receptive to her input. Tiye and her mother centered their attention to that handful of consorts born in neighboring countries. This conversation could have a most profound import upon these Royal Women. Conversely, it could be the ultimate end to mother and daughter if the word spread to Harem wives more secure with their future.

"My daughter has been telling me of the upcoming celebration to anoint the Pharaoh with the spells for his continued health. I have never seen such an event. It must be quite a remarkable occasion."

The gathered women readily agreed and many suggested the Royal Mother of the Lesser Queen should attend. The woman refused politely, alluding to other pressing matters.

"As I understand, and perhaps I am woefully misinformed, Pentawer will not be receiving such protection."

This statement brought about a great many comments and concerns, all of which the Queen and her mother took to heart and, in fact, flamed the embers of worry in the room.

"It is the truth of which she speaks," voiced Tiye sadly as she took up the rehearsed tale. "I have sought out Ramses who has confirmed this travesty. The concern you voiced earlier is quite true. Of course, as Pentawer's mother, I dreamt of my son sitting upon the Throne as Pharaoh. It is not to be, however. The Pharaoh gave his final word on the subject and is not approachable to more discussion. It is a pity, really. I believe — and I say this not as a mother but as a loyal Egyptian woman — that Pentawer is better suited to the Throne than Amonhirk."

"He is very intelligent," said one older woman, "and has often joined with me in lively discussions. He was fascinated with tales of my birth country."

"Yes," said another, "and he has always been most friendly to me. To us all, I believe." The women nodded and agreed with her. While Amonhirk seldom visited the Harem, Pentawer found comfort with the children and the fussings of the women.

"I wonder," said Tiye's mother, "what is fated for a wife of a Pharaoh when he passes from this life? Are you allowed to remain in the Royal Palace living a life of luxury and safety? Or perhaps you are given a regular stipend and forced to live elsewhere."

The women glanced at each other with some consternation. It was apparent they had never spoken of this. Perhaps they did not know of their fate should Amonhirk sit on the Throne. One woman finally spoke up. "When Ramses passes, many of us will be given to others for remarriage. I have heard of some returning to their native country, if they are not born Egyptian, to marry a man of means."

"I was not born here yet I consider this my home. I have lived the life as Consort to the Pharaoh. Yet you say this will no longer be so? I do not wish to marry a man of mere wealth," stated another.

"This is the only home I have known for many years," voiced a wife with pain in her voice. "I truly do not wish to go to my home country. My brother is now ruler and I would have no place within the royal household there."

"I wonder," began Tiye slowly, "if there is not a solution to this difficulty. It is a great pity Amonhirk will have the seat of the Throne. I believe Pentawer would not treat you so unjustly. He loves you all, as you know. If you were forced to leave he would be incensed."

"The Pharaoh must change his successor. Can you not speak to him My Queen?"

"Alas, I have tried many times to no end. He will hear no more of it. I took great risk by doing so once too many."

"Yet what are we to do?" asked one.

"Yes, something must change," said another. Murmurs of apprehension were running through the women.

One woman spoke up with something other than distress. "I refuse to leave. To think we may be discarded is unjust. I for one am extremely angry and decry any decision Amonhirk will make against us, Pharaoh or not."

The other wives felt her anger and expressed the same. "You are quite correct, Sister. He cannot determine our fate."

"I am of royal blood from another country with means and influence of my own. This will not stand."

"I too am not without links in society and within my birth country. We should alert our friends, telling them of what to expect when Amonhirk is crowned."

"Of one fact I am quite certain, however. Amonhirk plans to raise taxes to our citizens. I imagine that would include the Harem women as well since you have income solely your own, do you not?" commented Tiye. She had learned much from her son yesterday and planned to use this new knowledge to her benefit.

The women were most vocal in their disrespect for the man, their future ruler. "In truth, I have never trusted or liked the man. He will be a harsh and unfeeling Pharaoh if his lack of care for us is an indication of future concern for his people," remarked one younger woman.

"I have heard Egypt is currently in financial trouble. Now you say he could banish us to other parts of this country and tax us further? Despicable."

"I hear people do not have enough to eat and the harvest will be low again this year. Can this be true?" said another.

Tiye said, "It would appear the gods do not favor us this year. The Nile shall not flood enough to enrich our soil. It is true; people do not have enough to eat. Additionally, some citizens are without homes. If such existence continues, I do not know how many more will suffer.

"There is talk of increasing trade prices as well, blaming it upon the drought and poor crops. My son informs me that Ramses' many prayers and sacrifices no longer appease the gods as they have in the past." Lowering her voice she continued, "And what of the vast amounts of acreage he has given to the temples and priests. You are aware this is some of the best farming land in the country. Oh, I do not mean to disparage any gift to the gods yet our people go hungry and homeless. With the continued lack of water to the Nile from the melting snow, should we not be utilizing the best of the terrain for growing more crops, raising more animals? People come first, do we not?"

Tiye and her mother sat back and observed what they had wrought. The situation had far exceeded their expectations. Both had believed many such conversations would be needed to bring about this result. Yet here they sat, listening to this talk of a treasonous conspiracy. It was at this point in the dialogue they sent forth the final kernel to find growth.

It came from her mother. "This sounds drastic, I know, yet I can reason no other way. Perhaps one of you intelligent women may arrive at a different solution and as I say, I would be most obliging to other ideas. However, I can really see no other option to your future happiness and stability than to have Pentawer become Pharaoh. What say you, my daughter and Queen? Would not Pentawer guarantee these women, who have so blessed this Palace and home, the choice to do what is right for them?"

Tiye feigned sadness at their fate and said, "Knowing how my son is drawn to you I am assured he would not banish you from your home. He would come to you personally to assure this fact. He voiced that from his very lips to me. This is indeed your home. You have made it such and given great joy to us all. Something should be done."

"Our Queen is correct. We should take control of our own lives and fate. We must do something," said the eldest of the women.

"I wonder," said Tiye's mother with feigned thoughtfulness, "what would the result be if this protective magic was not given to Ramses? Do you know?"

Two of the women spoke up. "I believe he would be susceptible to diseases. The Pharaoh is quite old. To have lived so long proves such magical and divine involvement."

"Yes, I believe my sister is correct. Would he not also be susceptible to a grave accident if he did not receive such protections from the priests?"

One woman finally hit the mark Tiye and her mother had been hoping for. "And if he did not meet with an accident? Something more . . . forthright? Foul play for instance."

A young wife leaned in and said with shock, "You are talking murder, are you not. Murdering the Pharaoh of Egypt?"

Silence descended upon the women with only the noises of the children filling the room.

Tiye decided to ease their fear somewhat. Perhaps it was too much for this first gathering. This was a notion that needed sleeping upon. "Allow me to question one of the Royal Magicians," she began. "He could supply the answers we seek. After all, we really have no comprehension how complicated the magicians' spells truly are. They keep this information quite unto themselves and have never shared such things with us. Perhaps we can do nothing at all for your situation. I suppose it depends what I shall learn." They all nodded in unison. It was a perfectly plausible idea to determine where to begin.

"However, I would have you listen to your children, laughing and playing together as siblings, never having a care in their lives as Royal Children. Would you not do anything possible to protect them from exile? Why should they suffer from complete banishment, from the only home they know, and the love of their siblings? As a mother I commiserate with you. I would do anything I could for my son." This would give them something to chew upon, she thought.

Following a visit to a Royal Magician, she promised to meet with them again. With a word of warning to avoid gossiping of this topic, she and her mother took their leave from the Harem. The women showered them with gratitude for understanding their plight. It had all transpired very well.

## Chapter Eight

Tiye's mother was leaving later than she had anticipated. She opted to spend more time with her daughter and visit her sister the following week. She thoroughly enjoyed the pampering only a Royal Palace could offer and would never receive such indulgences at her sister's. The aunt of Tiye had received a reprieve while the Queen was forced to deal further with the curse that was her mother. The woman was now rushing about, wanting to begin her journey before the extreme heat of midday arrived.

Tiye entered her mother's guest quarters and watched her flitter about the room, making an attempt to look busy. The woman acted flustered while she issued orders to her tormented servants. She was, as usual, taking an excessive amount of time to gather her women and belongings to leave. Tiye was helping as much as she could, something as Queen she was not familiar with.

"Daughter, let the servants be. They are perfectly aware of which item goes in what case.

If that were true, why did her mother continually take out items and place them in other baskets? The Queen tired of this grab-a-bag and hide-the-item game they seemed to be playing without benefit of rules.

"No, no. This case holds the green jasper pieces. That one is for the lapis lazuli. I abhor packing. Far too much effort is given over to bundles and baskets. I am exhausted"

Enough, Tiye thought and said loudly, "I am taking my mother. When we return you shall be finished with the packing and waiting to travel. Come, Mother. We must find a cool place to talk before you leave."

To a servant her mother warned, "Handle that with caution. My dear departed husband presented that to me."

"Dear departed?" asked Tiye sarcastically. "Mother, he is not deceased. He resides a mere four towns away from yours." And, thought Tiye, he lives quite happily with his mistress. Her mother glared at her.

"Daughter," said her mother with concern, "I truly must supervise the servants. I shall have no idea where they have placed my clothing or jewelry."

"That is something you need no knowledge of, Mother, since these same servants will unpack for you at my aunt's. Feel free to supervise them at great length at that time if you so desire. I have duties I must see to and delicate conversations in which to engage." Tiye took her mother to a small garden nook next to the guest quarters. Any passerby was in plain view from the bench upon which they sat.

"Then I shall accompany you. You shall need me for any conversation."

"It is not necessary, Mother." By the gods, she should become dim-witted if she had to spend another hour with the woman. "Everything is well in hand."

"I pray so, Daughter, as our conspiracy has commenced and care is needed with the type of associates we require. The Harem seems most agreeable, however."

"So it would seem. We now have two handfuls of women ready to storm the Palace to murder the Pharaoh and his son," said Tiye with sarcasm. "Perhaps we should just simply burst into his chambers now since we have so many capable warriors among us."

"I agree our numbers are not without disappointment. Some of these women have leverage yet within their own countries as they said. It would be well to nurture those contacts. You would agree, would you not, that some neighboring countries are not overly fond of our current Pharaoh? Perhaps they too look for an excuse to replace Ramses."

"I would not have our country overthrown, Mother, no matter if Pentawer sat on the thrown."

"Naturally. Yet hear me out. No one need send warriors. Wealth in the correct hands will provide incentive for established families to join. That merely depends upon words in the right ear and payment to the most helpful hands. Promises or favors will succeed when gold might not. The social connections of mine do not require such crude enticements. No, I rather think they would like a position as a new Royal Advisor or perhaps a meaningless title bestowed upon them when Pentawer succeeds. That is not over-reaching and Pentawer is not committed to keep any promises we make."

"Mother that would be a deception to our friends and those in power. They might seek a reckoning if we do not honor our promises."

Her mother laughed cruelly. "Daughter, we sit here discussing the murder of the Great Ruler of all Egypt and you are concerned with a miscommunication between ourselves and the future Pharaoh? You are the Queen of Egypt. No one has power over you save the Pharaoh."

Her mother was quite correct in her remark; she did indeed have sizeable power as Queen. And while honesty was greatly valued in an Egyptian's life, breaking that trust was minor to the designs of their plotting.

"Who is the soldier I have seen with you? His connections to generals and others of stature might be used as an asset to us."

Her mother was referring to Akar. "I do not trust that one and I doubt his loyalty. He is also greatly admired by the Pharaoh and occasionally has his ear," expressed Tiye.

"If a man is loyal, we would not seek him for our purpose," replied her mother sagely. "We should never expect permanent loyalty. Greed is much easier to sustain. I suggest you speak to him gradually. Offer him what he wants."

"He has exceptional quarters within the military barracks, dines with the Pharaoh, and wants for nothing. There seems to be little I could offer him, Mother."

"Men always want something. Women, power, wealth — they repeatedly seem to favor one of those three and are quite foolish over them. Promise him a post as general or Royal Commander of a forgotten military division. Provide women to him. It matters not what you promise, only that you do.

"Additionally, I have been considering our initial plan and believe we might discuss the abandonment of it. Death by poisoning in your private chamber is much too risky. It is not an entirely controllable situation and too many unknowns could be at play. The amount of poison could be immediately fatal or not strong enough. We could leave that as an alternate choice yet I would reject it altogether.

"I offer another solution. We shall utilize the Harem wives who are incorporated into our desires. Clearly there is little love among them for the Pharaoh. If Ramses could meet privately with the group — and you as well— the deed could be committed jointly."

Tiye tentatively agreed. She had not been comfortable trying to poison her husband while alone with him and said as much. "Despite his age, he is yet stronger than I. It would take all of us to subdue him."

Her mother contemplated this fact. "So let us disregard the poison entirely and move on. You shall take him by force in the Harem chambers. The entire Royal Family and the wives will be enjoying the feast, correct? If you are able to entice him to, shall we say, a private celebration of debauchery, he should not stand a chance against seven women. Especially if he were under the influence of a sleeping draught or another calming potion. This could be planned beforehand, while the frivolities are still at their peak. Set a time and entice him into joining you. Have wine and his favorite sweets on hand, dress seductively, and prepare to cater to his every whim. A narcotic to lower his defenses and make him weaker could easily be introduced while he is drinking with you and the wives."

"Then the motive of death? If not poison, what?" asked Tiye.

"Weapons," her mother said simply, "small sharp weapons within reach of you seven women. Daggers, knives, hatchets — whatever you may be able to procure."

"What you are discussing is a bloodbath, Mother. The wives may be quite squeamish with this notion. It would be detrimental if our clothing were discovered covered in blood. There would be little time to discard it adequately by burning."

"Then there shall be no clothing. What better way to seduce the man than with your nude bodies? The guards must be handled, however. They cannot be within hearing."

Tiye considered the idea before replying, "I have in thought a certain magician as an ally. I wish to consult him regarding the removal of protections upon Ramses and Amonhirk. He might also provide us with magical protection against security guards. I believe I can convince him to aid us.

"Might he also provide you with the suitable calming potion for the Pharaoh?" Tiye nodded. "Excellent. You shall need an object in which to hide such a drug. Something that would not bring undue suspicion to have on your person, even unclothed.

"Ah, I have arrived at a most wondrous solution. I shall visit my jewelry maker. He has a collection of mystery boxes and trinkets that secretly open. He will certainly have something on hand. If not, he shall create one for me in necklace form. Sending jewelry to you will never arouse suspicion."

She looked sideways at her daughter. "You have plans to visit the priests, correct? Hmmm, I should truly extend my time here further, Daughter," her mother said thoughtfully. "I shall leave on the morrow. I am sure you could use my assistance with a holy man."

"I shall handle them, Mother," said Tiye. The very last person she needed on that undertaking was her mother.

"When?"

"Soon, Mother. The day is late and you are nearly packed for the return home."

"So be it," replied her mother with an irritated sniff. "Mark my words, Daughter, the appointed time is nigh. You must put forth a convincing argument to those with whom you converse."

Tiye remained silent, giving her mother to believe she had lost her nerve.

"If you do not possess the mettle to proceed tell me now, Daughter. I refuse to continue this treachery is you are not committed."

Now it was treachery? She had referred to this idea as a 'situation of need', and 'for the good of her grandson', thought Tiye. Suddenly it was treachery. By the gods, this woman would be the end of me, she thought. "Mother," she said sweetly, "I am quite stable in this."

Her mother looked at her and nodded. "Good. As it should be. I have labored incessantly for you, preparing the way for your final act. Please remember all I have done for you," she said in a huff. The time for her mother to leave could not arrive swiftly enough for the Queen's pleasure.

"Come, Mother. Let us see to your servants and your baggage. Now that we have set a date for the deed, there are other important conversations to be had. Only you are able to speak to your friends in society. It is a task you are worthy of." A flowery excuse yet Tiye did not stray far from truth. They had reached the point when their supporters must be handled gracefully. Working them into a lather of hostility was an ideal task for her mother. Indeed, her mother had that effect upon Tiye each time they met.

"Yes, that is true. Very well, I shall leave. I shall naturally return to you on the date we have selected. You must arrange a magnificent feast with an abundance of food and deep wines that increase a man's lust. Naturally, you must persuade the other wives in this. I shall pay a call to you on my return journey from my sister's home. Unfortunately, I shall only have time to spare for a family meal. I shall not stay overnight at that time. I must return home to begin my discussions with others we wish to incorporate." Tiye refrained from a smile of relief.

Shortly thereafter, Tiye was waving to her mother in the midst of the caravan of camels and servants setting out to beleaguer her unsuspecting aunt and society. A multitude of baskets filled with her belongings swayed precariously atop three transport camels. It was a relief to see her mother's backside.

Finally, thought Tiye, she has departed. She turned and leaned against the cool Palace wall. She rolled her head from side to side attempting to relieve the tightness she felt in her neck. She must remain in control and calm if her visit to the priest would prove effective.

## Chapter Nine

The priests in the Palace Temples were of service solely to the Pharaoh. Nevertheless, today she must bargain or issue threats for one's assistance. She would like to have utilized the aid of an elder priest. He was the perfect choice were he not so old and loyal to Ramses. She held such wonderful secrets on the man — visits to widows for other than religious comfort, for example. She would be forced to settle for one of the others, one with some unholy action to account for.

She began with a Royal Holy Priest named Perneb. He was not yet a High Priest but currently one rung below in stature and knowledgeable in Royal protection enchantments. She found him praying in the small temple of Amun near the Pharaoh's own memorial. She waited quietly for him to finish yet inwardly she was most anxious. He might be at his prayers for hours, she thought, or he could be called away before she could speak. She abhorred waiting for anyone. The priests expected everyone other than the Pharaoh to pause for them, even Queens. She disliked most priests she had spoken with. In addition to debauchery, she had suspicious of their theft and underhanded dealings. The passing of each year saw more gold around their necks and rings upon their fingers. Their legitimate income would not warrant all those bangles.

She had not procured the necessary weaponry against this particular man yet she believed him to be more pliable than most. Perhaps he was not so corrupt as his brethren. She had, however, noticed his lascivious glances at her body and hope she could use this unholy interest as an inducement against him. To this end, she opted to wear a very diaphanous garment, something she disliked donning yet hoped it might aid in her quest. The shoulders were gathered in soft wide pleats across the bodice and she wore a bevy of gold chains across her waist low enough to cover her more personal areas.

He finally rose from his prayers and before he had the chance to become otherwise occupied, Tiye approached him. He had the very good sense to bow before her. He did, however, give her nearly naked body a lengthy perusal. "My most revered Queen," he said, "how pleasant it is to see you here."

"My dear Perneb, I offer you the blessings of the gods on this fine day. If you have a moment, I would speak to you privately. Perhaps your personal quarters?"

He looked surprised at this suggestion yet did not negate it. Her expensive scent was intoxicating and he replied, "Whatever My Queen desires."

Smiling seductively as she slid her arm through his, she replied, "Indeed, I have several desires I would like to share with you, dear Perneb." They walked arm in arm to his room.

## Chapter Ten

I wonder how often my body has been at the disposal of these cleansing ministrations since I became Queen, Tiye thought. Perhaps we should have engaged a Royal Counter to the Queen's Bathing, she thought with a smile. It was now late morning, much past the time for her normal cleansing routine, yet her mother had continually tangled her schedule with her second untimely arrival and many demands. Naturally, her return visit for one family meal had turned into several more days. She could not, however, complain of her mother's acquisition of powerful members to their conspiracy or her performance with the Harem women and her explanation to Pentawer of the scheme. Both conversations and impressive procurements were quite agreeable.

She was in an exceptionally good disposition today. Perhaps it had been the delicious morning meal, she thought, or the sight of her mother returning home. That was reason alone to rejoice. Ah, she thought, I know. She plucked the reasoning from her thoughts as a farmer might pluck fruit: it was the anticipated particulars of one who was a menace to her.

Her thrill of emotion surprised her slightly. After all, Ari had been closer to her than any other yet she felt little remorse in destroying him. She was past sentimentality where her safety was concerned. Admittedly, they had a history together. She had considered him a friend, a confidant, and a lover. Yet now he betrays her. Did he really believe I would simply submit to his desires one day and allow him to bleed me of my belongings and position the next? He was a fool.

Akar sent a message late last evening informing her of his return from his investigative assignment. They would convene following her afternoon meal today. She was anxious to hear of his discoveries and learn the truth to Ari's treachery. Secretly she hoped Ari was not as deceitful as he had seemed yet she no longer held her previous delusions of his character.

The morning ablutions were nearly completed when the Queen happened to glance at Asim. As usual, the girl was quite drenched with water yet something had changed. She seemed quite wan and pale. Then the Queen's glance traveled down the body of her maidservant.

In horror, Tiye grabbed Asim's wrist and screamed at the Palace Woman also in attendance. "Out. Leave the room this instant."

Looking into Asim's face she spat with venom at the younger woman. "Who? Who is the father? Is it the Pharaoh? Do not lie to me, girl. I can plainly see you are with child."

Asim looked at the slight bulge in her stomach and her swollen breasts with understanding and fear. The explanation for her constant weariness and unsettled stomach was explained. Yet she attempted denial. "I . . . I am not. I can not be."

Tiye drew back her hand and slapped Asim across the face, causing the girl to slip and fall upon the ornately tiled wet chamber floor. "Traitor! Liar! I can plainly see the state you are in. Has the Pharaoh visited your bed?"

"No, My Queen. By the gods, I swear to you, he has not."

"I do not believe you, Asim. I had great promises in store for you and you dare to defy me in this manner. No man of means shall have you now, I shall see to that."

Asim drew herself from the floor and lifted her chin. "Which means you shall not acquire whatever you stood to gain by selling me to the highest bidder." As soon as she uttered the words, she knew of her error. The Queen's face was flushed with wrath, her two pupils becoming pinpoints. Asim had never seen such hatred emanate from her mistress and she cowered in the cold corner of the room, hoping to survive this ordeal.

In a low, threatening voice, Tiye said to Asim, "You shall leave my chambers and remain in your room until I decide what is to be done with you." Draping herself in a linen bath sheet, Tiye called loudly for one of the near-by sentries. "See that she is locked in her room. She is not to be released until I give the order. You will remain outside her door to ensure she makes no attempt to escape. Is that understood?"

As the guard dragged Asim through the exit way, Tiye clutched at the toweling around her body with hands so tightly clenched her knuckles were white. In a fury, she picked up a red glass bottle filled with expensive lotion and flung it against the wall, reducing the beautiful hand crafted item to shreds and covering the wall in white goo.

Pacing the room, she muttered to herself, "First Ari and now Asim. I am surrounded by betrayal at every turn. How dare she. How dare *they*. Two trusted people have turned against me. I shall not stand idly and watch as others fall into this habit of deceit." Her interview with Akar had best occur without difficulties. Someone would pay if obstructions arose where Ari was concerned.

She raged as she paced the room. "The Pharaoh! He is another who turns against me, against our son. This must not stand. If my son was Pharaoh I could easily have the revenge I seek. Now I must put great effort into my satisfaction."

Her Official Woman of Dress peeked around the doorway to see if safe entry was possible. "You are late," said the Queen, "As am I. It is time for me to be dressed. And have someone remove this mess from the wall."

## Chapter Eleven

Akar was glad to be back from what he called the desolation of Egypt. Actually, the area to which his Queen sent him was no more desolate than other areas of Egypt. The entire country had many remote spots and the whole was nothing but sand. It was amazing such a thriving empire and culture could be erected from such a simple foundation. Admittedly the town in which he spent the past seven days had not been without its more enjoyable aspects. Some of the women had been single, luscious, and as fond of the more intimate sports as he. Pity he had not brought with him a few of his accessories made for such activity. Although in hindsight perhaps it had been for the best. Some of his articles were quite vicious in their usage. He was, after all, engaged in a specific undertaking for His Queen and could not let his personal proclivities interfere. It would not have been sensible to become involved in a complaint and have his connection to her be known.

Ah, but now he was home, for he truly considered the Great Royal Palace and its grounds the only abode fit for him. If only he were Pharaoh. He began whistling a little tune as he strode through the various hallways on his way to confer with his guards. He was sure they had coped efficiently without his presence yet he had been absent a week, after all. He could not have them think he had grown slack or soft. He ruled by fear and must be in attendance for them to fully taste that which he could instill. For that reason, he believed, his troops were the best at what they did.

As his sandals slapped against the stone floors, he saw Asim at the end of the long hall accompanied by a guard under his command. She looked disheveled and was dripping water upon the floor as she walked.

Reaching her, he commanded his man to step aside. "Asim, my lovely, what has happened? Why," he said while cupping her chin, "you seem to have been shedding tears."

"Away, Akar. I have no wish to converse with you. It is my business."

"Now, Asim, that is not the manner in which to speak to one who only has your interest at heart. Come," he said leading her away to a small niche around the corner. "Tell me why you are so obviously upset. And wet." He drew her close in the small surround for lack of space. She gathered the folds of her dress about her wet body and tried to push him away. He only tightened his hold and bared his teeth. She was a trapped animal in his clutches.

"The Queen has become displeased with me. I am to be locked in my room until she . . . calms herself." She was not about to admit her true fears: that she would be sent away from the Palace.

"Ah, she has a temper that one. Come. I shall escort you." He was about to turn and order his man to leave when Asim interjected.

"My gratitude for your concern Akar," she said respectfully as not to incur his anger, "yet the Queen gave explicit instruction to this guard. I do not wish to place him in harm's way should he not do as she bid."

At this statement, Akar's man spoke. "Captain, I am more than able to do as ordered. I swear to remain at her door until Queen Tiye sends for her. I shall give you no cause to be concerned. Should Queen Tiye know of you vacating her direct order, you could be blamed equally as myself, my Captain."

"Yes, Akar," said Asim, grateful that the guard had noted this problem. "She would hold you responsible."

"Since it appears no instructions were given against visitors," he looked inquiringly at his guard who shook his head from side to side, "perhaps I shall call upon your chamber with a slight repast for you. You would like that, would you not?"

Naturally she would not like that yet she was too frightened to voice her true feelings. She nodded her assent with no other choice available. He would be quite displeased if she had responded with a 'no'.

"Excellent. I am most pleased." He pulled her hand to his lips, and stared into her eyes. It was only by the grace of the gods that Asim did not shiver within his grasp. "I have some business with Queen Tiye following my meal yet I am at your disposal immediately afterwards.

"Off with you both, then. I patiently await our time together, Asim." Other men might say those words with warmth and as a welcomed lover. Akar meant it as a warning. And now, she thought, I do not have the protection of the Queen to prevent such a visit.

As she turned to continue to her room of captivity, she heard Akar whistling a happy tune as he left.

## Chapter Twelve

"Ah, my returning sentinel," quipped Queen Tiye. She had put her foul mood aside with the aid of the wine upon the table. For now, details of Ari were all that mattered. Asim would be dealt with later.

She was elegantly ensconced in her audience room with plump pillows and delectables upon the low table. "Come. Sit. I have a small jug of wine to smooth the way for speech while I listen to all you have to tell. Did you find the route difficult?"

"No, My Queen. The journey was easy enough by camel. I set up a small tent with a few comforts yet it did not exhibit any surprise or curiosity.

"I must return to you the overage of stipend you supplied. I did not require it all." He began to dig into his pouch when she halted his action.

"Keep it. There cannot be much remaining," she said magnanimously. He was not about to contradict her assessment. While he did not use all she had given him, he had actually made money off her stake. A quite respectable amount, in fact. Gambling had been available and lucrative.

He began his tale with his arrival to the town. After only minor inquiries, he found the man he sought. He was, in fact, having an argument with a debt collector when Akar first found the Ari.

"From what little I overheard, I gathered their difference of opinion dealt with the value of an item with which he was bartering. It looked to be a plate of some sort. Ari demanded more and the dealer would not change his offer. Eventually, Ari left with the trade completed. He was quite crestfallen. It was ordained by the gods, this opportunity of mine to pose as a caring man.

"Agreeing with him that all debt collectors were thieves, I offered him a drink — an extremely strong beer — from my leather flask. I do not know if he drinks excessively yet he was quite prepared to do so this night."

The two men spoke about life's hardships with Akar letting Ari take the lead and agreeing with his edicts on life: debt collectors were dishonest, business men were cheats, and the gods were all against him.

"I asked him what trinkets he had been trading yet he was not very forthcoming. A few pieces of jewelry that belonged to his mother, he said, or household items owned by the family for many years. I mentioned how sad it must be to part with things that would surely conjure up memories of his parents and he merely nodded while pouring more drink. He did not have much to say on that subject.

"He did mention that his current financial position was due to his father, a degenerate gambler. This, he said, was the cause for his lack of worth and loss of family heirlooms.

"After drink loosened his tongue, he told me of a friend who was having a social gathering that evening. The entertainment involved several games such as Senet, Hounds and Jackals, and Mehen among others. It was an evening among friends and acquaintances, he told me. Additionally, he said, one was free to gamble within the premises. I asked about the allowable limit, to which he replied it depended upon the game and the table at which one sat.

"He inquired if I would like to attend with him. He said he would vouch for me yet I noticed he did not offer to pay for my gaming as his guest. It mattered naught, of course, as I was following a golden chance to learn more about him simply by watching."

"Quite a blessed occurrence," said the Queen.

"As I say, the gods were clearly with me," said Akar.

The home at which they arrived was not overly ostentatious yet it was obvious the owner was a man of some means. Akar wondered if those means were derived from the gambling within.

Small stools and tables filled the rooms of the home and Akar soon learned which tables and limits his new friend preferred. They began at Senet with a limit that was reasonable. To ensure this continued camaraderie with his subject, Akar offered to give Ari a small allotment with which to enter the table. He described it as a small fee for bringing him to such a fine site. True to form, Ari grabbed it greedily. He also grabbed at a passing tray of wine, sloshing a bit of the choice vintage upon the polished floor.

"I said to him, 'Perhaps you should keep your wits clear for the plays, my friend,' He would not hear of it, insisting he was quite good at the game, having played it as a child."

Yes, thought Tiye, I know he did. More often than not he lost. She could see him even now performing the most dangerous of stunts to settle a bet.

"How was his play? Did he win?"

"No, My Queen. He was in debt with his host from the moment he entered the house. Truly, the host initially refused to allow him to play. When I offered my first allotment, he was permitted inside."

"Your first allotment?"

"Indeed. He lost it almost immediately at the nearest table. As we moved to tables with higher limits, I afforded him two more allocations. He gained enough to offer encouragement yet lost more than he won. The same story is true for most habitual gamblers, I have been told.

"Finally, at the end of the night, all guests paid their due with the exception of Ari. I was about to offer my services to cover his bets when the owner firmly gripped his elbow and drew him into another room. I decided to linger and overhear as much as possible. If the man was truly in any physical difficulties, I planned on stepping in."

Akar stayed out of sight yet within hearing distance. Apparently, the owner was insisting Ari pay his past due amounts immediately while Ari declared he could not.

"The truly interesting part was yet to follow, My Queen. Ari was quite delighted to inform the owner of an anticipated blessing, as he called it, soon to come his way with enough wealth to pay that man in full as well as other creditors. It was made quite clear in the conversation that any financial hardship he was suffering was at his own hand and not those of his father."

"Did he explain from where this 'blessing' was originating?"

"The owner asked that very question. Ari was extremely vague in his answers. I do not believe it is from any business interest. The owner had indicated he knew of Ari's misfortune in those areas. Apparently he has very little business income remaining within the family name. Certainly none in his own. Perhaps he has a benefactor? I am sorry, My Queen, I do not truly know the answer. He indicated merely another month or so was required before he would settle all debts."

"Were you able to determine the amount of these debts and to whom they are owed?"

Akar mentioned several men known to her and a staggering sum. "How is it possible for one man to accumulate such an extraordinary debt?" asked the Queen.

"Most gambling losses are owed to so-called friends. Knowing their activities are legally frowned upon, one friend does not speak to another of this side business. Some men are professional lenders who do not always know of other debts until it is too late. Apparently, Ari has been borrowing from one to pay another, just enough each time to fend off inquiries. And he has been performing this dangerous dance for several years."

"Dangerous. What do you mean by that term? Would he suffer physically over his debts?"

"He may very well suffer bruises as a beginning. It would seem, My Queen, a lender has several means to ensure payment. Eventually he will loose his home and possessions to satisfy the debt. He may consider selling himself into private service. His master will pay all debts in return for work completed in a debt-bondage system. Based on the current amounts he owes, it could take many years before he could work off a new sum to the master."

"In the meantime, could he acquire more debt by gambling?"

"Quite unlikely in his city. It seems he has been finally found out. He is unable to secure new loans without incurring exorbitant interest amounts and he will not be admitted to any established gaming table. He may yet attend other social gatherings where his reputation has not yet reached. I believe that to be unlikely. The word is out on the man locally.

"He did make mention of a sporting event in a nearby town he wished to attend. If his need to gamble is as great as I imagine, he will travel there. Bets are often placed at such events."

Attending sporting events was a great pastime for Egyptians, rich and poor alike. Physical fitness was greatly admired in Egypt and sports not only provided an outlet for nationwide entertainment, but a chance for the athletes of the day to prove their worth. Tournaments in archery, boxing, high jump, handball, javelin throw, weightlifting, soccer, and gymnastics were among the favorites. Since most cities and towns were located along the Nile, it made sense the various water sports of fishing, swimming races, and rowing events were frequently held.

Egypt had no proper building or amphitheater where such events were held; the many open sandy fields served for competition and viewing. Whole towns turned out to cheer on their favorites with some attendees traveling from nearby settlements. Some competitions were held impromptu, others took great planning.

Pharaohs proudly funded many teams by furnishing neutral referees, uniforms, and equipment. Not only were they keen on attending, Pharaohs and their Princes often competed in archery contests. While providing an enjoyable activity for the Royal men, it also provided their subjects to see the physical fitness of the ruling class.

The people of Egypt eagerly anticipated pre-planed sporting competitions. On the lighter side, it was more than an occasion for family fun; it offered camaraderie among fans and conversations in local gossip.

On the darker side, sporting competitions offered a chance for profit. Wage takers were always available at these social festivities to accept bets. Some waged upon their favorite team, others bet based on assurances of a sure thing. Some gambled great amounts due to a dream they had the night before or an answer to a prayer. Whatever the reason or strategy for laying down a bet, some attended these competitions simply for the thrill of gambling, not for the sports.

Apparently, reasoned Tiye, Ari was one such person. He had become so addicted to the excitement of the occasional win he constantly sought it out again and again in whatever form presented.

"Unless he has a secret benefactor or his upcoming blessing is true — none of which I can discern — he is in a great financial dilemma."

Tiye reflected on all she had heard from Akar. "When is this sporting event to occur?"

"Less than three months hence." He gave her the exact date. She yet had time before he expected the 'blessing' he demanded of her. She would have to act quickly, however.

Queen Tiye was well satisfied with the outcome of his investigation and she told him as much. Naturally she did not present compliments to the man — it would not do for him to become more conceited than he was. She did, however, offer him further amulets in payment.

He bowed politely to her, thanking her for the opportunity to be of service, and asked if he could assist her further. Quite out of character for Akar but perhaps, thought the Queen, he was learning his place within the Royal Palace.

"Not at this time," replied His Queen as she granted him leave from the room. She would need time to ponder her next move yet she was sure to require Akar's services again.

Entering her suite of rooms, she told the servants to leave until she recalled them. So, she fumed, Ari lied to her yet again. It was by his own hand — by his own *stupidity* — he had come to this financial low. How his parents must be suffering to know the damage their son has done to their good name.

Making her way to her dressing room she began rummaging around in her jewelry cases until she found what she had been seeking: the lapis lazuli necklace from young Ari. She held it in her hands, delighting in the blue and gold-flecked stones. Had this truly been a gift of affection? Now she wondered if he had purchased the piece for her or won it in a game of chance.

Clutching the piece tightly, she flung it against the heavy wooden door. Bits of it shattered and flew about the room. She allowed herself to cry one final time over Ari.

## Chapter Thirteen

Akar left the discussion with His Queen quite elated. She seemed pleased with his recitation of the discoveries on the man called Ari. Very pleased indeed. And why should she not? He had accumulated an excellent accountability of the man's activities and habits. That bit of luck — meeting the man on his entry to the city — was unpredicted yet quite welcome. It had halved his searching time in the accursed town, as he had been anxious to return to the great city of Thebes. He had shown His Queen respect, not one sneer had he presented, and she had been grateful.

And now to the most adventurous part of his morning: the visit to his lovely Asim. He was fully aware of her lack of fondness towards him yet it mattered naught. He had enjoyed many women who disliked him. Some had even screamed their objections toward his actions yet, again, it mattered little to Akar. If truth were told, he actually favored the fight. A show of spirit was preferred to a woman under him cold as a Nile perch.

He hoped Asim was so spirited. He would have her no matter her disposition towards him. He took a moment to wonder why the Queen had confined her. With his usual self-centeredness he then thought "How convenient for me, however, to find her so restricted. Easier prey."

He also reflected momentarily over his recent trip for the Queen. Who was this man, Ari, and why was his financial standing significant to Queen Tiye? He was nearly to Asim's door and put aside such contemplation. Instead he thought of the generous payment he had just received and the enjoyment ahead.

Whistling the same little tune as earlier, he approached his man guarding the great door that kept Asim prisoner.

"Have you experienced any difficulty with her?" he asked his man.

"No, Captain, none. If I had not turned the lock upon her myself, I would not know she was within."

"Ah, a quiet prisoner. We should pray they would all be so."

His man laughed at that and handed him the long solid key at Akar's request. "I shall keep it with me," said Akar. "I will not require your services. Perhaps you would like a morsel from the pantry areas."

The man looked worried. "My captain, the Queen gave me implicit instructions. I was to remain at my post at all times. She did not mention time away for nourishment."

"And you have done well. Surely the Queen does not expect you to collapse from hunger. You have only to fill your belly and return. I shall be inside the room with her. Nothing can go awry."

With that, Akar inserted the large heavy key into the equally large locking mechanism and twisted it. He heard the pins slide, releasing the lock and allowing him entrance.

Waving off his man, Akar entered.

He had barely put his face through the opening when something sailed past his head and crashed on the wall behind him.

"By the gods, woman," he roared. "What possesses you to such an act?"

Asim stood in shock staring at the man in her doorway. "Akar! My sincere apologies. I did not know it was you."

"So it was my guard's head at which that pottery was aimed! You would render a man senseless who was simply following orders from Our Queen? Or were you only waiting for me to keep my promise of a visit?"

She was cowering against the wall. "I swear I did not remember our appointment. You did not specify a time. Truly, I thought it was your guard."

"You wish to escape? You have no safe refuge, my sweet, especially from me. Nevertheless, it would seem you need tutoring on manners. Fortunately, since I am present, I shall assume those duties." Slamming the door behind him and locking it, he angrily strode forward, the bulky key clanking in his hand. The room was small and he reached her in two steps while tucking the key ring into the top of his pleated *shendyt*. "I suggest," he said reaching for her neck, "we begin such instructions now."

Her shrieking screams stunned him yet only momentarily. When he did not pull away from her, she began to kick and flail her arms, punching and scratching at whatever parts of his body she could locate. "Enough," he hollered in her face, "I will have you with or without your objections."

He squeezed tighter upon her throat. She felt as if she were soaring as her feet left the floor and the room began to swim before her eyes. She was still striking and kicking yet the blows were less intense as she felt herself slowly slipping into blackness. Her fingers touched something solid protruding from his tunic, something with sharp edges, and she grabbed at it. Using what little conscious thought she had remaining, she raised it and began thrashing at his face with the jagged side of the brass key.

Akar suddenly released her while shouting curses. She fell to the ground and quickly crawled to the opposite wall. Asim grabbed a large shard of the broken pottery she had thrown. Someone outside began banging upon the door and yelling Akar's name repeatedly. Asim lifted herself from the floor and held the sharp wedge of pottery before her like a dagger.

"If you come closer to me I shall stab you with this. I swear it." The banging upon the door became louder and her fingers dripped blood from the sharp earthenware clutched in her hand yet she did not back down. "Get out of my room. I am still a member of the Queen's household and this is my room. You are not welcome here." Her neck was bruised and her voice was hoarse yet she stood her ground. Her chin was thrust forward defiantly and she shifted her weight from foot to foot like an animal prepared to strike.

"Away, Akar. Depart my room now and never return!"

Picking up the key, his eyes never left her face. Even while he inserted it and unlocked the door, he continued to stare at her. The guard behind him was peering in the room yet Akar pushed him aside.

"You have bested me this time, Asim," he told her while holding his bleeding face, "yet this has not ended. A victory in one conflict does not win the entire war, my sweet."

She heard the key relock the door. Lying across the bed she sobbed and rubbed her neck. *If only I had escaped and found Pentu or Joba. I would have been safe with them.* At least Akar had left the room, she thought, yet she believed what he said; he was not finished with her.

## Chapter Fourteen

Tiye's Palace Woman had been diligently tutoring the new servant girl in the ways of bathing the Royal Queen efficiently and without incident. She was not having notable success.

After dumping a water jug into the Queen's mouth and eyes, Tiye took the Palace Woman aside to question her. "Whatever is amiss with that girl? Either she manages to abuse my skin with the scraper or tosses water upon me in all directions. If I wished to drown I would jump into the deepest part of the Nile and do so."

The woman informed Her Queen that the girl was frightened of performing poorly. "You have honored her with this new position yet she is a nervous lamb. Asim was able to learn quickly yet this one . . ." she trailed off and simply shook her head.

"Asim is no longer here," Tiye said sharply. "This one shall either learn or return to the cleaning of my garments." She looked at her scraped arm and continued. "I feel I shall be worn to the bone if she continues in this manner. See to it."

Tiye, too, missed Asim's abilities yet the Queen would not have the girl in her presence. It had taken years to train her in the manner to which Tiye deserved, the Queen reflected. All that time wasted. The Queen gave a great sigh. She had always disliked change especially when it proved an inconvenience to her. Punishing Asim by emptying the various toilet rooms for the Palace staff had somewhat satisfied the Queen's need for revenge. She had been saving the girl for the ultimate favor. And now, she thought, with the conspiracy swirling about, I might have wielded power from the most influential citizen in Egypt: the Vizier. She had hoped to include him in their pact. Since he had no secrets to flaunt in his face, she was prepared to offer Asim as motivation for his attachment. That idea — one that would have brought great credibility to their cause — was now moot.

She sat at her dressing table in frustration, toying with her scarab mirror. Curse Asim. How dare she betray me in such a fashion? Tiye had seen the way the Pharaoh had glanced at her yet the girl swore the child was not her husband's. If not the Pharaoh then who? She sighed deeply. Truly it mattered naught. She was no longer a virgin, that was plainly obvious, and bartering her away as a wife was no longer an opportunity for Tiye.

Her eyes narrowed as she remembered another devious traitor: Ari. She had received the information she sought and must now find a solution to end this man's torment upon her. Ari would surely participate in the grand sporting event. Luckily, the event was scheduled prior to when I promised the payment to him. Many more payments would undoubtedly be expected, I am sure.

What nerve, she thought, to extort the Queen of Egypt in such a deliberate manner. To use her feelings for him with such *treachery*. She was surrounded by deceitfulness at every turn she made. She wanted to scream in aggravation yet held herself calm in the presence of her women attendants.

Enough, she thought. I shall not tolerate such mistreatment. Not to my son or myself. I shall do away with the three of them — Ari, Asim, and Ramses. It will be a great triumph to have my son upon the Throne of Egypt. He will be a wondrous Pharaoh.

She will take her mother's suggestion and send for Akar. She would approach him with their cause and initiate the first phase of her retribution. Ari would be first.

## Chapter Fifteen

Pentu was frantic with worry. He had neither seen nor heard from Asim for nearly a fortnight. Had she grown tired of him? Could she be in trouble? Or — hopefully — she had merely been too busy to visit him. Yet she would have sent Joba a message if this last rationale were true. He had decided to visit Joba today and ask his friend if he had news of Asim.

The gods were with him this morning as he found Joba entering the Royal Palace and walking towards his post. "My friend, it gives me great pleasure to see you. It has been some time since last we spoke. How are you, Pentu?" remarked Joba.

"I am concerned, my friend. I am troubled over Asim. She did not arrive at our last appointed moment and I have been frantically searching for her. I was hoping you could enlighten me as to her whereabouts."

Joba merely shook his head in sadness. When first they met, he attempted to tell the young lovers to be wary of their association. Actually, he had instructed them to forget about each other. That was futile when he saw their obvious mutual attraction. As far as he knew they had been quite discreet. Joba had been concerned for their safety and rightly so, even agreeing to act at their intermediary for messages between the two.

"I have distressing news for you, Pentu. She has been assigned to the toilet rooms in another area of the Palace. The servant's quarters, to be exact. There is little chance you will see her within our location, which is reserved only for assigned staff, the Royals, and official advisors. In short, she is not permitted in this part of the Royal Palace. You know this to be true." He touched his friend upon the shoulder. "My sincere condolences, Pentu. It would be best if you could remove her from your memory."

Stunned, Pentu pressed the point. "Never. I can never forget her. I should seek out the Queen and ask her to intervene. Asim was a favorite of Queen Tiye's and was most accomplished in her duties."

Joba shook his head while still gripping Pentu's shoulder. "It is the Queen who has banished her from her own Royal Chambers. You will find no recourse there, my friend."

"The Queen! What reasoning could she have for doing so? There has never been conflict between them.

"That I do not have privilege to. Again, my apologies for my lack of knowledge."

"I could speak to Pharaoh Ramses when we are in conference yet the other advisors will be present. Shall I seek a private audience with him?" he said, thinking aloud. "The Great Ramses can intercede on her behalf."

Joba again shook his head. "You must not. The Great Pharaoh Ramses does not lower himself in attending to household routines or staff.

"Additionally, Asim was a gift to Queen Tiye from Ramses himself. She is free to do as she sees fit with all her personal staff especially one freely given. There is no hope there, either. To think otherwise is to court the wrath of the King and your position in the Royal Palace."

"I cannot go through life without her, Joba. I love her dearly. To whom can I turn for help?"

Joba knew Pentu was far beyond listening to his advice. "There is no one. Yet I offer you this bit of hope, however small it is. If you are terminated you will surely be returned to Set-Maat and loose any chance to see her again. Bide your time and follow the rules and a chance meeting between you two might come to pass."

Pentu was crestfallen. "You are correct — that is little hope. I have no reasoning as to how this occurred. I can see no sense to it. My poor love."

"I will do my best to find added information for you, Pentu. It will take time. I must approach other women in Queen Tiye's care. Even then, it is doubtful they will know. Her banishment seems to have occurred quite rapidly yet I shall try, my friend. I shall try."

## Chapter Sixteen

Akar was vexed. For what purpose did Queen Tiye again send for him? Since he had fulfilled one task for her — and under coercion at that — did she now think him her personal servant? Still, she was Queen and he must as least attend this audience.

"Ah, Akar." She was flounced upon a long padded recliner with slices of melons at her side.

Akar bowed as expected. "At your pleasure My Queen."

She offered a nearby seat and instructed him to sit while waving away her extraneous servant girl.

Tiye neither liked nor trusted the man beside her. He was, in a word, revolting. Asking him to complete this assignment was going to be difficult. He could inform her husband or the Vizier. He could also ask for the moon yet never complete the deed she would set before him this day. Taking a deep breath she began reciting the request she had been rehearsing, choosing each word carefully. It truly pained her to be congenial to the man.

"Akar, I have a very delicate duty for you." She noticed angry red, scabby marks along his cheek yet looked away. Mentioning them was not part of her script. "It further involves the man you trailed last month. The man Ari." Akar remained silent. "Are you familiar with this sporting event he will be attending?" He nodded yet remained silent. "You know of its location?" Another nod. He was making this much more difficult than she had imagined. "I wish for you to travel to this city and locate him. Do not let him know you are in attendance. In fact, it would be best if he never set eyes upon you. You need only to familiarize yourself with the city, the streets, the marketplaces, and secluded areas. Find the paths Ari will take."

"If I do not resume my acquaintance with the man, what am I to do?" said Akar.

As last, he lent voice to thoughts. "This man is a great threat to our Pharaoh's empire and the state of governmental affairs," Tiye replied.

Akar looked skeptical. Ari was a habitual gambler who had nearly lost his family fortune. How could such a man even the gods had discarded threaten the Mighty Pharaoh of Egypt? She saw the sneer on his face and knew he did not believe the threads she was spinning.

Yet she pushed on. "I am told this grand sporting event will last three days. I feel quite certain Ari will attend for the entirety. He may seem harmless yet I assure you he does not have proper intentions towards our Pharaoh. He uses the excuse of gambling to meet with others who wish ill-will to our Great Ruler.

"Because of this, the man must be removed. I am counting on you to find the most inconspicuous time and place in which to commit the deed."

Akar leaned back and crossed his arms across his considerable chest with a gleam in his eyes. "You are instructing me to murder this man." It was not a question, yet a statement for which Tiye felt she must offer an answer.

"If you wish to put it so crudely, then yes. I prefer to think of it as an execution.

"Either way, the man shall die," replied Akar. "If this is for the Pharaoh, why am I not ordered to do so in an official capacity? Why here in My Queen's Private Audience Chamber?

"I am taking it upon myself to protect him. He is not always fully aware of the many threats to his rule." She was beginning to falter and he saw that. "This is one such threat that must be eliminated. I wish it to be completed without witnesses, quietly and with undue suspicion to yourself or this Throne. Of course I shall demand proof the deed is done. You shall bring me his gold ring. It has a family crest engraved upon it, a large crane with a fish in its talon. He never removes it.

"Is this a *duty* you will be able to perform?" stressed Tiye as Akar continued to stare at her without speaking. He must think of it as a 'Royal Sense of Duty' rather than eradicating someone on the sly.

"I am *able* to," said Akar. "*Willing* to is another matter.

Tiye chose to interject her Royal Anger at this point in the conversation. "I am *Your Queen* and this is a task I order you to complete. You have no say in the matter, only to embark upon it. Do you not understand this? I could have you charged with treason to the Royal Pharaoh," she said arrogantly.

"You could, yet I do not believe you would. Let us be candid with each other, My Queen. The reasoning for this order is yours alone and has naught to do with our Pharaoh. I do not pretend to know why — nor do I care. This is a deed you wish another to commit, ensuring your hands remain clean of the matter so demonstrated by this clandestine meeting. Only the two of us here, side by side. You believe since I accomplished your last decree, I must do so again

"It would be an easy task and one in which I could engage. Murder, however, is quite different than simply following a man. The punishment for murder is death in kind, as you well know. You must make it worth risking my skin should I be discovered. Indeed, I cannot be certain you would save your own hide by relinquishing mine.

"Oh, I could turn the table and inform upon your directive here today. However, I am known as a bit of a renegade and merely a captain of one simple guard unit. Would the Pharaoh believe me or his lovely second-wife and Queen? We both know the truth to that: my word would be tossed aside. I could cause you some bother or possibly peril if I chose to speak of this, however. We both realize that. No, My Queen, ordering me is not adequate. I believe we must arrive at another reason for my silence."

So Mother was correct again, curse her. He did want something, thought Tiye. She had no choice in the matter. Ari must never again trouble her reign as Queen. "What is it you want, Akar?"

Akar leaned in to his Queen and said, "I want your servant girl, Asim."

The Queen was amazed. Could this be true? Could this be a solution sent to her by the gods to rid herself of the hated Asim while guaranteeing the riddance of Ari? Apparently, Akar did not know of the girl's banishment from her service or the reasoning behind such action. "You wish to take her as a wife?"

Akar shrugged his powerful shoulders. "Not necessarily. I choose to possess her for a time. A marriage is up to the gods."

She must not be too eager to grant him this desire. She must play this with caution. "She is one of my most trusted handmaidens, Akar. I do not think I should part with her. I care little if you do not marry the girl, yet I would have her reside in comfort. How am I assured you shall provide for her adequately? Are your earnings enough to allow her to live the life she now leads? Indeed, she has lived within these Palace walls as a servant to the Queen of Egypt. That post holds many advantages and luxuries. I am aware of your yearly stipend Akar. It is not enough."

She allowed him time to contemplate her statement. It was obvious he wanted the girl. Tiye wondered just how greatly he wanted her. Would he be willing to enter the conspiracy brewing against the Pharaoh and Amonhirk? Of course, she might have to up the ante for his participation in the plot.

"Perhaps," said Tiye with a purr in her voice, "there is a way for this to be satisfying to us both. I believe the income of a General is more than sufficient to support Asim in grand style. Do you feel such a position would be sufficient for you and my favored servant? If so, let us discuss this further."

## Chapter Seventeen

Tiye was about her morning plans early. She was setting into motion the promise made to the Harem wives. To do so, she was making a visit to a certain Under-Magician to the Royal Family with the pretext of seeking a potion for a painful throat. She had chosen a time when her maidservant had other tasks assigned. Normally, a servant under her orders would seek a doctor who specialized in such discomfort yet another's hand would not suffice today. This needed tending to personally. She felt the need of a magician for this ailment.

All was proceeding better than she expected. With Akar on their side and his subsequent inclusion of other military staff who were disenchanted with Ramses, quite a respectable number were engaged in their plot.

The magician was surprised to see the Queen at the door of the magical depository and as such bowed and fawned over her presence as she entered. He was especially pleased that she knew his name: Samut. How wonderful and caring of her, thought the young man.

Large though the room was, it was obvious more space was needed to accommodate the many professional necessities. It smelled medicinal and dusty and the Queen fought against sneezing. Baskets and tables were crammed with herbs, potions, scrolls stacked to the rafters, bits of bone in small bowls, and diagrams of the human body. Cloth and papyrus pieces edged their way from between storage baskets while the whole seemed about to burst apart.

"Perhaps I should have sought a fully trained physician for my throat yet I have been told you are quite knowledgeable in ointments and liquids. Some are used in magical spells, are they not? Imagine my surprise to find you present, ready to assist me."

Samut assured His Queen that he was indeed knowledgeable in many of the tonics located within the room and willingly gave her the necessary medication for her symptoms. Rather than take her immediate leave, she lingered in the room, determined to fulfill her true intent. She began slowly by seeking his experience and skill.

"The time is almost upon us for the annual visit by the Chief Royal Magician. I am sure you know of this. It is when he renews or adds his protective spells upon the family. A fortnight hence, correct?" The young man nodded. The Queen remained quite casual by wandering from table to table, picking up bits of glass and vials of colored liquid.

"I am wondering, is it true our mighty Ramses is given much more potent protections?" Samut nodded. "Ah, that is excellent. Quite excellent. While his spirit is that of a god, his current form is that of a man and subject to human frailties. See how healthy he is and the length of his reign. The spells upon him must be very great indeed to be so effective.

"However, a thought has troubled me of late. You appear to be a talented apprentice. Perhaps you might ease my mind."

The young man was obviously most eager to help in any way he could. This was a Queen of all Egypt, here in this study, asking for his help. He prayed he knew the answer to her question.

"If something should happen to the Chief Royal Magician, who would be able to administer such magical incantations over the family? Could you, for example, perform the spells?" She replaced a piece of papyrus and picked up a dusty bird beak from a small plate.

"My Queen, it is the sole duty of the Chief Royal Magician to recite the spells. He is the eldest and most experienced. However," he said with great importance, "several of his assistants — myself included — are fully capable of the yearly care. The Pharaoh and the Royal Family must always be protected."

"Although," said the Queen in a contemplative voice, "magical spells are only part of maintaining our Great King's health, is that not correct? I believe the Royal High Priest makes special sacrifices to the god Amun and prays for his Majesty's health and wisdom as well."

"You are very learned in the protection of Our Great Pharaoh, My Queen. That is exactly correct."

"So I suppose," said the Queen amiably, "the reverse is true." The magician looked confused. Either that or he was horrified by what he presumed she was asking. She would have to tread lightly. She looked closely at something dried and brown in the palm of her hand. "Incidentally, what am I holding?'

When he told her it was a dried frog's leg, she hastily replaced it in the bowl from whence is came and brushed her hands together.

"Let us suppose an enemy of the Pharaoh wished to do him harm. Perhaps he bribed one of your fellow magicians or had a magician of his own. Could the protective spells be removed from our beloved King? Or worse yet, could another magician put spells causing death upon him?"

Samut looked relieved at her explanation. "Such a thing is unheard of yet it could be accomplished. If protective spells were removed, Our Great Pharaoh could be consumed by the same illnesses that plague us all. Also, if certain spells were incanted against him a mere mortal could cause him harm."

"Would my husband need be present if these dangerous spells were afflicted upon him? He would surely know of such danger if he overheard the incantations, would he not?"

"No," said the magician thoughtfully, "no, I do not believe that would be the case. Such a heinous act of magic could very efficiently be placed upon him from afar. That is, of course, if one had the talent and correct ingredients."

Tiye picked up a vial with an inscription upon the label and toyed with it. "Saw dust, acacia leaves, galena, goose fat. Bandage with it," she read aloud. "These instructions do not indicate where to place the bandage nor the duration. Other labels are more specific."

"Ah. That, My Queen, is for several types of eye maladies. Once it is applied, the bandage is affixed for a period of five days and then removed. It is one of the oldest remedies in the room," said the magician with pride that His Queen should take such an interest in his craft.

"How do you remember such a vast amount of information? It is quite a talent you possess. You seem to be fully equipped here for anything," she said while continuing to wander. "You mentioned the needed ingredients that could do my husband harm. Would the supplies in this room suffice for placing spells from afar? Perhaps someone could enter and pilfer such ingredients. Would it not be prudent to have a guard on duty to prevent such an occurrence?"

"My Queen, a sturdy locking mechanism has been installed upon this door. It is the single access point and only fully trained magicians have keys. That amounts to nine. Additionally," he reached out to indicate a scroll upon the table nearest the doorway, "we are required to sign the scroll when entering and leaving. Usually, this room is fully occupied with men, further educating themselves or searching for ingredients. It is difficult to find oneself here alone."

"And yet," said his Queen slowly, "you were here alone when I knocked upon the door, were you not? As a Junior Magician I believe you are not allotted a key." While peeking through a piece of round flat glass she continued. "I happen to know you are quite often here alone."

"I assure you My Queen, this is an abnormality. I . . . I borrowed the key. I am simply earlier today than others."

Tiye gave him a pitiful look of disbelief. "I imagine this room contains many dangerous and intoxicating elements. Some might fetch a considerable sum in non-sanctioned trade. Black Market, I believe it is called. I have heard of people using certain substances for personal use. Oh, not just for health remedies but for their hallucinatory and euphoric properties. This room surely contains such chemicals as well stocked as it is.

"Ah. An idea just occurred to me. I believe it may be prudent for the Pharaoh to assign an official accounting clerk to monitor the singing of that particular scroll you mentioned. Perhaps he should also administer a tally of the many resources here. A ledger, if you will, of incoming and outgoing products and to whom they are issued. The supplies should always be fully stocked and tracked. It would not do for someone to accidentally remove more than needed. How does that sound to you, young Samut?"

The terror on his face let the Queen know she had found her mark. "Good. Now we have perception between us and I shall be direct in my true desire.

"I would see my son, Pentawer, sit upon the Throne rather than Amonhirk. For that to occur, certain safety measures must be removed from the Pharaoh and his appointed heir. What I require from you is simple: remove the protective spells from Ramses and Amonhirk. They must become vulnerable to death. It shall be your responsibility to see it so.

"When my son is crowned I shall see to it you want for nothing. You shall have the distinction of becoming the first Superior Royal Magician to the King. Additionally, no one shall ever know of your medicinal thefts or your reasons for doing so. This I swear upon the gods."

The young man was now looking quite horrified. The color had drained from his face and his eyes were searching for a way out of the room like a cornered sand rat. With a sigh, Tiye realized another tactic would be needed. Bribery was not going to reach this fool.

"Tell me, Samut. Do you ever watch those gentle creatures of the skies?" she began softly. "Those soaring birds calling that blue space their own? Nature can be fierce if the situation calls for it. I have seen small mother sparrows fending off hawks to protect their chicks. The mother soars after the hawk, diving at him again and again to peck at his soft underbelly with her sharp beak. She will never retreat and will risk all for her children, flying at him relentlessly, pulling at his feathers and flesh until he can stand the harassment no longer and leaves the nest in peace.

"The decision is yours to make, of course. Only know this: there are two possible outcomes for you in this scenario. Should you refuse this request, another magician will gladly take what I offer and my son will yet succeed the Throne.

"There will then be no grand position for you. Indeed, there will be no position for you at all when Ramses hears of your pilferage. Naturally, restitution must be made on your part, whatever that may be." The man was keenly aware of several means of repayment. Stealing from the Pharaoh was a monumental crime and would receive a monumental penalty.

"Know this too: I shall not annoy you with simple harassment. No, you shall not escape me that easily." She leaned forward and said in a hiss, "I am that mother bird, my dear magician. I do not withdraw and I would risk everything for my son, even my very life. Or yours, for that matter. I shall sink my beak into your belly until I see your life's light escape from your eyes."

The man was shaking yet had the insolence to respond to his Queen in an attempt to save himself from either outcome. "Yet, My Queen, even with my counter spells the prayers, sacrifices, and perhaps other holy incantations by the Royal Priests might yet save the King's worldly body. I cannot promise you that my assistance alone would complete your needs."

"Do not worry yourself over the priests. I shall see to them. All I ask is that you perform your magic — your most powerful magic. I may also require an item or two from this room at a later time. Oh, nothing fatal, I assure you. Merely a sleeping draught. In return, you shall receive all I have promised you today."

He held no alternative proposal to her statement. Samut contented himself by believing any spell cast would not offset the long lasting attentions from the priests. All he need do was his best. For that he would receive riches beyond measure in this life. And yet, if she succeeded in her plan, would she implicate him later? Again, he said to himself, what other choice did he truly possess? The man sadly nodded his head.

"I am quite pleased with your decision, dear Samut." She looked at the medicine packet in her hand. Handing it to the Junior Magician she said, "It would seem my throat has improved. I shall not be needing this after all."

## Chapter Eighteen

It was sheer drudgery for Asim. Each morning she had an early meal then went about her job. The household servant chambers were in one of the many Palace outbuildings. An area attached to this contained their toilet rooms. The seat itself was carved from limestone and each was positioned on planks atop a clay pot of sand. Carrying each pot from the room and dumping them out of the Palace area, filling each with clean sand, then replacing each bucket was now her daily duty. This was seen to each morning and each evening.

It was back breaking work and a far cry from the life of comfort she had known with Queen Tiye. Her soft linen gowns were replaced with coarser shifts that became wet and soiled during the day. Her styled wigs were also taken from her and she went about with a short uneven cut of hair.

If she could only see Pentu once more to explain she had not abandoned him, she would gladly suffer this unpleasant situation. It had been shocking to discover she was carrying Pentu's child yet the baby grew large and strong within her belly. In spite of everything, she took joy in the life within her.

Pentu was not aware of the pregnancy and she longed to share the news with him. The question was how? Her life existed within a remote portion of the Royal Palace while his was in the most restricted. Those two areas seldom entwined. It was ironic, she thought, he had once worried of her high social status compared to his. Look at me now, she thought wryly. He sits with the Pharaoh and I have been reduced to the unsanitary service of toilet buckets. If she had been assigned to the toilets of the Royal Family, she might stand a small chance of seeing Pentu. Here such a meeting would never occur. His position held no dealings with those of scullery women just as field workers did not mingle with Royalty.

She was in the rear of the Palace grounds emptying a bucket of feces-filled sand when a sentry guard called out to her.

"Are you Asim? Former servant girl to the Royal Queen Tiye?" he asked her. She nodded in return. "You have been summoned. You are to come with me."

At last, thought Asim. I am to receive a reprieve from Queen Tiye. She would have me return to her service. I shall swear fidelity to her and work hard. I shall see Pentu again.

She followed behind the guard deep in these happy thoughts. When she would turn right towards the building exit, he continued straight. "Are we not to turn here? This is the way to the exit you seek."

Wrinkling his nose in disgust at her reeking smell, the man grabbed her arm briefly to direct her and answered, "That is not our route. Do not linger. We continue on this path."

Straight along the corridor, the guard finally stopped at the entrance to the women servants' community cleansing room. "You are to enter and wash the stench from yourself. Clean clothing has been placed inside for you to wear. You are ordered to take great care with your cleansing. You cannot enter the Royal Palace Chambers smelling as you do. Do not loiter with the duty. I shall wait here to escort you further." Handing her a bath sheet and a small vial of scented oil, he moved to the side for her to enter.

Seeing the simple yet adequate area made Asim remember the private wet room of Queen Tiye's. Limestone and marble lined the walls of the Queen's wet room while a gold painted ceiling glistened overhead. How wonderful it will be to care for Her Queen once more, she thought, for she was sure that would be today's outcome. She agreed with the guard — she could not enter the Royal Chambers looking and smelling as she does. Naturally, this cleansing room was her only option. She saw to her ministrations as quickly as possible, using the oil and removing any trace of odor

As promised, her guard was waiting and directed her to the area she was familiar with: the quarters of the Royal Family. Finally stopping at the audience room of Queen Tiye, her escort knocked upon the massive corridor door. "Enter." Asim recognized the voice of Her Queen and grinned as a child might when offered a treat. At last, she thought, at last I shall be in my previous position, able to meet with Pentu. All shall now be well. All has been forgiven.

Pushing open the door, Asim entered the familiar chambers. Light was streaming in from an overhead open-framed window and the Queen was reclining on her lounge. She was slicing small sweet cakes with her tiny knife, and popping them into her mouth. Asim rushed to her and knelt. "My Queen, my deepest apologies for offending you. I am overcome with gratitude that you would receive me in your service once again."

Queen Tiye indicated that Asim should rise. "Turn around," she ordered. "Slowly and completely." Asim was curious yet did as told, pivoting full circle with her head slightly bowed. "Yes, your shape has indeed changed. Carrying a child will do that to a woman. Apparently, some men find it appealing. Well, we shall see." Asim was confused at that statement. Did Her Queen know of Pentu? Was she about to see him here? Were they to be punished?

Slicing another piece of cake the Queen continued. "It pains me to say this," she said with no sign of distress in her voice, "however, you are mistaken in your assumption. You shall not be welcomed into my service. Henceforth you shall be servicing the Harem in whatever those women require. I doubt the work shall be an overburden for you. Less so than the toilets I should think. You will not be residing within the Harem, however. I have arranged other accommodations for you," finished the Queen with a cruel smile.

Sitting upright upon the overstuffed sofa she clapped her hands and cried, "You may enter now.

The man striding forth to Asim was not her beloved Pentu. It was the most hateful of men: Akar. He allowed a moment to smirk at the frightened girl before attending to the Queen and bowing low. He then moved and stood next to Asim.

"Asim, from this day forth you shall be belong to Akar."

It cannot be, thought Asim. Not Akar. She put her thoughts into words, pleading with the Queen, begging on her knees, not to allow this to occur. "Please My Queen, the man attempted to take me by force. He will surely do me harm. I swear by all the gods I will obey you in all things, only please do not give me to this cruel man."

Nothing passed Akar's prevue and he had been staring at Asim with narrowed eyes. Speaking with annoyance, he said to Tiye "It was not mentioned she carries another man's child. What am I to do with a babe?"

"If you reject this gift, so be it. Only know that I expect you to keep your other accords with me.

Akar was pondering his choices. He wanted Asim for many reasons, the least of which was to recriminate her for his humiliation.

He was not about to leave here empty handed. "I want more," he finally declared to the Queen.

"Indeed? And what would that be?" They scowled at one another, two scara beetles hissing in conflict. Neither wanted to concede to the other. The Queen thought of a compromise. "Would you be satisfied with a house in which to reside? My father owns a small home in Thebes, empty at the moment, yet you may occupy it rent-free. I shall not transfer ownership to you at this time yet you may call it yours as long as you require it. Will that suffice?"

Before Akar could reply, Asim began screaming and running for the door. Akar caught her and grabbed her around her thickened waist while she kicked and shrieked, "No, I shall not go with him. Release me, Akar. I shall not let you take me. My baby. I shall not allow you to harm my baby." By now she was frantic, flapping her arms trying to catch a piece of Akar's face — anything to escape this nightmare. "My Queen, please do not do this. I shall inform the Pharaoh. I swear it." At this, Akar released her and slapped her across the face with obvious pleasure, causing her to fall back against a wall.

Queen Tiye rose from her seat and approached Asim, grabbing the girl's face with one hand. Leaning in close, the Queen said bitingly to Asim, "For one so close to motherhood, you place little value upon your life or that of your unborn child. The Pharaoh does not care about you, Asim. You have always been in my possession to do with as my mood strikes." She roughly loosened her hold on the girl, showing finger marks on her cheeks. "However," said the Queen returning to her cushions, "I have no wish to harm a child," she said. "Akar, I see no reason why this mother-to-be should not see the birth of a fit child, do you? Or that care not be given to it and the mother after childbirth. At least for a time. Agreed?" It was as though a secret passed between them. Akar seemed to give her question a great deal of thought prior to his agreement.

"So it is done. Take her away." She waved her hand in dismissal to the two of them. Turning away from the scene, Tiye handed over her glittering knife to a servant and commanded, "Have this sharpened," she instructed as she dipped her fingers in the water bowl. "It is dreadfully dull." Asim continued her pleas as Akar dragged her from the room.

Halfway along the corridor, Akar stopped and turned Asim towards him. Holding her tightly by both shoulders he whispered in her face, "I have agreed to care for you and your whelp temporarily. I did not agree you should remain free from <u>all</u> physical harm. Do you comprehend my meaning?"

She finally relaxed within his hold. Wiping away tears of fear and frustration she said, "Yes, Akar. I understand."

"Very well. I urge you to think often upon that knowledge. We shall now proceed to my chambers. On the morrow we will be taking up residence in Thebes."

## Chapter Nineteen

After a particular grueling day catering to Pharaoh Ramses bellowing at the council members, Pentu finally exited the Great Council Chambers adjacent to the Audience Room. He was beginning to find his way through the many passages and ornate rooms designated specifically for the Pharaoh's routine. A room for eating, a room for meeting with council, a room with his Audience Window overlooking his people and gardens, one for his morning meetings, another for the council elite to meet, and offices for all members of his advisors. As a former stonemason, he was amazed at the imagination behind the designers of this massive complex. Gold, gems, and colored glass were prevalent everywhere: ceilings, floors, pillars, walls, chairs, tables, and even platters with food served during the meetings. Every wall and ceiling was so filled with paintings, limited empty space remained. He thought he had grown accustomed to such artistry and opulence yet he was agog at every turn throughout the Royal Palace.

Today he barely noticed the splendor he was walking past. He had only one thing upon his mind: Asim. It had been an eternity since he had seen her, had smelled her fragrance, had kissed her full lips. Joba had been conducting his own search among the servant girls he knew. Luckily, Joba had the acquaintance of many servant girls. Women were always attracted to Joba with his wit and ready smile. They clamored for his attention like bees to blossoms. Pentu had never seen a time when they refused his polite advances. To each one he offered adoration, attention, and flattery. In dealing with lovely women, Joba's friends considered him extremely lucky.

And I, thought Pentu, am extremely unlucky at the moment. He had met his eternal love and now she had vanished like a magician's trick. During the little free time he was given, he had spoken to dozens of people throughout the Palace. He had also made a trek to the local prison. Thankfully, she was not held within those walls.

Joba was not in attendance today at the Palace yet had agreed to meet Pentu in the Temple Garden. True to his word, he was indeed waiting, leaning against a column and speaking to a woman. How ironic, thought Pentu; I am unable to keep one in my sights while his friend juggled dozens.

Upon seeing his friend, Joba gave a kiss on the lady's wrist and walked to greet Pentu.

"My sincere gratitude in meeting me here today, Joba, along with my apologies for interrupting your time away from court."

"Ah, no matter. I have just had a most delightful conversation with a lovely lady. The day is not lost, I assure you.

"Now, as to Asim, I know you are anxious over her. I, too, am concerned. She has always been a dear friend. It is most fortunate I am on such friendly terms with so many servant girls. They tend to know all the Palace gossip. I have learned that Asim is no longer on the wretched duty of toilet and wet room cleaning. From that point I have hit a stone wall.

"One young girl saw her escorted by a guard from a wet room and travel along a servant's corridor. Another older woman thought she might be among the Harem servants. If so, she does not have quarters among them for I have heard nothing regarding her evenings spent in the Palace."

"Is it possible she resides in the city of Thebes."

"Possible yet unlikely for it begs the question of why. Single staff members without the benefit of family normally reside within the servant chambers. If she yet works within the Royal Palace, why would she live alone over a mile away?"

"I am confident Queen Tiye's hand is in this."

"That is possible. Indeed, highly plausible. She would have the power to dispatch Asim to whatever duty or dwelling of her choosing. Yet we do not know why."

"Then I must speak to Queen Tiye."

Joba put his hand on Pentu's shoulder. "No, my friend. Again I say to you it is folly to think the Queen would enlighten you to Asim's fate. And why should she? To the Queen you are nothing more than another council member to the Pharaoh. She would never lower herself to answer your concerns or your accusations.

"I beg you, permit me time to make further inquires. As a guard, I have the luxury of less restrictive access in portions of the Palace you do not. A minister wandering in staff areas would surely stand out. The Royal Palace employs hundreds of people. Someone must know something. I swear to you on the gods I shall find that person."

Chapter Twenty

Her duties in the Harem were less arduous and much less odor filled than the toilet rooms. Sometimes Asim believed she could yet smell the rank of those buckets upon her person. Though the demands of the wives were many, they were not burdensome.

The days were long and she had little time to herself. Certainly not enough time to root through the Royal Council Chambers for Pentu. She was restricted to the Harem and could think of no plausible excuse to travel to any other part of the Palace. Even her meals were taken with other servants to the many Harem women. She prayed one of the wives had a need for her to journey to the main Palace where she could either find Pentu or Joba.

She would prefer staying in the Harem quarters throughout the night, continually at their beck and call, rather than what awaited her at the house in Thebes. Any assignment was preferable to nights with Akar.

He met her every evening at the Harem entrance to escort her to their domicile. They appeared the perfect couple to the Harem of Ramses — she heavy with child and he most attentive to her after the long day. They knew naught the truth of their 'union' and she was too mortified to enlighten them. Akar acted the devoted lover when others were in view. The attention he paid towards her behind closed doors, however, was anything but devotion.

The bruises and scratches he inflicted upon her were placed where her garments would conceal the damage. The threats he issued against her and her baby were never uttered within another's hearing. She became adept at using powders and creams to hide any slaps across her face.

It mattered little what she did or said — he beat her because he enjoyed it, not because he was provoked. She learned of his proclivity the first night as he took her by force from behind, pulling at her short hair, and biting her shoulder blade so fiercely she bled. "Consider this, my sweet. We shall enjoy many such pleasant evenings together," he said as she cried in their bed. "You shall never deny me again." And so she did not, ensuring his every request was met, becoming a mouse to his cat, desperately attempting to avoid another 'pleasant' evening. She learned to sense the signs of an impending beating or perverted act in the bedchamber yet could not outrun them. She was nearly shackle-bound to him and would remain so if the gods did not take pity upon her.

He was leaning against the wall of the Harem building, whistling his favorite tune and waiting to escort her to the house in Thebes. He seemed to be in an exceptional mood this evening and she cringed inwardly wondering what new activity he had planned for them tonight. Gripping her elbow tightly, they made their way to the house in Thebes. She was walking slower these past days, the child within sitting heavier in her belly, causing her to walk much more duck-like. Using this as an excuse, she slowed her pace even further, hoping to delay his evening fun.

"Quicken your step, woman. I have obligations needing my attention to this night."

"My apologies, Akar. The child is causing me fatigue." If he had dealings tonight, perhaps that was the reason for his nearly pleasant mood. She did as directed and waddled a bit faster.

"I shall be leaving early on the morrow and shall be absent from my home for five days. I have assigned a junior guard to escort you to the abode each evening. I would not have you wandering off in my absence."

She could have leapt for joy. Five complete days without this man's abuse and presence. She questioned not the reason for this good news yet had one inquiry she must couch carefully to him. "And who is this guard?"

"It matters naught to you. Why are you so inquisitive?"

He was becoming suspicious to her intent and she strove to put that horrid whistle back upon his lips. "I merely ask since I must know whom to meet and where."

He grunted his satisfaction to this reasoning of hers and gave her the name of a young guard she had met while yet in the service to the Queen. When she happened upon the man now, he often gave her a look of pity. As Akar's subordinate, the man was surely aware of his cruelty. If he had sympathy for her, perhaps she might find a path to save herself or at the very least contact Pentu.

"I would ask permission of you to attend the play honoring the great god Amun. We discussed attending this together. It is to be held in three evenings hence in the temple complex and its gardens. Perhaps your guard could accompany me and keep me safe."

It was true he had intended to show himself at this religious play. It was important, he felt, to have citizens see him as the general he would become. He looked as Asim's swollen belly and frowned. Yet he was not fond of having Asim by his side in her current condition. She would only forestall his mingling with the crowds. And among beautiful women, he thought. Additionally, Asim's body did not lend itself to a satisfying sexual encounter. The stoic mood she had adopted during his sadistic actions caused his pleasure to wane as well. Akar finally grunted his acquiescence.

Only the tune emanating from Akar's pursed lips broke the silence. At last, thought Asim, the gods have shown sympathy to me.

## Chapter Twenty-One

Pentawer had been visiting the wives of his father since he was a child. Some would tell engrossing stories of their own countries: of the foliage covering their land, of their customs, and unusual foods. To a boy, hearing of far away lands was as though traveling there himself. The wives loved him for asking questions of their homelands while listening with wide eyes only a child could possess. He had continued his visits to the Harem as he matured. Here he could be himself and not put on airs of Royalty. As an adult, he asked questions of their nations' laws and beliefs, of their treatment of women, and the care of their elders. This understanding of other people and traditions aided him if his father asked for diplomatic advice when meeting with other rulers. He believed this understanding would continue to serve the next Pharaoh, his brother Amonhirk.

Now he knew the truth of that belief. Amonhirk would neither require nor want his advice. He would be known in this Palace as one who once held the ear of a Pharaoh then callously tossed aside as Amonhirk's reign flourished without him. He would be treated as a Prince, doted upon by servants, and every whim met. In return he would no longer engage in details of state or thought provoking discussions with members of the Royal Council. The shattering of his dreams and all he hoped to become saddened him beyond belief. His mother and grandmother forced him to see the truth of his future yet he was not sure if he felt gratitude or simply a great emptiness. He only knew the rage he felt towards Amonhirk, the man who would steal his purpose in life.

Initially he was quite shocked at his grandmother's suggestion. Kill his father, the man he loved above all others? Outrageous. And yet as they spoke further he came to the same conclusion as they: he would be superfluous in this life, almost comical, if he did not attain the Throne. He was in accord with the two women and their solution and would see it through.

To this end, he and his mother paid a visit to the Harem. The women and children were overjoyed to see him. "You have always been such a dear boy," voiced one.

Ending play with his many half-siblings, discussion turned to the crowning of a new Pharaoh. Six wives joined them, eager to hear what Pentawer had to say. On the lives of his children, he said to them, and by the gods they honor he would never force them to leave this sanctuary. This would be their home as long as they desired it to be so. Some began crying with relief. Others bowed to him in gratitude and honor.

Queen Tiye had more news to share with the women. "You are acquainted with Pebekkamen, the Chief of the Chambers to Ramses III, are you not?" They nodded in assent. They were very familiar with him. It was by his tacit approval any message from the Harem was either accepted for delivery or deemed too radical to leave the Harem.

"He is now in agreement with us. If you wish to send letters or suggestions to your birth nation, he shall see to the delivery. The same is true in your receipt of messages. There shall be no scrutiny involved."

She did not mention to these women or Pentawer how she acquired him as an ally — her sexual favors had been the trade for his devotion. Indeed, she was successfully juggling both the Chief of Chambers and the Royal High Priest with less than holy pursuits for the past several weeks.

"We thought," continued the Queen, "you might wish to inform other family members in authoritative positions of our stand. They should be aware of the rise in trade prices, the probable increase of taxes, of the agreements Amonhirk shall not uphold, and your desire to see Pentawer upon the Throne."

The women were quite pleased. To think they might finally make uncensored exchanges with their family. It was more than they had hoped.

"My brother is the Commander of Nubian troops. I shall request his calculated interference among his countrymen," volunteered one wife.

"My brother sits upon the Throne in my home country. Surely this information is important to trade agreements. He shall know of this," said another.

Pentawer kissed each woman upon their wrist thanking them for their confidence and guaranteeing his promises to them. Mother and son left in regal fashion.

## Chapter Twenty-Two

It was a full day's journey to the location of the massive sporting event. These events were a chance to prove one's prowess to the sound of cheering crowds. While Thebes would enjoy players on stage for the tribute to Amun, these three days of athletic prowess were also dedicated to that magnificent god. Citizens from near and far away would attend both sets of festivities.

Akar would likely have made the ride here without the insistence of Queen Tiye. He, too, enjoyed these events that gave him the opportunity for good food, sports, and the chance to place a few bets on his favorite players. For him it was mere pastime, betting a small pittance at a time. Certainly not like his prey, Ari. He wondered at the weakness of the man's character to gamble his entire wealth away in such a tawdry manner.

He would begin on the morrow in search of the man. Tonight he would secure accommodations and a meal. If the man arrived today, he would certainly be here then. Perhaps, thought Akar, if I locate him on the first day of festivities, I would have the following day for my own enjoyment. It would make no difference to the Queen as long as he completed the job. He only needed the man's ring as proof.

In fact, he thought warming to the notion, I might postpone the murder until the third day. There was an off-chance the man might actually have some winnings upon his person. It would be a simple task to relieve him of those as well as the ring. Akar saw no reason why he should not come away with a fuller pouch. It would also confirm that the kill resulted from a robbery.

Once again the gods were with him. Akar saw Ari that very evening, seeking shelter before the festivities began early on the morrow. Akar was almost tempted to approach Ari as he wandered down the road. Akar could reacquaint himself with Ari as an old friend who just happened to be at the same event. Surely it would be more simple to observe his movements if Akar was at his side. He discarded that thought immediately. When the body was discovered, Akar would be remembered as a companion. He could not take a chance of capture or eventual connection to the Palace. That was unlikely, to be sure, yet life could be quite peculiar at times and the gods occasionally took vengeance in spiteful ways.

He began by searching out the most likely places Ari would frequent on the morrow. Asking a few relaxed questions he located drink stands that doubled as bet-takers. While several permanent taverns were operated in the town, those fragile stands quickly thrown together for these three days were more accommodating. It was brilliant: sell alcohol and take the wagers. If a man consumed enough strong beer, he might be convinced to bet upon anything.

He wandered among the many booths of people trading wares and then to the nearest temple. Many were gathered here, no doubt praying for healthy gains from their wagers. Fools, thought Akar. I have worked too hard for my wealth. Never would I whittle it away into someone else's hands for such a brainless pastime. There was little skill involved to bet upon the outcome of another's physical prowess. A bet was placed — one team lost, the other won and that was the extent of it. He preferred to bet upon himself and his skill with a sword or a knife. Winning or loosing on the battlefield involved ability and cleverness. If a soldier did not learn his trade or did not train until he dropped, he died. Simple.

His eyes slid over those penitents kneeling and bowing in prayer, hoping to spot his quarry. He turned to walk from the temple when he suddenly smiled. Ari stood and gathered his possessions preparing to leave the great room. Akar quickly dashed behind the nearest pillar, remembering his orders to remain unseen by Ari and anonymous to all others.

His feeling of elation began to ebb. Ari was here with three other men. This could be more problematic than he had believed. Drunk and boisterous, the four wandered the streets and sporting tents as one. He must wait until Ari had separated himself from the pack. Only the gods knew when that bit of luck would come his way.

He watched as the four men wandered away. They had made their pleas to their god and felt sure they would leave as winners. All Akar could do was to follow from a distance and hope Ari would part from the other three men. He required merely a few minutes alone with the man yet how many hours might he spend waiting for those minutes?

## Chapter Twenty-Three

Tonight was the much-heralded Play to the Glorious Amun held in the courtyard of the temple of Karnak. Live story-telling stage performances were popular throughout the world, although other countries told tales of a fictional type — love, loss, and conquests. The Egyptian performances were strictly of a religious nature, telling the tales of the gods and their glorious beginnings. The actors in tonight's play were well known and the evening was greatly anticipated by the citizens of Thebes. Asim was also excited by tonight's performance. She was not, however, concerned with the actors or their portrayals.

She would be using the time to search out Pentu. Her guard would be present, as Akar commanded, yet she hoped by meandering among other audience members and socializing with those from the Palace she could avoid any undue suspicion from the guard. Above all, she must keep her wanderings casual and remain in sight of her escort. If she did not see Pentu, she was certain Joba would be in attendance with one of his many female conquests.

She was going to be late if she did not hurry. The hour to leave was growing near and she was missing a sandal. She began rummaging through baskets, chiding herself for this tardiness on her part. Time is precious, she told herself; forget the sandals. Yet in her current clumsy state, those bits of cloth and straw helped maintain safe steps. Her final option was under the bed yet she hesitated. Akar was less than careful with his clothing, often tossing it anywhere he stood, expecting Asim to tidy up. She had recently shoved many of his clothes under the bed out of sight. Now she must poke and push his items around to locate the errant footwear. She detested touching anything that belonged to Akar yet she braced herself to search under his clothing. She had no choice but to get upon her hands and knees to search, not an easy task with her awkward belly. It was a most ungraceful maneuver.

After moving aside a shirt and belt, she saw the shoe clearly. Ah, the gods are with me, she thought. As she reached for it, she saw a small decorated box and stretched out her arm for it. Pulling it towards her, she heard the sound of small objects rattling within. Certainly not what she was seeking, she thought, yet decidedly interesting. Could it be something of value? Might there be enough wealth in this box of Akar's to see her freedom with Pentu?

The wooden box was not tightly fastened and the small latch was easy to lift. Curiosity got the better of her. Opening it, she saw many tiny nodules that looked like dried up beans. She picked up a couple and moved them around in the palm of her left hand with her right index finger. What could these be, she wondered. And why would Akar keep them secreted in such a manner? Looking into the box again she noticed some were a bit softer and not as dried as those she held in her hand. She picked one up and closely examined it. Her eyes opened wide with horror when she realized what Akar's collection box held. She quickly tossed them back into the box and agitatedly wiped her hands against her clothing. She reclosed the lid fiercely as though she would become tainted by its contents.

Asim fought back the bile reaching into her throat and sat back upon her heels. Demon, she thought with revulsion. The man with whom I share this abode is truly a Demon. Those poor women. What else did he do to them? One or two looked 'fresh' she thought with a shiver. Was he yet maiming women in such a manner? How is it he has never been accused of such depravity? He has risen through the Pharaoh's most trusted of men and yet these . . . these *things* he keeps as treasures or fond memories. She was careful to shove the box to its exact former position when she noticed more closely its placement: directly under her head as she slept. Was it his private joke or was it something more sinister? Would a piece of her join this box one day? She placed her hand upon her belly. I cannot raise this child in the same house as this demon. Speaking to her unborn baby she said, "If I cannot attain freedom for us both, I shall somehow provide safety for you, my sweet one."

There was no further time to contemplate the many questions running through her. She would miss the opportunity to see Joba or Pentu if she continued to dawdle here. Her escort was knocking upon the door. Taking a deep calming breath, she approached the young guard with a forced smile and thanked him for taking the time to see to her safety. She must arouse no suspicion of her plans to him. She apologized for her clumsiness as she stumbled upon a pebble yet he steadied her and did not chide her, as Akar would have. He explained his wife had recently given birth to a baby boy. He understood her discomfort and promised to walk at an easy pace for her. She smiled and thanked him again. Hopefully she could loose him with her prepared excuses to complete what she must.

As per Asim's wishes, they were early to the event. She had used her pregnancy as an excuse to find a safe place in which to enjoy the show. Apparently many others had her same thought. As they approached the enormous temple complex, the streets became more crowded with people, carts, animals transporting the revelers, and various food stands. While she had hoped to quickly part ways with her companion, in truth she was grateful to have him near as he grasped her elbow to guide her through the throng.

Most visitors were placing stools or woven mats around the great courtyard upon which to sit and Asim with her guard did the same. She was grateful she would not be forced to stand upon her swollen feet for the lengthy performance. The smells of spices and hot spitting meats assailed her nostrils while voices of happy visitors echoed against the mammoth stonewall.

Sitting comfortably, she began to look around the crowd to search for anyone she might know. Several mats away to her right sat women she recognized who served the Queen. "Sir," she began to her guard, "I see some friends nearby. I would very much like to converse with them if you think it safe. I shall not stay long and there is much time before the actors begin." She pointed to the spot where her friends sat. "I shall remain in your view for the entirety."

Looking to where she pointed, he agreed yet insisted upon escorting her. That action was not planned on her part yet she knew it would look odd to object. He was a decent man and only performing his duty, she reminded herself. Standing with his assistance, she waved and called to her friends. She began stepping over legs and other body parts thrust in her path towards her acquaintances. She preferred traveling to them rather than they to her. The conversation she wished to conduct was private.

The ladies stood as she approached, commenting on her condition amid hugs and congratulations. They aided her to the ground and Asim spoke again to her most attentive guard. "Truly, I am safe here among friends," she said attempting to have him leave her side, "Perhaps you should return to our space. I would not want our location or belongings to be pilfered." He agreed yet not without eliciting a promise for her to signal him when she wished to return. As he left, the women began gossiping and laughing.

One young lady asked Asim about her current life. They all knew of Akar and wondered if he was a great lover. Asim merely gave a shy smile and shrugged her shoulders. What could she tell them? The truth? This was neither the place nor time.

"I noticed Akar had several appointments with Queen Tiye of late," said one pretty lady. Asim looked at her with wonderment and another lady nodded in assent. "Oh, do not worry Asim. It is not for physical gratification. They meet in her private audience room. The meetings never last long enough for anything other than conversing." The ladies laughed and Asim smiled at the small joke. They were assuming she would be jealous of another woman occupying Akar's time for sexual pleasures when, in truth, she would welcome such a dalliance. Anything to remove him from the bed they shared and that box underneath it. She shuddered at the memory of it then redirected her attention to her friends.

The observation made of such conversations made Asim question further, "Why do the two of them meet?" It was the lady's turn to shrug her own shoulders and mention, "I heard he shall be promoted in rank although it might be rumor. Yet their meeting is quite odd, do you not think? I cannot find reasoning why Queen Tiye need converse with him. She does not promote soldiers and certainly not in private."

"Decidedly it is strange. Yet the Royal Family is often strange," another young lady finished with a laugh.

Asim stayed for a moment longer before she inquired if they had seen Joba in the crowds. If anyone knew Joba it would be this clutch of pretty women. "Ah, Joba," said one woman while licking her lips to the amusement of the others. "He is quite a man, is he not?" It was apparent they had all enjoyed Joba's talents at one time and they gleefully added details of his prowess and his physical attributes with which he had been blessed. "I last witnessed him near that small potted fig tree," she answered as she pointed behind her, "with his arm around a woman's waist. Naturally." They all chortled good-naturedly. "He may yet be there as he seemed in no hurry to leave. The girl seemed the obliging type."

"As we once were," said another with a large smile. More giggling ensued.

Thanking them and wishing them well, she rose and caught the attention of her guard. He was about to rise when she signaled him to be seated and pointed to the area behind her as if she had found more friends. To make this pantomime complete she turned around and waved to her imaginary friends. Once again, she began to tread upon bundles containing food, children's toys, and the haphazard arms and legs. To forestall the guard from leaping to her service she moved as quickly as her protruding stomach allowed.

Finally reaching the elusive fig tree, she searched for Joba. Please, please, she prayed, let him be near. Turning her neck around and around she searched the ever-growing crowds. Nothing. She concentrated her search upon the people planted upon the ground. Still nothing. A braying laughter in the opposite corner caught several revelers' attention and she could not help but look to that area as well. Thank you gods, she said quietly. In the midst of two lovely women sat Joba. He apparently said something humorous, eliciting donkey-like laughter from one lady.

She made her way to the three-some and plopped down unceremoniously next to Joba's elbow. Turning to see who had joined his little party, Joba was caught by surprise.

"By the gods," he said realizing who the interloper was, "Asim. Where have you been? Pentu has been wild with fear and concern. We have been searching for you these past months." This was said to her with a great smile upon his face until he noticed her belly. His face became one of surprise and shock.

"Please, Joba," began Asim. "I must speak with you. Privately."

"Ladies, another time perhaps. It has been a most enjoyable visit. My sincere gratitude to you each." With that he kissed each one on their delicate wrists explaining, "I must speak to my Old Friend." Asim smiled at his stressing of the last two words. It would not aid his cause with the ladies for them to assume her full belly was a result of his actions.

Prior to telling her story, she asked after Pentu. "He is quite healthy," replied Joba, "yet most anxious about you. He is in Set-Maat today ensuring all is well with the employees' pay. He shall return on the morrow."

She interrupted him when he would speak further, apologizing for her rudeness. She did not have time on her side, she told her friend. She spoke quickly, telling him everything succinctly. He was not surprised to hear the baby's father was Pentu yet his face was filled with rage when he learned the actions of Akar and the Queen. "I assure you, my dear friend, I had no hand in the matter. The Queen gave me to him. I never returned to my own chamber nor had the opportunity to speak to Pentu. What am I to do? Akar is violent, sadistic. Something is amiss with him and his actions against women." She told him of the box under the bed. "He promised Queen Tiye he would see to my well being and a healthy birth yet afterwards I know not where his intentions lie."

To Joba's credit, he had remained silent during her tale yet felt the desire to find Akar and thrash him viciously. "Are you yet in service within the Royal Palace? Yes? Ah, the Harem. A fine station in which to be assigned. The women of the Harem shall surely help you. They are very like-minded and charming. Or so I am told," he finished with a mischievous grin. "Go to them. Explain your circumstances."

Asim shook her head. "I cannot. If Akar discovers I have revealed anything of him to others, my safety could be at risk. I am not allowed to hide within the Harem. It is only my position, not my home."

Joba contemplated this for a moment. If the man was as brutal as Asim hinted, she might indeed be in jeopardy. "When do you give birth? Soon? Excellent, that is excellent. And Akar shall be absent for five days. Perhaps the time shall be upon you while he is gone. Upon the fourth day you should do more." She looked quizzically at him. "When you are at the Harem, you might feign whatever it is you women do," he waved both hands frantically at her abdomen, slightly at a loss for words, "when you start the birthing process. The clutching of one's stomach, the bending over in pain while crying out: all of those movements. That could provide you the needed time until the baby truly. . . um . . . arrives."

"Stay at the Harem until I give birth. Is that what you suggest?" He nodded with great relief that she had grasped his meaning. The need to discuss womanly matters had been difficult for him. It could be possible, she thought. She had been experiencing a frequent tightening of her belly and the baby was most decidedly positioned lower than a few days past. "What then, Joba? Again I say to you that I cannot live at the Harem. And I shall never allow Akar to harm my child," she finished while holding her belly protectively.

He touched her arm slightly. "Let us take one detail as it presents itself, shall we? First we must contend with the birth. The rest we shall decide when the need arises. I suggest you find the Royal Consort Tamin. Do you know her?" Asim nodded. "She is calming in any situation and exceedingly kind. Confide in her completely. She can be trusted, I swear. If memory serves, I believe she is currently experiencing the same upcoming event as you." He pointed to her abdomen.

"By your doing?" she asked coyly.

"Decidedly not. Although she is quite tempting I am fully aware of my boundaries," he laughed.

She smiled at him gratefully. "I knew you would have solutions for me, Joba. You have always been a true friend. And now I must ask of you another favor. I must speak to Pentu. I wish to meet him in the Palace Temple courtyard on the morrow's evening. He knows of the precise place and time. Are you able to get such a message to him when he returns? Yet I beg you, he is not to know our full conversation. I would tell him all face to face."

"I swear I shall safely deliver your request with certain facts eliminated. I shall tell him you are alive and well and nothing more."

"I have no words to express my gratitude, Joba. You are my most trusted friend. Now I must leave. My guard is surely suspicious or searching for me at this point. I have been absent too long." Joba helped her to her feet. As she turned to make the return walk she turned to him and said with a smile, "My sincere apologies for interrupting what would have been a most enjoyable evening for you."

Joba smiled back. "I assure you it was no hardship. There are many beautiful ladies here who would welcome my companionship."

Laughing, Asim began her laborious path back to the guard. She was a mere five groups from her guard when she saw him standing and looking about frantically. She called out to him and saw utter relief cross his face.

"I offer my great apologies to you. Our conversation grew long and I became confused with the correct direction. It is very easy to become turned around among this crowd. I am quite well, I assure you." She did not want him to tell Akar of her lengthy absence. To do so would not bode well for either of them. With this in mind she said, "Please do not worry about your position with Akar. I know you were ordered to be at my side throughout the evening. Yet my tardiness away was entirely due to my own confusion. I swear by the gods, I shall say nothing to Akar of the error on your part." The poor man was so grateful he nearly knelt before her.

With her task completed she could enjoy tonight's entertainment at ease. Upon the new day she would see Pentu. Would he be pleased with the child? What would his reaction be to Akar as her keeper? He could discard her knowing she shared a bed with someone he hated. For now, she must push such questions aside and have this pleasant respite from her home life and the Palace. The gods would provide her with the answers she sought when they deemed the time was true. They could not be rushed in their plans for her.

## Chapter Twenty-Four

Cataloguing the supplies sent to Set-Maat had been time consuming, forcing him to stay the night in his town of birth. It had been a joy to see friends and sleep within his own bed. Yet he missed Asim by his side. He could not recall a time when he did not love her. He lay upon his pillow for hours staring at the sky from his window, imagining how their life could be in his village. The home was small yet large enough for a family. He was the second son of five and they had all lived and played within these walls. Perhaps, he thought, to please Asim I could have a second story added. He was one of the lucky few to not have abodes stacked upon each other as kindling.

Pentu believed he could retrieve his former position among the tombs. If not a foreman, he was skilled at masonry and reliefs. His wants were few and they could be happy here. Although, he thought with alarm, perhaps Asim's wants were many. She had, after all, been in the Queen's service since her youth. She was familiar with softer garments upon her skin and fine jewelry around her neck. She might be shocked at this simple mud-brick domicile.

Your thoughts lead to nonsense, he chided himself. Had he not described his life here in detail to his beloved? And had she not shared his dream of living here by his side? No, she was willing to sacrifice all she had known to be his wife. The word had a pleasant feel to it as he rolled it around his mouth: Wife. The gods had given his life a distinctive twist to the one he imagined. They had unlocked the doors to the Royal Palace and opened Asim's heart to his own. He listened to insects chirping and heard palms rustling, thinking how desperately he wished to share these evening sounds with her.

Providing he could locate her. Joba had heard nothing of her well-being. No one had seen her in the Palace for months. He knew she was yet alive, felt it within his being. The gods could not play such a cruel trick to remove her now. He was most anxious to return to Thebes and continue his search for her.

Although he began his trek early enough, Pentu returned to the Royal Palace later than he had hoped. He traveled upon a much-used hauling cart, an equally used donkey, and a man who saw no need for speed.  The man had left at the height of an argument with his wife and he rejected Pentu's plea for urgency, which would only throw the driver back into the family squabble sooner than he wished.  Pentu explained his reason for haste yet the man cared naught.  He was clearly more terrified of his wife than the Pharaoh.  With the conveyance, man, and animal conspiring against him Pentu did not reach the Palace entrance until midday.

Pentu's first bit of Palace business began with The Pharaoh's Royal Court Minister of Proceedings.  This man held the daily schedule of all court appointments and meetings with Ramses.  By the luck of the gods, Pharaoh Ramses would not require Pentu for any appointments at this time.  He was positioned upon the calendar for a full council meeting after the noon meal.  He had ample time for his second conversation of the day with Joba.

Pentu had been concerned he would have difficulty locating his friend yet as he approached his own chamber, the very man he sought was knocking insistently upon his door.  "Joba, I am here."

Joba turned grabbed both of Pentu's shoulders and said, "I expected you hours ago."  As Pentu began his tale of the donkey, cart, and unhappily married man, Joba cut in.  "No matter.  My friend I have news.  I have seen her.  Asim is well."

"She is alive?  And well, you say.  Tell me all, quickly."

Joba told only what he had promised: her struggle in the toilet rooms and her current assignment in the Harem.  Nothing was said of her co-habitation with Akar or the impending birth.  The tale was no less lengthy with these exclusions, however.  Pentu voiced concern to learn of Asim's banishment and the anger of the Queen. "Queen Tiye has wrought her vengeance, my friend.  I believe she has dismissed her from thought entirely.  Asim would meet with you tonight.  She said you would know the place and appointed time."

Pentu nodded happily.  "Yes, I know whereof she speaks.  My friend, you are loyal to us both and we commit the same to you.  We can never repay your kindness.  I shall keep you informed."

As they parted Joba said, "Pentu.  Asim has had much sorrow of late.  I urge you to remember this as you speak with her tonight." Pentu had little time to inquire into this cryptic warning as Joba was nearly at the end of the corridor.

He had never suffered through such a prolonged and anxious day.  His many duties did nothing to urge the daylight hours ahead faster. The goddess of love was tugging at his heart as a prank. The quicker he moved throughout the day, the slower time seemed to pass.

Finally, the sun had retreated from the sky and the stars had awakened. The Palace was nestled in slumber and the moonlight guided him to the temple courtyards. He heard her as he entered their favored cloistered area of palms and ferns. To hear her voice set his heart racing. The moon shone upon her lovely face and he held her face in his hands to kiss her.

"Pentu, my darling. I have missed you so." To his surprise, she stepped back before he could wrap his arms around her. "Please. Stay where you stand. I have some distressing news. I tell you now I do not hold you to your promises. Only know that I love you more than I believed possible." As he once more stepped closer, she retreated into a beam of moonlight and stood in profile. He looked at her with concern and confusion until she dropped one hand to her burgeoning waist.

"You are with child," he said in wonderment. Then with a full grin he exclaimed with glee, "*My* child. We are to have a baby. I have no words, I am so overjoyed." With that he reached around her expanded waist and held her close. "This is a most wonderful turn of events. We shall be married now and raise our family." As he said these last words she began to cry and stepped away from him yet again.

"There is more to tell, Pentu. Much more." Wrapping her arms around herself and bowing her head, she began her tale from the first moment Queen Tiye had banished her to the toilet rooms until last evening's conversation with Joba. As she spoke Pentu became more livid with rage and clenched his hands when she mentioned Akar's name.

"I shall kill him," he finally remarked with ferocity. "Akar shall not see the light of another day upon his face."

"Please, you cannot. He is favored by not only Pharaoh Ramses but by Queen Tiye as well. The Queen and Akar have had several closed meetings of late. I believe she has promised him a rise in position. I have no reasoning as to how or why she is able to do so yet he has become a powerful man.

"Please, Pentu, this is my punishment and I do not wish you to become lost to me with punishment of your own. Ramses would truly become enraged if Akar were harmed. I cannot express my deepest apologies to you. I no longer expect your love yet I swear to you this is your child I carry. I pray you may find it in your heart to forgive me."

"I am fully aware of the parentage, my sweet. You have not committed a misdeed against me. You have no cause to beg my forgiveness. It is I who should be on my knees before you. I did not find you in time to spare you this pain. In truth, I was not the man who came to your aid; it was Joba. To him I have sworn my fidelity for all time. To you, even if I walk upon these sands longer than our Great Pharaoh, I shall never absolve myself for your mistreatment.

"Yet while I happily await the birth of our child I cannot forgive Akar or Queen Tiye. I shall bide my time as you request, my love. Do not think me incapable of revenge upon those two miscreants. I swear by the gods Akar shall see death at my hands.

"As for the Queen, I shall not rest until I have toppled her. I shall find any misdeeds she may commit, any slights she offers. By what ever means necessary we shall see her separated from the Pharaoh's protection."

Asim looked troubled at this merciless attitude yet Pentu took her hands in his to calm her. "Block it from your thoughts, my love. Do not concern yourself with either of them. For now, my only concern is for your safety and that of our child. Perhaps Joba's suggestion to seek aid in the Harem is sound. Until Akar returns, we shall make the most of our time and devise your protection and our escape. If you shall have me."

In response, Asim began to sob again and bury her head into his shoulder, whispering repeatedly how much she loved him.

## Chapter Twenty-Five

Akar swore softly at the gods yet apparently not softly enough. Several passers-by looked at him in horror at his blasphemy. With his foul mood, he nearly cursed back at them yet forced himself to temper that response. His orders had been anonymity while in this town. If the slightest hint over the demise of Ari should reach the Royal Palace, Akar would suffer severely. He did not wish to loose the current status he now enjoyed.

Yet he had wasted time watching Ari who was seldom apart from his companions. Whether the other men were friends or financial lenders Akar knew not. Nor did he care. His only concern was to complete the deed and find enjoyment for the remainder of his time here. Each evening he honed his long bladed knife yet had not the opportunity to test its sharpness. He was determined to resolve this intolerable situation.

As Akar stood by, he witnessed Ari loose yet again in a wager made. The fool! If Akar did not proceed swiftly, this idiot's last possession would be his family ring. And Akar must have that particular piece of jewelry. Queen Tiye insisted upon it as proof of his successful undertaking. At the rate Ari's debts were mounting, he would have little choice but to bet — and probably loose — that very ring. Akar sighed. Following Ari about town was leading Akar only to his wit's end. He must devise another plan.

Further sporting events were not scheduled until the following morn. Night had fallen and crowds were considerably thinner making his prey easier to find. Ari and the three men were standing under a crooked tent, one of the few establishments open at this late hour to enjoy a final beverage. Ari had obviously over imbibed as he stumbled out of view to relieve himself at the rear of the tent. When his three companions stumbled away, Akar decided to strike before he came to his senses. This was against all he had been ordered yet he pursued his impulse.

Akar came around the back corner of the tent as nonchalantly as he could and greeted Ari with over enthusiastic surprise. "By the gods, it is my good friend Ari. It has been some time, has it not? Since you invited me to the home of your friend for games, if memory serves me. I provided you with the stake to enter, do you recall?"

Ari turned and lowered his garment looking unsteady and bleary-eyed. It was evident by the dubious look in Ari's eyes the man did not remember much at the moment. His face suddenly cleared and he exclaimed, "Ah, yes. My good friend. You were my benefactor on that evening. The door would have been slammed in my face had it not been for you." Then he guffawed loudly. "Although if truth be known perhaps I should never have entered that domicile. My losses outweighed my wins. As they do now, I am pained to admit." He leaned toward Akar and placed one arm sloppily over his shoulder. "Tell me, my good and clever friend," he said while laughing at his small quip. Akar could smell the wine upon his breath yet stood staunchly in place. "Do you have any suggestions for me on the morrow's games? I fear I am out of ideas."

"Perhaps," replied Akar. "Shall I offer you a beer while we discuss matters?"

"Ah, that is most excellent. I must introduce you to my friends, my very agreeable friends with the most excellent taste. And wealth." In a conspirator's whisper he said to Akar, "Best not mention their wealth. It would be rude. We must behave as gentlemen. Our station in life dictates that, you know." Looking Akar directly in the face he explained further while wagging a finger in the air. "My father informed me of that. He so informed me and I have never forgotten his words."

He looked around in a daze for the other men. "I do not see them. My affluent friends must have retired to their beds. They would not abandon me completely as I owe them the last three wagers, you see," and he began to wobble around the corner to the beverage tent that had by now closed for the night.

"Ari," began Akar recklessly. "I believe the gods have led me to you. I happen to have something for you, you see."

"For me? How good of you. What might it be? Whatever it is I cannot repay you," he finished laughing uproariously.

He is much too loud, thought Akar as he looked about. He was pleased to see they were the only two upon the deserted streets. I must do this now no matter the cost. He spoke into Ari's ear. "It is not from me. It is from Queen Tiye."

"Queen Tiye? Indeed. Ah, she has not forgotten me, that delicious little tart." He laughed at his wit, slow though it may be, before succumbing to curiosity. "Now, tell me. What is it you bring from her? Show me."

"This," and with that one word, Akar thrust the finely honed blade into the soft underside of Ari's jaw until hilt met bone. For a brief moment as Akar held the man upright he saw an incredulous look in Ari's eyes before they became blank and lifeless.

Lowering him gently to the sand, he tried to release the damnable ring from the finger. It would not budge. He was out of time and could not afford decency. He sliced through the finger with ease. Taking the forefinger, he dashed off to his bed for a restful sleep. The deed was done. He would enjoy his remaining time here before returning to Thebes. As he drifted into slumber he briefly remembered a comment by Ari. In essence he had called the Queen of Egypt a harlot.

## Chapter Twenty-Six

Asim and Pentu had not slumbered last night and while the time had been enjoyable, she was paying for it with extreme exhaustion this morn.

Under the bright stars last evening, they had discussed the quandary in which they found themselves. Akar was to return soon and there would be no further assignations with Pentu in the gardens.

"My most pressing concern is your safety, my love," said Pentu, "Yet I have another solution. Let us flee, travel to Set-Maat and have a life we can call our own. We can do so now, this moment. Never shall you have to look Akar in the eyes again or serve other women. Please, Asim, see the wisdom in this notion."

She shook her head. "I cannot. I am much to close to the birth. Additionally, we have voiced oaths to serve our Pharaoh and his Royal Palace. Akar shall leave no stone unturned to find me, I promise you that. My flight and your 'coincidental' disappearance would not only be suspicious, but easily reasoned. Akar, his subordinates, and the Pharaoh's Royal Guards would be at our heels. The first area searched would be Set-Maat. It would place danger upon the town as well."

"Your nature is most generous, my love. So be it. I do not wish upon us a life of pursuit and hiding. We shall bide our time with that thought."

He, too, had seen the wisdom in Joba's suggestion and said as much. "Perhaps the Royal Consort Tamin is the key to your safety. If she provides you the aid we hope for, you shall be confined to the Harem for some time. You would be protected among the women yet how shall we communicate? I must know if your request of the Consort had been met with favorably. I would be sorely tempted to storm the Harem if I thought otherwise."

Asim agreed; it was indeed the fly in their ointment. "Messages from the Harem are carefully reviewed before they are passed to the guards for distribution yet only from the Royal Women. Several handmaidens sleep in the Palace servant quarters and are permitted to leave the Harem. Perhaps one might be induced to bring a word to you."

"That would be much too risky. We cannot chance a connection between us."

"What of Joba? Perhaps he might act as our middleman. Would he object?" asked Asim.

"He would not object. However, I do not wish to see him become entangled in risk, remote as it may be. If Consort Tamin agrees to your request, perhaps you could send a vague message to him by way of a handmaiden. A friend of yours."

"What if she does not know Joba?"

"My love, all the ladies in the Royal Palace know of him. Joba ensures as much," said Pentu with a smile. "Now as to the message." He considered many various statements from Asim to Joba without success. "It would seem any message from a Harem servant to a guard for the Royal Audience Room is not without suspicion. I am at a loss."

"True. It is more difficult than I had thought." Mulling this over for a moment, she finally asked, "What if she inquired after his mother? A simple phrase would be best. 'Has your mother recovered?' Is that appropriate?"

"Excellent. I shall inform him on the morrow. If he relays such a message to me, I shall know all is well with you. Following that assurance, I shall do all I can to release you from the Harem and Akar."

With this conversation in Asim's memory, her foremost purpose this early morn was to seek out Consort Tamin. While she was a member of the Harem wives and a Royal Consort to the Pharaoh, her title was not Queen. That was reserved for his first two wives. Asim did not know her personally yet did indeed recognize her. If Joba gave testimony of her compassion, than it was so. She trusted Joba implicitly.

Asim found her sitting by the pond playing with children. Older than many of the consorts, she was lovely with a round, innocent face. Her eyes were friendly and crinkled at the corners when she was brought to a smile. Bowing low before her, Asim spoke with nervousness. "Royal Consort Tamin, I am Asim, a servant here in the Harem. I offer many apologies for my impertinence yet I wish dearly to speak with you. I have a close friend, Joba of the Royal Audience Room Guards, who suggested you might offer aid to me."

"I have seen you about. Yes, I know who you are. You are with the large guard, are you not?" With head yet bowed, Asim nodded. "I see you are in the same clumsy condition as I," she said with a laugh. "When is your birthing time?" Asim told her when she believed her baby would arrive. "I, too, am close to that date." Asim looked in wonderment at the woman. Tamin laughed good-naturedly. "I admit I am much larger in girth than you. This shall be my third birth and I have never been so rotund. This baby is quite a miracle from the gods as I was thought to be beyond childbearing years. Our Pharaoh is quite pleased to welcome another child into his world.

"One Royal Physician suggested I might be birthing two babies. That would truly be an event to celebrate, would it not? Yet I tell you in confidence — I believe my size is merely due to my overwhelming love for good food. Your first, I assume?" As Asim nodded again, Tamin put out her hand for assistance in rising from the low stool. "As Egyptians, we seem to be very fond of these low seats. Clearly it was not a woman heavy with child who designed them." Again she laughed. Asim smiled, taking an immediate liking to the Royal woman. "Come; let us retreat to the corner with the great palms. It is cooler."

As Tamin became comfortably seated, she said, "Now, tell me of what you wish to speak."

Asim began speaking, quickly and with detail, often needing to backtrack and insert a fact she had forgotten. Through it all, Tamin occasionally interjected a question yet remained quiet for the most part. She repeated Joba's suggestion to seek out Tamin and beg for safety. When Asim finished, She found herself exhausted from the effort of the narration. Relating her shameful circumstances to a woman she had just me had been difficult.

Sitting thoughtfully for several minutes the Royal Consort finally spoke. "Have you been examined by a physician? No? Then we must summon one to our chambers for that purpose." Leaning forward a little she tapped Asim on her hand. Those friendly eyes turned shrewd as she said slowly and with great significance, "I believe it is quite possible he shall suggest you remain here. I should also imagine you are much too delicate for the daily trek from Thebes and back." Staring intently into Asim's eyes and holding her hand tighter she continued, "In fact, it is highly likely you might place yourself and your child at great risk if you were not to remain here in complete rest. You should be surrounded by women who have experienced your same condition."

Leaning back in the seat and with a great smile upon her face she said, "Of course we cannot truly know this until my favorite physician has paid you a call. With his written rendering upon your condition, no one — not even a mate," she said pointedly, "would have the ability to remove you from our sanctuary. Why, it is entirely possible that after the birth our Physician of Royal Infants might deem it best for you and the child to continue with a prolonged confinement among us. That learned and good physician never chances the safety of mother and child for someone as inconsequential as a man." Tamin's eye were sparkling mischievously as she asked Asim, "Do you not agree with me, my dear?" Asim began to weep, nodding her head and interjecting her gratitude between her blubbers. "Then it is settled," declared Tamin.

"For now, sit here in the cool shade until our physician arrives. I shall request his presence and inform my sisters of your stay. Akar returns on the morrow, correct? Excellent. I shall have an official message sent to him that evening informing him of your unfortunate decline into poor health thereby necessitating a physician's care. Oh, and non-Royal visitors to our Harem are strictly forbidden." Asim assisted Tamin once again in her rise and watched the magnificent woman walk slowly away to organize Asim's stay.

## Chapter Twenty-Seven

Akar returned the previous evening and sought an audience with Queen Tiye. He completed his task, he stated upon entering her domain, and presented her with the familiar crested ring of Ari. Dried blood was yet affixed to it and she shuddered in revulsion yet accepted it gladly.

She wondered slightly — yet caring little— at the unusual mood of Akar. He did not linger to request further payment: uncommon for the man. Their business was concluded in a matter of minutes and the man left in haste with a scowl upon his face. No matter. Ari was dead and she need no longer worry over his treachery. She clenched her fists and cursed under her breath. Even now, after he had betrayed her, she could yet feel his warmth. The thought of him brought familiar tingles to her body and she wondered if she might ever experience such love again.

With a heavy sigh, she turned her attention to other matters. Today she had received by messenger the anticipated pouch from her mother. Reaching inside Tiye drew out a beautiful necklace composed of two alternating beads of amethyst and lapis. A large scarab beetle carved from a piece of amethyst was centered within the double strand. Deep purple flashed within when turned to the sunlight. It was a most beautiful and unusual bit of stone.

Shooing away her servant girl the Queen began to carefully inspect the beetle. Her mother had messengered a magnificent piece of jewelry. The wings were intricately carved and each leg was individually created of gold to make the whole quite an enviable necklace.

Her mother had never before sent a gift to her daughter and this was no exception. Tiye realized this was more than elegant jewelry. She knew this center stone must open in some manner. Inside she would place the cache of narcotic intended for the Pharaoh. Naturally her mother did not include instructions in the pouch thereby protecting its secret from prying eyes. Yet it was maddening to poke and push upon it to no avail.

Turning it over she squinted her eyes searching for a clasp. Nothing. Then she ran her fingers along the sides hoping to feel a pressing point. There seemed to be none. Tracing her fingertip around it once more she felt a nearly invisible seam around the sides. So, it was not one piece of stone after all, she thought. "This is becoming exciting," she said. "Rather like a puzzle game."

Next she pushed and twisted at the head of the scarab. It never moved. Then she began to tap each leg, finally attempting to bend each one without breakage. As she did so with the lowermost leg, she heard a small click and the winged section swung away from the body. Peering closer at the interior she saw the mechanism — a small hinge located at the base of the beetle. It was made of gold like the legs and Tiye marveled at the complexity of such a small trinket. She snapped the lid closed and opened it repeatedly until she need only feel the piece to find its catch. Inside she would place the drug intended for the Pharaoh. She could easily obtain it from the Junior Magician she had wound around her finger.

"I shall wear it tonight at the evening meal," she thought aloud. "A piece this large shall surely gain attention. It would be best to have questions asked tonight rather than the evening I plan to utilize the contents."

The evening of the Pharaoh's demise was quickly approaching. For many days, she had been planning the finer details for the feast in which to honor his reign. She relied upon the habits of Ramses to overindulge in both drink and food. She would instruct servants to serve a more intoxicating blend of wines and exceedingly sweet final courses. Ramses had a penchant for sweets that, coincidentally, made him thirstier for wine.

Tonight would be a test for the scarab necklace and any undue attention it might bring. "No one must suspect it is any more than a gift from my sweet loving mother," she said in mockery. At least that is the lie she would relate to any who asked.

## Chapter Twenty-Eight

Akar stomped out from Queen Tiye's chamber in a vicious mood. He had been angry upon entering and even more so now. So angry, he failed to remember his planned conversation with the Queen. On his journey from the sporting event Akar had thought out the entire exchange he would have with her.

First, he planned to test the Queen's reaction by relating Ari's personal description to her. She, naturally, would begin by asking how her name was introduced into the conversation between the two men. She would then remind him of her command to commit this kill unobtrusively. Akar would merely shrug and smile, taunting her into further speech. She might ask why he had initiated their meeting. She might also ask for further comments made by the dead man. This last would be her telling question. Why concern herself with the comments of a stranger if she held no fear? Naturally he would be forthcoming to her inquiries, perhaps even embellish upon Ari's remark.

She would have difficulties denying what Akar had long suspected — her prior acquaintance with Ari. Akar knew it to be the truth: the dialogue with Ari established it. He considered himself adept at analyzing people. That talent had propelled him far in this life. The fear would be present in her eyes, no matter how haughty she might act. Yes, he had the complete conversation designed in his thoughts.

Yet, as carefully as he had prepared the entire dialogue, he remained silent. This was the fault of Asim, he reasoned with anger. He could have secured further wealth from Queen Tiye if he had his wits about him. Instead, he had engaged in a superficial conversation with her and stormed from her chambers.

It had been a day's hot journey from the sports event. The sun was past its peak upon his arrival at the house in Thebes. Asim's duties in the Harem had long ended this day, yet his abode was empty. His instructions had been clear to her — duties in the Harem during the day, home at nightfall. He had been far too lenient in his teachings of late and his wife must learn a lesson tonight. He decided he should not have accepted the wretched pregnant girl from Queen Tiye, conveniently forgetting it was he who had demanded

Asim. "I swore a healthy birth to Queen Tiye which I shall honor. Yet upon its birth, I shall send it far away. Far enough so Asim shall never find it. I do not want the cries of an infant and the coddling of its mother to disrupt my life. Asim shall soon forget. If she does not, I shall force her to do so." Yet he must first find the defiant girl.

As he stood in the center of the abode, a small knock came upon the door. Flinging it open he was confronted with the insignia of a Royal Harem Guard. He had a verbal message, the man informed Akar. Due to a sudden complication in her pregnancy, Asim had been ordered by the Royal Consort Tamin and the Elder Royal Physician to remain within the confines of the Harem chambers. This position would be maintained until the birth and, depending upon the new mother's health, perhaps longer.

Akar was furious. How dare a mere woman, Royal Consort to the Pharaoh or not, inflict such an order upon his house. Did she not know his own status with the Pharaoh? Hollering at the man upon his stoop proved useless as he was merely fulfilling orders of his own. Finally he instructed the man to bring a reply to the Royal Consort. "Tell her Akar shall arrive later this eve to retrieve Asim. I am first obligated to another Royal appointment."

This, then, was the mood in which he arrived and exited Queen Tiye's chambers. Now he stomped angrily through the Palace garden to the entrance of the Harem structure.

Two Royal Harem Guards stood at attention, flanking the official entrance to the living quarters of Ramses' many wives. Bringing himself up to his full impressive height, he demanded of them, "I wish to see the Royal Consort Tamin. Immediately. Tell her Akar, the man of Asim, is here."

One guard looked at Akar with pretentiousness, replying, "Her Royal Consort Tamin is unavailable to the general populace," he said insultingly.

"Unavailable? I am Captain of the Royal Guards to the Pharaoh. I am not to be dismissed in this manner. I insist upon retrieving Asim this very night."

"I shall inform her of your attendance. Perhaps I may bring you a message." With that he turned upon his heel and entered the sanctum to inform The Chief to Ramses Chambers of this man's presence who would then inform Consort Tamin of the situation.

The entire process would be put in reverse should the wife have a message to be relayed.

The second guard moved to block the doorway, staring straight ahead, never flinching when Akar took exception to this compromise. "What is the delay? I shall not wait at this door all night." The second guard remained staunch in his assignment, looking over Akar's head as though he were invisible.

Akar paced back and forth, waiting impatiently for the first guard. After he had nearly walked a crevice into the mud-brick floor, the first guard exited the domicile. "I am to repeat to you a message from her Royal Consort to the Pharaoh, Tamin. The Royal Physician's examination stands. The servant Asim shall remain within the guarded and protected Harem unit. Visitors other than the Royal Family are strictly forbidden within these walls. Furthermore, Asim and her baby shall receive excellent medical care. They shall be healthy and safe during their duration of confinement."

No amount of threats, screams, or bribes could sway these two men from their duties. "I shall speak to The Pharaoh directly," Akar finished.

The first guard smirked at him with disdain. "You are most welcome to do so." With that, the two men retreated into their silent statue-like position.

## Chapter Twenty-Nine

"Does he yet remain at the entrance?" asked Asim. Tamin had informed her of Akar at the entrance and now returned with the outcome.

"No, he has retreated with tail between legs. He threatened the guards and attempted bribery to no purpose. Now I believe he is about to try his luck with The Pharaoh. Ramses might speak to him yet shall not grant any favor upon him. Our Pharaoh does not involve himself with the choices and problems of Palace women. Truly, he should not. Does not the ruler of our wonderful country have better pursuits and challenges to meet with? Do not worry, Asim. Akar shall find no satisfaction there."

Thanking her, Asim went about her duties for the many wives and children of the Harem. For several days she had found peace and support within these walls. To hear of Akar demanding her release forced her into reality with a shock. He had left for now yet Asim believed he would try again. She longed to see Pentu once more yet thought better of it. Akar might persuade a fellow guard to stand watch at the Harem entrance, waiting for her to leave this safe interior. Akar did not like his plans thwarted and was perfectly capable in having her followed.

She was happy here, feeling as though she was among family for the first time. Silly, she thought. I must be wary of such emotions. I am a servant whom the gods and these women have taken pity upon. Nothing more. As she told Joba, she cannot withdraw to this paradise forever. Indeed, she would be blessed if she could remain another week after the birth. Then she and the baby would be forced to face Akar. He would be angry and vindictive. "Assuredly with me," she thought, "yet what of my baby?" Again she remembered Akar's promise to Queen Tiye to ensure a safe delivery. Yet no mention was made as to care of the child after the birth. What twisted ideas lurked within him towards her baby?

As she reached down to retrieve a toy for a royal child, she found herself doubled over in pain. As she gave a little cry, a Royal Wife came to her aid. "What is it, Asim? Are you ill? Is it the baby?"

By now, Asim was upright and smiling. "I do not know. Yet I am now recovered. My apologies if I startled you. Here is the toy your daughter dropped." Then she was bent over again, feeling her stomach harden and tighten.

The wife called over her shoulder for Tamin and the Royal Physician. "Have you been feeling thusly for a time?" Asim could only nod before finding herself standing within a small puddle at her feet. "Ah, it is indeed a wondrous moment. It is your baby, wanting to face the world. Come. I shall aid you to your bed." While the two women plodded slowly along, Asim continued to offer apologies for the disruption. At her side appeared Tamin.

"Thank you, Sister," Tamin said to the other wife, "I shall assist from here on." To Asim she instructed, "Take long deep breaths, Asim. Yes that is correct. Lie upon your bed. My physician should be here momentarily. Come. I will assist you with your clothing." To nearby servants she ordered blankets, a bowl of water with a soft cloth, and a small table.

The physician entered the room and began laying out various instruments of his trade upon the narrow table. Tamin was gently offering Asim small droplets of water in her mouth while laying a wet cloth upon her forehead. The man at her feet was instructing her to hold from bearing down. Poking and prodding her while she began to cry out in earnest, he continued his verbal instructions.

"My friend," began Tamin to her physician, "she is becoming hot to the touch. She seems to be in an unusual amount of pain. What is transpiring with the baby?"

While Asim shouted in pain, and began to push, the man said, "Something is amiss with the baby. I believe it is turned around in a position that shall prove most difficult for her to give birth. I must aid with my hands by turning and drawing it out. My dear," he spoke louder to Asim, "Refrain from pushing. I must give you a tonic for the pain. The baby is in difficulty and you shall feel considerable distress if you do not take this." He offered her a bottle with clear liquid for her to ingest.

Between the tightening of her stomach and her cries of pain Asim asked of the medical specialist, "My baby. Shall this bring harm my baby? Nothing must happen to my baby."

"This medicine shall not harm your baby," said the man patiently. "Yet your baby shall die if I cannot get to it quickly. Here, take this now."

"Where is the Royal Tamin? I wish to speak to her."

"Here, Asim. I am by your side. Do you feel my hand in yours?" The Physician retreated slightly while the two women spoke alone. "I swear, Asim, upon the god of infants and the goddess of motherhood all shall be well." She turned to the medical man and said, "Give it to her. She is ready now."

Asim opened her mouth bird-like and took the substance. Almost immediately she became light headed and felt as though she fell into a dream. She heard voices and knew people were standing about her yet she felt nothing and could not speak to them. There was pressure upon her stomach yet she felt no pain. She was floating further away when she heard the sound of a baby's cry. Then she was in darkness.

Night had fallen when Asim awoke. Tamin was asleep on a pile of floor pillows, her head leaning against the stone wall. Asim struggled to regain full consciousnesses, opening and reclosing her eyes until finally keeping them wide. Reaching to her abdomen, she felt only a slight bulge where her baby had been. Her small cry of alarm awoke her benefactor who quickly took Asim's hands.

"Ah, you are awake. I am here," reassured Tamin.

"My baby. Please tell me of my baby."

Tamin held Asim's hand tighter. "My good Physician said you are well. You have been asleep for nearly a full day yet you shall recover. The gods have looked favorably upon you, Asim. My dear physician said you shall be able to carry another child."

Asim struggled to sit up, yet only made it to her elbows. "Yet this baby. Tell me please. I must know. Male or female?"

"A girl, Asim. You birthed a girl."

Asim lay back upon her bed. "A girl. I heard her cry just before I fell into blackness. When might I hold her?"

Tamin held on tight and lowered her head, shaking it slowly. "No," cried Asim. "No, I want to hold her. Please, please."

"You do not want the vision of her in your eye for all eternity. Believe me when I say to you it is better this way. I vow I shall see to all necessary details. You need not worry. I shall handle everything personally." She suddenly grimaced and clutched her own belly. "By the gods, I am not to give birth for several days hence. Babies do have their own plan for us however, do they not?" She called to a hovering servant for her physician once again. "He is yet within these walls, thankfully. I shall return to you, Asim. Do not worry. I shall send a servant to you in the meantime. Request from her anything you require."

"Thank you gracious Tamin. I do have one request," said Asim, remembering the message she must send to Joba. Her labor and delivery had begun so quickly she had not the time to arrange for a servant to speak to him. She would do so now.

"Please remain still and rest. My good physician shall return to you soon. He shall answer any questions you might have. You have been through much more of an ordeal than the one in which I now embark. This is my third birth, remember. It should happen quickly."

With that parting comment, the medical man arrived and began assisting Tamin to her own Royal Chamber for yet another birth this day.

## Chapter Thirty

For the second time in this long and irritating day, Akar found himself pacing in front of a massive set of doors. To and fro, to and fro like an anxious tiger in an enclosure. Two Royal Chamber Guards stood tall and straight at this entrance to the Pharaoh's Audience Room. One guard had the gall to offer Akar a rather hostile look when Akar expressed his need to speak to Ramses immediately.

"Our Grand Pharaoh is occupied at the moment. Perhaps you could return on the morrow," said Joba coldly.

Akar had had his fill of lowly and insulting guards this day. "Do you not know to whom you speak? I insist upon entering."

Joba looked at the large belligerent man standing in front of him and said with less admiration than Akar expected. "Yes, I know who you are. Yet I care naught. The Pharaoh Ramses is involved with more senior officials."

It was clear to Akar that this guard was neither afraid nor impressed by him. "Upon the completion of his meeting, inform him I wish an audience. I shall wait. Do not fail me."

Joba smirked at him and nodded his head slightly. He would naturally inform His Pharaoh of Akar's presence. Yet the cabinet members must first exit the room before he could make Akar's request. By then, the Pharaoh could quite possibly retreat through another doorway. Akar could pace until the morrow, thought Joba.

One by one, the officials exited the room through the carved double doors. Joba finally entered the grand room to express Akar's request to The Pharaoh. Further time ensued before Joba returned to inform Akar of the Pharaoh's decision. "The Pharaoh permits you to enter."

Akar strode fiercely through the entrance, filling the space of both doors with his bulk. He had the good sense to kneel before his Pharaoh, expressing gratitude for allowing him this late visit.

"Ah, my good Akar. Rise, my faithful man, rise." The Pharaoh descended his mighty Throne to stand in front of Akar. "How good it is to see you. I understand you have been on an assigned task for my lovely wife, Queen Tiye. Good, good. It is time you two mend the barriers between you. I am glad you are able to work together.

Come. My appointments have been completed this day. Let us retire to more amenable chambers."

The ornate sitting room adjacent to The Pharaoh's bedchamber was replete with drink and food for the Great Ruler to enjoy. Ramses was gracious enough to bid Akar to sit and enjoy the food upon the center table. Their relationship was casual enough that Akar be allowed within Ramses innermost chambers yet not so informal for The Great Pharaoh to remove his layers of regal garments and crowns. Within any public view Ramses would always remain the leader and god among his people. Centering his bejeweled chest collar and adjusting the large crown upon his head, he spoke to Akar. "I was informed there was some urgency in this request. I have little time remaining before the evening meal. Yet time enough to hear you out."

"My Great Pharaoh, my woman, Asim, is held against my wishes within your Royal Harem. I have been informed your Royal Consort Tamin insists Asim remain within those confines until her birthing time arrives. I would ask of you, My Pharaoh, to order her release to me."

"Ah, a great event, the birth of a new infant. I share your joy, as my admirable Tamin is to present me with another child soon as well.

"However, I do not interfere with the lives of my Harem wives. It is their domain and as such — baring any governmental interference — they are free to officiate their own affairs. Perhaps your woman is unwell? That is reason enough to confine her within the Harem walls."

"Great One, I have been told a physician is of the opinion she should rest prior to her ordeal. However, I believe she could do so within our home in Thebes."

Ramses looked at Akar thoughtfully. "I shall not order her release. However, in setting this to rights I shall send a messenger to the Harem to garner the full import of this situation."

The Pharaoh rang the small bell upon the table. Within minutes a servant entered who bowed low and awaited his ruler's pleasure. "Send me a swift messenger," he ordered. Such a person quickly appeared in the form of a young boy. "I wish you to take a message to Her Royal Consort Tamin in the Royal Harem chambers. You are to tell the guard at the entrance to deliver these words to the Consort

Tamin. 'Her Pharaoh wishes to know the condition of the servant Asim.' Is that understood? You must wait and memorize her reply. If need be, and if so instructed by the good Tamin, you shall repeat this message to her physician and wait for his reply as well. Now repeat this instructions to me." Astonishingly, the young man did so practically verbatim.

After Ramses sent the messenger on his way, Akar could not refrain from commenting. "I am quite in awe at that boy's talent. Can he repeat anything?"

"Very nearly," replied the mighty Ramses. "He is quite fleet of foot as well. We should have a response shortly. Let us partake of the refreshments offered while we wait."

Lending truth to this Royal prediction, the boy returned swiftly, barely short of breath. He leaned low and whispered into The Pharaoh's ear for some moments. A lengthy message, thought Akar. He wondered if it would be to his advantage.

"I wish you to remain," said Ramses to the young boy. "I may have further need of you."

Turning to Akar, Ramses began to relate the information the boy had brought. "I would offer the pleasantries first. It seems my lovely Tamin has given birth early. I am the father of two girls. Twins. Quite an achievement, would you not agree?

"Now, as to Asim. She too has given birth to a baby girl. Alas it is my unfortunate task to inform you of the baby's death almost immediately following her birth. I offer my sorrow to you, Akar.

"Fortunately, Tamin's personal physician is yet tending to both women and the following information is his statement. He is quite certain Asim shall be able to bear you another child. Very good news indeed.

"However, the birth was strenuous and complicated. Therefore, he instructs Asim to remain within the Harem in complete rest to fully recuperate. He also promised to continually care for her to complete this recovery."

Akar frowned yet kept calm. "What length of time must she remain?"

"The Physician estimates at least a fortnight although two such time periods might pass before he shall set fit to release her to your care."

"A fortnight. Perhaps two." Akar thought a bit before finally stating, "That amounts to a minimum of fourteen days. Women do not take such time to recover after birthing. The Queen Tiye gave her to me. Asim is mine. I wish her home now."

Ramses was beginning to loose some patience with Akar. "This information is from the physician's own mouth to this young boy," he said and pointed at the messenger. The boy nodded in assent. "This medical man is most astute and very capable. Asim could not be in better hands than his for a swift recovery."

Pushing this completed subject aside, Ramses brought up another. "Additionally, my dear Consort Tamin assures me she shall made the arrangements for the preparation of your baby's remains. All you need do is provide the location of your tomb for her burial."

At this, Akar discarded any attempt at polite conversation. "I care naught if this child is buried in a tomb yet I assure you it shall not be set in mine. This baby is not of my blood. I would not have claimed it alive nor do I claim it dead. Asim is free to do what she wants with it."

Ramses looked at this man with emotion leaning toward anger. "A child brought into my land is a blessing. Any child. I feel more sorrow for the loss of this little life than do you. Your kin or not, Asim carried this child and as such you should feel shame at your attitude. I am quite disappointed in you, Akar. Asim shall be free to make her own decision as to when she wishes to leave my Royal Harem. It is my judgment she is better cared for within those walls than within yours.

"As for now, I wish to enjoy my evening meal with my family and rejoice in the new births. You shall remove yourself from my presence. See to your duties. Do not request from me again such a favor or late appointment."

Akar had no choice. He rose from his seat and bowed low before making a hasty exit. Nothing he said would have changed the Pharaoh's decision. He had seen the scowl and dislike upon Ramses face. He would have been a fool to continue his pleas. Banishment from the Royal Chambers was less chastisement than what could have been. Yet he may never again see respect and friendship in the eyes of his Pharaoh. That, perhaps, was the ultimate punishment

This entire wretched day and the anger thrown upon him by His Pharaoh was Asim's doing. He should, at least, be grateful for the death of the baby. It solved any further action on his part. He decided to wait one fortnight and make his presence known again at those sturdy doors. He would then retrieve Asim and she would pay for such insolence.

## Chapter Thirty-One

Pentu had not seen Joba for two days and longed to tell him of the message he would receive from the Harem. Apparently, Joba had changed his duty hours with another guard and their paths had not yet crossed.

Today the gods were with him as the two met over their first meal of the new day. "Ah, Pentu. How have you been?"

"Joba, old friend, I have news for you. Perhaps we could speak after you have been properly fed."

"It so happens I have just completed my meal. Would now suffice?"

Pentu was glad he was so accommodating and grabbed a small loaf of bread for sustenance as they strode outdoors. Initially, Pentu thanked his friend for his kindness to Asim at the festival in Thebes. "Also for your wonderful suggestion as to her safety in the Harem. She made haste to ask Consort Tamin for her assistance. We have hit upon a means of communication should she be granted the request." Pentu told his friend of the coded message he should receive in a day or two amid apologies for assuming he would be their go-between in this subterfuge. "I have been searching you out only to learn you had changed hours and sites."

"Ah, so that is the explanation. As it so happens, a lovely young lady approached me yesterday asking after the health of my mother. It would appear Asim has found the assistance she required.

"I admit I was perplexed by her question. I had thought it a jest from another guard. The girl was quite pretty, however, so after assuring her my mother was well we arranged some time together that evening. I must thank Asim for sending such a lovely flower my way."

Pentu laughed. Only Joba had such blessings. "You are quick-witted, my friend. I am relieved her approach was not an annoyance to you."

"A beautiful lady is never an annoyance. And now I have some news for your ears. Akar spoke with the Pharaoh regarding Asim. What an insufferable man, by the way, making outrageous demands to enter the Royal Audience Room. Although I have heard of him, I had never dealt with the man before.

"It so happened the Pharaoh was occupied at the time. He was forced to wait, unfortunately, while I entered and made his request to our Ruler. Actually, I found my self in need of the toilet room prior to speaking to the Pharaoh so I am afraid his wait was lengthier than most. When I finally admitted him, his mood was, shall we say, bleak. He does not seem the type of man to hold his tongue when riled."

"Do you know the outcome to his request?"

Joba shook his head. "They retired to the Pharaoh's personal sitting chamber. Yet this I know — the Pharaoh never interferes in the inner workings of the Palace of the Harem. It would be demeaning for him to meddle in the affairs of staff and their families. I believe it is quite safe to say Asim is yet within the Harem until you are able to arrange extrication from the Palace and your duties to the Pharaoh. I would see the two of you have a long life together, my friend, away from these questionable activities."

"It is my hope as well," said Pentu. "I pray blessings from the gods are yet with me. Upon the approval of the Pharaoh I plan to seize the first opportunity for us to flee."

## Chapter Thirty-Two

Asim had enough of her self-pity. Lying in her bed with little companionship save the physician, only accentuated her invalid status. The birth occurred ten days prior and she began completing small tasks for the women and their children.

To hold conversations with other servants and to be around the life of the Harem should aid in her recovery, she thought. Yet she found upon approaching others, conversations sudden lagged, smiles turned to faces of sorrow, and the words spoken to her were those of condolences. Neither of her options seemed to alleviate her sadness yet she was feeling stronger by simply conducting her duties and walking in the Harem.

Upon the last visit from the Royal Physician, she was told her progress was very encouraging. Once she was strong enough to make her daily trek from Thebes, he told her, she could return home. The medical man believed he had presented happy news to Asim and could not reason why she did not accept it as such. When she burst into tears, the Physician left hurriedly saying he must attend to Tamin's babies and their new wet nurses.

For the aristocratic woman, breast-feeding their newborn was deemed unfashionable and beneath her image. Tamin had been assigned two wet nurses to take up this task for each baby. While some lactating women were wet nurses by profession — earning more than their husband did in some cases — a Royal wet nurse required other credentials. These two women had given birth to healthy surviving children, an excellent endorsement in the face of high child mortality. Therefore, the Royal Physicians concluded these women's milk had excellent nutrients for Royal newborns to grow healthy and strong.

The Royal Consort Tamin was mending in health yet remained within her chambers since the birth. The Royal Physician To Infants dutifully examined the babies and declared the girls vigorous and robust. Asim learned of this welcome news from others who visited the nursery. While she missed her friendship with Tamin, she knew it would be too painful to see her with the infants.

To avoid awkward and painful conversations with the wives, Asim was not attending them directly in chambers opting instead to serve in the laundry rooms or cooking area. The enormous kitchens and ovens of the Royal Palace had always been a source of fascination for her. Common Egyptians cooked outside in open air to avoid excessive heat in the living quarters. Homes of wealthy citizens had separate kitchens placed in courtyards. Those of the Royal Palace and the Harem Quarters were several paces away from the main building yet enclosed within the massive mud-brick wall encompassing the Palace grounds.

Egyptian ovens consisted of large clay domes varying in size depending upon the household or need. A stone shelf was constructed within this dome and the fire was lit under the shelf. The baking and roasting surface of the oven contained open holes and circular depressions of various thickness and sizes. These allowed food to be cooked at different temperatures and times. Meat was often slow roasted for hours while bread needed much less time to bake. Food was roasted, boiled, baked, or fried in plant oils or the fats of animals. All classes of people used Egypt's plentiful spices yet only the favored rich could afford the rarest of seasonings.

The kitchens in the Palace were enormous, containing many ovens since hundreds of people needed feeding every day. Some of these contraptions were a double level design for baking large amounts of food or bread like commercial bakeries. These were often utilized for large banquets or celebrations.

Food was important to all Egyptians for celebrations of any kind, not simply sustenance. They loved any excuse to have a party by celebrating such official events as the Nile Flood Day to The New Year Day, from weddings to anniversaries, from births to deaths. Food brought loved ones together in moments of joy and those of sorrow. Meals taken with family and friends were a source of pleasure and comfort for all Egyptians, rich or poor.

Asim was making her way to the kitchen of the Harem to aid with today's food preparations. She could already smell the pungent spices and baking bread. As she neared an archway, she heard the slapping of sandals against the stone pavers. Truly, she thought, I do not wish to see another pitying face. She quickly snuck behind one of the painted pillars until the person passed.

The slapping sandals moved past her hiding space and Asim watched the retreating figure. She was about to emerge when the movement of the woman caught her eye. The walk was recognizable and familiar. She looked again. Of all the women she might expect to see, it was not this one: Queen Tiye.

At the edge of the water-lily pond, several women were gathered, speaking in soft undertones. Their voices were much too low to clearly hear their words. Giving into temptation Asim tiptoed to the foliage behind the women and peeked through the large leaves to satisfy her curiosity.

She had never known this Queen to converse so amiably with a handful of lesser wives. She seemed to be the main orator in this unusual gathering and the other six were listening intently to everything she said. The Queen leaned further into the group and handed each of them some indistinguishable items.

It was Asim's mistake to have sought a better view within the foliage and the leaves of a fig tree rustled because of it. Queen Tiye's head snapped towards her direction and Asim barely had time to retreat before discovery. Noticing Tiye's movement, the wives quickly concealed the items under their pleated skirts out of Asim's sight.

Asim sat back upon her heels. This is decidedly peculiar, she thought. Why would the Queen hold such a furtive meeting with these six wives? The Queen had often voiced her dislike for the Harem women yet now she was behaving in a very friendly manner towards them. What items did she hand to them? She reasoned their size was small enough to fit under their garments yet that realization did nothing to indicate the item itself. It could have been almost anything, she thought, any ordinary object. One woman held what appeared to be a small square of paper, carrying it nonchalantly it in her hand as they exited their enclosure and went about their separate ways.

After casting one more glance at the fig tree, Queen Tiye left as well, bearing towards the gardens of the Royal Palace proper. Should I follow her, Asim wondered. Yet to what end? Whatever her cause, she had accomplished it. Asim had never known the Queen to perform any act altruistically and her thoughts would never give rise to unselfish benevolence. Try as she might, Asim could find no reason for the Queen's behavior yet she believed the Queen must have a monumental incentive for her actions.

She decided to keep this information to herself for now. She knew this visit was of grave import and it must eventually reach the ears of others. Only two people could she trust with this information: Pentu and Joba. That proved difficult in her current situation within the Harem. Messages out were seldom allowed. The matter would be more difficult if she returned to Akar. He would make her pay physically for the time away from him while keeping an even closer watch upon her.

For now, she would observe the actions of the wives who had engaged with Queen Tiye. Perhaps she could glean more wisdom from quiet scrutiny, even discerning the objects that had been passed between them. Once she had more details and answers to her questions, she would seek an opportunity to reveal all.

Chapter Thirty-Three

A few moments earlier, Queen Tiye strolled through the elegant Palace Gardens towards the Harem. With servants trailing behind her, she carefully walked over the damp wooden bridge to the secured doors of the establishment. These doors were guarded with reliable locks and dutiful guards yet she passed through without difficulty. She was Queen Tiye, after all, and faced no restrictions. She left her servants standing upon the intricately designed bridge ensuring them her visit would be brief and she would not require their services.

She carried with her a wrapped cloak, seemingly to keep splashing water from her expensive gown. Pebekkamen, The Chief of the Chamber, greeted her within the antechamber of the quarters. Naturally, he allowed Tiye to enter, honoring her with a deep bow and without scrutiny to her bundle. He did, however, remind he of their private appointment later in the day. Tiye smiled seductively and nodded. She would be glad when these tiresome duties requiring her sexual talents were no longer needed. Although the services she offered kept him dedicated within the conspiracy.

It was a simple matter to catch the eyes of the women within the conspiracy. They had all received an earlier message from her informing them of the approximate time of day she would call upon them.

She walked to the semi-enclosed area of foliage and sat to wait. Situated far into a corner and seldom visited, it was excellent for their needs. One by one, they arrived with eagerness to hear what the Queen had to tell them. She did not disappoint their expectations.

"My Sisters," she began quietly, "We have witnessed the protective ceremony for Ramses and his son. In a matter of weeks the feasts in Egypt and within the Palace shall commence. That is the appointed date upon which I move into action. I shall not ask you to soil your hands with any physical attack yet I would ask of you another favor." She unwrapped her cloak. Seated upon her lap were five wax figures, each carefully constructed to appear as men. Under those was a small piece of papyrus paper, sorely worn and tattered like a favorite blanket.

She handed the dolls to five of the women. "I have received these from a Royal Magician. While he swears to perform incantations to remove all protection from Ramses, he asked that you aid him with these." She handed the same women several long thin pins. "By chanting precise incantations over each doll, we shall further lessen his god-like immortality. Reciting a different spell while using the pins upon the figures shall render the Harem guards' limbs useless. Even if they should overhear a cry for help, their legs shall not carry them into the garden. This is merely precautionary, however, as I plan on positioning our allied men at the doors.

"I have saved this for you," she said to the sixth wife and handed her the paper. "You are chosen for an important responsibility. When your sisters are utilizing their dolls, you must read aloud the two spells marked by the magician. He indicated they were simple yet powerful spells and easy to read. He voiced this warning — the dolls shall not be effective without the spells, nor shall the magic be successful without the utilization of the dolls. On the third day prior to the feast you must begin this task one time per day using both magical chants. I have provided them to you at this early date so you are able to review the writings and handling of the dolls."

Suddenly Tiye stopped speaking and turned her head quickly. "Did you hear a noise?" The other women shook their heads. Tiye continued to stare between the leaves of a fig tree. "I thought a sound came from that area." She and the other six women listened carefully yet heard nothing. The women hurriedly hid their dolls within the folds of their garment. "No matter. We have nearly completed with our discussion. Remember, once you receive the package of weapons, you shall arrange various blades to be hidden within reach. We need them near.

"Follow my lead upon the chosen day. You shall arrive wearing only necklaces and magical amulets for protection. Wear as many as you feel comfortable with. Remember this is our husband. We are to entice him and remove any suspicion before striking.

One woman looked frightened. "My Queen, if I should miss with the blade or bring it out too soon . . . "

"Have no fears. I would not place you in the position of the fatal strike. That is my task. I shall consign Ramses to history by drawing the blade from behind. I merely require you to keep him fully occupied from the front. You must do your best to keep him visually entertained. You shall only use your weapons should I fail with my strike. Yet I tell you this, I shall not fail. Know you all, by this act we vow to protect our home and country."

She rose from the edge of the fountain and finished saying to them, "May the gods be with you, my Sisters. If you have concerns send me a message through our Chief of Chambers. He is our humble ally." As they entered, so did they leave — discreetly and one by one. Finally the Queen took a last glance at the fig tree in question and turned to leave.

At this point, all was proceeding according to their preparations. The magician and priest guaranteed their parts would be fulfilled. When they finished with their magic and prayers, the Pharaoh would be as human as any other person in the kingdom. Allies within the Royal council had agreed to overlook the death of Ramses or his son. With the monetary promises made to them, they would dissuade any formal investigation into the matter as well. Akar enlisted a general into the plan who would surround the Palace with troops to further discourage the Pharaoh's own personal guards if need be. Mother's many allies had received their pledges of titles and property and were prepared to gather at the Royal Palace after the assassinations to support Pentawer if their voices were needed.

And her mother, she thought, would reappear in five days to review the details. Tiye had no idea how long the woman would remain in the Royal Palace following the assassinations. She hoped it would not be an indefinite stay.

# BOOK THREE
**Murder**

## Chapter One

True to her plan, Asim had been carefully approaching the foreign Harem wives whenever she found an excuse. When they were gathered as one, she would bring fresh drink and food hoping to see something of note. Often she would retreat from the group only to hide behind a massive pillar or the ever-present foliage. Striving to remain within hearing distance while not appearing to do so was maddening. So far it had been for naught. Their conversations had been normal and dull.

She was becoming frantic. She was completely restored to health following the birth and realized her remaining time in the Harem was limited. She could be sent away at any moment. It was imperative she find truth to the actions of Tiye. She knew in her heart a black deed had been hatched by the Queen. It was her duty to know of the details before it was too late.

Today she lingered longer than the norm at the entrance of one of the foreign wives. This particular wife seemed in command of the other five. The others often approached her with concerns or companionship. As she took a step forward, she overheard several voices emanating from the room. Praying she would not be seen, Asim leaned against the door to listen.

"Do you have what is required of you?" asked the owner of the chamber. Apparently there was assent from the others. "Good. Bring them forth. Our Sister shall recite the words from the paper while we repeat them. We have only three days hence and must continue with this until the day of the feast. We cannot fail in this. He must fall."

Asim heard one voice mumble a chant or mantra. She had no idea what the words meant only that each woman repeated them.

After they had done so individually, they repeated the words again in one voice. Then another set of gibberish was recited and the circle of chants began anew. The low voices, speaking unintelligible words from behind the door raised the hairs along Asim's arms. They sounded as a coven of witches might.

Their prayers — if one could call them that — did not take overlong to complete. Asim heard the sounds of stools scraping the floor with further instructions by the residing wife. "Take heed and remember what we have been told. We are to come to this chamber from the evening feast to prepare. We walk as one to the central garden. Remember your holy amulets. Wear nothing else. Blades shall be sharpened and at our ready." As the women assured her they would be prepared, Asim quickly ran from the door to find another task with which to occupy herself.

She reviewed all she had heard. She did not believe those chants were of a holy nature. If so, their joint efforts would not have been hidden. All Egyptians prayed throughout the day, freely and openly. This was something sinister, Asim believed. Something evil was taking place in three day's time at the Feast of Heb-Sed. Someone, she realized with a jolt, was about to die. These women were discussing murder, she was sure of it.

"On Pharaoh Ramses' feast day," she said. "Why then?" The day would be filled with festivities throughout the country. Thebes would be filled with well-wishers and those hoping to see the Pharaoh. Confusion would be the theme of the day. Important representatives from other countries would join in the celebration at the Palace feast while the Pharaoh and the Royal Family would be situated near their honored guests. Could that be the answer? Could they be plotting against a foreign diplomat at the feast?

She sat upon the low stone garden wall to reason further. If that is truth, what could Queen Tiye gain by such an action? Killing a dignitary within the Palace walls could mean war. At the very least, treaties of trade and peace could be damaged. The Queen would not want war to come to Egypt. Nor would she wish to have trade routes halted. She greatly valued her pampered way of life. Either of those choices would put her affluent lifestyle in a precarious position.

If war came to our land and the Pharaoh died in conflict what then? She knew Amonhirk would become Pharaoh and attempt to rectify the situation. What might he do if it should be discovered the wives of his father brought war or poor trade to Egypt? Punishment, naturally. Execution? Perhaps. Amonhirk and Tiye did not like each other. He could make her suffer tremendously. The Queen would never suffer, the thought idly, if Pentawer sat upon the Throne.

*If Pentawer sat upon the Throne.* She sat up straight and felt a tremor long her spine. No, she thought with fear. It cannot be so. She is determined, to be sure, yet she would never be so foolhardy. Murder the Pharaoh? Impossible. Yet it fit into place like a childhood puzzle. All the pieces formed a complete picture of what Tiye had always sought: her son upon the Throne of Egypt. I must be mad, she thought. The Pharaoh could surely reason this out. He might confirm my madness or lock me away for telling such a heinous lie of his wife. It mattered little to her. It was her duty. The question facing her was how.

## Chapter Two

"Ah, Grandmother has arrived. I believe she has more baggage than upon her previous visit," said Pentawer. "Enough to last a lifetime."

Pentawer and Queen Tiye were upon the canopied rooftop watching as her mother traveled from the Nile River to descend upon their regulated and relaxed life.

"My mother does not arrive, my son; she invades," replied the Queen.

The woman was sitting in what appeared to be a new carry litter held by four strong males on each end of the inserted poles. Following this flamboyant display were several flat litters for the express purpose of carrying her many chests, boxes, and bundles. Tiye sighed. It was obvious her mother planned on staying for some time although hopefully not the lifetime her son had mentioned.

"Come, Mother," said Pentawer, softly touching Tiye's elbow, "she is nearly upon the Royal Grounds. It is time to greet her."

Carefully traversing the steep mud-brick steps to the lower lever of the Palace, the three met in the main garden area. Pentawer was hugged firmly by his grandmother. Over his shoulder the woman said to Tiye with a casual nod in greeting, "Daughter."

"Mother," the Queen replied, nodding in return.

Situating the many servants of her mother was not an easy task, tasking the energy of several Palace staff. Finally ensconced in luxurious guest quarters, her mother became serious. "Ah, Daughter, please be seated. I have some distressing news for you. Ari is dead," she said bluntly and with noticeable excitement. Never before had a murder occurred to one within her social group

Tiye had almost forgotten of Ari. She looked suitably shocked. "Dead? Whatever do you mean? Was he ill?"

"No, not at all. He was *murdered*," she finished with gruesome delight. "He had been stabbed in the throat. It was immediate, I am told. Apparently it was in a vital area. Directly here." She pointed under her jaw line.

"How dreadful," Tiye stated. "Have they apprehended the culprit?" Tiye was nervous. Based upon her mother's tale, Ari had been assailed from the front. That would imply he had seen his murderer, undoubtedly recognizing Akar. The man had clearly disobeyed her orders. She tried to focus upon her mother's answer yet was incensed at Akar for taking this risk.

"There have been no suspects nor witnesses, although the sporting even at which he attended was quite crowded. It was late and the day's festivities were completed, I understand. A terrible shame. He was such a wonderful man."

Believing she had mourned Ari long enough in this conversation, her mother quickly switched topics. "Now, let us discuss the business at hand. All has been arranged with the Harem wives? And others?"

Tiye detailed the many members of court she had won to their side — the priest Perneb, the magician, the Royal Chief of Chambers, the Pharaoh's butler, his physician, the Minister of the Treasury, a general with several of his men, as well as others of note. True to their word, the Harem wives had alerted powerful family members in their birth countries of the plan and many were quite prepared to lend support. The brother of one Royal Consort was a captain of the Royal Egyptian Archers. He and his fellow archers would incite the people against Ramses III by whatever means at their disposal. The priest and magician would remove all charms and protections from Ramses on the morrow. "At that point, he shall be as mortal as any other Egyptian."

Mortal or not, thought Tiye, he would never be simply another Egyptian. He was the Supreme Ruler and had dozens of guards at his command. Truly, Tiye was terrified of the plan going awry. Even with their most meticulous details, the tiniest snag could mean their downfall.

Additionally, she had suffered dreadful nightmares of late, some in which she found herself bound and gagged, starving in a cell. In others she had been sentenced to death and waited the blade of the executioner. For several nights, she awoke in a cold sweat. Were these warnings from the gods or merely her guilt rearing its ugly head while she slept? She cleared her thoughts of such nonsense. She gave no credence to nonexistent gods hence they did not control her dreams. And she held no guilt. This was for the good of the country, she told herself convincingly, nothing more. Dreams were random bits of memory from the day's activities and of no concern to her.

"Wonderful. And the wives? They are aware of their part in this? How are you to excuse yourself from the feast and ensure the Pharaoh shall follow?"

"He is my husband. Do not concern yourself with that problem, Mother. I know of his desires and have it well in hand." Cooing in his ear, telling of the wine and sweets awaiting him, cool empty gardens at his disposal, and the planned debauchery with six other wives would be enticement for any man. Ramses could not resist the invitation.

"Excellent. Our financial benefactors have contributed enough to provide respite to those who are hungry and homeless. Following Pentawer's succession to the Throne, these shall be distributed to citizens in his name. Think of it; my grandson shall be Ramses IV, ruler of all Egypt.

"I believe it advisable to visit once more with the Harem wives. Pentawer should accompany us to ease their minds should any be too nervous to execute their portion of the bargain. This afternoon would be best, Daughter. You must contact Pentawer and see that he has time available.

"Now, I wish to rest and prepare for the afternoon meal. Leave me now." Having been majestically dismissed from her mother's presence, Tiye set upon another course the woman had put her thoughts upon — Akar's disobedience. Afterwards, she would visit her son, informing him of her mother's decree.

Chapter Three

Akar had been summoned while Queen Tiye was waiting in her audience room, fidgeting and growing more incensed as time passed. *Why is he not here? I have no time for this. Mother was more demanding than usual, fellow conspirators must be spoken to and coddled one final time, and now I wait upon this* soldier *to arrive.*

At long last the door opened and Akar was ushered into the room. "Do you not know I have been waiting for you? I am the Queen. I do not wait for the likes of you. Sit," she commanded.

"My Queen, I had many duties for My Pharaoh today regarding the celebration."

She narrowed her eyes at him. *So, he chooses to outrank me with the duties to the Pharaoh. After tomorrow, as Mother of The Pharaoh, I shall show him my wrath at his insolence.* "As to *My Husband*," she began sweetly and with emphasis, "is all in order? The general and his men shall keep watch for the appointed signal from you and swarm the Royal Palace, correct? And you. Where shall you be?"

Now it was his turn to narrow his eyes. *Did she think me dense? Did she think I am unable to remember my assigned post?* "I shall stand guard at the Harem entrance," he began. "Those normally assigned at the door shall be allowed to partake of the celebration and I shall offer my services in their stead. I shall monitor the two men you have assigned to the door, ensuring they do not falter in their duty. I shall make short work of anyone who interrupts." This was a post beneath his skills yet one he was anticipating with pleasure. *After the Pharaoh was down, he intended to enter the Harem and take what was his by force: Asim.*

"Excellent. And you shall provide small weapons for us — sharpened daggers, small axes — something easily wielded by women."

"They have been prepared." He took a deep breath and plowed ahead. "I would have a moment of your time, My Queen, if we have concluded."

"We have not, yet I shall listen before I continue. Speak."

Succinctly he explained Asim's confinement and her absence away from him.

"And what am I to do regarding these circumstances?"

"I wish her returned to me. I hoped you could intervene with the Harem."

"Why should I intervene? I care naught for the girl. Tamin is very clever. I am sure her hand is in this. You have managed to loose her to someone with great manipulation skills. She is yours to regain, not mine. I have finished with her."

Akar's face grew dark with fury yet he held his tongue. He would carry on with his own plan to retrieve Asim. If opportunity presented itself, perhaps he would see to the meddling woman named Tamin.

"Now I have another topic upon which to speak." While she continued to look upon him with sweetness, she said with venom, "You disobeyed me, Akar."

When he looked confused yet would issue a denial, she interrupted. "I have learned details of Ari's demise. He was stabbed under his jaw. That meant, dear Akar, the blow would have been from the front. Face to Face." Her anger was simmering. "You were explicitly told to avoid contact. He was not to recognize you. Yet you did exactly that. He saw you and knew you were his murderer. You put yourself and the Royal Palace at risk. There may be witnesses."

"There were none," Akar said in some confusion.

"Indeed? Someone knew of the murder. These details came from a person who was not in attendance at the sporting events. Not even close to the city. Explain how this person knows such accurate details."

"I am at a loss to do so. Yet I assure you, I was alone with him."

Tiye leaned forward slightly so she would look him in the eyes. "I care naught for your insipid explanations. I am concerned of your need to improvise the direct orders you receive. *My* direct orders. We have carefully reviewed the morrow's events. The timing is crucial. I shall not have you taking your own initiative in these designs, operating when and where you please.

"I have found many details of your life, Akar — the prison, the torture, even the attempted disfiguring of your younger cousin. Do not look so surprised. I am Queen. I have many resources and personnel available to me.

"I am inclined to believe with these misdeeds in your past, and those you may have in your present, there is little likelihood you shall reach an Afterlife. It is, after all, a matter of caring for your fellow Egyptians, which you do not. In spite of the eternal damnation you have surely created for yourself, I shall make it fact."

He acted contritely yet was teeming with fury inside. "My abject apologies, My Queen. I shall follow your wishes. I swear by the great god Amun."

"As I swear by Montu, the god of war, if you disobey, or do not see this through, you shall not have the title of General nor any other." How nicely she brought forth the memory of that particularly vicious god, she thought. "I shall have you cut from neck to groin, feed your guts to the vultures, and burn what is left of you in the desert sands. Do you have comprehension of what I speak?" He nodded.

"Do not wrong me, Akar, for I shall bring absolute carnage upon your head. I speak truth to this pledge. You would do well to heed me."

## Chapter Four

She cursed Akar upon his departure and wondered if he could truly be worth the exasperation she felt. She loathed and despised that man yet needed him to fulfill his agreement. She came to the conclusion she hated Akar even more than she did her mother.

Tiye hoped her second appointment of the day would be more enjoyable than her first. Spending time with her son was sweeter to her disposition than honeyed wine, even with her mother in tow. Eradicating Akar from her thoughts, she concentrated upon her son sitting upon the great Throne of Egypt as the three walked to the Harem.

They entered unhampered into the domicile. Pentawer was behaving as a true ruler, greeting the wives they passed and stopping to chat with his younger half-siblings. Queen Tiye smiled as she watched her son basking in his element among people. Everyone found him to be approachable and sincere, thought Tiye. He shall be a good Pharaoh to his people.

Eventually, the threesome made their way to the area concealed by thick foliage. Within moments their six cohorts joined them. Several of the women seemed edgy. Have they decided against us, thought Tiye. Pentawer noticed their unease as well and opened the discussion.

"As your future Pharaoh, I wished to take a few moments to express my appreciation and gratitude to you. Your actions shall not only ensure my seat upon the Throne, but also your safety here in your home. Your children shall be at your side until they seek families of their own. You shall enjoy your children and grandchildren for your lifetime.

"I wish to ease any tension you might have towards this glorious end. Be assured no harm shall come to you if you simply adhere to my mother's instructions. Afterwards, my gratefulness shall know no bounds. You shall never be forced to marry another unless you choose to do so." The women were moved by his attention to them. Their bodies relaxed and smiles warmed their faces.

Until now, her mother had remained silent. That was about to change. Oh no, thought Tiye, her mother was about to speak. There would be no stopping her. "Perhaps," her mother said conspiratorially to the women, "my grandson might be willing to take you into his own Harem."

Pentawer was usually prepared for his grandmother's outlandish statements and he handled this one with great aplomb. "Perhaps," he said with a slight smile.

After making their excuses and paying further compliments, the three walked across the bridge to the main Palace. "Splendid," said his grandmother. "A most splendid result. Grandson, you were magnificent. They actually believed you."

"I do not wish to see the women cast out. We shall increase the size of their quarters if needed yet they must always be welcome in the Royal Palace. I told the truth, Grandmother."

"It matters little if you did. Your speech was clearly the encouragement they required," said his grandmother, patting his arm in a conciliatory manner.

## Chapter Five

Asim must leave the Harem. She had witnessed with astonishment Queen Tiye, her mother, and Prince Pentawer enter the Harem. Those three Royals visiting the Harem together was an extraordinary occurrence, one that could only point to one reasoning — something illicit and evil was to transpire. At one point she thought she had been recognized. The Queen's mother looked her way yet did not seem to notice Asim. She admitted to her change in appearance since they had last come in contact. Yet Asim thought the non-recognition was due to the woman's conceit. She was the Queen's Mother, after all, and as such would never recall a mere servant.

After the scare she received today, Asim knew it was imperative she warn the Pharaoh. Coupled with today's mysterious Royal visit and the previous conversations, she must address him directly with her concerns. Her hasty conclusion was probably incorrect yet only the Pharaoh would truly know. She finally realized she needed an ally. Since she had no means of knowing how many other wives might be involved in this odd occurrence, Asim had no other choice. The only person in these chambers she could trust was Tamin, yet she hesitated to endanger her with this knowledge. Queen Tiye held more power than these lesser wives, almost as much as the Pharaoh. She could squash them like insects absent all emotion. She decided to keep Tamin safe and not divulge all.

Knocking quietly upon her chamber door, it was opened by a familiar servant. They greeted each other kindly before Asim took a deep breath and began. "My grave apologies for arriving unannounced yet I was hoping Her Royal Consort Tamin might spare me a few moments. I do not wish to interrupt her should be sleeping or engaged."

The servant bade her enter the small waiting area while she left to make the request of her mistress. She was smiling when she quickly returned. "My mistress voices pleasure in your company."

Tamin was reclining in her sumptuous sofa near a window. "Ah, Asim. How well you look." Asim sat upon a stool facing the Royal Consort. To keep her hands from shaking, she held them tightly together upon her knees.

"My apologies for my tardiness in paying you respect. In truth, I was not strong enough to face you or the babies." At that moment, the cries of infants were heard in the adjoining chamber.

The wince that floated across Asim's face did not go unnoticed by Tamin. She gently touched Asim's hands and looked with pity upon her. "Yet I am very glad you did so." Changing the subject, Tamin began, "Akar has again made a nuisance of himself with our guards. Naturally they rejected his many requests. From all you have told me of him, I should very much like to keep you by my side. Perhaps my physician could be called upon to extend your stay."

"I am much too healthy for him to do so and I do not wish him to lie on my behalf. In truth, I believe I should be permitted to leave. Even if I am released for a day or two, that would be sufficient."

"Sufficient? Sufficient for what purpose?" asked Tamin.

"It is a matter of great importance. To that end I must achieve an appointment with the Pharaoh immediately. I know of one man capable of adding me to his calendar yet it would prove risky if Akar saw me. Yet it is my duty."

"The Pharaoh? Why must you see him?"

Asim shook her head. "My humble apologies, my Royal Tamin, I am unable to tell you of the purpose. I do not wish to place you in harm's way. You have been my most gracious benefactor and I shall not chance your safety in any manner. I swear by the gods I would impart upon you this information if I could."

"Asim, you sound frightened." Asim nodded. "Perhaps," said Tamin as she reached for a slice of fruit, "there is a way for you to gain admission to his great chamber. Under normal circumstances, he would come to me if I requested he do so. The upcoming celebrations would delay that, however, perhaps for several days. We have many dignitaries in attendance and they require his personal touch. Meetings, meals, casual conversations. It is quite exhausting for him."

Asim was amazed. "He is the Pharaoh of all Egypt. Can he not meet with them at his convenience?"

Tamin smiled at her. "These foreign dignitaries are not in Thebes for the celebration alone. Treaties need to be examined, requests presented from their kings, supplies traded, and prices set upon them. To be a good ruler to our country, all these matters and more must be carefully handled.

"Yet, we are two capable women, are we not? Between us a solution is waiting for us to find. I wish to ask of you something very private. You have said the baby was not Akar's. Does he know who the true father is?"

"I never revealed the name to him. As long as my pregnancy did not interfere with his desires, it mattered naught to him."

"Have you told anyone? You need not mention names."

"You are aware of Joba. He has knowledge of the father. I trust Joba completely. He would not have given the information to another. I have, naturally, informed the father."

"Does he reside within the Royal Palace? Yes? Ah, that is good. How pressing is this audience with The Pharaoh? Must you speak with him today or shall tomorrow suffice?"

Asim considered this. Tomorrow was the day of celebration. Tonight would be preferable. Waiting until the morrow might be risky yet could be possible. "Early on the morrow would suffice. Yet that is the final day in which this information would be of use to him."

"Then we must not delay," Tamin said. "Now think carefully upon this: would you be safe in the quarters of this other man? Excellent. Then it is only a question of leaving the Harem and proceeding to his chamber unseen. Or at least unnoticed. We shall proceed tonight. Now, hear me on this solution."

## Chapter Six

The handmaiden exited through the doors of the Harem and strode into the lush gardens of the main Palace. Copper braziers atop metal stands provided a glow by which she was able to maneuver. It was an extremely dark night, near blackness with only a sliver of the moon and the twinkling of stars in the sky. She was dressed in a pleated shift with gold threads running through, a long black wig, and excessive kohl makeup around her eyes. Her appearance was that of one in station to a Queen, rather than a servant who simply fetched and cleaned. Because of her attire, she would not likely be stopped as she went about her business. She walked with assurance and steady purpose, yet felt little of either. Asim desperately prayed she would not be recognized.

Looking straight ahead she met no one's eye and appeared aloof and unapproachable, as Tamin had instructed. "If you move with entitlement to walk those halls, one shall assume you do. Pay no heed to anyone who might challenge you. Perceive them with arrogance and self-importance and they shall back down. Superiority is in one's attitude." She walked through the halls and celebratory rooms in which she was accustomed. Chambers off limits to most had been open to her while she was in the attendance of Queen Tiye. After tomorrow she would never have the privilege of service to a Queen. Indeed, she may be banished completely from the Royal Palace if the Pharaoh believed her to be meddling where she was not wanted.

She had never been within these corridors at this hour with so few guards on duty. To Asim, it felt as even the walls of the Palace were in slumber. Only the mounted oil lamps sparked and spit at her as she walked past. Nary a night bird could be heard and even the mighty Nile was flowing with subdued splashes. When the Great Pharaoh slept, so did the rest of the world. The atmosphere was quite eerie yet she would have it thusly rather than the crowded daylight.

Passing the Audience room of Ramses III, she made her way around a sharp turn and found herself within the chamber area of government officials. By the light of an oil lamp, she made her way to the door of Pentu's room. She began by gently tapping upon the door, waiting for a response from within. Nothing. She tapped with slightly more force, hoping he was merely in a deep sleep and not absent from his domicile. "Yes," she heard his voice. "Who is there?"

Now she was faced with a dilemma. Should she announce herself and chance a neighboring resident to hear? Or simply continue tapping until he opens the door. She chose the latter. Tap, tap, tap.

"By the gods, what can not wait till the morn?" Pentu flung open the door wearing nothing but a frown. Asim could not abate her laughter.

Squinting at the strange woman at his doorway, a look of recognition and surprise came across his face. Grabbing her arm and drawing her into his room, he exclaimed, "Asim. My love. How are you here? What has happened?" He looked at her stomach and asked, "The baby. Tell me of it." She lowered her head and shook it slowly from side to side.

He took her in his arms and held her. He had no words of great wisdom or condolence to offer her. She finally looked up at him and said, "I have come for sanctuary, for shelter within your chambers." She related to him the reason for her presence. "I ask for your assistance. I must speak to the Pharaoh early on the morrow."

His reaction was not what she had expected. "And place you in further danger? Akar has seen the Pharaoh regarding your consignment to the Harem. He took your departure as a personal rebuke and requested your return. The Pharaoh refused yet if you were to appear before him, he might easily rescind his decision. We must leave this place of deception and cruelty. Tonight I shall take you to my home of Set-Maat. You shall be safe there."

She considered this wonderful solution for a moment. "Consort Tamin has provided instructions I must present to the Pharaoh. In it, she requests he hear my concerns and consider them carefully. She mentions only my name, not another's. I cannot pass this to you, Pentu; it is for my use only. Please, I know Queen Tiye is contemplating harm to our Pharaoh. I must inform him of this, even though he might think me mad."

"Harm? I do not wish you to be in close proximity to harm's way alone. I shall accompany you. Have you any objections to that?" She shook her head. "Excellent. Now, come and sleep; the hour is late. It would appear we have much to accomplish and discuss on the morrow."

This was the attitude of a great many people that gathered in Memphis, the first stop of the Pharaoh's Royal Procession. People were discontented with their lot in life and angry at the regime. Mix anger generously with hunger, and hostility would surely rise.

## Chapter Eight

Pentu made his way hurriedly to the quarters of Joba the morn of the great celebration. Naturally, he was not within his room. Next, he walked to the Royal Audience Room where Joba was normally assigned. Again, no sign of Joba. His last choice of location was the garden and temple area within the center of the Royal Palace. Just as he was about to give up, Joba emerged from one of the smaller temples.

"Greetings, Pentu. I have just finished my early prayers within," he pointed to the entryway from which he had just exited.

"I am so relieved to have found you. I have news for you." He lowered his voice and glanced around making sure they were not overheard. "Asim has returned. Even now she is hidden within my chambers. Alas, our baby — a baby girl — has been lost."

"My great apologies for your loss. A tragedy for you both. I shall pray to the gods for you both and the baby's *ka*." Pentu nodded and thanked his friend. "Yet, Asim; she is well? Shall she remain with you?"

"She is well although saddened over the baby, understandably. Truthfully, I am not completely sure how long she remains with me. She was released from the Harem to speak with our Pharaoh. She has overheard some distressing conversations and fears for the Pharaoh's life."

"His life? She is positive of this?" asked Joba

"So she says. Personally, I am not sure — it seems so outlandish to consider — yet she has become quite agitated over this. At any rate, I am hoping to seek an audience with him as soon as he has availability. The conversation should not be too lengthy yet it is necessary she speak directly to him."

"That shall be most difficult today. He and his entourage left extremely early this day. He is traveling along the Nile River to share in the celebrations. He shall be presented in various Royal Processions in the nearby towns. This evening he shall do so once more in Thebes before the feast."

"I was aware of his journey yet did not realize he was planning such an early departure."

"Have you called upon the Royal Court Minister of Proceedings?" asked Joba. "He is always in possession of the Pharaoh's complete schedule for the day."

Pentu nodded. "He was the first minister I sought. I was told he is with the Pharaoh which means neither of them shall return soon. I must speak privately to the Pharaoh as it could be dangerous to do so with others present."

"Perhaps you might wait at the main Palace entrance for them to arrive. I have no idea when they might return."

"Then I shall wait at the gates for him. There should be time enough prior to the Thebes procession to catch his ear."

"Why not postpone this until the morrow? The celebrations would be complete and the day less turbulent."

"Ah, my suggestion exactly. Yet Asim is quite unyielding; we must speak to him today. Tomorrow, she said, shall be too late."

"Are you expected at the Royal feast tonight?" Pentu nodded to Joba's question. "Perhaps that is your only opportunity. You have had his ear before, my friend, when others have not. Perhaps the gods shall be with you this evening."

"I pray it does not come to that. I would do well not to interrupt his feast day. Celebratory banquets shall be served to guards and servants as well," said Pentu "Are you to attend? The entertainment should last well into the early morn, I am told."

Joba smiled. "I shall partake of the meal, naturally. Afterwards I have other activities planned."

Pentu smiled in return. Of course he did, thought Pentu. "Then I shall inform you of my success in this quest for Asim. Pray it does not result in an interruption of his feast day or my head upon a platter."

## Chapter Nine

"When *shall* we see the Pharaoh? It is imperative, Pentu. His very life may depend on the delivery of this message. What are we to do?" Asim was frantic. Pentu had never seen her in such a state and it was beginning to worry him.

"My sweet, please calm yourself. Take a deep breath and we shall discuss this. Better? Good. Now please sit and I shall broach my thoughts. I have an invitation to the great banquet tonight in the main dining room. The Pharaoh shall be with dignitaries from other lands, our ministers, and the upper echelon of the ruling class. He shall be surrounded by people, hundreds of people. Additionally, his food taster shall perform his assigned task before handing the platter to our Pharaoh. He shall be safe, I assure you."

Asim shook her head vehemently. "You are not appreciative of my fear. I do not believe harm shall befall him at the banquet. I believe it is to be later. I do not know the exact moment yet I truly believe it shall be tonight. I must speak to him."

"Perhaps," Pentu said slowly, "your sorrow over the baby has driven your thoughts to such turmoil. Could there be a more rational explanation for what you believe to happen?"

"No, Pentu. I have not become so bereaved I cannot distinguish between grief and threats to our Pharaoh. I love and trust you above all things. Yet in this steadfast resolve of mine I ask you to place your trust in me. Please do not discount the import or truth of which I speak."

Pentu nodded. "Yes, you are quite right. My great apologies. You are not prone to fantastic imaginings and I shall do all I can to aid you in this task. To begin, I shall wait at the main entrance to the Royal Palace. Perhaps I shall catch a word with him in the gateway. I am sure his advisors and ministers shall pounce upon him when he is within the Palace. You would stand little opportunity to see him at that point. If I cannot have a moment then, I shall do so at the banquet. Perhaps you should accompany me there. That could be a solution."

"How am I to enter? I am no longer a part of the Queen Tiye's staff. Even then, I should be segregated to the servant's banquet area. Is Akar invited as well?"

"I assume he shall be present."

"I cannot possibly be in the same room with that monster. Additionally, if he saw me it could be our ruin. He yet visits the Royal Harem seeking my return and would most assuredly create an altercation at the banquet. Additionally, I believe he is involved in this threat to the Pharaoh in some manner. He and Queen Tiye have become quite cozy and genial of late."

"Akar," he said with venom. "That does not surprise me. Very well, then I shall require the note from Consort Tamin. It may provide me with leverage in approaching him, at least. I shall start there."

That said, he tucked the bit of papyrus paper in his *shendyt* and walked down the mud-brick stairs. Grabbing a pitcher of water and a loaf of bread, he prepared to wait perched under the main gatehouse. He sat just within the tall rectangular opening against the thick cool walls. It was nearing midday and the sun crept higher in the sky. He watched as the heat rose in waves from the sand, giving the land a look of rippling water. Few people were out in this heat yet he saw some travelers upon camels. Those dependable beasts of burden were always part of the Egyptian landscape.

He would wait all day if he must. Anything for Asim. He drank the water and ate his bread while he sat. He looked to the horizon once again, and was rewarded for his patience. The tip of the Pharaoh's largest barge was easing through the private Royal Canal preparing to dock at the Palace harbor. He need only wait for the Pharaoh's disembarkation.

Nearing the entrance before the Pharaoh were several guards who had accompanied the Royal party. They spoke sternly amongst themselves, each shaking his head in obvious concern. Pentu had a sinking feeling. Perhaps Asim had been mistaken in her facts. Perhaps something has already happened to the Pharaoh. The guards entered the gatehouse and stood at attention, flanking the walls for Ramses' entrance.

Pentu could not help yet ask, "Something has happened. Are you at liberty to tell me?"

Guard One said, "It was most disrespectful and dangerous. I do not know what they hoped to gain by their actions, do you?" he asked Guard Two.

The second man answered, "No. I was taken aback by their violent behavior."

"Who?" asked Pentu fearfully. "Who was violent?"

"The crowds of people," answered Guard Three. "In two different cities," he said with amazement upon his face. Taking a deep breath, he turned to Pentu and explained further. "Our Pharaoh wished to visit other towns and cities by providing further processions. He felt it important for the people to witness his health and ability to continue his sovereignty. The major city was pleasant, even reverent in their greetings as they lined the roads. Then we approached the farming communities. The atmosphere there was very different."

"Yes," took up Guard Two, "as we led the procession in formation, people in the crowds began to shout at the Pharaoh. They demanded jobs and food. Someone actually began hurling rotten fruit at the carrying chair."

"Actions were worse in the next town," continued Guard Three. "Some threw rocks with their insults and demands. One found its mark upon the cheek of the Pharaoh. Several of us attempted to break rank and chase the culprits down. Either they were extremely fast, or other troublemakers sheltered them."

"By the gods, I wanted those men. I would make them pay," hollered Guard One

"The Minister of Proceedings cancelled the remaining processions to provide the Pharaoh medical care. He thought it best in eliminating further disruptions. That is why we return earlier than planned."

"What of Thebes?" asked Pentu. "Our city has prepared for his grand entrance. Shall he eliminate that procession from the celebrations?"

"Our brave Pharaoh wishes to carry on. Thebes is our capital and the people within love him. We shall double the guards, of course, surrounding his litter if need be. Pharaoh Ramses may choose to close the draperies on his carrying chair, however. He has suffered a nasty gash upon his cheek and shall wear an obvious dressing upon it. His people should not see him so."

"The fabric is sheer and the masses shall yet have a view of him. We shall know later of his ultimate decision. Ah. He arrives."

The King walked the short distance from the barge through the entry pylon flanked by his personal guards. Men were shoulder to shoulder even in this large space, each having a say in the deplorable antics of the day. As the many conversations echoed within the confines of the walled interior, Pentu slid past the throng and moved towards the King.

This is most ill advised, he thought. Chances were slim he would have the chance to speak to the Pharaoh at all. Certainly not in private. Yet he pushed on until he had reached the men surrounding the Pharaoh. Bowing low, he greeted his Pharaoh with exclamations of sorrow for the violence he experienced.

"Pentu. It is good of you to greet me. I have seen much worse in battle. It is merely a scratch. Yet I have never seen such unrest among my people. I was not informed of the extreme hardships they are suffering. On the morrow we must gather the council and speak of this."

"Yes, My Pharaoh. I shall pass the word to the others. I have one request, my Great Pharaoh. Do you have a moment for a brief discussion in private? I assure it is most important." He reached into his garment to retrieve the paper from Tamin. He began to explain the note and its author when the Supreme General of the Royal Army approached. Next to him was Akar, the highest-ranking officer of the Pharaoh's Private Guards.

The general bowed and directed the Pharaoh's attention to his own conversation. Pentu slipped the note into his garment. There could be no privacy now, he thought. Still he attempted to gain the Pharaoh's eye and ear. He waved his arm behind the military men and said, "Your Majesty, if I might only have a moment . . ."

"Pentu, I have not the time to spare. I must meet with my personal physician and prepare for the procession in Thebes. Perhaps later. Or on the morrow." With that he was led away to the interior of the Royal Palace.

Pentu tried once more, saying loudly, "Please, My Pharaoh, this can not . . ." yet Ramses was gone and Pentu finished his sentence softly to himself, ". . . wait until the morrow." He sighed. He must tell Asim of this development. Tonight he must interrupt any and all festivities the Pharaoh would be a part of. Pentu must convince the ruler to listen to his message. If need be, Asim would be at his side. Perhaps she could reinforce the plea for a modicum of privacy. The procession would soon begin in Thebes followed by the great banquet where, he prayed, he could approach the Pharaoh.

## Chapter Ten

Queen Tiye was attempting to relax within the luxuriant gardens within the first enclosure of the temple. She had been served a bowl of fresh fruit and she was attacking these innocent delicacies with her fruit knife.

She was frustrated with her mother who was currently sleeping through the heat of the day; Akar for his persistent insolence; and the Crown Prince who continued to lift his nose in superiority to those around him. She stabbed at her fruit repeatedly until some pieces were nothing more than mush. Having lost her appetite, she set the bowl aside.

There would be food enough at the banquet for nourishment, she thought. Her mother's appetite, on the other hand, was abundant to the extreme and ate as thought murdering the Pharaoh and his Crown Prince tonight was not a cause for worry. She was never one to pass up food, especially if it came at no cost to her. With so many exquisite and unusual delicacies in the Palace, it seemed the woman continually had a bowl or plate in front of her. Oh please make her leave after the deed was completed, prayed Tiye to no one in particular. She had been here nary a week and I am nearly deranged by indulging her every whim. And the woman had many: from roasted goose before slumber to seeded pomegranates before she rose and sweet wines in between. Asim, admitted Tiye, had been more adept at handling her mother's orders than her other servants.

Tiye took a long deep breath. She must sort out the details for tonight. Thoughts of her mother could wait. She picked at the mangled fruit beside her and popped a piece into her mouth absent thought. She had a new, intricately designed gown for tonight's occasion. With it, she would wear topaz at her ears and wrist, she decided. Her gown was gold so the yellow stone would be complimentary. Additionally, the gem protected the wearer from evil spirits and she did not want to encourage them to gather about her tonight.

In addition to the amethyst puzzle pendant, she would have at her throat a choker strand of Egyptian turquoise beads with a golden medallion of the goddess Baset, the fierce feline warrior. Her protection and strength would be warranted this night. Providing she is real, thought Tiye. However, it was best not to rely strictly upon luck. Atop her plaited wig, golden chains would hold another medallion in the center of the hair.

She must encourage her husband to consume drink. The special wines at tonight's feast would lull him into comfort. She had already secreted another jug of the same wine within the Harem wives' possession. Once they met in the Harem gardens, they shall present the wine to him along with his favorite sweets. He shall be so enamored and occupied by his wives, she thought, I could easily open the scarab locket and deposit the substance into his wine.

We must be coy and cautious with him, waiting till the moment is ripe. This was not to be rushed, she thought. He must be properly intoxicated. He may be old yet he could still overpower the seven of them, call loudly for assistance, or attack one of the women. She must bide her time.

Pentawer shall make his way to his brother's chambers while death overcame Ramses. The guard stationed at Amonhirk's door tonight was part of the conspiracy. A cry of alarm would not be answered. It would be simple for her son to find Amonhirk within his private quarters. The Crown Prince was not comfortable with parties or large groups of people and would leave the festivities as soon as it was proper. A poor trait for a leader, thought Tiye, since a Pharaoh met with more people than one could imagine. Well, thought Tiye, at least he shall be spared such groups in the future. After tonight, the embalmers shall have him.

In her thoughts, she began ticking off the other members of their chosen cohorts, a diverse group of people from walks of life she did not normally associate with. Still, she was pleased at the large number of allies she and her mother had accumulated. It was more than she had believed possible.

Several of their sympathizers — various soldiers, a Captain, and a General — had been ramping up the locals against Ramses III and Amonhirk. Several wives of social status were inciting those within their own circles using the probability of higher taxes with which to do so. The Harem wives were prepared with their part to play. They promised diligence with the magic chants and the wax figures to render any extraneous Harem guards useless. Their family members located in Libya, Nubia, and the Hittites were to lend their international support of Pentawer after the assassinations. Various interior guards and servants were at the stand-by.

Akar — she thought of him with revulsion — promised to supply the weapons and oversee the guards at the Harem entrance. The Pharaoh might think it odd for such a high-ranking officer to stand guard at the door — especially one he called a friend — therefore he would stay out of view until the Pharaoh entered. Ramses must notice nothing out of place. Most importantly, she had negotiated the cooperation of the Magician and Priest. They had already completed their part of the bargain. Ramses was mortal, subject to the hand of death tonight.

It would take some time to prepare for tonight's dinner, she thought: bathing, makeup, hair, nails, gown, and jewelry. She had a few choices for the remainder of the day facing her. She could travel by her husband's side during his procession in Thebes, occurring in an hour or so. However, she had heard of this morn's trouble in neighboring cities and towns. While it was an excellent show by those in their conspiracy, she did not relish the notion of experiencing possible injury.

The other option would be to visit the Harem wives, confirm their preparedness and the whereabouts of concealed weapons from Akar. That too, seemed fraught with difficulties. She had been seen in the Harem more often than she could convincingly explain. Additionally, she did not expect any weapons to be on the site at this time of day. Akar was to present those sharpened items to the other wives just prior to the feast.

Her last alternative for the day was one that made her cringe: visit her mother. She knew the woman would insist on reviewing the details — yet again — before the banquet began. The woman never seemed to tire of this topic. At least, thought Tiye, I shall be seated at the Pharaoh's table and not forced to converse with her while eating. She looked at the discarded bowl of fruit now covered in flies and decided to leave this area. The garden failed to provide her the calmness or serenity she had sought. She stood with a heavy sigh. She was quite sure those emotions would elude her until the morrow.

## Chapter Eleven

By the grace of the gods, the Pharaoh had returned to the Royal Palace unscathed and jovial. The citizens of Thebes had behaved in a most respectful and reverent manner. Their words of encouragement and occasional cheers almost eradicated the memory of this morn's events. Almost. The Pharaoh was well aware of the duty he must perform on the morrow. Those towns, which had brutalized him in words and actions, would find punishment. It was a recognized and sanctioned fact an example must be set for such treachery and disloyalty against the Crown. Even now, as he waited for his butlers and handlers to complete his readiness for tonight's celebration, he barely understood the anger emanating from his people. His advisors and council members withheld the truth of his country's condition, he concluded. If I had been properly informed of homeless and starving citizens, resolutions might have been found. Now, he thought, it seemed too late for simple modifications. Needed now are drastic measures, measures I shall enforce.

Not tonight, however. The entire Palace is anticipating tonight's celebration and banquet. Weeks had been spent with the details to the point of near exhaustion to his staff. Dignitaries from Egypt's trade countries would be in attendance. He could not call a council meeting to thresh out financial solutions now. Tomorrow would be soon enough. By then he might be persuaded to forgo any punishment.

Putting such thoughts and worries aside, the King viewed his reflection in his mirrors. I am yet a most regal sight, he thought, ruler of the greatest country in the world, feared by many, and loved by all. Stepping from his Royal Chambers, he was met by a division of his personal guards, dressed in their military finery. Flanking him front and rear, the troops escorted their Pharaoh to the grand banquet hall. Further enhancing his power, the many guards would stand at attention throughout the evening and line the wide hallway leading to this massive dining chamber.

As he walked slowly to the beginnings of a great celebration, he saw his newest minister, Pentu, gesticulating frantically to him from the edges of the corridor. Waving in return to Pentu, the Pharaoh noticed the desperate look on the man's face. Ah yes, he recalled, I must have time to speak to Pentu on the morrow. It would be best, he decided, to hear him out prior to a full council meeting. He would inform his Royal Court Minister of Proceedings of this decision during the celebration. Naturally, that minister would be present. His Royal Advisors, Royal Family members, and aristocrats would all be present in this main banquet hall. After all, tonight's request for attendance was not an invitation: it was a Royal Command.

## Chapter Twelve

Pentu rushed to his quarters where Asim was remaining out of sight. "Asim, I have yet to speak a word to the Pharaoh. He noticed me during his procession to the great banquet yet he did not yield. We have no choice. I shall have to force my way upon him tonight before the meal begins."

"Is that wise? Queen Tiye will be seated at his side. If she should overhear any of what you say to him, she might order your arrest or order Akar to remove you. That man would not simply escort you from the area, you may be sure."

"There is no other way. I must go to him directly, present him with your note, and pray that he will agree to hear us out. To do so in private entails leaving the family table. Indeed, he must exit the entire room. You must be present, Asim, somewhere nearby. I have no notion what you are to say to him or why you are so compelled to speak yet it must be from you own lips."

Asim thought a moment and said, "Across from the banquet room is a passage leading to the chambers of a council minister. It has a strange canopy structure jutting out above the door. I have often noticed this oddity, wondering the why of it. Yet it is perfect for our needs. The entire doorway protrudes into the hall to some depth almost as a small angled tunnel. There is space enough for me to stand in its enclosure. The passageway is lit with oil lamps yet this space remains in shadow."

"Then we must leave at once. The Pharaoh has entered the celebration and the guests are present, awaiting the feast. We should not be hindered in our short walk."

Asim and Pentu walked swiftly down the stone steps, along the corridor framing the Audience Room, and on to the banquet hall. Asim quickly turned a narrow corner and pointed out the peculiar shaped entranceway.

"There it is. Quite odd, is it not? If I stand thusly," and she stood sideways with her back to the corner they had just turned, "I do not believe I shall be seen."

Pentu backed away from her and looked toward the large stone overhang that projected into the passageway. "I see naught of you," he whispered. "I shall return as soon as I am able. When you hear

## Chapter Seven

The entire country was under the spell of the great commemoration. This was the opportunity for every person in Egypt to celebrate the reign of Ramses III and pray for his continued rule. From the smallest of villages to the largest of cities, parties would thrive well into the dawn.

As the capital city, Thebes was not to be outdone in grandeur. Food and drink were being consumed, pathways cleared for the Royal procession, and tents raised for long lasting enjoyment.

The Palace as well was in a flurry with excitement and preparations. All the formal dining rooms were to be utilized, so great were the number of invited guests and dignitaries. An unlimited amount of roasting meats were already sizzling upon the grill while fresh fruit and vegetables were placed wherever space was found. Flowers had been picked and strung into garlands or placed in watered vases. Tonight, the largest baking and preparation rooms in the country were not large enough.

While the aristocracy was anticipating a joyful night, another faction of people had concerns that differed. Over the course of several years, more and more people found themselves homeless and hungry. The sight and sounds of this revelry only brought to home their suffering. For weeks, members of the conspiracy had been seeking out these poor wretches and inciting them into action during the Royal Procession through the streets. Their poor status, they were told, was a direct result of the Pharaoh's splendor and self-indulgent spending. The welfare of Egypt's people should be foremost in the eyes of the Pharaoh.

Several disgruntled people took up this mantra of 'people first'. Egypt had never seen such hard times. The wealth spent on today's celebration could feed many families for a lifetime. The crops failed and water levels were low. Jobs were lost yet the portly bellies and bloated coffers of the Pharaoh, his ministers, and priests grew wider with their greed. Cloistered as they were among the grandeur of the Palace and temples, how could they realize the poor man's plight? Why do they not look with seeing eyes at the lives of this disregarded group? The rich, said the agitators, continue to grow richer while the poor become poorer.

me call out, walk around the corner into the main hallway. Pray for me, my love." With a quick kiss, he was gone.

The row of guards at the large opening to the banquet hall was a daunting sight yet Pentu was glad to see them in easy view. If he could somehow convince the Pharaoh to enter this corridor, he might do so more readily with this small division nearby. The noises were great from within. Music was playing, people were clapping, and conversations were spoken loudly over the din. He had never seen such a display of fresh flowers, glittering jewels on women and men, abundant exotic foods, and oil lamps lighting the whole. He was so overtaken with such splendor he could only stand and stare before gathering his wits to proceed.

The Pharaoh sat at the long main table upon a raised dais with his two main wives, the Crown Prince, and several dignitaries from neighboring countries. The Harem wives, other emissaries, citizens of stature and wealth, and noblemen of Egypt were positioned about the large room as their status dictated. To cause a scene among so many powerful people would surely be Pentu's downfall. He must tread lightly as he spoke to the Pharaoh while convincing him to leave this celebration honoring him. Not an easy task, thought Pentu.

He made an approach to the dais yet had barely taken three steps when a guard stepped in his path. "This area to the Pharaoh is only for a chosen few."

"I understand, yet it is vital I speak with Pharaoh Ramses. I am of his advisory council. I believe my presence shall be allowed."

"His Royal Pharaoh Ramses III is scheduled to stand before his guests to offer blessings upon them. You cannot proceed further."

Pentu looked up at the serious man. "Then I choose to wait on this spot until he has finished. Then I shall proceed."

The guard grunted at Pentu. "That is a matter for the Pharaoh. We shall see."

Before Pentu could offer a word of further argument to the guard, the music ceased and the Pharaoh rose from his chair. He was greeted with great applause and the Pharaoh graciously lowered his hands with a smile. The people took to their seats and became attentive to their ruler.

Pentu heard naught of the Pharaoh's blessings. His thoughts remained on speaking to Ramses, convincing him to leave the table and his friends, and allow Asim to inform him of whatever detailed secret she held. He had not seriously reasoned the outcome of this conversation he was attempting to instigate. He only prayed Ramses would not punish Asim for her intrusion.

He looked at his ruler, standing so straight with the crown of both Upper and Lower Egypt upon his head, the man who governed all, the god to his people. He had seen the Pharaoh when he was joyous and when he was consumed with anger. Through it all, he remained a good man, Pentu decided, and a ruler he was honored to protect if warranted.

As the Pharaoh regained his chair and the ensuing applause broke into his thoughts, he turned his attention to the guard impeding him from the task at hand. "So," began Pentu with some aggression, "It would seem our Pharaoh has completed the blessing. I demand you to step aside or I vow by the gods above I shall ensure the Pharaoh knows it was at your hand I was halted."

The skeptical guard called another to his side. "This man wishes to see our Pharaoh. He insists he has important information for him. I do not trust him, however. I shall stand in his path while you obtain the Pharaoh's permission."

The newest member to this farce looked askance at his superior. "Sir," he began, "I cannot approach our King. I have not the rank to do so."

"And you never shall unless you reason out the order of protocol. See the soldier wearing the gold belt? It is he whom you need approach. Pass the message to him and he in turn shall see it passed to our Pharaoh." The lowly guard nodded happily and went off.

By the gods, why so much protocol in all things Royal? Thought Pentu. If I had only captured Ramses' attention, I might now be in full conversation with him. Pentu watched as the guard approached the soldier at the end of the Pharaoh's table. The man looked at Pentu yet took no action other than speak to another sentry two steps away. Pentu groaned. The infuriating line of command, he thought. Shall this entire proceeding be set in reverse? As if watching a relay stick being passed down the line of men, he finally saw the hand-off to the Pharaoh. Ramses looked in Pentu's direction who was frantically waving to his ruler hoping to forestall any further delay. Thankfully Ramses smiled and, with a slight motion of his hand, the guard stepped aside and allowed Pentu to pass.

"Ah, Pentu. How good of you to join in the festivities. I have arranged our talk to commence early on the morrow. Then I shall require all ministers and the full council to convene for an important discussion." With that decree, Ramses turned away from Pentu to speak to another.

"Your majesty," Pentu began. The Pharaoh did not hear him. Pentu began again leaning closer to the Pharaoh. "Your Majesty, my sincere and abundant apologies. The morrow shall be too late. I must speak to you now."

Ramses finally turned a cold eye upon Pentu. "You *Must*?" said the ruler meaningfully with a frown. "I think not, Pentu. You are excused." Again, Pentu was ignored with a turn of the great man's head.

Praying for strength and the preservation of his head, Pentu plowed ahead. "My Noble Pharaoh," said Pentu in a whisper near Ramses' ear, "I have a message from your Royal Consort Tamin." He held the note below his waist to avoid attention from the others at the Royal Table.

The Pharaoh turned his head back to Pentu and glanced down at the bit of paper held in his hand. Taking it, he read it quickly and raised his eyes to Pentu's. "This woman of whom she mentions. She is known to you?"

"Yes, My Pharaoh. She is waiting beyond the great arch of the banquet hall entrance. She is most anxious to speak to you and indicates she has knowledge which could save you from harm."

Ramses looked skeptically at Pentu then glanced back at the note he held. "The trust I have in Tamin is unconditional. Yet I would ask you, why is the woman mentioned not presenting me this information here and now? Why do you carry this message and not she? I would have you bring her to me instantly."

This request is what Pentu had feared. What he had learned in diplomacy and protocol would now be put to the test. He bowed low to his ruler and said, "My Great Pharaoh, she could face danger within this room. Indeed, she has been in hiding for these past three days. If others witness her speaking to you, immediate action could be taken against you both. Please, your Majesty, if you feel uncomfortable leaving this room with me, several guards at your side might ease your concerns."

Ramses stared long and hard at Pentu before responding. "You have always been honest with me, Pentu, even when others would not. I shall attend to her." He rose from his chair to the astonishment of those present. His table of Royal Family members rose as he walked off the dais. As a ripple extending upon the Nile River, groups of celebrants began to rise a table or two at a time until all the guests were upon their feet, waiting for their Pharaoh to exit. Ramses motioned four of his nearby guards to accompany him as he walked ahead of Pentu into the large hallway.

"Now, Pentu, where is this woman?"

Pentu called out and pointed to the corner where Asim emerged. The Pharaoh looked at her with recognition and said, "You are a handmaiden to My Queen, are you not?"

"I was, my King," said Asim bowing low. "I am currently serving the Harem. It was there I made acquaintance with Consort Tamin. I am Asim."

Ramses opened his eyes a little wider. "Tamin instructs me to listen to your words. Very well. Quickly, then."

Pentu began to walk away when the Pharaoh halted him. "You shall stay, Pentu. Guards," he called to them, "Position yourselves behind the pillar. I shall call if you are needed."

Turning once again to Asim, she took a deep breath and began her tale as succinctly as she could, beginning with the first overheard conversation to the last visit of Queen Tiye to his Harem. "Our abject apologies for this intrusion yet this could not wait till the morrow. Whatever they plan, it shall occur tonight, My Pharaoh. Queen Tiye is most anxious for Prince Pentawer to sit upon your Throne. When the Queen, the Prince, and the Queen's mother last spoke to the other wives, they were confirming the details," she concluded with her eyes lowered in respect.

Throughout her recital, the King had remained silent, wisely contemplating all he had heard from her mouth. Now he began questioning Asim. "My beloved Pentawer," he said sadly. "Are you aware of any others involved?"

"I believe Akar is one of them, my King, and of course the six Harem wives. Yet while I am sure many others exist within the Palace, I am not privy to those names. My reasoning was to deliver it to you personally though you may think me mad. I did not trust others with this information. I believed you would know the truth of it. Again, my apologies for this intrusion."

"Akar," said Ramses. "Yes, I know of your relationship to him. I also know of his temper and that of My Queen. Her mother is extremely forceful as well. Perhaps these accusations are merely a ploy to punish them for misdeeds committed upon your person."

Asim looked shocked and frightened. "I swear by all the gods, my King, I speak the truth. My concern is only for your safety. Akar is not the man he portrays himself to be." She informed her Pharaoh of Akar's treasure trove she found beneath her bed. "He is vicious and quite capable of any deed to meet his needs."

"I had no notion to this brutality. I assume you are able to lay hands upon this box for proof if I should require it?" Asim nodded. "I believe you, Asim. As apparently does my good Tamin. Without this corroboration from her," he waved the note in the air, "I should imagine the worst. I assume the trust is mutual between you and my Consort." Asim nodded. "That begs the question — why not relay this information to her? She would pass it to me in full."

"I was concerned for her safety as well, My Pharaoh. I told no one. I knew not how deeply this conspiracy was seeded. I wished no harm to come to another because of what I knew or told them."

"Yet you were willing to place yourself in harm's way," Ramses said with a smile.

Asim nodded. "I had the aid of Pentu; a loyal subject to you, My Pharaoh. I trust him with my life."

He considered the two people standing in front of him before continuing. "So, it is to be tonight. You stated I shall be lured to these gardens by the hand of my wife and Queen, Tiye." Again Asim nodded. "Seven wives against their Pharaoh; brother upon brother. While I am no longer a young man, I could yet call out for aid or damage one of them in the attempt. Tiye is clever. She assuredly has allies among the harem guards and must have made provisions for my inability to act."

Remembering another fact Asim said, "There was a mention of a favorite wine and sweets, served at the feast and within the Harem. Might that be of importance, My Pharaoh?"

"Yes, Asim, it explains much. At least I cannot be harmed by the meal with my food tasters at my side tonight." The Great

Pharaoh was silent as he thought. "I believe I shall not have a great thirst for any further wine brought to me this night, no matter the vintage. Perhaps water might be more quenching. Pentu, you shall sit by my side this evening. Firstly, you must locate a large pitcher and fill it by your own hand with fresh water. Bring an unused cup as well. Only from these shall I drink tonight yet no one is to know the pitcher contains mere water. To the others at my table, it shall be a special wine. Are you in complete understanding of what I ask? This knowledge is for the two of us alone, Pentu."

Pentu nodded and bowed. "As you command, My Pharaoh. Then you will not attend your Queen and Consorts to the Harem?"

Ramses smiled cruelly. "On the contrary, I intend to play their game. The rules, however, shall be mine.

"Asim, you and Pentu have exhibited much courage and served me well this evening. At a more appropriate time, I shall send for you both to properly show my appreciation. I shall not forget all you have done for my reign. For now, I think it best for Asim to return to her hiding. I shall return to the feast and await you there. Pentu, one last word: tell no one what we have heard from Asim. I wish to handle this personally." Pentu nodded and bowed. While he thought better of Ramses' decision, it was his to make as the Pharaoh.

"Guards," called Ramses to those four stalwart men who had accompanied him, "I would have a word with you before I enter."

## Chapter Thirteen

As the King re-entered the banquet hall, Asim began walking to their chambers. "Wait," said Pentu. "I should escort you."

"You must attend to the Pharaoh. I am capable of the walk and I swear to stay in the room until your return." That said, they made their goodbyes and Pentu began walking to a kitchen or storage room, hoping he could find a pitcher and cup.

Not knowing the layout of the servants assigned areas, he became muddled. He was about to stop any servant within the hallway when he saw Joba, leaving the second area of banqueting. Naturally, his arm was casually wrapped around the waist of a young lady.

Pouncing upon his friend, Pentu expressed his need for help. "Did you say you are looking for a pitcher and a cup? Have you become part of the kitchen staff, my friend?" he said with humor.

"It is upon the orders of the Pharaoh I seek these things, odd though that may sound. I have a long tale to tell you, Joba. On the morrow, however — I have no time tonight."

Joba finally took pity upon his friend and headed him in the direction of the elusive pitcher and cup. "Oh, I have seen Akar this evening. He is a contemptible man, that one. Do you know a reason for him to be guarding the Harem this night? Perhaps this lower duty is a punishment for some misdeed."

Pentu stopped mid stride. "What is this you say? He is at the Harem entrance? How do you know of this?"

Joba explained he saw the man walk across the bridge in that direction. "When I asked for his reasoning to be in an area not under his prevue, he said he had guard duty at the Harem and I should watch the manner in which I speak to someone with his rank. He followed this statement with curses and threats."

Pentu grabbed Joba and said, "Joba, I must speak to you in private. It is urgent." He pointedly glanced at Joba's companion. "Please. I assure you it is of the greatest import."

With a great sigh, Joba kissed the lady's wrist and made his excuses. Watching as the lovely girl walked seductively away, Joba turned to his friend and said, "I hope I shall not regret what you have asked of me. Pray what you say is important enough for me to forgo such a treasure."

Pentu dragged Joba around an empty corridor. He had promised the Pharaoh he would keep his tongue yet now he was afraid. He kept the details at a minimum, not exactly disobeying the Pharaoh and possibly assisting. "Asim spoke to the Pharaoh tonight. I have orders not to divulge this, Joba, yet I believe you can assist me. Akar is embroiled in a scheme to harm the Pharaoh. I know not what he plans while standing at the Harem entrance, yet I assure you he has ulterior reasoning behind it. I fear for Ramses life and Akar has a hand in whatever is brewing."

Joba stared at his friend intently. "Nothing that man does would surprise me. Allow me to see to Akar. I shall be my pleasure as a task long overdue. If by chance he is not alone, a few of my fellow Royal Guards would enjoy such action against him. Do you wish him dead?"

"I think not. The Pharaoh may wish to question him. Apprehended would be best. One thing more." Pentu described the house in Thebes where Asim had lived and the box under the bed. "Is it possible for you to retrieve this item? I fear for Asim's safety so I cannot send her. Only when you have time, naturally. The Pharaoh expressed an interest in it yet not immediately."

Joba replied, "Of course. It shall be in your hands on the morrow. Are you positive you do not wish him killed?" Pentu shook his head. "A pity," said Joba glumly. "Still, if he makes a move against me, I reserve the right to subdue him by whatever means necessary."

With that, Pentu journeyed towards the pottery he needed and Joba proceeded on his way to subdue Akar.

## Chapter Fourteen

Ramses arrived at his table and walked majestically upon the dais. The entire room stood until he took his seat. "All is well my husband?" asked Queen Tiye at his side.

"Quite well, my dear. A minor political matter in which to attend." He watched closely as his food taster sampled a bit of each item upon his plate before setting it in front of the Pharaoh. The man retreated into the background until he was again needed.

"I have ordered one of your most favored wines, My Husband. I shall have a cup poured for you," she said as she motioned a hovering servant to put her words to action.

Ramses shook his head. "I think not, My Queen. I have another vintage arriving. Ah, here is Pentu with said wine. It is a gift from a visiting crown prince. The man would be insulted if I did not partake of it.

"Pentu, I would have you next to me. I wish you to dispense the wine when my cup is empty. My dear," he said to Tiye, "You shall sit on the other side of Queen Iset. Another seat shall be forthcoming for you." He clapped his hands and put his words into action. Another chair was placed next to Ramses' First Queen.

If Tiye could have stabbed Ramses on this spot, she would have done so. "I am your Queen. By rights I should be seated to this side of you."

Ramses looked at his wife with derision, this woman who would have him dead. "And I am your Pharaoh god. I command you to vacate your chair," he said calmly. Bowing slightly, Queen Tiye did as commanded.

Throughout the meal, Ramses continually sipped upon the water from his cup. He kept it close to him and allowed no other to sample the 'special wine'. As he drank, he became slightly more vocal, laughing more often, and applauding vigorously for the musicians and dancers. Many guests were by now completely inebriated with the flowing wine that seemingly had no end. To their eyes, the Pharaoh was merely enjoying himself and imbibing slightly too much wine. To Pentu who knew the cup contained only water, the Pharaoh remained quick-witted while choosing to appear intoxicated. It was apparent the Pharaoh was playing into the Queen's hand until he could spring his own trap.

The evening had grown late and Pentu began to doubt the truth of Asim's knowledge. The Pharaoh was saying good night to the Crown Prince when Pentu noticed Queen Tiye approach her husband from behind. "My Husband, could you spare a moment of your time?" Ramses gave his assent and Tiye leaned into his ear speaking low and softly. She leaned so close her ample bosom was fully on display to him. So, thought Pentu, the enticement begins.

The Pharaoh smiled at his Queen. "Ah, a most wonderful idea, my dear," he said slurring his words ever so slightly. As he said this, Tiye motioned to six of his wives from a secondary table and they approached their Pharaoh, giggling and bowing. "So, my dear consorts, you are to be my private entertainment this evening? By all means, carry on with your preparations and I shall meet you there." He took another noisy gulp of his water/wine. He was, to all intent, quite drunk. "Off with you all. I shall have another drink of this excellent wine and follow you directly."

Queen Tiye smiled and bowed. As she walked away Ramses shot her a long calculating gaze. To Pentu he said, "I shall have no further need of you tonight. You have serviced me well." With that, Ramses reached for the jug in front of him, rose to thunderous applause, and exited the room encompassed by several guards. Now it begins, he thought.

## Chapter Fifteen

Tiye finished redressing in a most diaphanous gown for the occasion. The gown flowed behind her as she walked and exposed every curve and crevice. Tomorrow she would be the Queen Mother, she thought. My son shall sit upon the Throne of Egypt. Yet tonight she must keep her wits. All must go according to plan. So far, she was on schedule with her timing and hoped the others were as well. Taking a last look in her mirror and adding a dab of perfume to her temples, she traveled quickly and quietly to the Harem.

Her appointed two men were on duty at the exterior door. For an inordinate sum, they were prepared to ignore any noises emitted from the inner sanctuary. Akar was in the shadows and would oversee them to enforce their promise. He would venture forth only after the Pharaoh had entered. If the Pharaoh saw the Captain of the Royal Guards at this mundane post, he might become suspicious. She slid past them and into the gardens.

The remaining family members were attending the banquet and entertainment, the younger children were asleep, and the garden empty. Tiye walked swiftly, almost running, to the area they had decided to meet — the same secluded and foliage filled spot of their prior meetings. The elder of the six wives was organizing refreshments on a low table for the Pharaoh. Several oil lamps were repositioned, lending a more secluded and shadowy atmosphere to the area. "Perfect," said Tiye. "You have secured his favorites and more. Your sisters are prepared?" she asked.

The Consort nodded. "They are located opposite that pillar, unseen for now yet prepared to make a grand entrance once you call out. We are dressed much the same."

Tiye noted the wife who was nearly naked save for her jewelry and a bit of sheer cloth and beads tied about her waist. Tiye nodded at her attire. "Lovely," she said. "Our husband shall be unable to resist the temptations presented to his eye. And the weapons?" she asked anxiously.

The Consort pointed under potted plants and beneath stone benches. "Within easy reach yet unseen."

Tiye sighed with relief. It would seem Akar had kept his assurances. "You have arranged all with great skill. Find your sisters and I shall escort the Pharaoh directly." Tiye retreated to the entrance door to receive Ramses. She smoothed her wig and straightened her gown, hoping these simple actions might quell the twisting of her stomach. Reaching into the nearby pond, she dipped her wrists into the water and dabbled a few drops against her neck. The heat seemed to gather in this enclosed entrance or perhaps, the reasoned, it was anxiety she felt.

Outside the portal doors, she heard footsteps crossing the wooden bridge. Taking a deep breath, she brought a smile to her lips and one hand against her hips. The door opened loudly and her husband entered saying, "My Dear, I have arrived." He was a bit loud, teetering on his feet slightly and Tiye reached out a steadying hand to him.

"Husband," she said, "it pleases me to see you. We have prepared many of your favored foods and wines for you if you wish to imbibe further," she said with a laugh.

"Wonderful," he said. "I have brought the last dregs of my wine. I shall complete that prior to partaking of your delicacies."

"We have many delicacies tonight for you, My Husband, many of which are not upon platter or table," she said with a lascivious grin.

Tiye held his arm slightly while walking to the secluded area where his other wives greeted him, giggling and fawning over him. They engulfed him with kisses and tender touches, cooing in his ears and enticing his body in spite of his resolve.

Laughing happily, he said, "One moment, my precious ones. I must first relieve myself if I am to be of any use to you this evening." With that said, he wandered in the direction of the nearby toilet room, his jug in hand.

Tiye whispered to the other women. "All is in order, My Sisters. We shall ease him upon the recliner while we feed him sweets and ply him with wine before the deed is done."

Several minutes passed before one wife observed, "He is long absent. Perhaps he has fallen." It was at that point they heard him returning, rustling nosily through the fig trees and palms, obviously drunk and stumbling to find his way.

"Come, My Husband, relax upon the soft cushions we have furnished for you. We shall feed you fruit and sweet breads from our very hands."

One wife, resting her nude breasts upon his arm, offered him a slice of bread dipped in honey. Rather than open his mouth, he took the offering and presented it to that wife. "Allow me to honor your beauty by feeding you the first bite." With a smile, she did as asked without hesitation and bit off a portion of the bread. He then popped the remainder into his mouth. "Delicious. You have provided me with exquisite tastings."

While his movements were those of a fully intoxicated man, his senses were keen. He watched their every movement through hooded eyes, ready to strike as quickly as an asp when threatened. His six consorts were fondling and kissing him yet his attention was upon Tiye.

"My Husband, let me offer you some wine. I have your preferred sweet vintage upon the table and fresh cups." She had been attempting to supply his cup with wine throughout the meal to no avail. He insisted upon that dreadful jug, even bringing it here, she thought. How am I to ensure his collapse if I cannot slip the drug from my locket to his cup?

"A most splendid idea, my dear. This jug has been nearly emptied." It was time to see this farce draw to a close. His excuse to use the toilet had been merely that — an excuse. Instead, he had opened the outer door to admit guards to be near his side. He purposely created a clumsy racket through the foliage to cover that of the guards situating themselves in hiding and within vantage points.

Taking an unused cup from the table, she poured the wine. "Oh, I have spilled upon my new gown. It is of no consequence. The water should eradicate the mark. One moment, My Husband." She set the cup upon the stone edge of the pond and made to dip her fabric in the water. The other wives were keeping him well entertained yet she saw the Pharaoh glance her way. She believed him too drunk to realize her true purpose although that glance had seemed quite keen.

She became nervous and indecisive. The slice to kill would be easy if he were not lucid. If he had his senses, all would be lost. She opted to assure his incapacitation and not rely solely upon the influences of the wine. She clicked open her scarab cache and dumped it into the cup. It was wiser to err on the side of caution, she thought. Combined with the wine, this should have the desired effect upon him shortly. Splashing water on her dress to confirm the pretext of a stained garment, she was once again at her husband's side.

"My apologies for the delay, My Husband. Here is your wine." Ramses caught the telling glint in her eyes as she handed him the cup.

While he appeared to sip the beverage, he merely brought the cup to his closed lips, and then wiped his mouth in feigned appreciation. After repeating this motion several times he exclaimed, "I seem to have had more than my share of drink tonight. I am suddenly quite lightheaded." He shook his head as if to clear the dizziness and grabbed his head in both hands. He laughed and said, "I may fall asleep in this very spot. I am blessed to have so many beautiful wives to see me to my bed." He made a half-hearted attempt to stand then sat abruptly back upon the couch with a laugh. The ladies in front of him laughed with their husband, and assisted him comfortably upon the cushions.

Grabbing a short knife from a hiding spot, Tiye slipped to the rear of the sofa. Closer and closer she crept to his back. At that moment when she had positioned herself to act, the Pharaoh stood and tossed the cup of wine in her face, grabbed her wrist, and wrenched the blade from her possession. "Guards," he called loudly.

As if by magic, shadowy figures emerged from the foliage, quickly surrounding the women with swords drawn. Ramses dragged Tiye to his side and threw her to the ground. "You thought to do away with me. *Me* — the Pharaoh of all Egypt. You and your gaggle of women stood no chance."

Tiye began calling for Akar, hoping he and others would come to her aid. "Akar is gone. He and those you positioned at the door have been dealt with. This guard," and he pointed to Joba who was standing near, "and others from my Royal Audience Chamber arrived earlier and made quick work of them. Even now they are bound and gagged, prepared for prison."

Tiye lifted her head and said with surprise. "How is it you are so clear of thought? I saw you drinking from that jug. You were quite overcome with wine. I do not understand."

In response, the Pharaoh grabbed his jug. "This jug?" He poured the remaining contents upon the ground watching it splash on the stones. "Mere water," he said.

"You knew," Tiye said accusingly and with malice. "How?"

"You were overheard upon this very spot, you and my wives, conspiring against me. Moreover, while I have these loyal guards at my side, so to does Amonhirk. I have forestalled the attempt on his life as well as my own. Even now, Pentawer is being taken from you. You ask how? I shall gladly tell you. I have one person to thank for the courage shown to me this night. Your servant, Asim."

Something glittered under the sofa and Tiye reached for it. In one move, she reached the Pharaoh, screaming, "No," at the top of her lungs. The guards were not swift enough. Tiye brought the small sharp ax down upon Ramses large toe, slicing it through completely. Blood flowed upon the stone floor while the toe casually rolled away. Stunned, the guards and wives could only stare at that stubby piece of flesh rolling upon the floor.

Chaos suddenly broke upon the scene of flickering lamplight and naked women. The Pharaoh screamed in pain and collapsed upon the seat. As Tiye stood and raised her hand once more, Joba had the good sense to throw her completely upon the floor and touch his sword to her throat. "Do not move," he ordered the Queen.

The other wives screamed and scattered. Some turned to fight, holding a rock or potted plant in her hand. Some managed to lock themselves behind their doors. Each one found a guard upon her, beating doors inward, seizing some around the waist or grabbing at their hair. They were deposited unceremoniously upon the floor of the garden and encircled by the guards. The men resembled a predatory pack of animals waiting for their prey to attempt the slightest movement. Their swords were outstretched, daring them to do so.

From his seat, the Pharaoh placed a large pillow over his foot yet the blood continued to flow, staining the pillow with the sticky crimson fluid. The pain was dimming his attention and he felt groggy. "Arrest them all," he yelled. "Confine them to their quarters. Take this one," he pointed to Tiye, "to her chambers with a guard on full duty. Retrieve my physician immediately." He heard sandals smacking upon the floor as someone ran to fetch the doctor. Tiye was screaming at the top of her lungs as two men dragged her from the Harem, closing the heavy doors behind them.

# BOOK FOUR
## Trials

### Chapter One

Tales of an attack upon Ramses permeated the Royal Place. While it was spoken of in whispers and hearsay, it was the only topic of conversation worth repeating. Rumors flourished with accounts of Ramses suffering a severed leg, loosing his fingers on one hand, or the complete removal of his nose.

Only one fact was a certainty; Amonhirk was managing the situation in his father's absence until Ramses III was restored to health in his private chambers. To the amazement of the Royal Physicians, The Pharaoh was recovering quickly. After suturing the open wound, they had utilized their vast knowledge of herbs, poultices, and magic prayers. The Pharaoh insisted upon a seat in his private audience room adjacent to his bedchamber. With his carefully bandaged leg upon a stool, he continued to rule the country by providing Royal directives to his son.

Every Palace individual, even his Royal Physicians, were now suspect. Indeed, while the doctors were ministering to him, he insisted upon Amonhirk or his First Royal Wife Iset at his side. The only guards he trusted were those who had followed his every command on the night of the attempted murder.

Ramses had quashed the attempt upon his son's life. While he knew Pentawer was part of the conspiracy, he had not thought him possible of murder. For it was Pentawer, he was told, who had endeavored to murder his brother with a very long sword. Prince Pentawer was currently locked within his private quarters, guards placed at his door day and night, until his trial. He was sure to be found guilty of treason and collusion to commit murder among other charges, thought the sad father. How could this have happened within these very walls? The son I loved above all others would see me dead, thought the King, simply to gain the crown. What had he done wrong to conjure such hatred in the boy?

As he was in this contemplative state, Amonhirk arrived. "Father, the physicians have been of aid to you, I see. You have regained color in your face."

"I have suffered worse in battles," replied the Pharaoh. "This shall not halt me. Even now, artisans are designing a wondrous device; a toe fashioned of leather and metal to strap upon my foot. It shall restore my balance, they tell me, and allow an easier gait to my walk."

"I have come to inform you where we stand with the accused. Those arrested are talking, implicating others."

"Accused conspirators always talk, my son," said the Pharaoh. "Always."

Indeed, so many were talking it was becoming problematic to have them cease. They were as animals of the night, snarling and snapping at each other. When one began to howl and blame others, so did they all. Many conspirators had been named: his personal Royal Butler, Perneb the priest, a magician, servants, his trusted friend Akar, his General, members of the Treasury administration, scribes, several magistrates, the chief of the Harem Chambers, and six of his wives. Yet he had been in the dark, never suspecting such a plot possible. It had taken the small voice of a servant girl to alert him.

"They shall point a finger to anyone if it saves their own skin," continued Ramses.

"It is as you say, Father. Some individuals we have already cleared of direct involvement. Others are accused of providing capital in the way of bribes. The investigation process is lengthy yet I have put many men upon the task. We shall know which men were truly invested and those who are innocent."

"I would appoint a judicial panel, my son. Twelve men whom we know to be free from this scandal." The Pharaoh named many men from which to choose. He hoped these had been uninvolved in the conspiracy and would be above bribery. All but two, they decided, were sound. "I would speak to each prior to their assignment. I have an additional man I wish to personally assign to the task. He is above reproach.

"These trials must remain completely unbiased. Since I do not wish to influence any of the twelve, I shall not be present at the hearings. You shall attend in my stead and provide to me all that occurs. I wish to oversee the events from here. Ensure you remain uninvolved. The court alone must evaluate the information presented and arrive at the truth. The justice must be dispensed according to the laws designated for the crime. The court will announce to the perpetrators the following statement when verdicts have been passed — 'Your Pharaoh and His Court do not hold responsibility for your punishment. The blame lies upon the conspirator's head alone.'

"I would have these trials and sentencings be a cautionary tale for future generations. The people must never entertain a notion against their Pharaoh again. The court must show no favoritism, even to members of the Royal Family." He finished this final sentence with obvious sadness

"Father, if not for your quick thinking, we should both be dead. You are not to blame for Pentawer's actions."

"Yet I am saddened and even now mourn the death sentence that must be reached. I find this entire debacle beyond veracity. I am harshly brought back to reality by the pain in my foot. Only then do I realize such treasonous acts actually occurred."

He gave a sigh and asked of his son, "Of what details are the citizens and Palace personnel aware?"

"Only that an attempt was made upon your life and the culprits have been apprehended. No mention has been made of your severed toe. Yet rumors abound within these walls from your death to loosing major body parts."

"These rumors must be put to rest. I do not wish the people to know of the mutilation of their Pharaoh. It is of great import they know of my continued strength.

"Send a guard after my minister Pentu. Instruct Asim to accompany him. It is to these brave loyalists we must give our thanks. Due to their quick thinking, I was properly warned of the conspiracy against us. You shall remain while I engage in conversation. I wish your mother to be present also. She wishes to show her gratitude towards them.

"Send for a scribe as well. While we do not normally conduct Royal matters in this Audience Room, circumstances are anything but normal. What we discuss in this room while I am in recovery is no less official. It must be recorded and preserved as shall the complete trials, no matter how many papyri are used, no matter their length."

Chapter Two

With the protection of a guard, Pentu and Asim were escorted to the Pharaoh's private chambers. This area was familiar to Asim yet Pentu had not witnessed the family quarters. He had always marveled at the artistry and extravagance of the Palace yet these hallways and private chambers put the other rooms to shame. He was so intent upon his examination of the finely crafted door, Asim was obliged to pull him away.

They entered the luxurious outermost chamber, that of the Pharaoh's Private Audience Room. He was seated upon a chair nearly as grand as the Throne, his injured foot upon a golden stool cushioned with soft pillows. The bandages were thick yet blood could be seen seeping through.

They both bowed low and awaited His Majesty's pleasure. "Rise, my faithful two. Amonhirk, this is Pentu and Asim; the two of whom I spoke."

The Crown Prince was seated next to his father with two guards flanking their sides. It was clear the Pharaoh was not about to take any chances. "My father informs me of your warning. I humbly offer gratitude to you both. You have saved the lives of two Pharaohs with your heroic action. My father improves with each passing day and shall see his reign continue. Your bravery shall not be overlooked."

Queen Iset was less formal in demonstrating her appreciating. Presenting each with an embrace, she expressed her thanks for saving the lives of her child and her husband.

Pentu and Asim bowed again. Pentu said, "I did no more than any loyal Egyptian would do. Yet I would mention a third person, most instrumental to the safety of My Pharaoh and the Crown Prince: The Royal Audience Chamber Guard, Joba. He restrained Akar and two other guards at the Harem door prior to your arrival. He further saved Your Majesty from a second slice of the Queen's ax." He praised Joba and his constant assistance from the day Pentu and he met. "Without his advice, Asim would never have met Consort Tamin nor overheard the conspirators."

"Then we must offer our gratitude to him as well. With so many involved in this scheme, you three have honored me with your loyalty," said Ramses.

"Due to your selfless actions, I am prepared to grant you whatever you desire. Title, wealth — anything."

Pentu looked at Asim and she nodded to him. "My Great Pharaoh, we would like a life together, as husband and wife, in my town of Set-Maat."

The Pharaoh looked upon them with astonishment. "You wish to resume your job as tomb foreman? I had hoped you would continue to serve me in a much higher council position. You could name any title you wish."

"If you wish me — us — to remain in your service, we shall do so, My Pharaoh. I seek only to serve you in whatever capacity you wish. Yet Asim has suffered much at the hands of Queen Tiye and Akar. I wish her to be safe."

"Tiye is no longer Queen. She and many others have been arrested and will soon face trial. No one can harm you further, Asim, I assure you. Is Set-Maat your wish as well?"

"I bow to your will, My Pharaoh. Yet in truth I would live the simple life with Pentu as my husband." She looked meaningfully at Pentu and continued, "And our baby."

"Baby?" said Pentu in astonishment. "I believed her to have died at birth."

The Pharaoh took up the conversation with equal amazement. "As did I. Explain the meaning of this."

"I feared for the life of my baby, My Pharaoh, at the hands of Akar. Your Royal Consort Tamin was in agreement. Akar was making every attempt to remove me from the Harem. I was willing to return to him yet I knew not his plans for the baby. I would not chance that.

"I beg of you, do not place blame upon Consort Tamin. It was my idea to have others believe she had given birth to twins." Looking at Pentu she said, "In truth, one baby girl is ours. Your wonderful wife agreed to care for the babe as her own. She has shown nothing but kindness and concern for me, My Great Pharaoh. If someone is to blame for this lie, please place it upon my head." She was kneeling upon the ground. "I have no right to any consideration from you, yet I beg you to allow me to see my baby before you pass sentence upon me."

Mighty Ramses sat back in his grand chair. "You have not yet seen your child?"

"No, my Great King. She was taken from me immediately after her birth and placed in the care of your wife. I did not look upon her fearing my resolve would dwindle. She remains with your consort, safe and loved."

His Queen laid her hand upon his shoulder and said, "It is a baby of your realm, My Husband."

Nodding in agreement with his Queen, the Pharaoh smiled. "Ah, Tamin," he said shaking his head side to side, "she is a great one for clever trickery. I am proud to learn of her involvement in keeping a child safe. This was a noble and selfless act on your part, Asim. You are truly worthy of motherhood. You were willing to give your child away to keep her safe, never to see her face.

"There shall be no punishment in this matter. I shall have a few words with my lovely Tamin, however. Secrets should not be kept from the Pharaoh although, considering what I now know of Akar, I fully understand taking this precaution."

The Pharaoh moved his injured foot slightly with a grimace crossing his face. "I shall inform you of the second reason I have called you here today. I have created a council of judges to administer the trials of the accused. I wanted you among those men to form a panel of twelve. I trust no citizen more than you, Pentu.

"I shall grant you the request you choose. Live a long and happy life in Set-Maat, have many children. Yet I would hope you postpone such a journey to sit upon the panel. Several trials will commence and your time here could be extended by weeks. Perhaps longer. This is not a Royal command, Pentu. For today, it is merely a request."

Pentu again looked to Asim for guidance. When she nodded assent, Pentu turned to his ruler. "I shall be most honored, My Pharaoh. I swear by the gods to consider all information presented so I may arrive at fair decisions. We shall delay our journey as long as you need my participation in this honorable task."

"Excellent. You shall meet with the Crown Prince and the other judges later today. My son shall outline the importance and rules for objective proceedings.

"In the meantime, I shall have your daughter brought to your arms, Asim. Pentu, I shall assign suitable quarters for your family. I shall also have a trusted guard accompany you both at all times. No harm shall befall either of you within these walls. On this I swear as your living god."

## Chapter Three

Every movement of Queen Tiye's was watched. How had it come to this? She had been Queen of Egypt; every wish granted, every comfort imaginable. Now her title had been stripped from her and she was under arrest, locked within her private chambers. Perhaps I should have been content with my life, she considered. Her mother's criticism may have been correct: she was seldom satisfied.

Her mother, Tiye thought, was confined to the guest chamber. To be sure, it was a beautiful room. She had the obligatory servant to tend to her daily needs and her proclivity for exotic foods, and any other wants the woman had. Still, beautiful or not, the chamber was still a cage. She must be livid, thought Tiye. Her mother loathed restrictions of any kind.

That woman will be the death of me someday, Tiye thought. Then she laughed aloud, a callous maniacal laugh. As she finally has, thought Tiye with a touch of lunacy. Her mother's wondrous scheme shall surely land me upon the chopping block. Pentawer as well, she thought with sadness. Oh my son, I never meant you harm. I only wished the world for you.

Thankfully, she was not locked away in some hideous jail, shackled to the walls, and starving. Her one allowable servant informed her such treatment was Akar's fate — the confines of a jail cell. From the lips of her servant who was privy to the gossip mill — which was rampant on this topic — he had given away the entire plan upon his initial questioning, pointed fingers at Tiye, and cast blame upon others. How she hated the man. If I am called as a witness to his official trial proceedings, I shall voice several items of interest to the judges. He shall not remain unscathed.

She thought of Asim with bitterness. That wretched girl. I should have sent her to an outlying property or had her drowned in the Nile. I thought Akar was up to the challenge yet clearly he could not handle her. The weakling. I took her in, trained her, and gave her a life she could only dream of. All the while, she resorted to spy upon me, listen to my conversations with the Harem wives, and tattle to Ramses.

And Tamin, she thought. Of all the wives in residence within the Harem quarters, Tiye wondered how Asim and Tamin had found each other. Their partnership had proved fatal for the conspiracy. Tamin is a clever woman, thought Tiye with disdain. It was an uncomplimentary trait in her eyes, particularly since it directly affected Tiye's existence.

Her trial was to begin on the morrow, the third day of the court proceedings. Thus far, minor characters had seen the courtroom: the Harem Chamber Guard, butlers, magistrates, and the like. Supposedly, Ramses was not a party to the proceedings, yet she knew her husband's traits. He may be absent from the court room yet he was informed daily of the trials, witness statements, and punishments rendered. Of this she was sure. He would insist upon every detail, every word uttered. Did he have a hand in the punishments? She thought not. It had been made quite clear of the court's unbiased attitude.

She considered others she could implicate during the trial. That might lessen the severity of her charges. Perhaps a deal of sorts could be struck. After all, it had only been a toe.

## Chapter Four

Tiye strove for refinement in all things. Forced to enter the courtroom with two accompanying guards was no exception. With head held high and elegantly dressed, the doors were opened before her. Exiting was her beloved son. He looked pale and exhausted with head held low as he shuffled into the hall. The sounds of his bindings could be heard against the floor.

Tiye call out to him. "Pentawer, my son," she said and made to reach him. Her arm was brusquely slapped away. She looked at the offensive guard with dislike and reproach. "Those shackles are an affront to my son's position. He is the Prince of Egypt. Remove them immediately," she said with venom.

Pentawer shook his head slowly as though it weighed that of a boulder. "No, Mother. They must remain. So, too, whatever punishment they pronounce must stand. Patricide and fratricide are the most heinous of crimes."

Tiye cried out to him. "Your brother yet lives and you did not have a hand in your father's injury." Standing still, Pentawer looked his mother in her eyes and shook his head again with great effort and sadness. "I shall always love you, Mother. Know that as truth. I pray we shall be reunited again in whatever Afterlife we are granted." With that, he was led away down the hallway, clinking his chains.

"Pentawer. Pentawer, it was not your fault." She called frantically to her son, "It was only a toe," she shouted yet he never glanced back at her. He was prepared to accept his fate.

Standing straight and proud she thought, I am not so resigned. I am Queen. I am prepared to fight. She turned to her guards and said regally, "Let us proceed." The great doors of the courtroom closed firmly behind her.

As she walked down the aisle to the witness chair, some men rose from habit. They were quickly encouraged to reseat themselves. So, thought Tiye, some still have the respect for me that I deserve. She sat with haughtiness in the chair, waiting for this charade to commence.

While these men knew she no longer carried the title of Queen, they found it difficult to address her. One judge referred to her as 'Madam' early in the proceedings. Throughout the day, Madam it remained. Questions were hurled at her from the panel of judges with no consideration for her stature in life.

"Is it true you were the instigator in this crime of treason?"

"How did you convince the other members of your conspiracy to betray their Pharaoh?"

"We have heard testimony you arranged to have Our Pharaoh's protective spells removed from him."

"Who else was joined in this deed?"

The questions were never ending and she grew weary. Naturally, she told of her mother's hand in all this. Indeed, she said, it was entirely her mother's plan. She even provided Tiye with the puzzle amulet in which to hold the sedative. Had it not been for her mother, she said, life would have continued as usual within the Royal Palace. More questions followed.

"Is it not true you provided sexual favors to those you coveted for allies?"

"Was it not your voice that convinced the other wives to commit this act?"

"Did you not arrange to have Akar provide you with sharpened blades?"

"We heard testimony Akar was ordered by you to murder a member of Egypt's finest family."

"Is it not true you were quite promiscuous in your youth?"

Unending questions were tossed to her like handfuls of sand pelting her from all angles. There was no reprieve from them. It was quite clear Akar had revealed damning testimony in a prior conversation with the judges. It was also clear he had again lied to her. Akar had indeed exchanged words with Ari prior to death, as evidenced by the inquiry into her sexual encounters. She cursed him for the hundredth time, laying blame upon his head for her current state.

Enough, she thought. She stood and said loudly to the court, "I shall not be treated in this disgraceful manner. I refuse to answer any further questions. I shall be in my chambers." So stated, she walked from the courtroom and made way to her wing of the Palace. The two sentinels followed behind.

## Chapter Five

Her mother was called before the court on the fifth day. I should like to see that, thought Tiye. How the woman must have squirmed. Alas, her time on the witness stand had been brief. According to her gossip-laden servant, the woman swooned with distress upon the stand necessitating the Royal Physician to be called forth. She was ultimately sent to her quarters for complete rest. Such drama, thought Tiye. The woman had a calling for the stage.

On the sixth day, Tiye insisted on a meeting with the Pharaoh. Her method of insistence was to call loudly and often to the guards, bang upon the doors, and toss items at them when her door was opened.

Begging their Pharaoh — through the proper chain of command, of course — to ease their suffering from his wife, her plea was granted. She was marched into her husband's chamber accompanied by the same two guards. Their faces had become quite monotonous to Tiye.

She dropped to her knees before her King upon entering. "Rise," said Ramses. As she did, she noticed Amonhirk, Iset, and several guards gathered about Ramses. "As you can see, I am taking extreme precautions. Particularly when you are present.

"I was informed you abruptly left your first day of questioning. Without dismissal, I might add. Not unexpected from you yet I demand you fully attend any subsequent proceedings. I have issued the same command to your mother. Shall that be our topic of conversation, or have you another reason for this meeting?" Ramses reached for a orange slice and chewed upon it. He had already become weary of this dialogue.

"My Pharaoh, I have another reason for my visit. A personal request. For our son."

Instructing his guards to remain he ordered his Queen and the Crown Prince to leave the room. "Father, perhaps I should remain," said Amonhirk.

"I was thoroughly searched, Amonhirk," she said acidly. "I am not armed and pose no threat,"

Ramses waved him off and the Crown Prince followed his mother from the room.

Rinsing his fingers in the ever-present water bowl held by a servant he said, "Pentawer is *your* son, Tiye. He is no longer mine. His title has been removed as has yours. Neither of you have a stake in this reign. You remain in the Palace only to present yourselves for trial. Nothing more."

"Yet you have made my current stay comfortable and for that I offer my gratitude."

"Did you believe I would have you hauled away in chains? You were Queen and my wife. I loved you, Tiye. To respect your former title, you shall have comfort. Temporarily."

"Ramses, if only you had listened to reason, considered Pentawer for the Crown we would not be immersed in these trials and court proceedings."

"Me? You would blame this treachery on *Your Pharaoh?*" Ramses roared. "I consider you an intelligent woman, Tiye, yet in this one concern you are irrational. It was the law. Is the law. First-born sons inherit. I have no inkling as to the hate you hold for me yet you had no cause. I treated you more than simply a Queen. I treated you as someone I loved.

"All that is over. We must face what is coming. I shall have no hand in your sentencing yet we are both aware of your probable fate. And that of Pentawer's. The court shall decide the formal sentence and method of your execution. Knowing this, what is your favor?"

"I beg of you, Ramses, please allow Pentawer to be buried in your tomb. Permit him to await your arrival within the tomb so you may eventually rest together. The action against his brother was at my insistence. You said he was weak and impressionable. This is your proof. Do not hold those traits against him. I beg of you as his mother. Allow him to dwell near you, the father he cherished."

Tiye had found his guilt and brought it forth. While logically he did not fault himself for Pentawer's actions, emotionally he felt some culpability in Pentawer's impending death. He had loved him more than any other child, yet it had not been enough. He was the ruler of all Egypt and with the title came massive responsibilities including periods away from the family he loved. Perhaps if he had spent more time with Pentawer, ensured him a place in the Kingdom, praised his sound reasoning more often it would have made a difference. If only he could relive those early days.

"Such an act will show disrespect to the Crown Prince. If I grant this, you must be prepared for a sacrifice."

She was sure to die in any case, she reasoned. What more could she sacrifice? "Agreed," said Tiye.

Ramses turned to his closest guard and said, "Retrieve my son and send a scribe to me."

In a matter of minutes, his order had been fulfilled. "Scribe, I wish you to write all that I say. I enact a Royal Decree this date. It is so ordered: upon the death of Pentawer, his body is to be enclosed within my tomb.

"It is with a heavy heart I hereby order all further references to Prince Pentawer and Queen Tiye be stricken from official records. This includes references by either written name or Royal design on all public buildings, columns, edifices, or temple. No person shall alter or neglect this Royal Decree. I call upon those here today to bear witness. As this has been written, I shall affix my seal." Using his ring with the imposing Royal Seal upon it, he set it into black ink and pressed it upon the papyrus of the scribe. "So shall it be."

## Chapter Six

That evening, Amonhirk sat with his father to discuss current events of the court. "I would have a word with you before beginning, my son." Dutifully, Amonhirk sat and waited for his father to speak. "I realize you were taken by surprise at my decree this morn. Yet you must appreciate this; I love all my children. I never wish to cause them harm. This is yet a small request I granted today. A price need be paid to meet such favor and I choose to remove their memory from history. Some day you shall be Ramses IV and be known for eternity. Their names shall be eradicated."

"Yes, Father. Your will shall be done." Amonhirk said this with an attitude of harmony. He understood his father's decision yet he was angered by it. He would, however, ensure his father's directions as set forth. The prince was suddenly overtaken with a coughing fit. "My apologies, Father. I seem to have a tickle. Let us carry on. I have sensitive dealings to discuss with you.

"Father, it has come to the court's attention of a rather sensitive situation. It seems several of the assigned judges have shown a lack of judgment, to voice it mildly. As you know, your six accused wives are confined to guest quarters within the Royal Palace proper, not their Harem chambers. The women held a social gathering in several of the rooms. Seven of the magistrates who would preside over their upcoming trials attended."

"Are not guards upon their doors?" roared Ramses with anger.

"Indeed, yes, Father. However, the guards were in attendance as well. Apparently, many jugs of wine were consumed. Also, they engaged in fornication."

"With the accused wives of my Harem?" he yelled, thrusting himself forward.

"Move with caution, Father. You have not yet completely mended. Your sutures might burst."

"By the gods, can we not find a handful of honest and trustworthy men in my Kingdom? I find it difficult to grasp these atrocious events, my son. I urge you here and now, Amonhirk, when you are Pharaoh your eyes must remain open. I have always expected danger from outlying countries and scavengers. To expect it from your own family and administrators is — or rather was —

unthinkable. Gather to yourself a few loyal and intelligent men. Use their guidance in your reign. Do not rule with complacency as I have done. Reflect several times upon suggestions by others before your decision is made. Remember these simple truths and you shall be a strong and effective Pharaoh."

"Yes, Father. My gratitude for your insight."

"Now, as to the reprehensible behavior and stupidity of these men. A child could see the women's objective. Naturally, they hoped to persuade the judges to grant a favorable verdict to their trials.

"These men must be tried as well. Their least offence is inappropriate contact with the accused although the charge might entail possible collusion. I care naught when they are tried. That is the court's timetable and their responsibility.

"I assume the scribes are recording every proceeding in its entirety."

"Yes, Father. The length of this judicial papyrus has reached many feet in length. I anticipate it shall be the longest ever recorded in our court system." The Prince turned his head and coughed once again.

"Even if it grows in length to reach the center of Thebes, it must be completely accurate. Acquire more scribes if needed." He looked at his son. "And see to that cough. You must remain in the best of health."

## Chapter Seven

For several days, Pentu and his fellow judges sat upon their official seats listening to witnesses speak. Asim had been a key speaker in the courtroom, the accounting of her first-hand knowledge taking many hours. She overheard the conversations between members of the Royal Family, she could recite the time and place of each exchange, and she personally knew each person by sight and name. She also informed the panel of the aid she received from the Royal Consort Tamin and the exact time the Pharaoh was warned of the conspiracy. Her testimony was most damaging to the accused and Pentu was extremely proud of her calm manner and cool recitation of the facts. She did not flinch upon further questioning from his fellow judges, only provided details as she knew them. Her testimony was informative and damning.

The courtroom was an imposing chamber. Large wooden beams crafted from date-palms hung overhead lending support to the tall room. The inscriptions and artistry in this room did not match the serene drawings in the rest of the Palace. These renderings were of gods issuing judgment upon the guilty and the Pharaoh smiting his enemies. The men and women coming before the court did so in great fear and the room did nothing to allay that fear.

Official trial proceedings were extremely slow. The number of suspects continued to rise, all hoping to save their necks. Those on the docket prayed they might lessen their sentences by relinquishing names of other participants, real or imaginary. Some information was simply conjecture — one man saw another in the general area appearing suspicious. Another believed he heard a fisherman speak ill of the Pharaoh. These types of statements were useless to the judges. The panel demanded specifics.

A few official proceedings had concluded. To date, Ramses' Royal Butler, physician, and one guard had been found guilty of treason. Pentu learned the sentencing portion of a person's trial would be handed down at a later date. This, he was told, gave the judges an opportunity to discuss the punishment amongst them. This was, after all, an unprecedented situation and the judges swore to be thorough in their verdict.

Pentu diligently studied various punishments for each conviction as required by law. The primary offenders would surely receive a death sentence. While execution was not particularly common in Egypt — at least not as prevalent as in other countries — two unlawful acts sure to garner death were tomb robbing and crimes against the Pharaoh. Since the people were always under the watchful eyes of the gods, they were not to be killed upon the whims of mere men. The courts and Pharaoh relied upon divine intercession to serve the appropriate justice. The question, however, was not mere death but the method of said death.

Death by execution was not necessarily swift: Egypt had developed some appalling methods of capital punishment. The quickest method, however, was beheading. One mighty slice and life on these sands was over. Obviously, this was the most preferable to other methods of capital punishment if one was condemned to death. Other instruments of execution were far more horrific.

Flaying — the peeling of one's skin while the person was alive — was a most bloody and gruesome sight. With sharpened blades and appalling skill, a person's flesh was carefully sliced and peeled back from muscles and tendons. Usually held in public view as an example to criminal behavior, he had seen most offenders lose consciousness from the pain. Bystanders as well fainted from the gore.

If one was condemned to burn at the stake, their ashes were strewn across roads for men and animals to tread upon. He had heard people scream in unimaginable pain while their burning flesh blistered and burst. Pentu thought burning a double-edged punishment. Not only did one die a horribly painful death, they did so recognizing they could never reach the Afterlife. As further indignation, they knew their ashes would serve as road fill.

If one's body was not completely intact, it could not be embalmed. This was a standard truth among Egyptian teachings. The individual could not, therefore, enter the Afterlife — the eternity every Egyptian desired. Even after beheading, a body might be further eradicated if the crime demanded it. The remains might be fed to ravenous alligators in the Nile or pieces scattered in the desert for predators. Again, a double punishment — death in this life and none in the next.

Yet one manner superseded all others in viciousness: the impaling rod. Certainly not a new idea and used more frequently in other parts of the world, it was always a slow and excruciating death. A metal or wooden rod literally impaled the victim through the center of the torso exiting the person's back. The stake was then fixed into the ground where the person hung upside down like a cluster of dates upon a tree. Grease and a blood-clotting medication were first applied to the chosen entry and exit spot. This afforded easier access through the body while preventing a swift death by excessive bleeding. The implement was rounded at one end so as not to pierce a vital organ, which would cause immediate death. It was, after all, meant to be a prolonged and agonizing demise.

Of course, variations upon torso impalements had been 'improved' upon. Some condemned to this torturous death occasionally faced anal impalement — inserting the pole through the anus and out through the mouth. For the extremely rare punishment of impalement to a woman, the pole entered through her feminine organs. It took days for these poor wretches to die, all the while staked in public view along roadways or at the entrance to a government building. Artists had long been rendering images of this type of execution upon buildings throughout the country. Again, it was a dramatic visual lesson to all would-be wrongdoers.

Ironically, Pentu believed, if the average Egyptian committed such brutality upon another, it would be deemed as torture and judged as a criminal offense. When the same 'torture' is enacted within government sanctions, it was considered just punishment.

Some were allowed to commit suicide in a public spectacle, loosing their family honor and suffering degradation in the eyes of the people. Others, in cases of special leniency, were allowed to commit suicide in private. Egyptian religion showed no discriminatory treatment of people who found death at their own hand; upon proper preservation of their body, they could enter the Afterlife if the gods so decreed it. The only requirement for one's eternity was a complete body.

Some appearing before this current council of judges might be less actively involved in the assassination scheme than others. If someone donated riches to the cause, for example, their punishment might be less severe. Their sentence might be reduced to mutilation. As an indication to the world of crimes committed, noses or ears were partially or fully severed. Citizens occasionally discussed these tortuous procedures with horror, yet few people missed an opportunity to witness the scene. These varied public examples seemed to have been successful: Egyptians had not viewed a criminal execution for several years. Until now.

Pentu entered the small adjoining chamber to the courtroom while considering these various agonies he must hand down to the guilty. The judges gathered in this small room attached to the Royal Court Chambers prior to proceedings. Here they discussed previous testimony and reviewed the upcoming witnesses for the day. Occasionally, someone was completing a slice of bread or a handful of fruit. The courtroom proved stressful as the judges dealt with crying women, families begging for mercy, accused men emphasizing their personal importance, and others swearing they were innocent of all charges. Eating a meal was the most normal action of their daily schedule and they savored the simplicity of it.

Today, only four other men were present in the anti-chamber. "My apologies if I am past the appointed hour. I believed I was early," exclaimed Pentu

"You are," said one overstuffed judge with a protruding nose. "As are we all. We have had unfortunate information this morn. We shall be a panel of five henceforth."

"Five? What has happened to the other seven judges?" asked Pentu.

A third gentleman leaned into the mixture of his fellow judges and whispered the recent news. "It appears our other colleagues have made a grave error. The six accused Harem wives had a small, shall we say, *event* last evening. Our missing judges attended this inappropriate gathering.

"Extremely reckless behavior on their parts. I, too, was issued that invitation. I understand alcohol was plentiful and sexual favors were traded in the hopes of leniency," remarked the first man. One or two others admitted to an invitation as well, shaking their heads in disapproval.

Pentu was shocked. "Have they been removed from these duties?"

"It is much more serious than removal. They have been arrested for collusion and possibly accepting bribes."

"Arrested!" exclaimed Pentu. "Are we to sit in judgment upon these men? The same men with whom we served? I believe this places us in an awkward situation."

"Pentu is correct. This casts scandal upon us all."

"I have known two of these men for years. They are extremely just and loyal men. I find this difficult to believe. Perhaps a fault has been made."

One man shook his head. "They were all found within the chamber, engaged in rather questionable activities. A few of the men were naked. There is no error."

"How were they discovered?"

"I believe one man betrayed the others. When he entered the chamber and saw the gathering, he located a Royal Guard."

"That excuse sounds suspect. Receiving an invitation to the guarded chambers of the wives should have alerted him immediately to something unsavory."

"I agree," stated another of the remaining five. "It would appear he was in over his head and wanted to save his own neck. I heard he participated in the favors offered prior to summoning authority."

"Still, he made the correct move by alerting a guard. Perhaps he deserves credit for that act along with some mercy. A word of warning should suffice in his case," said the first pompous judge.

Pentu could not believe what he was hearing. These men were willing to excuse this man because he informed upon the others. "And the rest? What punishment would you suggest for them?"

"Naturally, we shall not know the entire situation without hearing their story. We must be receptive to their plight. Any of us could have succumbed to that invitation."

"And yet, you did not," remarked Pentu. "If you had the good sense to remain absent from such temptation, so should they. These men are intelligent individuals who surely knew the dangers of such a gathering."

The men looked slightly uncomfortable with Pentu's valid assessment. "We must listen to their explanations," said the elder judge pretentiously.

They mean excuses, thought Pentu. As with all things, even though their instructions specifically indicated fair and impartial trials, this sympathetic attitude towards their fellow judges could result in leniency. Pentu had a sudden cold sensation run down his spine. What of others who were well liked and held in high esteem? Specifically he considered the fate of Akar. He could be quite charming when he so desired and many thought him likable without knowing the true man. He also had great status as a fierce soldier. Akar was not beneath intimidation or threats to achieve a sentence other than death, Pentu believed, and might do so with these judges.

Knowing of the man's cruel tendencies, Pentu would not chance Akar's freedom. Something must be done to assure his deserved punishment is met when his trial is completed.

## Chapter Eight

By the evening on the seventh day of trials, Pharaoh Ramses III took to his bed. His physicians declared his foot infected and with fever, due to the impurities coursing through his body. Poultices were placed upon his wound to draw out the contamination, oral medications were produced every four hours for his pain and fever, and his dutiful wife, Iset, placed cool linen cloths upon his brow.

The Queen entered the Pharaoh's bedchamber to find three Royal Physicians tending to her husband. "I have a pan of fresh cool water for his head."

"Excellent, my Queen. We are in the process of cleaning and bandaging his wound." The Chief Physician was instructing his apprentices in the use of honey over the sutures. Not only did this act as a binding, it also effectively destroyed bacteria. Mixed with the honey was a slice of moldy bread, a product known to draw out the infection. Over this combination, clean strips of linen were looped snugly around the toe and foot. "We shall place a warm compress over his foot to further draw out the impurities from the injury."

The Queen took a seat at the Pharaoh's head and began to place the cold cloth against his forehead and cheeks. She looked at the physician and said with some pique, "I would like to know how this occurred. You were caring for him regularly, were you not? If so, then how could this infection set in?"

The man bowed low to her. "My Queen, Our Pharaoh dislikes wearing the bandaging, often complaining about the discomfort it causes. Apparently, he removed it before retiring for the night. I found him without it this morn."

"Then someone must tend to him during the night hours as well. Even if it is merely a servant girl applying coolness to his head. She can call for assistance if needed." She pointed to their ministration upon his toe. "Will this treatment be effective?"

"If he allows the poultices we prepare to remain upon his wound, then yes, he shall recover. His injury was healing quite well — the skin continues to mend — until he developed this fever. These medications shall aid in that recovery, I assure you, My

Queen. He is a very strong individual. We have no doubt he shall be restored to his natural good health."

"For the present, I shall remain here by his side. Occasionally I shall require fresh water. What additional assistance may I lend?"

"He should remain in bed and rest with the dressings intact upon his foot. Perhaps you may convince him of this need. As you can see, we have positioned additional pillows atop his headrest to elevate him further. It seems to ease his back and aids in his breathing. Additionally, he should drink water; plenty of it."

The Pharaoh opened his eyes and said grouchily, "You speak of me as if I am absent from your sight. I am able to hear your every word." He sat up straighter on his mattress. "The tonic they pressure upon me is foul tasting. I fail to reason why these many physicians cannot produce more flavorful medicinal liquids. At least they could infuse honey into it.

"It produces sleep as well. I would stay awake to rule my Kingdom, not lie about as an infant." Catching the look of concern upon Iset's face he continued, "Yet, for you My Queen, I shall behave as a docile child."

"Rest yourself, My Husband. I shall remain with you. Imagine the many conversations we may indulge in. You shall return to your busy schedule in a matter of days when I shall no longer have the pleasure of your unrestricted time."

Ramses nodded at her with a smile before nodding back to sleep. "I shall return directly," she said as she left her husband's side. From the bedchamber she entered the large private audience room of the Pharaoh. Several physicians and magicians were gathered here discussing the Pharaoh's health. Sentinels had been placed in the main hallway at the chamber doors admitting into these hallowed rooms only those allowed. From their point of view, it would seem everyone was allowed. Had they not been given specific names of those permitted in these lofty chambers? She stood for moment watching the many men gathered casually in her husbands' room, eating and drinking as if they were attending a grand midday meal. She decided she would see a change to these arrangements.

She exited the door into the hallway. Pointing to the first guard she saw, she ordered him to follow her to the Royal Audience Room. She spoke loud enough for the entire gathering to hear her voice. "Gentlemen, this guard shall remain in these chambers throughout the day. One guard is to remain upon that position at all times while the Pharaoh recuperates." She indicated a place against the wall near the adjoining door of the Royal Bedchamber. "While my husband is within his bedchamber, I am ordering this protection throughout the day and night. I shall speak to my son regarding a replacement for you," she said to the young man. "I should imagine he shall see to the organization of several different time periods for various guards.

"Additionally, every person entering my husband's room shall be searched." She raised her hand at a Royal Physician's interruption. "As for the magicians and physicians, you shall be allowed the various trappings of your profession, questionable though they be. However, along with your implements you shall enter with another in your profession. You must always have a second set of eyes accompanying you. My husband must be protected.

"Additionally, these rooms are reserved for Your Pharaoh, and for those men he wishes to see, not for men who seemingly have no responsibilities in life. As such, useless gatherings and inappropriate conversations in these chambers are no longer tolerated. You shall henceforth remove yourself from my husband's chambers and direct your talents to the Pharaoh's quick recovery. Upon this, I insist.

"Oh yes, one more item of note. The Royal cooks and additional Palace servants are not available to do your bidding. Such extraneous attendants are to be removed from these areas to avoid their harassment by those with unacceptable requests." With those final words, she re-entered the chamber of her husband.

## Chapter Nine

The court had diligently completed two of the trials at hand. These proceedings had taken seven days with two more full trials scheduled. After a full day of discussion, three sentences had been agreed upon. Someone in high authority must now inform the guilty of the court's decision. The man who volunteered was of the very highest authority. He was warned of the unpleasantness in this task yet he seemed quite eager to personally visit each of the three convicted individuals. Receiving the written decrees from the court, Prince Amonhirk — the man who volunteered — decided to first visit his brother.

He walked briskly along the residential chambers of the Royal Family and passed the two guards flanking the door of Pentawer's suite of rooms. He entered to find Pentawer sitting upon a stool, staring out upon the Nile River.

"I have always enjoyed watching the ebb and flow of this river," said Pentawer while not taking his eyes off the water. "It speaks to our existence, of new birth and growth. Do you remember when we played at the water's edge, begging our nannies to allow us to swim to the other side?"

"Naturally, they refused permission," said Amonhirk, remembering the fun. "As if we actually could do so. I remember the shock upon their faces. They believed us serious."

Pentawer looked upon his brother. "Were you not?" he said in surprise. "That is interesting to know after all these years. I was quite intent upon the swim." He turned again to gaze at the rushing waters. "Ridiculous, I know, yet I felt we two could do anything we set for ourselves. With you by my side, I had visions of standing upon the opposite bank, laughing and waving at our nannies."

Pentawer paused before stating sadly, "I loved you, my brother. What changed between us?"

Amonhirk withdrew from past memories abruptly. "We became men. It was time to put aside such childhood ideas."

"My love for you has not changed. You are my brother and I shall always love you as such."

"And yet," said Amonhirk with anger, "by your own hand you would have me killed."

"And you would see me ineffective and useless in your rein when I only wished to serve."

"I require no aid from you when I am King. I shall have more than enough ministers in my cabinet to guide me when that time comes."

"Indeed? You referring to the same caliber of ministers who plotted against our father?" Pentawer shook his head sadly. "I wished only to be of service to the land I love."

"I see. Your love for Egypt extends to murdering her Crown Prince?" he held up his hand when his brother would answer. "Enough. I do not wish to quarrel with you. Time for that has long passed.

"I am here for another reason. The court has rendered their decision against you. You have been found guilty of treason against the Pharaoh and attempted murder of the Crown Prince of Egypt."

"Naturally. I had no doubt as to their verdict. Tell me of my fate. I am quite sure it shall please you."

With reluctance, Amonhirk replied, "First, I tell you this — Father issued a decree on your behalf written in official records. Upon your death, he orders you be buried in his tomb, whether or not he has yet passed through this life."

"Indeed. This is a surprise. I see you are not so pleased as you had anticipated. Is this a decree you hope to overturn or does it stand?"

"It stands. One other point should be made. Your name and that of your mother's shall be stricken from every edifice and every written record throughout Egypt. No mention of your burial location shall be made. There shall be no mourners or prayers said for you at the tomb."

"Ah," said Pentawer looking keenly at his brother. "Now there is the satisfied face I expected to see. Yes, I imagine it is very agreeable for you to know your name shall be carved and etched into the bricks of Egypt for all eternity. While mine is reduced to scratches from a chisel and consigned to obscurity. There is more?"

"There is," continued Amonhirk. "In accordance with this Royal Decree you shall require your earthly body to entomb. For that reason, I have decided you shall be allowed to commit suicide."

"*You* have decided. I see. And my mother? Dare I hope she fares as well as I?"

Amonhirk answered him with a smirk. "She does not. I go to her directly with that information."

"I assume you shall not divulged it to me."

"You assume correctly. I leave her death to your imaginings. For you, I have brought two choices." He handed Pentawer a papyrus rope and a long bladed dagger. "Either of these shall see the task completed."

Pentawer took each in his hands and sighed. He looked at the sturdy support beam in his ceiling. "And which would you prefer, my brother? Strangulation by hanging or a blood soaked room?"

Amonhirk shrugged his shoulders. "It matters naught to me. As long as you are dead by nightfall tomorrow."

The two brothers stared at each other in mutual understanding. Pentawer finally nodded and said, "If you have no objection, I wish to linger at my window for a time. I would engrave these images to memory prior to leaving this world." He turned away from Amonhirk without another word to gaze again at the Nile and surrounding land.

The Crown Prince turned on his heel and strode out the door. He had two more visits planned this day.

## Chapter Ten

Amonhirk approached the guards alongside the chamber door of the woman, Tiye. He refused to consider her a Queen. She had committed the most heinous crime in the history of Egypt and no longer deserved such respect. Of course, she never had his. He had often observed her close scrutiny upon him as a child, and it had unnerved him. When he was chosen as Ramses' III successor, he found it unnecessary to treat her as anything more than a lesser wife of the Pharaoh.

He allowed the guards to knock upon her door and announce him to the lady within. As a female, it would not do for any male to simply barge into her private chambers, Crown Prince or not.

He was aghast at her rooms. More opulent than his mother's, they spoke to her greed and desires. "Oh, it is you." She said. "Welcome to my chamber, *Your Highness*," she said acerbically.

Amonhirk stood in the center of her receiving chamber, admiring the richly painted walls and ceilings. "You have done well for yourself, I see. Larger than Mother's, more richly appointed. That mirror is exquisite. I have never encountered one like it."

"Enough with the niceties, Amonhirk. Why have you come?"

He sat without invitation and said, "As you wish. I am here to inform you of the court's decision as to your fate. You have been found guilty on all charges."

"Naturally. I expected no less. As did my husband."

She responded dispassionately and did not rise to his bait as he had hoped. Additionally, he was annoyed at her offhand mention of his father, the man she tried to murder. Perhaps he could yet enjoy a reaction from her. "Your son said much the same when he learned his fate."

"Pentawer?" she said anxiously. "You saw my son? How does he fare?"

"Interesting," he said in return. "You care more for the fate of your son than your own. Ah, well, I suppose that is the definition of motherhood. You, however, also resort to murder for your child."

Taking a deep breath, Tiye let these insults pass. "What shall my son face? Please I beg you to tell me."

Amonhirk considered her request and decided to be magnanimous by agreeing. "I have allowed him to commit suicide in his private chambers. There will be no public display to his death. He shall do so by nightfall two days hence."

"Two days," she said with astonishment and angst. "Am I allowed a final farewell?"

Amonhirk raised his head and looked down his wide nose at her. He was not about to be *that* magnanimous. "I think not. I do not consider a need for such sentimentality."

She realized he was not about to be swayed no matter her argument. "Ramses decreed my son be buried in the Pharaoh's tomb. It was a written Royal Decree. You were present as were others."

"I am aware of my obligations concerning that decree. It shall be done. I shall personally see he is delivered to the embalmers following his death. Yet I remind you of the desecration which shall occur to the memory and images of you both."

Tiye nodded. "An Afterlife for my son is all that matters. Thank you." She looked him squarely in the face and said, "Now as to my fate. I am sure you have come to tell me of that as well. I assume it is death in public view, am I correct?"

"Indeed. A most public spectacle is scheduled in five days hence. Several executions are in preparation, involving the work of many men and several days. Hence your delay. Your execution shall be at the stake."

Tiye's eyes became wide and her stomach twisted into knots. She thought she might vomit. "Burned," she remarked in disbelief. "I am to be burned alive," she said in a small voice. It was not so much question as statement. "You would condemn me in this life and the next?"

"I would and I shall."

If all that remained of her were ashes, there could be no embalming. She and her son would not be reunited in the Afterlife. With some bit of hope, she reasoned that as a non-believer in gods who would condemn her, she might have a slim chance to everlasting happiness. It was her one wish; eternal life without the interference of false gods.

I shall not let him see me suffer, she thought. Prince Amonhirk shall receive no satisfaction from me. I shall not cry to him for mercy or beg for an alternative death. Sitting up straight she asked, "And my mother. Has her fate been decided as well?"

"It has. She shall also take the stake a day prior to you. I am attending to her following my completion here."

"My mother is a true believer in the gods and their reckoning," she said slowly while planning some small retribution of her own. "She will become quite overwrought with this news, perhaps to the point of collapse."

"Indeed?" said Amonhirk with interest.

"Before you begin to tread upon my ashes on the Theban roads, I would appreciate a final request from you be met." She leaned closer to the Crown Prince and said meaningfully, "I wish to inform my mother of this decision."

Amonhirk sat back and stared at Tiye. "Knowing her reaction, you do not find this objectionable?"

"On the contrary," replied Tiye, "I shall find it extremely rewarding." She narrowed her eyes and looked intently at Amonhirk. "Additionally, if you see fit, I would like to witness her execution. You may shackle me or tie me to guards if you so desire. Yet I wish to look upon her burning flesh."

"I see." After a lengthy pause, he said, "It is a curious and complex relationship you have with your mother, is it not?" He considered all she had divulged to him. With a twisted smile upon his face he said, "Very well. You may accompany me directly and be present at her death."

## Chapter Eleven

The procession of six people was a bit parade-like as they made their way single file to the chamber occupied by Tiye's mother. Amonhirk was flanked within his two Royal Guards at the front of the line; Tiye was centered between hers. They traveled in two groups of three each with a respectable distance between each pack. The sentries kept close scrutiny upon the former Queen to prevent any sudden attempts upon the Crown Prince. For a woman who plotted to overthrow the Throne of Egypt, she was considered a menace.

The guard knocked upon her mother's door, announcing the Royal Presence. Amonhirk, Tiye, and two personal Royal Guards entered her room. The woman was situated upon a luxurious down-filled sofa tended to by two servant women. One was gently wafting the air with a long feathered fan. The other servant was attending to the woman's fingernails. The table nearest her was filled with an abundance of rare food reserved for Royal Family members, certainly not prisoners of State.

"What is the meaning of this?" the Prince hollered angrily. "I happen to know this sofa is from a private reception room of the Royal Palace. How did you come by this?" He leaned low and scooped up a bowl filled with exotic fruits and salted meats, throwing it against the wall. "Such feasts shall no longer be permitted, is that understood?" He glared at the two servants and ordered them from the room.

Tiye's mother dropped to her knees in reverence to the man. "My Great Prince, my sincere apologies. When questioned as to my needs, I simply answered with my desires. It shall not happen again."

"Indeed, woman, your fare while incarcerated within these walls shall be meager at best. It is only through the generosity of my father, your Pharaoh, you yet remain near your daughter. If it is not to your liking, I am capable of transferring you to the prison in Thebes."

Tiye's mother crawled towards the Crowned Prince, sobbing and pleading, promising no further assumptions on her part.

Amonhirk nodded then turned his attention to Tiye. She had been standing in a nearby corner, clearly enjoying the scene as it played out. "Your daughter brings you a message from the Royal Courts."

"Tiye, you have come to see me. Oh, my dear daughter, I have been so concerned for you. I have missed you greatly. I pray you have good news for me. I am so overwrought and only wish to return to my home."

Standing with her arms folded under her full bosom, Tiye replied, "You have missed me? Indeed, I am here now yet you ask only of yourself. I am afraid the news is *not* good, Mother. We have both been found guilty of all accusations made against us."

The woman stood now in full fury. "Guilty! That is absurd. Surely you are aware of my loyalty to our Pharaoh. And to you as well, My Great Prince. I am nothing but a lonely woman, wishing to spend my remaining years with my daughter and grandson. I swear, something is amiss here. Someone has been planting lies within the court testimonies." She turned accusingly towards Tiye and said with venom, "Daughter, what evil have you spread? What tales have you told the court?"

"Mother, you forget I have been labeled with guilt as well. You are not the sole person to loose this day. Additionally, your grandson has been so branded."

"He, too, is guilty? That cannot be so. I wish to speak to the judges on my behalf. No, I shall speak to the Pharaoh. I am the mother of a Queen and I insist upon it." She stood haughty and proud, not about to let these indignities pass.

"Mother, do not continue with this tiresome pretense. I am Queen no longer. Within the court and the Pharaoh's good graces you have no standing."

"What is to become of me?" the woman wailed.

"Life no longer revolves around you, Mother. Indeed, it never did. You wish to know of your fate?" Tiye leaned in close to her mother and hissed, "In four days hence you shall be burned alive."

He mother screamed and wailed, thrashing at items within the room while Tiye continued to speak. "All of Thebes will be in observance, Mother. You shall be the ultimate entertainment of the day."

Her mother began to scream at Tiye, "This is your doing, your pact of treason. I had no hand in this. You wretched, ungrateful girl! How dare you, my only daughter, turn upon me so." The woman lunged at Tiye but was met by the strong arms of guards.

Tiye stood behind them calmly and complacently. Leaning in towards her screaming mother she said, "Ah, yet that is not all, Mother. By the good graces of the Prince, I am allowed to witness your death. I shall hear the sputtering of your flesh and see the blisters bubble up. Your screams of pain shall be as music to my ears," she said in a spiteful hiss. "Your ashes shall be scattered throughout nearby towns and cities, never to join together as one, never to realize proper embalming and prayers, never to reach the Afterlife."

The sounds emanating from her mother's throat were guttural as she struggled to break free from the guards. Tiye continued to taunt her mother with ghastly details. "Women and men will trample upon your earthly bits, animals will tread and empty their bowels upon your ashes, Mother, until you, the feces, and the sands become one. You shall be forgotten, Mother, except by those who suffered at your hands. Your sons will not mourn you, your husband has already forgotten you, and I shall curse your memory to eternal damnation."

The woman howled and thrashed against the guards, seeking to reach Tiye with her claws to no avail. "You seem to be a danger to yourself and possibly others, Mother *dear*. I believe it necessary to confine you alone to this room. Your servants are to be removed and you must tend to yourself. We cannot guarantee their safety around you, after all. An armed sentry shall provide you an assortment of bland meals." She turned to the Prince. "With Prince Amonhirk's permission, of course." He nodded his assent, marveling at the scene before him. "Do not fret so, Mother. It is only for your protection. And only for four days." To the tune of mad shrieking, Tiye turned away from her mother. Bowing to the Prince, the group left the room. From inside, her mother continued to shout vicious expletives after her.

The Prince turned to Tiye and inquired, "Was that all you had hoped for?"

"It was most satisfying. Thank you," answered Tiye graciously as she was escorted back to her chambers.

## Chapter Twelve

Two more days dragged along in the courtroom. Today, the ninth day, Akar was scheduled to appear before the judges as more than a witness — it was the commencement of his trial. This was uppermost in Pentu's thoughts as he bid goodbye to Asim for the day. Prior to his arrival at the Judicial Chambers, he made a point to seek out his good friend, Joba. The two had not spoken for several days and Pentu felt the need to do so.

Joba was in the eating area for servants and Royal Guards. He was extremely glad to see his valuable friend. "Joba, it is good to see you. Have you been well?"

"I am quite well, Pentu. I understand you and Asim have finally been united with your child. That is most wonderful news. I, too, have news and it is with gratitude to you both: I have been elevated in rank and responsibilities. Our Pharaoh requested my presence, thanking me for my part in ending the murder attempts. He said in this time of questionable allegiance among staff, he was most grateful for my loyalty when others would turn to greed. I have you to thank for placing the information into his ear."

"Truly, I am most gratified to learn he has rewarded you. Without your assistance, Asim would not have overheard the Queen's details."

Their further conversation reverted to gossip, the shamed dismissal of judges, and tales of the trials. "I am not permitted to divulge complete details of the trials, you understand. Yet I shall tell you this — Akar shall be tried this day. I have not revealed this to Asim. The mention of his name yet brings her to turmoil."

Joba frowned. "He is a pretentious pig. I was sorely tempted to create some damage to him that night at the Harem doors. It would have been most gratifying. Yet I enjoyed the look upon his face when I placed him into custody, tightly binding his hand and legs. He objected most strenuously, hence the cloth gag in his mouth. I thought the Pharaoh was most pleased to see him in such a predicament. I pray for a guilty verdict upon the man, Pentu."

"As do I. However, he has several friends in high authority he can yet rely upon. The judges often speak upon his battle triumphs and his closeness to the Pharaoh. I believe they are in doubt as to the extent of his participation. I am concerned he might only receive verbal censure or, at worst, a minimal form of mutilation. I am not prepared to allow that to occur."

"I urge you to take care, my friend. If you insist in having a hand in his punishment, do so with foresight and planning."

Pentu replied, "I swear by the gods I shall not move irrationally. I shall listen to all he says this morn and make an honest and unbiased conclusion.

"I plan on presenting into evidence the box you retrieved for me. It has little to do with his current charges yet I am praying the other judges will consider it regarding his overall character. If I am able to sway the other men to my way of thought during the midday recess, I shall do so with great reasoning. It shall, however, be difficult to see the man upon the stand knowing he might remain free, yet I have no intent upon jeopardizing my life with Asim."

"As to Asim — what of an impending marriage? Shall she initiate a divorce from Akar?" asked Joba.

"Akar never saw to the blessing upon a union with Asim and held no celebration to that end although those are not mandatory to form such a union. However, both people must willingly agree to bind themselves, usually through love, and Asim was forced to his side. Indeed, to my thoughts he held her as chattel rather than beloved companion. When these trials have been completed and we are free to return to my village, we shall have a marriage feast there. I am hoping you shall travel to Set-Maat to celebrate by our sides."

"I would not miss such a joyous event. I shall happily attend whenever you send me notice. Perhaps I shall even now begin to seek the appropriate lady to accompany me," he said with a grin.

"With so many servants dismissed or on trial, there is a bevy of new beauties waiting to catch your attention," said Pentu with an equally large grin.

The two men clasped arms and each went upon their way for the day with promises to see one another soon.

The conversation was fairly light when Pentu entered the secondary chamber for the judges. A few minor witnesses were to be heard prior to Akar. Pentu had never voiced his opinion of the man nor their connection. Indeed, Pentu had never officially met the man and was able to swear to that fact truthfully. As far as the remaining judges knew, Pentu had no knowledge of the soldier other than the charges before them.

Akar entered when announced; a large and imposing figure. He walked into the room with a distinct military marching gait learned through many years in the Pharaoh's Royal Army. Smiling and bowing to the judges, he accepted the proffered witness stand without concern.

Due to his status as a great warrior, he was treated with more deference than simple servants. Pentu was slightly surprised by the judges' collective tone — even the former Queen had been treated as a common criminal. The questions were not shouted out or shot at him repeatedly like arrows. Additionally, the judges waited patiently for Akar's complete answer rather than interrupt. Within the hour, several were chuckling or smiling at a witty statement from the accused. In Pentu's estimation, the trial was not proceeding as he had hoped.

Pentu attempted to dissociate himself from the malice Akar had shown to Asim and concentrate solely upon his testimony. With a sense of humor Akar carefully sidestepped awkward questions. The man continually referred to his impressive record in public service as tax collector and prison guard together with his unquestionable bravery on the battlefield. Pentu could see the awe upon the faces of the judges. It was time to tamp down this air of conviviality.

Pentu began to speak in a clear voice. "I wish to question this man," he said. Pentu had concerns of Akar's relationship with Asim coming to light. He must couch his words carefully. He began by asking of the house in Thebes where Akar resided. "Is it true you resided in this abode?" Akar answered yes. "Is it also true this house was let to you rent-free by the former Queen Tiye?" Akar answered in the affirmative once again. "Is it also true she afforded you these accommodations to engage your partnership in the assassination of the Pharaoh?" Akar was beginning to squirm, requesting clarification of this question. "Very well," said Pentu. "I shall rephrase. Would you consider this a bribe on the part of the former Queen?" Akar's face cleared; he was only to corroborate the Queen's efforts to gain allies in her plot. Yes, Akar answered, she bribed and threatened many people.

"This house has a sturdy door with a lock upon it, does it not?" Akar said it did.

"And the key was in your hands, was it not?" Akar was not sure where this conversation was leading yet these questions seemed harmless enough. He answered yes again.

"Upon moving into the house, did you find it vacant or furnished with supplies?"

Akar said, "The house was completely empty."

"So you furnished the home from your personal belongings?" Akar said yes again.

"I would inquire as to where you found such fixtures."

"Everything was retrieved from my personal quarters within the military barracks   I had been supplied my own rooms and furniture by the Pharaoh for my loyalty and outstanding service," he finished arrogantly.

"So you are telling this court that every fixture, every bag of food, the bedchamber furnishings, each chair, and cooking implements were yours completely. No one else had a hand in supplying these accessories to your abode, correct? Everything in that house was owned by you?"

"I have already said as much to you," he said irately.

While never taking his eyes from Akar, he reached under his chair and brought forth the delicately carved box. With pleasure, Pentu saw the look of fear cross the man's face and he turned ashen in color. He countenance quickly switched to rage and he opened his mouth to speak, eventually thinking it better to remain silent.

"Do you recognize this box?" asked Pentu.

"It is not mine," said Akar.

"I did not ask if it belonged to you. I asked if you recognized it." Akar said he did not.

"Indeed? I am prepared to recall before this court the Royal Audience Chamber Guard, Joba, for further clarification. He retrieved this box from the afore mentioned house. Did you not swear to this court that all items — each and every item — in that house were brought in and owned by you? This was found under the bed you said belonged to you. Beneath where you slept. Yet you do not recognize it."

"It is not mine," said Akar stubbornly.

"I would show the contents to my fellow judges," and he opened the box, passing it among the men. As they inspected and picked up the bits of dried flesh from the box, Pentu explained further. "I have it on good authority from the Pharaoh's Personal Physician as to what these bits are — or were. They are desiccated human female nipples."

The other judges tossed what they held into the box with repugnance upon their faces. Each man in turn looked at Akar with disgust.

"I say again, that is not mine," Akar said loudly, the blood rushing to his face.

"And yet," concluded Pentu, "When Joba and his fellow guards sought entry to this house, they found it firmly locked. They were forced to break the door as a solution to acquire entrance. You claim this box containing such horrific items is not your property. I say again, the door was firmly locked, broken down to gain entry. You testified to possessing the key and all property within belonging to you. If this is not your possession then to whom does it belong?" This was the question Pentu had dreaded asking. He said a quick prayer that Akar did not have the thought to blame Asim.

Again he was blessed — Akar merely looked puzzled and defensive. "It is not mine. You are confusing me and using trickery. I shall not speak to you further."

"No matter. I have finished with my questioning," said Pentu with a smile in Akar's direction.

## Chapter Thirteen

The judges began a cursory discussion regarding Akar's testimony while eating their noon meal in the attached discussion chamber. Pentu sat and listened, as he had in the courtroom. He wished to garner a feel for which direction the wind was blowing prior to stepping in with comments of his own.

One man appeared to share Pentu's thoughts and brought up the previous testimony of Asim. Thankfully, Pentu had never revealed his involvement with Asim. It had proven a sensible and cautious deed. He could agree with 'the servant woman's' information without acknowledging his connection to her.

Pentu casually agreed with his colleague. Her testimony seemed quite strong and he could find no reasoning why she should lie. A scribe was brought in to re-read her testimony — quite destructive when read aloud.

"What of the box of Akar's trophies, if I may refer to them as such," asked Pentu. "I believe it tells of his cruelty and desire for power. I also believe he committed to conspiracy for his own gain and not through her coercion. He was awarded the future post of General by her for his participation, after all."

"Hmm," said another judge, "that was the most revolting collection I had ever seem. Yet he insisted it was not his. Even if it belonged to him, it has nothing to do with the matter at hand. After all, what did he do except stand guard at her orders? Obeying the Queen does not connect him to her fiendish plot. We all have some oddity within our person, do we not? And we all must follow orders."

The discussion continued with men flipping back and forth over Akar's definitive guilt. Pentu attempted to convince them to the truth, yet he felt the overall impression of Akar was not to be blackened.

Towards the end of the meal and discussion, Pentu claimed stomach trouble. "My great apologies," he said seemingly in pain. "I fear I must spend some time in the toilet room. Something I have eaten does not agree with my internals."

They expressed concern, wondering if they should postpone the remainder of the day. Pentu assured them he would be attending shortly. He needed only a few minutes time. One gentleman declared his need to utilize the room as well.

As with many children, young Pentu and his friends had frequent contests in flatulence: he who could pass the worst stench and create the loudest noise was declared the winner. Pentu utilized that childhood talent now by making a great show of relieving his internal gasses until the other man quickly left.

Seizing the opportunity, Pentu dashed from the room and made his way to the isolation chamber where Akar awaited. Any accused individual who had not completed his questioning by the midday break was held nearby in a windowless locked chamber. The room contained one small table, one chair, and a lighted oil lamp. Akar was placed here until court reconvened for the second half of the day's trial. Although he was scheduled for further questioning, Pentu felt whatever more Akar said would matter naught to the judges. They had their opinions decided.

The room did not require a guard since the door was securely fastened with a drop beam and escape was impossible. It could only be opened from the exterior of the room by lifting the solid beam from its metal holders. Many guards had been reassigned of late or had walked to Thebes to observe the executions. There was a decided lack of security for useless tasks such as watching a barred door. He touched the long paring knife he had brought with him. It was an ordinary possession and several were on hand in the antechamber for bread and fruit. It would not rouse suspicion upon his person if noticed.

Standing in front of the door, he suddenly had misgivings. Would relinquishing the box to the Pharaoh provide enough harm to Akar? Ramses had expressed interest in it earlier. He would ensure Akar hold no position in his reign and would be a broken man. Yet he would live, thought Pentu, and that was not acceptable.

Quickly lifting the board and slipping into the room, he found himself face to face with his enemy. Akar looked up from his provided midday meal. "You!" said Akar with rancor. "You have twisted my tongue enough for one day. You have further questions? They must wait. I have not yet completed this meal. I choose to have no further conversation with you."

"Then we are in agreement," said Pentu. "For you, a would-be murderer and the violator of my Asim, there shall be no further conversation."

Realization passed through Akar's eyes and he sought to rise from the table. He was not swift enough. Pentu was upon him in a flash and drew his knife across Akar's throat. A most unusual gargling sound came from the man and blood poured down his broad chest. Exchanging the bloody knife for the clean one in the cell, Pentu stepped quickly out the door. After sliding the bolt into the corner hooks, he retreated to the toilet room. In a clean sand bucket, he scrubbed at his hands to remove smudges of blood. Finally, he made his way back to the discussion chamber to find his fellow judges gathering themselves to return to the courtroom.

"Ah, you have returned, Pentu," said the judge who had accompanied him to the toilet room. "Are you now well?"

"I have recovered, sir," said Pentu. "Abject apologies for my condition earlier. I was sorely in distress."

"I am relieved you are able to join us," the man said, remembering the sounds emanating in the toilet room.

The five men dutifully donned the garb of their assigned post and proceeded to their official seats. A nearby guard was instructed to escort Akar from his chamber. Moments later, he man returned quite alarmed and announced to the panel, "He is dead. The man, Akar!"

The panel was aghast, declaring disbelief and casting blame upon the lack of guards at the chamber door. They would see for themselves, they announced. There must be an error.

They made their way to the holding chamber and stopped upon the threshold. One man sarcastically commented, "With so much blood, I doubt the guard was in error."

"What should we do?" asked Pentu innocently.

"We must contact the Royal Prince and begin an investigation," said one.

"Might the Great Prince direct blame upon us?" asked Pentu. The last thing he wished was an investigation.

"Pentu is correct. I have seen the Prince when he is riled. We are charged with the safekeeping of the accused and witnesses. He will surely throw fault upon us."

"Then what are we to do?" Pentu asked again. "I shall follow any lead you wish to take."

The other men became silent. "Nothing," said the elder of the judges. "We shall alert the executioners. They shall dispose of him in whatever manner they wish. He is no concern of ours. This man committed suicide rather than face his guilt." He pointed to the bloody knife and looked at the other judges. "Since his trial is now a moot point, perhaps we can direct its eradication from the scribes' transcripts. The matter has been decided for us, after all." Each man nodded solemnly and returned to the courtroom to sum up the day's proceedings to the scribes.

## Chapter Fourteen

It was early morn on the tenth day of trials. The judges continued to slog through the many pleas of the accused and hear witnesses in a thorough manner. It was apparent to all however, they were becoming increasingly fatigued. In spite of the high security, the trials for treasonous acts were spread among the servants and citizens. Thebes was treated to public executions, suicides, and mutilations of the disloyal criminals. It was a clear example of the danger facing anyone who defied the Pharaoh.

Queen Iset had been diligently beside her husband for many days. Last evening the Royal Physician declared he was very pleased with the Pharaoh's recovery, telling the Queen that Ramses had passed through the worst of his infection and illness. "He is well out of danger, My Queen, eating and drinking well. He is conscious and alert yet still rather weak. He should continue with bed rest for a few more days. I expect Our Royal Pharaoh to be directing his ministers again soon. Perhaps this would be an appropriate moment for you to acquire rest as well. You have been most helpful in his recovery yet you must consider your own health."

The Queen shook her head. "I shall stay today, at least. I would appreciate a visit from my son, however. Perhaps you could instruct a guard to find him."

The physician smiled and bowed. "You are a most wonderful example to us all. I shall see to your request directly."

As she waited, her husband awoke from his slumber and smiled at her. "My Queen, you yet sit by my side. What a delight it is to see your beautiful face when I awake."

The Queen returned the smile and dabbed some cool water upon his brow. "Your Royal Physician announced your health has improved greatly. I am so very pleased. It shall be nice to see you up and about again."

The Pharaoh snorted. "I shall be 'up' yet I question just how 'about' I shall be without a toe. Why has the completed artificial object not been fastened to my foot?"

The Queen continued to smile. "Calm yourself, My Husband. The object has been completed yet could not be attached until the infection had withdrawn from the wound. In truth, you shall be walking soon. I am relieved to see your strong personality has returned." At that moment the stomach of the Great Pharaoh rumbled. "As well as your appetite, it seems. I shall have food brought to you." With that, she opened the chamber door and ordered the guard to fetch broth, bread, and milk with honey for the Pharaoh.

The Pharaoh was propped up in his bed and well into the plate of food when his son arrived. "Father, I am pleased to see you looking so well. Your face has color once again and your eyes are bright. We have been concerned for you."

The two men began discussing affairs of Egypt and renderings of the court trials when Iset interrupted them. "I shall leave you two alone, My Husband. You seem to have much to discuss. I shall be directly outside your door should you need me."

Iset had time to refresh herself with a cupful of wine and a small loaf of bread before her son entered the Royal Private Audience Room. "He slumbers again. He completed the entire plate of food, however. It is joyous news, is it not? I am so pleased to see his improvement."

His mother nodded. "We must give thanks to the gods. He has been blessed." She made to move back into the Royal Bedchamber when Amonhirk stopped her.

"Mother, you are looking very tired. You have not left his side for days. I wish you to slumber as well and regain your strength. The worst has passed, he has a guard at his door, and he is abed. Do you not agree this is a perfect opportunity for you to rest?"

Iset thought for a moment. "In truth I am weary, my son. Yet I do not wish to leave him unattended. Would it be possible for you to sit with him while I retire to my bedchamber? Only for a few hours."

Amonhirk shook his head and harshly cleared his throat. "I cannot, Mother. I have urgent affairs that need my attention. This visit to you left many men waiting for me. Yet I say again, what could happen for such a short time?"

"If he awakens and requires assistance, the guard might not hear his call through these thick walls and door. If I cannot be with him, I insist someone is. His head and neck must be soothed with a cool cloth. He seems to favor that."

Amonhirk smiled at his doting mother. "As did I when I was feverish as a young boy, which seemed irritatingly often. Perhaps a servant might be an answer. Anyone can sit quietly by his side and apply a wet piece of linen. I would see to your health, Mother."

Iset finally agreed with her son. "As I would see to yours, my son. When you have a moment free in your schedule, I ask you seek a physician and see to your throat. We cannot afford the luxury of you falling ill as well," she said with a tired smile and patted his cheek. "Please allow me to check once more upon your father. Then, if all is well, I shall summon a servant girl and instruct her."

"I suggest you instruct your servants to leave you in peace for a rest, Mother. You should not be bothered with silly problems they might bring to you. Would you please see to this request of mine?" His mother smiled and agreed. Her son kissed her upon the cheek, thanking her for this compromise, and left the chamber to attend to the duties of his father.

Passing the watchful guard, she quietly reinterred the bedchamber of her husband. He was indeed deep in slumber. She smiled at the sight and just as quietly retreated.

"You are to remain on duty." She told the guard. "I am summoning assistance for the Pharaoh in my stead."

With that, she left the guard and proceeded into the hallway. Apparently, a passing servant girl was not quickly found. Little wonder, thought the guard. Several were expected for questioning in the court. Most were placed elsewhere in the Palace or allowed to travel to Thebes to witness the executions. He would liked to have viewed such sights yet he was a loyal Egyptian and followed orders. He stayed his post.

A few moments later, he heard the voice of the Queen call out. "You, handmaiden. What is your name?"

The guard heard a high-pitched voice answer in a frightened tremor, "I am Vita, My Gracious Queen." Poor girl, thought the guard. It had been a shock to have The Queen single her out.

"I have a task for you, Vita. You are to fetch a clean bowl of cool water and a clean cloth. You will sit at the side of the Pharaoh's bed, ready to assist him when he awakens." He heard a little squeak from Vita. "Do not look so frightened, girl. You need only sit and wait quietly for him to awaken. When, or if he should do so, I insist you begin cooling his face and head with the damp cloth. The posted guard shall assist you if needed. Is that understood?" The guard heard Vita answer in the affirmative, ensuring the Queen she would do as commanded.

The Queen returned to the side of the guard. "You heard my discussion with the hand maiden? Good. She will bring the bowl of water and the cloths. You must search her and whatever she carries. She shall be here shortly. I shall retire for a few hours and return. Remain alert and vigil. Understood?"

Several minutes later, a young servant girl approached the guard. She was wearing only linen breeches and barefoot. Her hair was cropped short yet stylish. In her arms she carried a large pottery bowl half full of fresh water and several cloths tossed over her arm. Her head was down in deference to his position over hers.

"I must search what you carry," said the guard. The woman complied, extending her arms while keeping her head slightly lowered. The guard looked in the water bowl and shook out the two linen cloths. It was quite apparent from her meager clothing she carried no weapons although he instructed her to turn around to be sure. When he was satisfied, he unlocked the door for her to enter. "If you encounter a concern, knock upon the door and I shall enter."

The girl nodded and entered, walking softly to not wake the great man. The guard stood his post and all was quiet. No one entered seeking the Pharaoh and the entire Royal Palace remained eerily quiet.

Less than an hour had passed when the maiden quietly knocked upon the door. As he unlocked it for her, she tentatively spoke to the guard as she stepped from the room. "The Pharaoh still slumbers," she whispered. "My water has grown warm. Am I allowed to return with another bowl of cool water?"

The guard saw no harm in this. He told her to do so with haste as the Queen had specifically left instructions the Pharaoh was not to be left alone. "I shall run to the kitchens and return at once." True to her word, she exited the audience chamber on swift feet.

Time dragged on. The Guard was becoming concerned with the delay of the servant, Vita. He debated leaving his post and searching her out yet thought better of it. If the Queen returned and found them both absent she could, and probably would, be furious. Instead he continued to stand watch, hoping the errant servant would dash through the door at any minute.

When the hallway door finally opened his heart sank. Entering the room was not Vita but the Queen. She smiled at the guard and asked him if all was well.

With eyes downcast he answered evasively, "My Queen, the servant girl, Vita is gone. Actually, not truly gone just absent for a moment while she retrieves cold water. She said the bowl had become warm and she wanted to follow your instructions, My Queen."

The Queen looked at the lowly guard in dismay. "Gone? Are you telling me my husband is alone in his bedchamber? Quickly, unlock the door. How long has she been missing?"

"Oh, not long, My Queen." He was nervous and his hand did not seem capable of twisting the large key. "Several minutes, that is all." Finally, they heard the clicking of the tumblers in the lock and he opened the door allowing the Queen to proceed. When she began to scream, he peeked over her shoulder. The Pharaoh lay upon his bed, blood flowing from his throat, across the mattress, and pooling upon the floor. As the Queen rushed to her husband's side and continued to scream for help, the guard stumbled from the room and vomited in the nearest potted plant.

## Chapter Fifteen

By the time Amonhirk arrived at his father's chambers, he found his mother saturated in the Pharaoh's blood. She was cradling his head to her bosom and keening softly to him. When she saw her son, she said, "Amonhirk! See to your father. He has been wounded and I cannot stem the blood."

The look of anguish and disbelief upon her face was frightening to her son. Amonhirk walked to his mother and pried her away from her dead husband. Physicians began entering the room and as he handed the Queen to one, he said to her, "Yes, Mother. See, medical specialists have already entered." To the medical man he ordered, "Attend to my mother."

The Prince stood patiently in the room waiting for the Physician's pronouncement. Looking at his father, however, he already knew the outcome. The elder man looked up at the Prince. "It is with great sorrow I inform you, My Prince, of you father's passing. The Pharaoh is dead. The wound was clean and deep, slicing through his throat, almost to the spine. I would assume that," he said indicating a long sharp knife upon the floor "was the weapon used."

The item was partially under the bed as if it had been kicked out of view. Amonhirk bent and retrieved it. "My father's memorial blade from the last wars with the Sea People. This knife was displayed in the family's private hallway. He was most proud of it. How is it here in his bedchamber?" He tested the bloody edge. "Yes, it is extremely sharp. Someone has seen to the usually dull blade. It could easily have done the deed. Send me the guard from his door and when you have finished here, have the Pharaoh carried to the embalmers. He must be remade whole."

The guard entered, nearly shaking in fright. "You were the guard assigned to protect my father? Tell me how this weapon came to be in my father's room. Gather yourself, man. Time is of an urgency." The man swallowed twice, attempting to settle his stomach, and snapped to attention.

"The servant girl. The Queen ordered a servant girl to sit with the Pharaoh while she slept."

"Did you not search the her as you had been ordered?"

"I swear by the gods, I searched. She wore a transparent brief and nothing else. She carried only a bowl of water and clean cloth. She had not such a weapon upon her. I swear."

"And yet," said the Prince in anger, "My father is dead and there lay the knife. Tell me what you know."

Upon this further command, the young guard told what he could. He overheard the girl and the Queen in the hallway and provided a detailed description of the handmaiden. "I have not seen her prior to this day, My Prince, although I have not been privy to this part of the Palace until I began this duty."

The Prince walked into the hallway and called for guards and military men. Amonhirk summoned his many personal guards and members of the military to comb every corner of the Royal Palace for the woman or any clue as to her whereabouts. The calming paintings within the corridors and walls belied the current atmosphere of the Palace. A storm swept through the fortress as every building was searched for the elusive servant girl. Everyone was suspect of involvement or knowledge.

Men burst into personal chambers, public areas, kitchens, and even Royal Bedchambers. The Harem quarters were ransacked, every bit of clothing was inspected and shaken, wigs were ripped apart, food storage areas were torn through, and priests were searched as well as Palace temples. Servants huddled together in fear while they were searched and questioned.

Military personnel were dispatched to Thebes and outlying areas in continuation of the search. The Pharaoh's death must be made public in due time without the mention of murder, therefore the men were not told of the reasoning behind their search. The soldiers searched homes, businesses, and city temples with the excuse of apprehending a criminal.

Inquires were made of all possible escape methods: camels or wagons leaving the Royal compound, caravans of goods exiting towns, or a lone woman walking from the Palace. A full day and half with hundreds of men were spent upon the search to no avail. It was as if powerful magic had been performed; the woman had simply disappeared.

Shortly after the exhausting search, all Palace personnel were ordered to attend a speech held in the largest room of the Palace, the

Royal Banquet Chamber. Servants and officials alike stood shoulder-to-shoulder waiting for the speaker to enter.

Asim and Pentu were also in attendance. Pentu's arm was placed at her elbow and Asim held the baby, occasionally bouncing her up and down when the small child fussed. "I have difficulty in believing this has happened," began Pentu. "I understand the facts as I have heard them yet I cannot seem to absorb them. It is if I have become as numb as this stone wall beside me." Asim had been crying through most of the night and her eyes were rimmed with red. She shook her head sadly, unable to find words to sooth Pentu. "It was in this very room I approached the Pharaoh with news of the impending conspiracy. We saved his life, Asim, yet it made little difference. He is now dead. Why?"

"It was not a pointless act on our part, my love. We served our Pharaoh well and he knew of our deed. We also saved the Crown Prince who will now rule Egypt as the Pharaoh Ramses III instructed. If we had not, Pentawer would rule and Tiye would be the Royal Mother of the Pharaoh. He was fully aware Amonhirk would ascend to the Throne due to our warning.

"Even as we speak, he is being prepared for eternal life, knowing we were loyal to him, that we honored him. He realized we risked our own safety to save him. These are all special gifts to take with him for all eternity. We shall yet see him when it is our time."

"You are a great comfort to me, my love. Yet I miss him. Ramses III was extremely generous to us both. No man has shown me more trust."

Asim looked up at Pentu and turned the conversation. "I hear Akar is dead."

"Yes," was Pentu's only reply.

Asim pressed forward. "Some say he was murdered."

"The official ruling was suicide. It was quite a surprise."

"Indeed?" asked Asim. "To you all?" No reply was forthcoming from Pentu and she leaned her head upon his shoulder. She said softly in his ear, "I love you." Asim knew what Pentu had done for her yet it was a truth between them that would never be spoken of.

Murmurs were moving through the crowd and a man stepped upon the raised floor where the Great Ramses III had enjoyed his celebratory banquet. The thought brought a lump to Pentu's throat.

"Look," said Asim. "It is Joba." Indeed it was their friend, waiting for the people to calm themselves and become quiet. To see him in this new position of trust and power pleased his friends immensely.

"Good people of the Royal Palace," he began. "I am fully aware of the speed with which rumors fly in the service ranks. I shall state plainly the facts to you thereby eliminating false tales.

"Our Glorious Pharaoh Ramses III has died. He fell ill several days prior and succumbed to a grave illness." Moans and crying began from his listeners. "We have been searching for a maidservant who may have been present when he died. Her name is Vita. She is tall and slender with short dark hair." As he looked at his audience, he realized such a description fit nearly all the women servants on hand. "We believe she is a new servant to the Royal Palace," he continued, "and we are hopeful one of you good people may have seen this young woman. If you have, it is your duty and honor to report anything you may have seen or heard concerning her. Alert any guard at any time if you have word of her. The Royal Family wishes to know the Great Pharaoh's last moments and words." The truth of Ramses' murder was carefully deleted from this speech. It must not be thought a Pharaoh was vulnerable to such actions, especially by a mere servant girl. Joba also did not acknowledge the ongoing trials. No reference was made to a prior assassination attempt or the ruination the act had caused. While the people knew of the executions as punishments for treason, it was best not to dwell upon the scandal or the truth. "Our Pharaoh is beginning his time with the Royal Embalmers. He shall be entombed with his son, Pentawer, who also left this life two nights past." More murmurs and gasps from the crowd. "This is in accordance to Pharaoh Ramses III explicate Royal Decree."

"The gods have blessed us with a new Pharaoh. Upon the day of his coronation, he shall be known as Pharaoh Ramses IV. Coronation arrangements are under way. Various festivities to celebrate our new ruler will proceed as tradition dictates, long into the coming year.

"Pray the *ka* of our Great Pharaoh Ramses III may proceed swiftly to the Afterlife, to sit among his fellow gods. Pray, too, for the Royal Family and all who loved him. While this is a time of mourning, Egypt yet endures. Even now, our Crown Prince attends to Royal duties, ensuring a better life for us all. May the gods bless Crown Prince Amonhirk."

The crowd joined together in this sentiment. "May the gods bless Crown Prince Amonhirk." They were shattered by the news, yet life continues. They must have faith in the new ruler of Egypt and his reign.

## Chapter Sixteen

Tiye's mother was scheduled to die the day following the death of Ramses III. Some discussion was held regarding the postponement. The Crown Prince did not agree. He had seen how weary the judges had become. They were in the eleventh day of proceedings and could see no end in sight. Additionally, Egyptian life must continue as before. People would take note of schedule changes or the cancellations of executions.

As promised, the former Queen Tiye was allowed to view this particular execution. She stood quietly near the front of the crowd, surrounded by guards with wrists bound, ignoring those who would point and whisper at her dilemma. She saw her mother walk on shaky legs towards the middle of the onlookers. The crowds' attention was now focused upon the woman as she attempted a retreat while the guards dragged her to her fate.

Tiye could muster no pity for the woman, now terrified and haggard. The only person in her thoughts today was her son, Pentawer. He had taken his life by flinging a rope over a massive beam in his room and hanging. Her beloved boy, the person she had loved more than any. Now he was gone. She blamed her mother, of course. If not for her outrageous suggestion, her son would yet live. Uncharacteristically, she saved some blame for herself. It was she who had led him into the foray with her desire to have him as Pharaoh.

A large tall post was deeply sunk into the sands slightly away from the town center. The bulk and height of it was imposing. Men had been digging the hole and pounding the beam into it for days. With a thick mud and straw mixture as the foundation, it was now secure enough for her mother's conflagration and her own on the morrow. It would take many men to pull it from the sand afterwards, she thought. After I am burned.

Surrounding it was a cluster of small dried branches and wood shavings. Kindling, thought Tiye. The flames are meant to catch upon the first touch of fire. The wood post looked as if it had been planed into a smooth four-sided shape. The former Queen clasped her hand over her mouth to keep from laughing irrationally. How ironic, she thought, engaging a fastidious craftsman to plane the stake and eliminate excessive bark and branches. Even though we are burned at this wooden post, we should not suffer splinters.

By now, her mother was behaving in an undignified manner. She had seen the pyre and began pulling from the guards, screaming at the crowd who jeered her, and praying for salvation. It was all for naught; the guards increased their grip upon her, the crowd was angered, and the heavens did not open in redemption. The woman was forced upon a small platform attached to the base of the post, placing her slightly above the kindling.

Tiye smelled the fiery torch before seeing it, carried sedately by a man assigned to the task. The Royal Speaker of the Courts recited a verdict of treason to the crowd while she loudly denied all charges. The torch was lowered to the small bits of wood shavings, igniting them into tiny fingers of flame. As the fire grew higher and hotter, most people backed away. Not so Tiye. She wished to be close enough to see the terror on her mother's face. She would face more heat than this on the morrow.

The blaze gained momentum and licked at her mother's gown. She began to scream and kick her legs, hoping to snuff out the fire. Finally she spied her daughter and begged for water to stop the flames. As the woman continued to scream and cry for water, Tiye walked as close as she dared to the blaze.

"You wish water from me, Mother?" she questioned. Leaning closer to the fire she spat upon it and said, "That is all the water I shall offer you." With that, the flames engulfed the woman and bits of her clothing and hair wafted upward. Or, thought Tiye, perhaps those are charred fragments of skin drifting away. The acrid smell of burning flesh assailed her nostrils and the cries from the beam had ceased. What was once a person was now barely discernable from the scorched wooden post. It was done.

Turning to her guards, Tiye said, "Return me to my chambers."

## Chapter Seventeen

Queen Iset carried a small silver tray with a glass vial positioned precariously atop. There was no chance of disaster, however; her smooth glide along the hallway prevented the possibility of breakage.

The security guards at Tiye's door opened it for the Great Queen to enter. When one would stand with her, she instructed him otherwise. "Leave us," she ordered. "We would speak in private."

The two women stood facing each other. Tiye finally bowed yet it was Iset who broke the silence. "I offer my sorrow to you for the loss of your son."

"That is most generous of you, Queen Iset, and this visit is most unexpected. I swear to you on the life of my son, Ramses' death was not by my hand or knowledge. I assure you; those known to me who conspired have been apprehended. I am bewildered as to who drew the blade across his throat."

Iset set the tray upon a small low table. "As are we all. It would seem a handmaiden was the culprit yet she has vanished. My son believes she was bribed or threatened to act. We have no other reasoning."

"It was not I, My Queen. By the gods I swear it."

Iset sat and motioned Tiye to do the same. "My son knows you did not. You have been under close observation and locked within these chambers. You have met with no one other than my son. We hold no fault against you for Ramses' death. You could not have done the deed nor bribed another to do so for you."

Tiye seemed relieved. "I have little time remaining. Even now they are preparing the kindling for my burning."

"Which is why I am with you. I know of your attendance at your mother's fate. It must have been horrible to watch."

Tiye looked pointedly at the vial. "You have come to poison me instead?"

The Queen flashed her toothy smile. "No. I cannot go against the wishes of the court." She picked up the bottle from the shinning tray. "This is to aid with the pain and fear. It will not render you unconscious, yet you shall feel quite euphoric. As though you were floating and watching yourself from on high. Physically your pain should be lessened though not completely eliminated. I am afraid no drug is able to accomplish a complete lack of sensation." She handed the bottle to Tiye. "Drink the entire amount when you hear them coming for you. It is fast acting. It shall create thirst yet I believe the drug's benefit outweighs that small side effect."

Tiye looked at the murky liquid and asked simply, "Why? Why would you do this for me?"

Iset sighed deeply. "I understand the reasoning for your actions. I, too, would sacrifice many things for my child. I have prayed for the ability to forgive you, although admittedly I yet hold some resentment for the attempt upon my son. The courts have spoken and you are facing your just due. I must be content with that. As I continue to pray for my own Afterlife, I believe the gods have directed me to show you mercy. This, then, I so do. We were, after all, Sister Queens for many years. I choose to hold that to my heart."

"Words cannot express my gratitude. I am not worthy of your kindness," said Tiye with meaning. "If I may inquire, I have been wondering of my zoo. I realize you do not share this extreme tenderness I have for animals yet I would hope they shall thrive and bring joy to others."

Iset presented the teeth again. "My own grandchildren share your feelings. They have already begun feeding and playing with your collection. Some of the animals have grown quite plump from the attention. At the children's insistence we have no choice but allow the zoo to flourish. My son has decided the citizens shall have access to your pets regularly; news that has pleased the people immensely in these trying times."

The Queen glanced at a magnificent set of garments and bejeweled wig upon Tiye's bed. "You have chosen to wear your finest, I see. I would expect no less. A most dignified and stylish exit. I could assist you in dressing, if you wish me to stay." Tiye gratefully agreed. "Then let us prepare you. Time grows short."

Elegantly dressed and waiting upon a stool, she heard them coming for her. Taking the bottle and releasing its stopper, she drank it quickly. Before the drug took its toll upon her senses, she had one last clear reflection upon her life. How peculiar, thought the former Queen, I should think of Ari at this moment.

## Chapter Eighteen

The Crown Prince Amonhirk traveled to Thebes with his Royal guardians in tow. He was meeting with the embalmers, attending to his father with these specialized men. Following the expected bowing and show of respect to him, Amonhirk began discussing the prolonged mummification process his father would receive.

Canopic jars were placed close to the slab holding the body of his beloved father, Ramses III. As per the holy funerary rituals, the liver, lungs, stomach, and intestines of the King were to be stored in each appropriate jar. The four sons of the god Horus — the protector of Royalty — were depicted upon the sealed lids of each jar. As Pharaoh, Ramses' III jars were of the finest quality, hand-carved from alabaster with heads/lids of pure gold. Each stood at ten inches in height.

The Crown Prince stood silently near his father, observing the progress. The elder embalmer approached Amonhirk and bowed. "Would the Royal Prince care to hear of the progress we are making upon his father?" Amonhirk nodded.

The Prince and the embalmer walked closer to the slab. While the Prince would become the new Pharaoh of all Egypt, his understanding of the mummification process was that of a layperson. Therefore, the elder man began providing information as succinctly as possible. He chose, however, to eliminate the shock he and his fellow embalmers experienced when they first saw their Pharaoh. The inordinate amount of blood covering his body had taken a full day to remove. Underneath the sticky fluid they had discovered the massive gash at his throat. It would not do to converse with the Pharaoh-to-be as to the offensive condition of his dead father.

"We have drawn out the brain and discarded it, My King. This long metal hook was inserted through his nose to do so. Additionally, the internal organs were removed through that small incision in his side. They are now drying in a salt substance called natron before we place them in the canopic jars." He gestured to the beautiful almost translucent jars. "His interior cavity has been cleaned with palm wine and spices. We shall soon be filling the space and covering the body with more natron to render it dry and free from moisture. Afterwards we shall fill his belly with myrrh, cassia, and other sweet spices.

"We have some concerns of which to speak to you. Naturally, he must be made whole to sit at the hands of the gods. We have found two severe wounds to his body: his neck and toe. We have received the carved leather replacement toe." He showed the Prince the item. "The remarkable craftsmanship shall easy attach to his foot. We wish to include several powerful charms under the folds of the neck for protection. Amulets of The Eye of Horus hold great properties. We shall then repair the wound.

"In normal circumstances, we would pour resin over the body prior to wrapping it with linen strips, beginning with the head. This stage would then be repeated a second time. However, for us to conceal and secure these two damaged areas, we propose to first layer an abundance of resin with linen strips at the neck and around his severed toe. We propose to repeat this with several layers of resin and linen to each region.

"Additionally, so he remains as attractive to the gods in the Afterlife as he did in this world, we shall stuff his body with several types of exceptional packing materials. We use linen and sawdust along with frankincense, more natron, onion plants, and the like."

"Why is that necessary?" asked the Pharaoh.

"Ah, um . . ." The elder struggled to be as tactful as possible in the description of a body after the drying process. "The moisture in our body keeps us looking . . . curvy and smooth-skinned. When it is removed, a body becomes more . . . wrinkled and flat. The packing shall round out the Pharaoh once again before we carefully suture him together." The Prince nodded in understanding. "Prior to the wrapping process, we also apply precious oils, rubbing it into the skin to render it supple and soft.

"The priests shall select pages from the Book of the Dead to be placed upon his chest, arms clasped to it, before we begin the wrapping. Each finger and each arm is wrapped separately before we begin upon his body. As I say, we commence with the head during which the Royal Priests recite prayers for the Pharaoh's safe and swift journey to the Afterlife. The complete process — drying, ointments, stuffing, wrapping, and prayers — takes a full seventy days."

"When can we proceed with the procession and burial?"

"The estimated time is perhaps sixty-eight days hence, My Prince, since we have slightly begun the process. At that time we shall require his garments and casket in which to place him. The priests shall say their final prayers and spells in the burial chamber while placing him in the sarcophagus. I hope these arrangements meet with your approval. If you have a special request of us we shall satisfy it."

"You have made excellent solutions to problems given. My gratitude," said Amonhirk. "I have two requests. I am in the process of dictating a lengthy papyrus on the life and accomplishments of my father. I wish it to be buried with him. It is a formidable task to review our history and find a scribe who does not tire easily. However, I believe we shall see its completion within those sixty-eight days.

"Consider my second concern a demand: my father's wounds shall never be revealed. Not a single embalmer or priest shall divulge this information. This is not a matter of vanity. It is of government importance. Do you understand? You shall personally instruct the other participants in my father's preparation of this command. If word of this should be passed to the populace, I shall know from whence it came."

"Of course, My Prince. I shall guarantee their silence," said the little man knowing his head would be placed on that guarantee. "I wonder, My Prince, if I may have another word." Prince Amonhirk graciously acquiesced.

## Chapter Nineteen

One Hundred days had passed since the death of Ramses III. The trials of the conspirators had finally reached their conclusion. While hundreds of people were suspected of either complicity or simply aware of the plot while failing to report it, only thirty-eight people in four separate trials were charged and found guilty. The list of names had been staggering and weeks had been spent sorting through those guilty and those who were probably guilty yet without enough evidence to bring charges against. Families of good breeding and wealth, Royal Ministers, physicians, guards, butlers, military personnel, foreign dignitaries, priests, magicians, Royal Consorts, a Queen, and a Prince had been on the docket before the judges.

As to the judges who had recklessly attended the Harem gathering, one committed forced suicide, four had their noses and ears removed, and one — the man who betrayed the others — received a verbal reprimand. Pentu often wondered why one offender was sentenced to death. Did they not all attend the same party; participate in the same entertainment? He could find no reasoning for the ruling even though he sat in judgment.

Of the conspirators to the murder, ten were 'permitted' a forced suicide. Refusal meant execution and the possibilities were endless as to that method of demise. Prince Pentawer was allowed to commit suicide in private, the other nine either by hanging or by blade in a public demonstration. The remaining criminals were executed in open view either by beheading or burning at the stake. Thankfully, thought Pentu with revulsion, flaying of their skin or impalement were not directives.

The murderer of the Pharaoh had not located and no leads were forthcoming. The Great One had been laid to rest in the most stupendous display of a Royal Funerary Procession. Citizens followed behind the coffin to an allowable stopping point short of the actual Valley of the Kings. They paid their respects and honored Ramses III who had ruled their land for thirty-three years.

While the country was yet mourning Ramses III, the necessary coronation ceremonies of Pharaoh Ramses IV were conducted. Egypt must continue under a Pharaoh's rule. Yet before he could rightfully wear the crown, the Pharaoh-to-be was bound to complete several rites and religious rituals. These dedications, prayers, and public sacrifices could take months to complete. This particular new Pharaoh would see those requirements pass quickly. He had duties to perform, some involving retribution to those foreigners having a hand in his father's would-be demise. These were duties only a crowned Pharaoh of Egypt could tend to, hence the rush to be crowned.

Following one of many feasts occurring this coronation year, Ramses IV sent for Pentu and Asim. "I have not ignored my father's promise to you following the completion of your duties as judge. Although you wished at that time to return to your birth village, I now inquire if that is still your desire. You are welcome to remain here in the Royal Palace, as a minister in my new cabinet. This is completely your decision and I shall not take offense if you choose to leave. What say you, Pentu and Asim?"

The couple looked at each other, each knowing the other's heart. "My Great and Royal Pharaoh, we both wish a less . . . complicated life in the town of Set-Maat with our child."

"Ah, the ever-diplomatic Pentu. So it is agreed. I wish you a safe journey and a joyous life together. I assume marriage is in your future." They both nodded happily. "Then I also wish you a fruitful life. Children are a blessing to families and Egypt.

"Due to your bravery and loyalty to the Crown, my life and that of my father's was spared. While you remain in Set-Maat, I command you to hold a new position, one of prestige. You shall be my voice among your people. You shall communicate with me of difficulties, missed wages, needed supplies, and to all things related to life and work at your village. Naturally this means a rise in wages." When the couple began to issue profound thanks, he interrupted them saying, "It is a nominal reward for saving my life. If you wish to return to my service within the Royal Palace, a position in my court shall be made readied. You are always welcome within these walls. Safe journey, my friends."

Having received the Pharaoh's permission and blessing, they prepared to depart for Set-Maat. "One last goodbye to say, my love," said Pentu.

Carrying their daughter, he and Asim met with Joba in the gardens. They prearranged this location due to the memories for them. "This I shall miss," said Asim. "I spent my days here as a young girl to pray and find solace. The lush plants and splashing waters have always brought calm to me." She turned towards the walls of the Palace. "The Royal Palace is beautiful and grand. It is where I first set my eyes upon you. Yet I look forward to our new life."

"I shall never forget the day I saw you. You were a goddess from the heavens."

As they reminisced, Joba arrived. "My friends, it is with great sorrow I see you depart from here. Though I know you shall be blissfully happy together, I shall miss you."

"I shall see you more often than you know, my friend," and Pentu told him of the promotion. "I believe my new duties should involve frequent visits to the Palace. You shall return with me to my town for the wedding."

"And this little one," said Joba towards the baby, "is little no longer. Crawling and gurgling, I see. Soon she shall be of an age for me to woo her."

Pentu returned the joke. "Not if you value your life."

## Chapter Twenty

Queen Iset was walking through the Royal Family's hallway to the Pharaoh's chamber. A maidservant carrying a bowl of fresh flowers bowed to her as she passed. Stopping to take a deep breath of the mixed fragrances, she remarked, "These are a lovely arrangement. They shall look beautiful in the banquet hall tonight. You have an eye for placing the colors." The maidservant smiled at the Queen and handed her a perfect bloom. The Queen tucked it behind one ear and continued her graceful walk.

Upon the formal and private coronation in the temple of Karnack, Amonhirk officially became the living god of Egypt and Pharaoh Ramses IV. Today's celebration of 'The Appearance of the King' served as the confirmation of his right to rule. All of Egypt was now his.

Nodding and smiling to the Royal Guards at the Pharaoh's door, now belonging to her son, she entered the chambers. Her son was standing at his balcony, watching the mighty Nile and looking out over the sands. "Ah, Mother," he said as she approached. Taking her hand he drew her to the wide-open window. "A beautiful day for another celebration of my coronation, do you not agree? See how the sun glistens upon the river."

"It is my most favored view, my son. I am grateful we have this time together before you stand at the Window of Appearance. People are even now gathering for sight and sound of you. You shall appear to them as Pharaoh Ramses IV for the first time."

He grasped her hand tightly and smiled at her, enjoying this rare moment with his mother. "The entombment procession of your father was a wondrous event," said the Queen Mother. "I feel confident he is seated with the gods. He was a good and compassionate King and would have no obstacles upon his journey. Were you able to complete your written memorial to him?"

The Pharaoh nodded. "I included events found in ancient text, not only of my father's victories in war, achievements in building, and generosities to his people, but those of my grandfather's as well. The papyrus amounted to over 137 feet in length and took several men to roll it neatly. It is placed openly in his burial chamber where the gods are sure to read it."

There was a slight pause between them before The Queen mentioned, "Pentawer was not included in the procession, I noticed. Yet he has been properly interred within the burial chamber, has he not? I understand your feelings and while your father decreed all mention of him be stricken from history, he was most explicit as to his inclusion within the Royal tomb."

Ramses IV continued to view the landscape while he recollected the second conversation he had with the Chief Embalmer . . . . .

. . . . Prior to the Prince's departure from the embalmer's place of business, the elder embalmer had further information to relay. "We have received the body of your brother, Prince Pentawer, yet have not begun his embalming process. I have, however, been instructed by the priests to begin immediately. I understand he shall be entombed with your father and wished to speak with you regarding this time frame."

"I wish to see him," said Amonhirk. Amonhirk walked the direction in which the man pointed.

Pentawer was upon another stone slab in a second chamber. Neither holy priest nor embalmer had touched his body. Amonhirk stood staring down at his dead brother. "My gratitude for bringing this to my attention. He is indeed to be buried in my father's tomb, however I have a few special requests for preparing his body."

While Ramses III was yet living, Amonhirk had every intention to follow his father's decree regarding the burial of his brother. Yet following the Pharaoh's death, Amonhirk thought it possible to follow the written directive while still enacting his revenge upon his brother. He studied the decree carefully and completely for some ambiguity within this father's words.

"Of course, My Prince. Anything you wish. I shall see to it personally."

"His body shall not be part of the Royal Procession to my father's tomb. I wish him to be placed within the burial chamber in three days time."

"Three days," said the elder with alarm. "Great Prince, even the least expensive process of mummification takes weeks. The organs must be removed and salted and we have not yet been provided his canopic jars. And the entire body . . . the body cannot dry in three days. What course shall we take?"

The man received a withering glance from the Crown Prince. "I do not ask for a complete process and you shall not receive jars. Indeed, I do not wish him to be embalmed in any manner. He is to be wrapped in goat skin and his internal organs are to remain intact."

The elder man was astonished. "But My Prince, goatskin is an impure material. The Royal Family has exquisite quality linen reserved for them. We store that which is needed upon this site. Without preparing the body, your brother shall never reach the Afterlife. And his mouth, My Prince; it yet remains open from death. If it is not wrapped, it shall droop further down. Additionally, this long mark upon his neck has not healed. I require time to repair this damage."

The man was rewarded for his concerns with a condescending look. "You shall not make repairs. He shall lay here and dry from the heat in this room, wrapped only in goatskin," said Amonhirk with annoyance. "Only you shall attend to this matter. I shall have no other near him. No priests, no prayers, no spells. Upon completion, an unmarked cedar box shall be supplied for his body after which you shall deliver him to the tomb. No one shall have knowledge of this. Are you in complete understanding? I shall have your tongue if word of this passes your lips. If you have questions, ask then now." The little man shook his head sadly. It was a horrendous fate to cast upon another person, especially a former Prince of Egypt. "Excellent. I shall compensate you handsomely for this, providing all I demand is completed. If I am needed for further discussion of my father, send for me."

The Prince left this place of death and decay quickly. . . .

. . . To his mother awaiting his response, he answered her succinctly. "He is within his coffin and placed near my father. I have seen to the decree as it was written."

His mother studied his face for a moment before lightly saying, "I see. As it was written, you say." She threw a suspicious glance at her son. It did not go unnoticed by Pharaoh Ramses IV.

Changing the topic, the new Pharaoh commented, "I miss him, mother. While I shall continue his good work, certain arrangements must change. The flooding season is upon us. If enough snow fell in the mountains this year, we should have a glorious overflow. I pray it is soon. Taxes will surely be raised if this draught continues. I think of my father and wonder what course of action he would take." Ramses IV sighed and wiped his nose. "I truly miss him."

"As do I, my son. I believe he is proud of you, watching you from the Afterlife. You are quite equipped to rule your country. He saw to that."

"It would ease my conscience if the murderer had been found and tried. If not for that traitor, he would yet be standing here. Do you believe we shall ever find her, Mother?"

Images flashed through her thoughts of that night: blood filling the room, complete confusion within the Palace, and one servant girl who had vanished.

Yet those were not the only images pressing upon her. She had other memories unseen and unheard by staff or her son . . . . .

. . . What a stroke of genius it had been to order constant vigilance at Ramses' door and eliminate the many superfluous people constantly gathered in the outer chambers. As her diligence to the Pharaoh upon his sick bed lagged on, she knew her son would be concerned for her health. Due to his insistence, her servants had been removed so she might rest. The guards she personally chose for duty at Ramses' door were unfamiliar to staff in these private family quarters. Additionally, during the ensuing chaos of the Palace, the duties of many servant girls were switched from one chamber to another or from kitchen cleaner to handmaiden while the court questioned the hundreds of staff. It was not, therefore, surprising that Vita was unknown as an established servant in the Royal Family's residence area. She could have been temporarily assigned to this post from almost any area in the Royal Palace. A second reason for her ambiguity was more on point, however.

The servant girl named 'Vita' did not actually exist.

It was simple for the Queen to be quite certain the sentinel overheard her conversion with the nervous handmaiden. She spoke in loud clear tones while conversing as 'Queen Iset' then simply raised her pitch and spoke in a quiet voice for 'Vita'. With her bedchamber next to her husband's, she only needed to discard her wig and gown to reveal her own short hair and sheer breeches. Carrying the water bowl from Iset's own chamber, and not from the kitchens, the nervous 'Vita' approached the Pharaoh's chamber door. The need to search the servant girl had been stressed to the guard yet he would find no weapon upon her. Since family members were exempt from search, the Queen had brought the appointed knife into the Royal Bedchamber days earlier. With her constant care to her husband, and banishment of all but truly necessary visitors, it would not be found in his room. For a Queen, it was an easy task to retrieve the ceremonial knife from those displayed throughout the family residence area. One among many would not be missed and she carefully sharpened the blade while Ramses slept in a drug-induced slumber.

  The bowl of cool water carried by Vita was also not as it seemed — it contained the same narcotic she had given to Tiye upon her execution. Yet to the guard, it was as it looked; fresh, clear water. She held her head low in a sign of deference to his position over that of a mere servant girl. In reality, she hid her face from him, as he would surely recognize the Queen.

  Ramses was surprised to awaken and see his wife in the clothing of a servant. It was their private joke, she told him, meant to enhance his well-being and joviality. How simple it had been to squeeze a few drops of the tainted water into Ramses' mouth. The more he drank, the thirstier he became. In a matter of moments he was oblivious to his surroundings and would be unable to feel pain.

  She listened at the door for sounds other than the occasional shuffling feet of the sentry. All was quiet. Removing what little clothing she wore, she enveloped herself in bed linens. If the cloth caught blood, it would be easily explained when it mingled with more of the sticky liquid upon the Pharaoh's bed.

  Walking quietly behind him while he lay in repose with elevated head, she drew the blade swiftly and firmly across his neck. His withered flesh ripped and crumpled as though aged papyrus paper and his lifeblood issued forth in a great gush. Removing the bed sheet she wore, she tossed it over his lifeless body, ensuring the pools of scarlet fluid soaked the fabric. She set the knife partially under the bed, as though it had been kicked there in haste. Redressing in 'Vita' clothing, she gathered the near empty bowl and exited the room. As she closed the door firmly behind her, she made the acceptable excuse of fetching more water. In reality, she returned the water bowl to her chamber table and the ensuing two hours were spent reclining upon her bed. After redressing in her Royal finery, she began her act of the bereaved wife.

Her one moment of fear came as she noticed a droplet of Ramses' blood upon her arm. Thankfully the guard was too unnerved to notice as he opened the bedchamber door. Rushing to her husband's side in hysterics had been a clever maneuver on her part. The fresh blood of Ramses' that soon covered her blended with the old. The sight of her cradling her husband's body as the distraught wife was also in her favor. It proved both poignant and shocking to those who witnessed the scene — a scene often spoken of throughout the Royal Palace during the ensuing days — and reinforced the great love she felt for her husband.

For such a complicated notion as murdering a Pharaoh, it had been inordinately simple. One would have thought she did so on a daily basis. . . . . . .

. . . "Mother?" asked her son, bringing her back to reality. "I asked if you believed we might yet find the murderer."

"No," she said. "I do not." She paused before speaking again completely off topic. "I find it interesting the methods the gods use to play or interfere in our lives. Your father, for instance, was healing exceedingly well according to his physicians. With the strong constitution he was blessed with, he might have outlived you. Oh, I realize you are athletically strong, yet you were always susceptible to illnesses as a child. That is true even now as the adult you are. Your cough, for example, has not yet cleared.

"It would have been a tragedy for our country if we had buried you first. Pentawer might be wearing the crown and greeting the crowds today rather than you. I should have been immensely saddened at that turn of events."

The Crown Prince looked at her warily.

"You are quite correct about the day," continued the Queen casually as she turned to the window again. "It is indeed beautiful. Perfect for my son, the Pharaoh."

Epilogue

Cairo, 2012

The director finished reading the extensive results of the CT scans performed on the mummy of Pharaoh Ramses III. They were, in a word, astounding. His learned guests were talking at once and swarmed the stage to see the scans and written results for themselves. All these years of guessing and finally the questions were answered. A layperson overhearing the academics would have thought the conversations gruesome; they were discussing death with great enthusiasm and delight.

"So it was not poison. Amazing. That was always just an assumption, I know, but this! I could never hope for such exciting news."

"The slash was actually ear to ear. That took some force, I think. The incision severed his trachea, esophagus, and the large blood vessel. This two dimensional scan is quite easy to read." He pointed to the CT scan. "It's shocking to see it on the sheet. Death would have been instantaneous with so deep a cut. Messy too. All that blood. Imagine the embalmers reactions when they got a look at the old boy."

"Yes. It must have taken some force to slice that deeply. Still, if the knife was sharp enough and Ramses was not suspicious, I suppose a woman could have drawn the blade. The circumstances would have to be in her favor, though."

"Perhaps. Or the Pharaoh was caught off guard. Difficult to tell, really. But that extra mass of linen certainly kept the secret. Hah! A 3000 year old secret. And we've cracked it, Gentlemen, we've cracked it. The neck and foot were layered with excessive resin and linen strips. Small wonder no one could get through it. It dried like cement. They tried in the late 1800's, remember? Thank God they didn't just keep hacking away at it. Imagine what the world will say to this."

"His artificial toe fascinates me. What a remarkable achievement for the times. The leather has been shaped just like his other big toe. The metal support and straps are truly a work of art. This was not just a rush job, my friends. This mechanism obviously took some time to create. See how it fits his foot so incredibly well."

"It makes sense, really. According to their beliefs, if a body wasn't intact when buried, the person couldn't be raised to join the Afterlife. And since the papyrus indicated Ramses was alive to appoint the counsel for those trials, the fatal cut must have been later. Ten days later according to the writings. That would mean his toe was severed while he was alive. Cut off with what looks to be an ax, of all things, according to the scan. I wonder if they fashioned the leather toe before he died."

"Now that's an interesting idea and very possible. He was their living god, after all. The physicians and magicians might have assumed he would survive the ax cut. Their Pharaoh couldn't very well go through the rest of his life without a toe."

"Amazing care was given to Ramses in the embalming process. And yet the other mummy didn't receive any. His organs weren't removed and he was wrapped in goatskin. The marks around his neck could indicate hanging. That probably accounts for the screaming facial expression. That and his lack of proper embalming. Amazing to finally know the Screaming Mummy was really Ramses' son. The DNA proves that. We've had our suspicious but to actually know the truth is really satisfying. Pentawer do you think?"

"Well, we know where Ramses IV was buried and the other members of the Royal family so it wasn't any of them. Whichever son it is we can reason that Ramses III had a grudge against him or he wouldn't have that goatskin around him. But I think you're right — it must be Pentawer. That would explain quite a bit."

"But he was part of the conspiracy. The main reason behind it, really. And still he was buried with his father?"

"If it is Pentawer, the Pharaoh must have loved him dearly. Even with the accusations and guilty verdict from the court he could still have been buried with his father. And I don't think that would have been done without the Pharaoh's consent, do you?"

"Then that leads us back to the original question. If Ramses loved his son enough to share his tomb, why was Pentawer not properly embalmed? We know goatskin was considered unholy and a form of punishment after death."

The room became silent. That was a good point, they thought, and no one had an answer. The DNA proved it was a son of Ramses III. But buried in such a fashion would have made it impossible to attain the all-important Afterlife. Whatever the contradictory reasoning, it was a tragic end for the son.

"So, let us recap our findings from this scanning process," said the director. "We know Ramses III and his son were buried together. We assume the Pharaoh was attacked twice — one blow to the toe and then the fatal cut to the throat 10 days later. But we are no further in answering the most pressing question."

"Ah, yes," one man asked looking around the room. "Who drew the knife across Ramses' III neck? And why was the person never mentioned in any court transcripts?"

"Yes," said another in excitement "Was he tried in another court case? Only four trials are faithfully recorded in the Judicial Papyrus and other official texts. The sentencing of the Harem wives isn't even mentioned. The only woman written about is Tiye and then only briefly. Her punishment was never even mentioned. I mean, I'm sure she was executed but I'd like to know how. Perhaps there are missing documents."

"Look, scholars have known about the Judicial Papyrus for many years," explained another Egyptologist. "It's 17 feet long but it could have been longer when first written. It showed up at a market place in the 1800's looking as though it had been ripped into pieces. Chunks of it had probably been sold off for more money than just selling the whole thing outright. So how do we know it's complete?"

"We don't," said another scholar. "There might very well be other pieces but this is the only information we have. We're lucky this much has survived for 3000 years. We've learned a lot from the writings but I still wonder what happened to the killer, whoever it was."

"Maybe he was never caught," said another man. Silence took the room again as each man was mulling over these additional questions.

The director shrugged his shoulders. "We may never know. At least not in this life. Perhaps," he said with a twinkle in his eyes, "in the Afterlife."

Author's Notes

No official records have been found as to the cause of Pharaoh Ramses' IV death yet we know he ruled for only six and a half years. He continued his father's extensive building activity in an attempt to maintain Egypt's prosperity. He also began the construction of his mortuary temple, designed to be larger than that of his father's, but it was never finished. Most of his projects were uncompleted at his death, in fact, due to his short reign. His successor, Ramses V, is believed to be his eldest son.

It was the beginning of the end for the great Egyptian Empire as interior and external conditions began the civilization's deterioration. Positions of key High Priests to the god Amun were secured as hereditary posts rather than appointment by the Pharaoh. As priestly titles were passed between relatives, and greed grew within their ranks, the needs of the priests overshadowed those of the gods and Pharaoh. They became more and more independent from the Pharaoh's influence. With increased power to the priesthood, there was a lessoning of faith in the Pharaoh.

Below average annual flooding of the Nile continued for several more years. Drought, famine, and civil unrest continued to drain the government treasury. Several officials were involved in extensive corruption schemes that went unpunished for ten years.

And yet, Egypt would see the rein of five more Pharaohs before the invasion of Greeks, Romans, and finally the Muslims. Eventually, the glories of the ancient Egyptian civilization became obliterated under the sands.

In the early 19th century, the world was agog by the discovery of the Rosetta Stone (the key to translating ancient hieroglyphics and hieratic writings), the excavation of the Pyramids of Giza, and the untouched tomb of Tutankhamen. It sparked a frenzy for all things Egyptian and opened the doors to a new understanding in one of the greatest ancient civilizations.

As we decipher their writings, touch the clothing they wore, marvel at their beautiful artistry in golden artifacts and jewelry, and examine their mummified bodies we are left with a feeling of knowing these people and the lives they led. Further treasures are still being uncovered through excavation, including in 2018 when one of the oldest established villages was discovered. The settlement dates back to about 5,000 BC, predating even the Great Pyramids of Giza.

The ancient Egyptians were astounding astronomers, artists, architects, mathematicians, and sculptors. They were considered experts in the fields of metallurgy, weaving, cooking and baking, and irrigation. They created canals for their crops and water travel, designed the ox-drawn plow, and the sickle for farming. Their culture developed a yearly calendar, clocks, metal tools, ink, and papyrus paper. (In fact, the etymology of the word 'paper' is a derivative of the word 'papyrus'.)

They practiced the first known religion professing a life after death and believed in monogamy within marriage. We have discovered their exquisite literature containing topics such as love, teachings of ethical living, religious matters, tales of the Egyptian society, lives of the Pharaohs, the philosophical ideas of the time, and their rich imaginary in poetry.

Egyptians are now credited with inventing glass, formerly thought to be a discovery of the Mesopotamians. While a common feature to us in this day, to create such a clear solid surface was a monumental discovery and a rarity thousands of years ago. The remarkable product was considered as precious as gemstones and was first used in simple beads and amulets, then for small containers and figurines. When a method for colored glass was created, it was utilized in mosaics and inlays for furniture. The upper class often exchanged pieces of sculpted glass to form political bonds.

Records of the Egyptians are the earliest found for multiplication, division, and complex fractions. They mastered geometric shapes for land measurement and architectural calculations. The Pyramids of Giza are built with such precision in alignment of north to south, they have an accuracy of 0.05 degrees. Some of the stones casing joints are set so closely, a human hair cannot fit into the joint. Today's architects are still attempting to understand how the pyramids were built or the underground tombs dug with such precision using the crude tools (by our standards) of the times. Several theories have been offered yet none have been accepted as a completely satisfactory premise.

These imaginative people first developed the idea of a phonetic alphabet in 4,000 BC. It began with over 1,000 characters until they finally settled upon twenty-four. Their idea caught on with nearby civilizations and spread through Phoenicia, the Near East, and Greece through trade routes. It became the foundation for alphabets around the world.

The Egyptians recorded some of the most detailed medical logs we have ever discovered. The papyri outlined medicinal formulas and uses for healing as well as surgical treatments. One such text discussed various wounds upon each part of the body and the recommended treatment for each. It is the first historical medical record that doesn't use magical or religious methods to heal the wound. It is unique in this sense and scientifically sound for the times. And in the field of surgery, these ancients are credited with the earliest surgical tools used.

While philosophy is usually credited to the Greeks, the ancient Egyptians had their own philosophical celebrity. His name was Ptahhotep and lived in 2350 BC. His is the best-known and preserved text on Egyptian wisdom. His work, *The Instructions of Ptahhotep*, is currently in The National Library of France in Paris. While some translations differ slightly, most Egyptologists agree his text teaches the practice of moderation, kindness, justice, the treatment of one's wife, and promotes honesty in all things. His writings are dated over 1800 years before Confucius and Socrates were born.

Sports have existed since man first drew upon cave walls but many of the sports we play today were first officially recorded in ancient Egypt. Various drawings and translated inscriptions provided the games mentioned in this novel. Even with such a lengthy list, those clever ancients enjoyed one more sport: bowling. Records indicate it was played in 5,000 BC. The players rolled stones — probably the rounder the better — at various rows of objects to knock them over. Over time this ancient game became the one we know now.

I've always been fascinated with the achievements of the ancient Egyptians and the stepping-stones they provided for modern development. Their numerous accomplishments were clearly ahead of the time in which they lived. To put it simply, it boggles the mind. Not only did the extensive techniques and discoveries of these people astound the world then, they continue to touch our lives with methods and practices we use to this day. I often wonder what more these remarkable people might have accomplished if they had not fallen.

In my many pages of research, I found one universal truth that helped greatly in my character development: while our beliefs, practices, and cultures have changed over the centuries, human nature remains much the same.

My hope is you've enjoyed this slice of Egypt's ancient history.

# Bibliography

(2017, June 27). Retrieved July 2019, from The Secrets of the Ancient Egyptian Harem.

*25 Famous Pharaohs*. (n.d.). Retrieved May 2019, from Ancient Egypt Online: www.ancientetyptonline.com

*About Ancient Mirrors*. (2018). Retrieved May 2019, from Mirror History.

*Ancient Egyptian make-up*. (n.d.). Retrieved April 2019, from Ancient Egypt Online.

*Ancient Egyptian Medicine*. (n.d.). Retrieved June 29, 2011, from Wikipedia: www.wikipedia.org/wiki/Ancient_Egyptian_Medicine

*Ancient Egyptian Medicine*. (n.d.). Retrieved May 2019, from Ancient Egypt for Kids: www.egypt.mrdonn.org

*Ancient Egyptian Royal Regalia*. (n.d.). Retrieved August 2019, from Tour Egypt: www.touregypt.net

*Ancient Egyptian Technology*. (n.d.). Retrieved June 29, 2019, from Egyptian Diamond: www.egyptiandiamond.com

*Ancient Egyptian tombs and Death Rituals*. (2019, August). Retrieved from Nat Geo: The Story of God with Morgan Freeman/Beyond Death.

Andrews, E. (n.d.). *Eleven Things You May Not Know About Ancient Egypt*. Retrieved July 02, 2011, from History Lists.

*Attacks on Egypt*. (n.d.). Retrieved June 29, 2011, from Phoenix Data: www.phoenixdatasystems.com/goliath

*Yetterflies and Moths*. (n.d.). Retrieved June 2019, from Ancient Egyptian Bestiary.

*Cats Were Important to the Ancient Egyptians*. (n.d.). Retrieved June 29, 2011, from Eayptian Diamond: www.egyptiandiamond.com

*City Quarters, Residential Areas*. (2001). Retrieved September 2019, from Ancient Egyptian Town Planning.

*Clothing and Adornment*. (n.d.). Retrieved June 2019, from Mysteries of Egypt.

*Clothing in Ancient Egypt*. (n.d.). Retrieved April 2019, from Wikipedia.

*Crocodiles*. (n.d.). Retrieved June 2019, from Ancient Egyptian Bestiary.

*Crook and Flail*. (n.d.). Retrieved September 2019, from Wikipedia.

*Crook and Flail in Ancient Egypt: Definition and Symbolism*. (n.d.). Retrieved September 2019, from Study.com.

*Daily Life, Gods and Religion, Funery Custome, Orientation, Agriculture*. (n.d.). Retrieved June 2019, from Life in Ancient Egypt.

*Daily Lives of the Ancient Egyptian Queens*. (n.d.). Retrieved April 2019, from Ancient Egypt Online.

*Deir el-Medina*. (n.d.). Retrieved May 2019, from Wikipedia.

Denault, L. t. (n.d.). *An Introduction to Ancient Egyptian History*. Retrieved July 02, 2011, from Life in Ancient Egypt: www.watson.org

Denault, L. T. (2003). *History, Gods, Hieroglyphics, Phonetic Alphabet,* . Retrieved June 2019, from Life in Ancient Egypt: www.sptimes.com

Dixon, D. M. (1974). Timber in Ancient Egypt. *The Commonwealth Forestry Review , 53* (3).

Draux, D. (2016, January 12). *Water History*. Retrieved from Water Suupply of Ancient Egyptian Settlements.

Dukowitz, G. (2008, August 26). *Think lLke an Egyptian*. Retrieved from The first mention of the Brain.

Dunn, J. (2019, April). Retrieved from Ramses III, Egypt's Last Great Pharaoh.

Dunn, J. (n.d.). *Ramesses IV, Beginning the Empire's Collapse*. Retrieved September 2019, from Tour Egypt: www.touregypt.net

Dunn, J. (n.d.). *The tomb of Ramesses IIi, Valley of the Kings, Egypt*. Retrieved July 2019, from Tour Egypt.

*Economy During the Ancient Egypt Times*. (n.d.). Retrieved June 29, 2019, from Egyptian Diamond: www.egyptiandiamond.com/ancient-egyptian-economy

*Egypt- The Double Crown and the Three Kingdoms*. (n.d.). Retrieved April 2019, from History's Histories.

*Egyptian Civilization - Daily Life*. (n.d.). Retrieved September 2019, from Mysteries of Egypt.

*Egyptian Civilization Daily Life/Trades and Crafts*. (n.d.). Retrieved September 2019, from Mysteries of Egypt: www.historymuseum.ca/cmc/exhibitions/civil/egypt

*Egyptian Civilization Daily/Transportation*. (n.d.). Retrieved July 2019, from Mysteries of Egypt.

*Egyptian Cvilization: Daily Life*. (n.d.). Retrieved May 2019, from Mysteries of Egypt.

*Egyptian Diamond*. (2011, June 29). Retrieved September 2019, from Clothing That was Worn By the Ancuent Egyptians: www.egyptiandiamond.com

*Egyptian make-Up*. (2018). Retrieved May 2019, from www.historyemblmed.com

*Egyptian Symbols: Crook and Flail*. (n.d.). Retrieved August 2019, from Eqyptian Gods and Goddesses.

Encyclopedia Britannica. (n.d.). *Ramses III*. Retrieved June 2011, from Encyclopaedia Britannica: www.britannicacom

*Faashion in Ancient Egypt*. (n.d.). Retrieved June 2019, from Ancient Egypt Online.

*Facial Hair*. (n.d.). Retrieved February 02, 2019, from Tour Egypt: www.touregypt.net/featurestories/beards

*Facts About Ancient Egyptians*. (2019, October). Retrieved from Ancient Egyptian Toilets.

*Fashion and Jewelry in Ancient Egypt*. (n.d.). Retrieved June 2019, from Casoro.

*Fashion in Ancient Egypt*. (n.d.). Retrieved April 2019, from Ancient Egypt Online.

*Fertility, Family Planning, Pregnancy. Childbirth*. (n.d.). Retrieved August 2019, from Procreation in Ancient Egypt.

*Furniture*. (n.d.). Retrieved October 20, 2019, from Tour Egypt: www.touregypt.net/featurestories/furniture

*Garments,, Production, Fashion,Laundering*. (2011). Retrieved May 2019, from Ancient Etypt:Clothing: www.reshafirm.org

Ghosh, B. (n.d.). *Contribution of the Eqyptian Civilization to the World Civilization*. Retrieved August 2019, from History discussion.

*Gods and Religion*. (n.d.). Retrieved June 29, 2011, from Carnegie Museum of Natural History: www.carnegiemnh.org

*Harem Conspiracy*. (n.d.). Retrieved May 2019, from Wikipedia.

*Hat-hetep Sunusret, a Planned City*. (n.d.). Retrieved September 2019, from Ancient Egypt: The Planned Town of Kahum.

history, J. *www.toureegypt.net/featurestoreis/furniture*.

*House and Garden*. (2010). Retrieved Septembeer 2019, from Ancient Etyptian Acciomodation.

*Housing in a Workers' Villiage: Deir el Medine*. (n.d.). Retrieved June 2019, from Ancient Egypt.

*How Linen was Made.* (2011). Retrieved August 2019, from Ancient Egyptian Clothing: www.dragonstrike.com

J Paul Getty Trust. (1998). *Oxygen-Free Musuem Cases.* Retrieved April 2019, from The Getty Conservation Institute.

*Kalasiris.* (n.d.). Retrieved July 2, 2011, from Fashion Encyclopedia: www.fashionencyclopedia.com/fashion/The-Ancient-world-Egypt

*Karnak Temple.* (n.d.). Retrieved June 2019, from Discovering Egypt: www.discoveringegypt.com/karnak-temple

Klimczak, N. (2016, December 16). *Fast Money: the Egyptian Economy, Monetary System, and Horrendous Taxes.* Retrieved August 2019, from Ancient Origins.

*KV11: Burial Site of Ramses III.* (n.d.). Retrieved July 2019, from Wikipedia.

Laura Leddy Turner, Demand media. (n.d.). *What was a Pharaoh's Life Like in Ancient Egypt.* Retrieved May 2019, from Synonym.

*Life in Ancient Egypt - Daily Life.* (n.d.). Retrieved June 29, 2011, from Carnegie Museum of Natural History: www.carnegiemnh.org

*Life in Ancient Egypt - Orientation.* (n.d.). Retrieved June 29, 2011, from Carnegie Museum of Natural History: www.carnegiemnh.org

*Life in Ancient times: the Slave/the Laborer/Merchant/.* (n.d.). Retrieved June 29, 2011, from PBS-Secrets of the Pharaohs: www.pbs.org/wnet/pharaoh/life

*Loeb Classical Library Edition, 1933.* (1933). Retrieved may 2019, from Library of History of Diodorus Siculus.

Loktionov, A. (2015). *Convicting Great Criminals.* Retrieved October 2019, from A Neew Look at Punishment in the Turin Judicial Papyrus.

*Maat: ancient Egyptian goddess of Truth, Justice and Morality.* (n.d.). Retrieved June 2019, from Ancient Origins: www.ancient-origins.net

Mark, J. (2016, November 14). *Ancient Eqyptian Literature*. Retrieved 2019, from Ancient History Encyclopedia.

Mark, J. J. (n.d.). Retrieved July 2019, from The First Labor Strike in History.

Mark, J. J. (2017, July 17). Retrieved June 2019, from Tomb Robbing in Ancient Egypt.

Mark, J. J. (2013, January 13). *Ancient Egyptian Culture*. Retrieved May 2019, from Ancient History Encyclopedia.

Mark, J. J. (n.d.). *Ancient Egyptian Religion*. Retrieved june 2019, from Ancient History Enyclopedia: www.ancient.eu

Mark, J. J. (2019, January 20). *ancient Egyptian Religion*. Retrieved May 2019, from Ancient History Encyclopedia: ancient.eu/egyptian_religion

Mark, J. J. (2017, September 20). *Definition*. Retrieved June 2019, from Ancient Egyptian vizier.

Mark, J. J. (2017 , March 13). *Dogs in Ancient Etypt*. Retrieved October 2019, from ancient History encyclopedia.

Mark, J. J. (2017, April 11). *Games, sports & Recreation in Ancient Egypt*. Retrieved 2019

Mark, J. J. (2016, March 18). *Pets in Ancient Egypt*. Retrieved August 2019, from Ancient History encyclopedia.

Mark, J. J. (n.d.). *Ramesses II*. Retrieved July 29, 2019, from Ancient History Encyclopedia: www.ancient.ey/Ramesses_II

Mark, J. (2016, September 26). *Love, Sex, and Marriage in Ancient Egypt*. Retrieved June 2019, from ancient History Encyclopedia.

Mark, J. (2009, September 2). *Sea Peoples*. Retrieved May 2019, from Ancient History Encyclopedia.

*Medinet habu*. (n.d.). Retrieved September 2019, from wikipedia.

*Military of Ancient Egypt*. (n.d.). Retrieved July 2, 2011, from Wikipedia: www.en.wikipedia.org

*Monkeys*. (2007, February). Retrieved May 2019, from Ancient Egyptian Bestiary.

Morris, J. (2018, November 13). Dozens of Cat Mummies Are Discovered in Egyptian tomb. *Contra Costa Times*.

Muillburn, N. (n.d.). *Banquet Hall Set-Up Ancient Egypt*. Retrieved September 2019

*Myth/Fact Sheets*. (2013). (E. University, Producer) Retrieved 2013, from Holocaust Denial on Trial: hdot.org/en/Leaning/myth-fact.html

Parsons, M. (n.d.). *Ancient Egyptian Royal Regalia*. Retrieved May 2019, from Tour Egypt.

Parute, E. (n.d.). Retrieved May 2019, from Perfume cone: the Mysterious Fashion Accessory of Ancient Egypt: www.fashionologiahistoriana.com

*PBS-Secrets of the Pharaohs*. (n.d.). Retrieved June 29, 2019, from Life in the Ancient times: www.pbs.org/wnet/pharaoh/life_pharaoh

*Peasants and Slaves in Ancient Egypt*. (n.d.). Retrieved June 29, 2011, from History Link: historylink101.net/egypt

*Personal Adornment*. (2011, July 2). Retrieved September 2019, from Ancient Eqypt.

*Personal Hygiene and Cosmetics*. (n.d.). Retrieved June 2019, from Ancient Egypt.

Peters, S. (n.d.). *Kids Ancient Egypt*. Retrieved September 2019, from Fun facts About Ancient Egyptian Wigs.

Pharaoh's Murder Riddle Solved After 3,000 Years. (2012, December 18).

*Planning*. (n.d.). Retrieved September 2019, from Building in Ancient Egypt.

*Preventative and Curative Health Care*. (n.d.). Retrieved June 29, 2011, from Ancient Egypt medicine: www.reshafim.org.il/ad/egypt/timelines

*Pylon (archetecture)*. (n.d.). Retrieved September 2019, from Wikipedia.

*Pyramids and Temples*. (n.d.). Retrieved May 2019, from Incredible Ancient Egyptian Architecture.

*Rameses III - 1187-56 BC*. (n.d.). Retrieved June 2011, from Rameses III.

*Ramesses III*. (n.d.). Retrieved June 29, 2019, from Wikipedia: http://en.wikipedia.org/wiki/Ramesses_III

*Ramesses IV*. (n.d.). Retrieved May 2019, from Wikipedia.

*Ramses III*. (n.d.). Retrieved September 2019, from 20th Dynasty Medinet habu.

*Ramses III*. (n.d.). Retrieved May 2019, from Ancient Eqypt.

*Ramses III*. (n.d.). Retrieved June 2011, from Wikipedia.

*Ramses III Pharaoh of Egypt*. (n.d.). Retrieved May 2019

*Religion and Everyday Life*. (n.d.). Retrieved May 2019, from Ancient Man and His First Civilizatioins-Egypt 2: www.realhistoryww.com

*Rramesses III*. (n.d.). Retrieved June 2019, from Wikipedia.

*Sea Peoples*. (n.d.). Retrieved May 2019, from The Global Egyptian Museum.

*Sea Peoples*. (n.d.). Retrieved May 2019, from Wikipedia.

Seawright, C. (2001, February 10). Retrieved May 2019, from Egyptian Women, Life in Ancient Egypt: www.thekeep.org

Shaw, G. (2014, March 11). *What did Egypt's Pharaoh Do Each Day*. Retrieved May 2019, from Garry Shaw: www.garryshawegypt.blogspot.com

*Slavery in Ancient Egypt*. (2019, May). Retrieved from Wikipedia.

Snape, D. S. (2018, December 16). Retrieved July 2019, from Palaces in Ancient Egypt: Cities for Kings and Gods.

Snape, S. (n.d.). *Palaces in Ancient Egypt: Cities for Kings and gods*. Retrieved November 17, 2019, from Brewminate: A Bold Blend of News & Ideas: brewminate.com/Palaces-in-ancient-egypt-for-kings-and-gods

Teeter, D. J. (1999). *Marriage and the Family: Egypt*. Retrieved June 2019, from Fathom Archive.

*The Harem Conspiracy*. (2017, February 21). Retrieved September 2019, from Just History. Plain and Simple.

*The Last Great Pharaoh - Ramesses III*. (n.d.). Retrieved June 29, 2019, from Discovering Ancient Egypt: discoveringancientegypt.com

*The Time of Pharaoh Ramses III*. (n.d.). Retrieved June 29, 2019, from Speciality Interests: www.specialityinterests.net/ramses3

*The Villiage Workers*. (2017, November 02). Retrieved June 2019, from Historical Investigation: dier el-Medina.

*Thebes Ramesses III, The Last Great Pharaoh*. (n.d.). Retrieved June 29, 2019, from Great Dreams: www.greatdreams.com/thebes/ramiii

*Thebes Ramses III the Last Great Pharaoh*. (n.d.). Retrieved September 2019

*Tiye (20th Dynasty)*. (2004). Retrieved JUne 2019, from Wikipedia.

*Topics: Beliefs/Myths/Religion and Spirituality/Religious Leaders*. (n.d.). Retrieved July 02, 2011, from Eternal Egypt: www.eternalegypt.org

*Topics: Government.* (n.d.). Retrieved June 29, 2019, from Eternal Egypt: www.eternalegypt.org

*Topics: Government/Bureaucracy/The Military.* (n.d.). Retrieved June 2019, from Mysteries of Egypt, Egyptian Civilization: www.historymuseum.ca

*Topics: Military.* (n.d.). Retrieved July 2, 2011, from Eternal Egypt: www.eternalegypt.org

*Topics: Society and Culture/Family/Food and Drinks/Sports and Entertainment.* (n.d.). Retrieved July 2, 2011, from Eternal Egypt: www.eternaletypt.org

*Topics: Textiles.* (2011, July 2). Retrieved September 2019, from Eternal Egypt: www.eternaleqypt,.org

*Trade in Ancient Egypt.* (n.d.). Retrieved February 13, 2019, from Egypt Trade: www.egypt-trade.wikidot.com

*Tyti.* (n.d.). Retrieved May 2019, from Wikipedia.

*Ultramarine Blue.* (n.d.). Retrieved June 2019, from Egyptian Lapis Lazuili Uses as a Pigment.

*Weapons.* (n.d.). Retrieved July 02, 2011, from Weapons in Ancient Egypt: www.reshafim.org.il/ad/egypt/weapons/index

*Weapons.* (n.d.). Retrieved July 2, 2011, from Tour Egypt: www.touregypt.net/featurestores/priojectileweapons

*What was Egyptian Blue?* (2019, October). Retrieved from Ancient Pages.com.

*Who Were They?* (n.d.). Retrieved June 29, 2011, from Egyptian Slaves: ftp.aa.edu/lydon/egypt/Fleischer

Made in the USA
Columbia, SC
05 March 2020